Bren set foot on the flo... battalion of reporters trie... assault of cameras failed ..., as Tano and Algini directed him and his entire party aside through the plant manager's office. There was the smell of heated wax, a wax-jack waiting for him in the office. Lord Geigi and nand' Borujiri, and a number of other officials came pouring through the door with the news services clamoring outside.

He signed and affixed his seal in wax to cards while his security fumed and clearly wished a quick exit. But there were moments at which haste seemed to create worse problems than apparent lack of it; and they hadn't yet flung him to the floor and drawn guns, so he supposed it wasn't critical.

"The car is waiting, nand' paidhi," Tano said, the moment the last card was stamped.

Escape lay out the door: the news services hadn't yet outflanked them. Algini went out first, surveying the Guild-provided car which procedure had dictated would never leave the personal surveillance of the paidhi's own security. Tano held the door for him, a living shield against what he had no idea.

For two seconds in that position they were without any locals at all in earshot. "Lord Saigimi is dead," Tano said to him, low and urgently. "Unknown who did it."

So *that* was the emergency. Bren took in his breath, and in the next firing of a neuron thought it likely that lord Geigi, stalled on the other side of the same door, was getting exactly the same news from *his* security.

The lord of the Tasigin Marid, the circle of seacoast at the bottom of the peninsula, was dead, *not* of natural causes.

C.J. CHERRYH
INHERITOR

Foreigner #3

DAW BOOKS, INC.
DONALD A. WOLLHEIM, FOUNDER
375 Hudson Street, New York, NY 10014

ELIZABETH R. WOLLHEIM
SHEILA E. GILBERT
PUBLISHERS

For Elsie

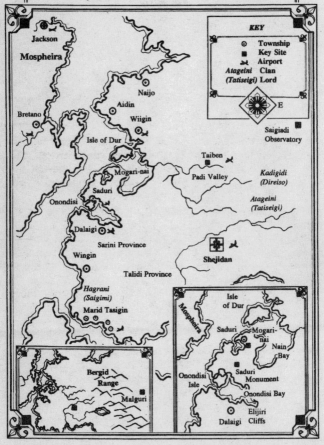

Mospheira and the Aishi'ditat

KEY

- ⊙ Township
- ■ Key Site
- ✈ Airport
- *Atageini* Clan
- *(Tatiseigi)* Lord

Jackson

Mospheira

Bretano

Naijo

Aidin

Wiigin

Isle of Dur

Mogari-nai

Saduri

Onondisi

Dalaigi

Sarini Province

Wingin

Hagrani (Saigimi)

Marid Tasigin

Taiben

Padi Valley

Kadigidi (Direiso)

Atageini (Tatiseigi)

Shejidan

Talidi Province

Saigiadi Observatory

Bergid Range

Malguri

Mospheira

Isle of Dur

Saduri

Mogari-nai

Nain Bay

Onondisi Isle

Saduri Monument

Onondisi Bay

Elijiri Cliffs

Dalaigi

1

The wind blew from the sea, out of the west, sweeping up to the heights of the balcony and stirring the white tablecloth with a briskness that made the steaming breakfast tea quite welcome. The view past the white-plastered balustrade was blue water, pale sky, and the famous cliffs of Elijiri, from which, the thought had crossed Bren Cameron's mind, wi'itikiin might just possibly launch themselves.

But no, the sea was surely too great a hazard for the small, elegant gliders.

"Eggs," lord Geigi urged with a wave of his fingers. It was a delicate preparation, a sort of crusted soufflé, eggs of a species the cook swore were innocent of toxins for the human guest.

Bren trusted himself to his staff, Tano and Algini having made his sensitivities to certain native spices quite clear to the cook; and having made equally clear, he was sure, the consequence of such an accident to the reputation of lord Geigi, who had a personal stake in not poisoning him. He allowed the servant to pile on a second helping of the very excellent spiced dish. Rare that he found something he liked that he dared eat in quantity—it was a piece of intradepartmental wisdom that the way to survive atevi cuisine was to vary the intake and not allow the occasional trace of an objectionable substance to become three and four traces at the same meal—but Tano and Algini thought this dish should be perfectly safe.

Geigi was pleased, clearly, at his enthusiasm for the

cuisine, pleased in the crisp, clean air of a seaside morning, pleased in the presence of an important guest. Geigi's appetite ran to another, far larger helping of the soufflé. Black-skinned, golden-eyed, towering head and shoulders taller than any tall human, besides being gifted with an alkaloid-tolerant metabolism, Geigi, like any ateva of the mainland, viewed food as a central point of hospitality, the consumption of it a mark of confidence and assurance of honesty, understandable in a society in which assassins were an important guild, and a regular recourse in interpersonal and political disputes.

Such, as happened, were Tano and Algini, watching over Bren's shoulder, standing near this breakfast table on the balcony; such, Bren was very sure, were the pair who hovered on Geigi's side of the table, near the balustrade. Gesirimu, Tano had said, was the woman's name, and Casurni, her senior partner—the pair in a dark, fashionable cut of clothes perfectly in character for a lord's private security. And one assumed Tano knew. One assumed that, among the thousands of members of the Assassins' Guild, the highest did know each other by reputation and, more importantly, by man'chi—that word something like loyalty, that meant nothing to do with hire, or birth, or anything humans were equipped to understand.

But it wasn't necessary that humans understand the passions of atevi minds and souls—at least, it never had been necessary that humans understand, so long as all humans in the world—save one—occupied the island of Mospheira, which lay some distance across the haze of the blue and beautiful strait the other side of that balcony.

That was the state of atevi-human affairs under which Bren had begun his tenure in office not so many years ago. Translator, Foreign Affairs Field Officer, he was, in atevi terms, the paidhi-aiji, the *only* human permitted by the Treaty of Mospheira to set foot on the mainland.

He, Bren Cameron, descendant of spacefarers stranded for nearly two centuries on the earth of the atevi, was the one human alive who walked and lived among the atevi, and Bren, at twenty-seven, had it as his lifelong business and sacred trust to mediate the differences between atevi and humans.

Until last year that business had been much the same as that of his predecessors. Most of his days had been spent in the atevi capital of Shejidan, rendering the vocabulary of atevi documents into the one permitted human-atevi dictionary for the human University of Mospheira, for use in the training of other paidhiin. A years-long program from which the twenty percent who did go all the way through to the degree in Foreign Affairs disappeared into the bowels of the Foreign Office, all but the one scoring next highest marks: the paidhi-successor, the other tenured graduate of the program (and usually not a voice of any importance at all), who waited in the wings for the Field Officer to quit, die in office, or need a two week vacation. As all the others waited, in the order of their scores, as the paidhi's support staff in the Foreign Office. That was the program. That was one job the paidhi did. Train one successor and write dictionaries.

The other job was to serve as the conduit through which the Mospheiran State Department made a slow transfer of human technology into the atevi economy. The paidhi did have definite importance in that regard. And he served as his government's eyes and ears in the field. He reported what data he gathered; he took requests from the atevi government and relayed them; he handled customs questions, and the occasional legal tie-up or bureaucratic snag. Based on what information he passed through, the University of Mospheira and the Mospheiran State Department slowly made decisions about what technology to release—debated sometimes for years over the release of a *word,* let alone, say, microchips. The goal was to keep the technology compatible, to keep, say, the standards such that a grade of wire produced on the continent could be connected inside a toaster built on Mospheira with no thought of difficulty.

He'd never looked for things to change appreciably

in his lifetime, not the toaster, not the society and not the level of technology. Steady, economically stable progress: that had been the design for the atevi-human future. Interlocked economies, meshing just like perfectly standardized nuts and bolts.

Now, just since last year, there was one more human on the mainland, one Jase Graham, born lightyears removed from the earth of the atevi, and certainly not a product of the University's Field Officer candidate program.

And Jase Graham's arrival was why he, Bren, was sitting on lord Geigi's balcony eating a soufflé of spiced eggs and relying on two assassins' professional judgment that there was nothing by design or default harmful in the dish.

The situation and his job had changed radically overnight when the starship had turned up, the same starship that, two hundred years ago, had left his ancestors to fend for themselves among the atevi. The atevi government (which had elevated intrigue to an art form) had consequently suspected the human government of Mospheira (which Bren well knew couldn't site a new toilet in a public park without political dithering) of double-crossing atevi high, wide, and with considerable cleverness for nearly two hundred years.

It was not the case, of course; there had been no human double-cross of the atevi, though for a time even the paidhi had had to wonder whether his own government really had been more clever than his park-toilet estimate. The humans on Mospheira had had no idea that the ship would return. They had, in fact, believed quite to the contrary.

As it had turned out, the State Department on Mospheira had truly reacted as desperately and as ignorantly as he'd feared. They had tried to contact the ship directly, and in secrecy, to secure its alliance exclusively for Mospheira.

They'd tried, in short, to shut the atevi out of the dealings.

If they'd asked, Bren could have told them they were

fools, that you didn't double-cross the atevi. To be sure, the State Department at first had been unable to secure his advice; but they hadn't listened to him once he did get through, no—since his advice hadn't agreed with what their fears and their biases said they should do in responding to the Atevi Threat.

The atevi government had, of course, found them out. Sharp atevi eyes had spotted the new star that attached itself to the abandoned space station in the heavens, and atevi antennae had intercepted the communications between Mospheira and the ship. The atevi had promptly taken action, in which Bren had been inextricably involved, that had placed them in direct communication with the starship.

Mospheira's maneuvers hadn't won the sympathy of the starship, which had turned out willing to deal with the atevi and with the human enclave on an equal basis—*anyone*, the starship maintained, was welcome up in space, but the one thing they wouldn't agree to was time.

The ship wanted help, manpower to repair the station abandoned two centuries before, and they wanted it immediately, or as immediately as a world without a manned spacecraft could build one. The ship cared nothing about the careful work of centuries not to destabilize the atevi government—which in turn supported the atevi industrial base, which in turn supplied the factories and shops on Mospheira and the *human* economy.

But with the mutability of self-interest, Mospheira's attitudes had shifted. Of *course* the State Department supported the atevi government, and of course it was more than willing to work with the atevi to obtain materials the atevi needed to go into space equally with humans, and of course it supported the paidhi, any paidhi the atevi wanted, just so the Treaty stood firm.

Meanwhile the average human citizen was both scared of the ship in the skies, which bid to change a way of life they'd thought would go on forever, and scared of the atevi, who had defeated them once in war and who were alleged in popular understanding to be utterly incomprehensible to humans—this at the same time atevi were supposedly growing more and more like humans, having television and fast food, skiing and soccer—which of course defined everything.

So somehow, without destabilizing the atevi, as they'd been taught all their lives would happen if someone slipped too much tech to atevi too fast, they were going to merge the cultures instantly and have universal peace.

No wonder the population of Mospheira was confused.

As a result, Bren Cameron no longer exclusively served the President on Mospheira who'd allowed that state of confusion to develop. He damn sure no longer exclusively served the higher-ups in the State Department, who'd tried to browbeat the Foreign Office and to use the situation for domestic political leverage.

The Foreign Office within the State Department, well, yes, he was loyal to them—if the commotion his actions had caused had left anyone of *his* staff and *his* superiors in office.

He'd last heard from his old chief Shawn Tyers two months ago. His personal bet was that the President wouldn't dare jerk Shawn out of office, because without Shawn, the Mospheiran government had *no* chain on the paidhi. But even the two months since he'd last talked by phone was a long time, and the silence since implied that Shawn had no power to call him as often as he'd like; or, evidently, to send him mail.

And by now (unless Shawn had somehow protected within the system the computer codes Shawn had ingeniously slipped him on his last trip home) the Field Officer's access codes to the Mospheiran computer net were useless. His access to Shawn himself grew increasingly less assured.

He didn't know the true distribution of power in Mospheiran governmental offices any longer. He knew who *might* be in charge. And for that reason he wouldn't link his precious computer to Mospheiran channels right now for all the fish in the briny sea—

because without the protection of updated codes and the access they gave, some electronic disease might come flashing back to its vulnerable systems from people who really didn't want his computer to hold the records it did.

A situation that half a year ago had had the Foreign Secretary hiding computer codes in a cast on the paidhi's arm didn't inspire the paidhi to confidence in the State Department even at that time, and his government having since then reacted in internal partisan panic and having done things and issued statements which, unmediated, could have blown the fragile peace apart, he didn't think the situation had improved.

So with Shawn and every living soul in the Foreign Office who actually knew the atevi seeming not to have power to prevent such folly, the paidhi, Bren Cameron, loyal to the previous regime, but damned sure not to the present one, conceived it as his personal duty to stay in his post on the mainland and *not* to come home.

The paidhi counted himself lucky to be sitting on this balcony, in that consideration.

The paidhi reflected soberly that humans and atevi alike were extremely lucky that the situation, touchy as it occasionally became, had never quite surpassed the ability of sensible humans and sensible atevi to reason with one another.

The fact was, their two species *had* reached a technological level where they had a common ground for understanding. It was possible that the threatened economic and social destabilization was no longer a justifiable fear. The trouble was—it was a deceptively common ground. Or a commonly deceptive ground—again, that interface was the paidhi's department.

Fortunately, too, the essential interests of both species were not incompatible, meaning that both of them could adapt to space—and it had been the aim of both species and the better-thinking members of both governments to get there some time this century, even before the ship reentered the picture.

But the common ground was treacherous in the

extreme. There had already been moments of extreme risk: a particularly nasty moment when he lay senseless in a Mospheiran hospital, when conservative political interests on Mospheira, led by Secretary of State Hampton Durant, had sent in the paidhi-successor to replace him, hoping to make irrevocable changes while their opposition in the government was having a crisis.

And they'd nearly succeeded.

Deana Hanks, dear Deana, daughter of a prominent conservative on Mospheira, had within one week managed to founder two hundred years of cooperation when she'd used the simple words faster-than-light to lord Geigi of Sarini province.

The same lord Geigi with whom and on whose balcony Bren shared breakfast.

Simple word, FTL. Base-level concept—to human minds. Not so for atevi. Through petty malice or towering folly, Deana had managed in a single phrase to threaten the power structure which governed in this province and the sizeable surrounding territory, which in turn held together the Western Association, the Treaty, and the entire industrialized world— because FTL threatened the very essence of atevi psychology and belief.

The atevi brain, steered by the principal atevi language (a chicken or the egg situation), was *ever* so much more clever than the human brain at handling anything to do with numbers. The atevi language required calculation simply to avoid infelicitous numbers in casual utterance.

Math? Atevi cut their teeth on it. And questions abounded. There could not be paradox in the orderly universe on which atevi philosophy depended.

Fortunately, an atevi astronomer, a despised class of scientists since their failure to predict the human Landing, had been able to find a mathematical logic in the FTL paradox that the philosophical Determinists of the peninsula could accept. Vital reputations had been salvaged, the paidhi-successor had been bounced the hell back across the strait where she could lecture to conservative human heritage groups to her heart's content and harm no one.

But as a result of Deana's brief foray onto the continent, and thanks to the publicity that had flown about atevi society on what had otherwise been a quietly academic question, the FTL concept had leapt into atevi popular culture last fall.

He'd had to explain to the atevi populace on national television that the human ship which had come to their world had entered their *solar system* and come from *another sun,* which was what all those stars were they saw in their skies at night, and about which most atevi had never wondered overmuch. Yes, humans had fallen down to earth on the petal sails of legend (there were even primitive photographs) and no, humans were not originally from the moon. But the difference between a solar system and a galaxy and the dilemma of the origin of humans, until now shrouded in secrecy from atevi, was up for question.

Yes, he'd said, there were other suns, and no, such suns weren't in this solar system, and yes, there were many, many other stars but not all of them had life.

So now the atevi, who had been building a heavy lift rocket launch system, in an undeclared space race with Mospheira, were building an earth-to-orbit spacecraft that would land like an airplane, thanks to the information the ship in the heavens had released to them. That spacecraft under construction was what his entire trip to this province was about.

And he had to admit he was far less worried about the spacecraft and its materials documentation dumping unconsidered tech wholesale into the atevi economy (although a year ago the proposed import of a digital clock had—justifiably—raised storms of concern in the Foreign Office) than he was about the work of the gentle, slightly daft atevi astronomer who'd come up with that mathematical construct that let them translate FTL into atevi understanding.

The elderly astronomer, Grigiji, who might be the most dangerous man to come out of those mountains since the last atevi conqueror, had been the guest of lordly choice throughout the winter social season, feted and dined, wined and elevated to legend among the amateur philosophers and mathematicians who were the hangers-on of any lordly house—Grigiji, the gentle, the kindly professor, had taught any hearer who would listen (and the respect accorded him approached religious fervor in atevi minds) his quietly posed and philosophically wandering views.

Now Grigiji was back in his mountain observatory confusing his graduate students. And the paidhi, who had survived the social shocks of the paidhi-successor's adventurous offering of faster-than-light, didn't even want to *imagine* what was going on in atevi universities all over the continent in the last several months, as that faster-than-light concept, along with the mathematics that supported it, hit the lecture halls and the ever fertile minds of those same atevi students, who were neither hangers-on nor amateurish.

Considering the excitement the old man had raised, and considering the ability of atevi to take any mathematical model and elaborate on it, the paidhi on certain bad nights lay awake imagining atevi simply, airily declaring at year's end they'd discovered a physics that didn't *need* a launch vehicle *or* a starship to convey them to the stars, and, oh, by the way, they didn't truly need humans, either.

The paidhi, who thought he'd had a very adequate mathematics education in his preparation for his office, thank you, had had six very short months to study up on a branch of mathematics outright *omitted* from the Mospheiran university curriculum for security reasons—mathematical concepts now spreading limbs and branches in other areas of atevi academe besides the lately fashionable astronomers.

And all this brain-bending study he did only so he, the paidhi, who was not a mathematical genius, could laboriously translate the documents of atevi who *were* mathematical geniuses—to humans on the island and on the ship who didn't half suspect the danger they were in from a species they thought dependent on them.

He hoped at least to keep well enough abreast of matters mathematical so that conceptual translation remained possible between two languages, and two (or counting the ship's officers, *three*) governments; he also had to translate between what was formerly two, but definitely now three, sets of scientists and engineers, all of whom were flinging concepts at each other with a rapidity that numbed the sensibilities.

Now humans who had never met atevi face to face— the crew of that ship—were proposing to bring atevi into space and to hand atevi the kind of power that, by what he understood, couldn't be let loose on a planet.

Only last year the University advisory committee on Mospheira, who did know something of atevi, had maintained that nuclear energy, like digital clocks and the concept of time more finely reportable than atevi numerologists were accustomed to reckon it, was still far too dangerous to put into atevi hands. And humans up there proposed to bring the technology of a stardrive into atevi awareness.

What the humans on that ship still had difficulty getting through their heads was that it hadn't been just a bad day on which the space age humans who had landed on the planet had legitimately *lost* the war they'd fought with the then steam age atevi. Humans had really, militarily *lost* the war, so that, indeed, and by the resulting Treaty, Mospheira had been surrendering their technology a step at a time to the atevi of the Western Association—Treaty mandate, not a voluntary choice.

And in all those years, a process mediated by two centuries of paidhiin, technological change had been deliberately slowed and managed so that atevi and humans could achieve technological parity without ever again destabilizing *atevi* society and starting another *atevi* war.

The ship, by the conversations he'd had with its captain, and with Jason Graham, with whom he shared quarters back in the capital, seemed convinced atevi would adapt.

He hoped they were right. He was by no means convinced.

As it was, certain factions within the Western Association of the atevi were viewing with considerable suspicion the flood of knowledge and engineering pouring down on them from the sky, knowledge and space age science that could be turned—very easily—against them, in their regional and historical quarrels with the capital of the Association, situated at Shejidan.

The current aiji, Tabini, the atevi president, whose capital was at Shejidan, was ethnically Ragi, a distinction the ship didn't understand. Tabini-aiji, whose position was both elective and to some meaningful degree hereditary, was also clever, and bent on taking every bit of power he could get into the atevi central government, for good and foresighted reasons, by Bren's estimation; but tell that to the provinces whose ancestral rights were being taken away by this increased centralization.

And in that light, damned right the atevi of the Peninsula had a reason to worry about the space program in the hands of the Ragi atevi; most of the atevi of the Peninsula weren't Ragi—they were Edi, who had been conquered by the Ragi five hundred odd years ago.

While lord Geigi, across the table from him, likewise sipping his tea in a dawn wind, wasn't even Edi: he was Maschi, which was a complete history unto itself, but he was an Edi lord. And, to add to the puzzle—which neither the ship nor his roommate would understand—until lately, last year, in fact, Geigi had been in a very uncomfortable position, trying to do well economically and legislatively for his district, trying to be a moderate in a region of well-armed hotheads who were almost-but-not-quite his ethnic relatives, while trying not to lose what humans might call his soul in dealings with Tabini, who headed the Ragi atevi, the Western Association, and the civilized world.

Tabini, even before the advent of the ship, had been dealing with Mospheira hand over fist for every piece of human tech he could get his hands on. Now Tabini dealt with the ship instead, wanting whatever technical diagrams and materials information the ship would send down to the great dish at Mogari-nai and into his control. Tabini was hell-bent on new tech, and all it implied about central power and respect for the traditional mathematical philosophies which still constituted the atevi view of the universe.

Geigi had been the one provincial lord who, thanks to his unique position as technologically and mathematically educated, *and* a Lord of the larger Ragi Association, *and* a philosophical Determinist (as the peninsular atevi generally were), suddenly had had to find honest answers to the FTL paradox that Deana Hanks had posed.

FTL was a devastating challenge (via a mathematics implied in its new universe-view) to the philosophy by which lord Geigi and all his Edi neighbors lived and conducted their affairs: if something could move faster than light, science, which thought it had understood the universe, was wrong and the peninsular philosophers and all the Edi who had been part of a philosophical rebellion against Absolutist number theory had been made to look like fools.

Yet Geigi, tottering on the brink of public embarrassment and a loss of respect that could collapse his financial dealings, had sought the truth face to face, had challenged Bren-paidhi to answer for him the mathematical questions Deana-paidhi had raised.

The support and resources Bren-paidhi had gotten from Tabini himself had enabled him to answer that question, and that answer had undoubtedly saved Geigi's reputation and probably his life, counting the financial and political chaos that would have erupted in the province.

Bren rather *liked* the plump and studious lord, this man who posed courageous questions of his universe because if it killed him, lord Geigi wanted the truth: baji-naji, as atevi put it, turn the world upside down, lord Geigi didn't want some surface assurance that would let him ignore the universe. No, he *was* a scientifically educated man, not because an atevi lord had to be, but because he wanted to embrace the universe, understand it, see it in all its mathematical beauty.

Understand the human side of the universe—maybe Geigi could even approach that.

But lord Geigi would not, on a gut level, understand being *liked,* his language having no such word and his atevi heart feeling no such emotion. What went on inside Geigi was equally complex, it might produce the same results, but it was not human; and that was the first understanding of all understandings the paidhi had to accept in dealing with atevi.

As a human, he *liked* lord Geigi; he also *respected* Geigi's courage and good sense, and that latter sentiment Geigi *could* understand, at least closely enough to say there was congruence enough between their viewpoints for association (a very atevi word) of Geigi's interests and his—in the way atevi looked at things. Geigi also seemed to respect him, the paidhi, as the one official of Tabini's predominantly Ragi household ironically most able to understand the tightrope Geigi walked as a Maschi in an Edi district in a Ragi nation. That was another point on which they were *associated,* that atevi word of such emotionally charged relationship.

Or their mutual numbers added, giving them no cosmic choice but association.

It was a lot *like* friendship. The human in the equation might *like* the man. But add them up to equal friendship? That wasn't what Geigi's atevi nerves were capable of feeling, let alone what Geigi's atevi brain thought was going on; and that very delicate distinction was true of any atevi, no matter what. Basic law of the Foreign Service: *Atevi aren't friends. Atevi can't be friends. They don't like you. They're not capable of liking you. The wiring isn't there.*

Never forget it. *Never* expect it. Start building that construct to satisfy *your* needs and you're dead. Or you'll *be* dead. And the peace will be in shambles.

Based on his own experiences, he'd add, if he were,

like his own predecessor Wilson-paidhi, talking to a university class in Foreign Studies, Don't lead them to expect too much of you, either.

He hoped Geigi didn't attribute Tabini-aiji's shift of attitude and the grant of manufacturing in this district directly to the paidhi's doing. That would be a mistake, and dangerous. Tabini's actions were for Tabini's reasons, and he never, ever wanted to get between the aiji of Shejidan and any of the lords of the Association. A human had no business whatsoever in the lines of man'chi, of loyalty between lord and lord, and, taking that one element of his predecessor's advice greatly to heart, he never intended to stand there.

A brown lizard whipped along the balustrade. *It* feared nothing. Djossi flowers were in bloom again with the coming of spring, and the little reptile dived in among the blooms and heart-shaped leaves, on the hunt for something tasty.

Humans came and humans might go. But the land went on, and the sea washed the rocks, and atevi, like Geigi, who knew such rhythms of this world of their birth in blood and bone . . . were a force to be reckoned with, wherever it regarded this planet.

He was glad, seeing this dawn, that he had opted to guest in lord Geigi's house. His security had had very serious misgivings about his accepting Geigi's invitation to stay with him in his ancestral home rather tran in the Guild-guaranteed hotel. It was unprecedented that a person of Tabini-aiji's household (and so the paidhi was accounted, socially speaking) should guest in this house, which until recently had not had the status, the resources, or the security clearance to receive such a visitor from the court at Shejidan.

Well, the considerations once in the way of such a move had changed. And clearance had come from the aiji himself for the paidhi to accept Geigi's invitation.

One couldn't say lord Geigi was particularly in the paidhi's debt for that latter change of heart, either. In that, Tabini had been informed and had decided for his own reasons to change Geigi's status.

Figure that lord Geigi, too, was risking something in

having such an unprecedented guest, since it certainly would be talked about—talked about on the evening news, coast to coast if it was an otherwise quiet day—and would set lord Geigi at some odds with the politics of his Edi neighbors: not seriously so, Bren hoped.

But personally the paidhi, by taking this very sip of tea (out of a kitchenful of herbs lethal to humans), bet his life that Geigi was exactly what he seemed. He had bet it last night and he had slept quite soundly under this roof. Wilson-paidhi would hold that he was in danger of transgressing common sense, and that a paidhi who started having such confidence in his assessments of atevi was headed for serious trouble, but, ah, well, here he was.

On the other hand, where *did* he invest emotionally? His treatment of the paidhi-successor and his refusal to knuckle under to the head of the State Department meant, effectively, that he couldn't go home. Meant he would have no more chances to sit by the sea on the other side of this strait. Meant he would have no more breakfasts on his brother's front porch—and this place, this moment, this *association* in an alien government was what he'd traded it all for, in some very real sense: the chance to sit here, in the position he occupied with an alien lord. He had a mother, a brother, an estranged father, and his brother's family all over there in that haze that obscured the strait, and there was a chance he'd never see his mother again, considering the troubling reports he'd gotten on her health this winter. He was bitter about that penalty his government made him and her pay; he was angry, and he asked himself at odd and very dangerous moments like this one, if it wasn't psychologically or professionally acceptable for him to build careful little fences around certain atevi in his mind and, one-sidedly, *think* about liking them, what in *hell* was he going to do?

He had a human roommate. He had Jase Graham. There was that.

He could *like* Jase Graham. That was permitted, psychologically, politically, in every way approved by the State Department; that was permissible.

But he didn't dare quite turn loose of his suspicion of a man from a human culture centuries divorced from his own, a man who didn't, on his side, offer deep confidences to him. Geigi had flung his *life* into Bren's hands when he welcomed him and the aiji's Guild members under his roof with every evidence of delight. They'd spent the previous evening and this morning discussing sea shells, architecture, and Geigi's marriage prospects. Jase, who had lived under the same roof, shared dinners and spent the majority of the last six months with him, had trouble talking about his home or his family or his ship's whereabouts over the last couple of centuries.

And that seemed a significant reticence.

It takes *time* to travel between stars, Jase had said. And, We did our jobs, that's all.

But where *were* you? he'd asked Jase, and Jase had taken a piece of paper and tried to draw him a diagram of the ship's location for some significant period of time relative to a star he couldn't identify, but he'd made no sense of it. Then they'd gotten a bottle of shibei and tried to talk personally, but Jase said, I don't know, to all questions of how that star where Jase said they'd been sitting for years related to where they were now.

And to, What's out there? Jase had said to him, It's just stars. It's just stars, that's all.

Well, maybe it wasn't what a human who'd dreamed of seeing the space station, who'd dedicated his teen-aged years, his romantic hopes and his adult life to the hope of advancing the planet just to the edge of space, wanted to hear from a man who'd been born to it.

Maybe it had turned things just the least bit sour in the relationship that Jase, after all the excitement with which he'd welcomed him to the world, hadn't had wonders to tell him. He didn't know why he felt put off by Jase Graham.

But he hadn't been happy since the world changed and since he'd shared his world with an unhappy, often scared young man. He knew that.

He didn't like to think about that fact on this pleasant

morning when his mind had been intermittently, though they were talked dry by now, trying to manage the intricacies of conversation with an atevi lord he admired but didn't know all that intimately.

He most of all didn't like to think about the fact that, while he was on this side of the strait coaching Jase in a language that wasn't easy to learn, his own mother was suffering phone calls in the middle of the night from crackpots who hated him, crackpots the government over there couldn't seem to catch.

He didn't like to think about the fact that his almost-fiancee (whom he wasn't totally sure he loved, the way he wasn't totally sure nowadays he *liked* anything in the world without checking his subconscious) had gotten tired of waiting and tired of his absences. So she said. His belief now was that she'd grown scared of similar midnight phone calls.

But whatever the reason, she'd married a man she didn't in the least love; and there went another tie he'd once had to Mospheira.

Barb was safe now, off his conscience, and married to Paul Saarinson, who was well-placed in the government. He was sure she didn't get threatening phone calls nowadays.

His brother, Toby, on the other hand, had no such refuge. His brother had suffered phone threats against his family until his kids were afraid to walk to school in their quiet, tiny town on the north shore of the island, a mostly rural place where behavior like that didn't happen and people hadn't been in the habit of locking their doors.

He didn't like to think about the fact that if he did go home for a visit and to try to defuse the political situation via consultation with the State Department and the President, he might find himself arrested right at the airport.

Oh, he didn't think the Mospheiran government could hold him, for one thing because the aiji in Shejidan would threaten global war to get him back, and for another because Tabini-aiji definitely would not accept Deana Hanks as his replacement. He reckoned either one was a sufficiently powerful incentive for the government of Mospheira to behave itself on that surface level, and had toyed with the idea of a few hours' visit to try to straighten matters out.

Over all, however, he wasn't willing to bet his life or world peace on his own government's common sense the way he bet it right now on Geigi's cook's choice of teas.

Trust that he was safe on this exposed balcony, drinking this tea maybe seventy miles from an atevi resort area overlooked by radar installations looking for illicit human airplanes? Yes. Crazy as the world had become, he did trust that he was safe here. An ateva who'd conspired against him and then changed his mind had changed his mind not because of the law (which allowed assassination as an alternative to lawsuits) but because it was no longer in Geigi's interests to do him harm.

A human enemy on Mospheira, especially a crazy one, was another matter entirely; and the members of his own species who'd started calling his brother and his mother at three in the morning to threaten them because of actions he took on the mainland were liable to do anything.

So if he did have to visit Mospheira before they got a ship into space and made all issues moot, who knew? Certainly there was reason that chief presidential advisor George Barrulin and others high in the administration would feel the heat of their under-the-table, bribe-passing supporters if they found him within their reach and had to yield him back not only to the mainland but back to hold the paidhi's office again, bowing to atevi pressure. They'd done that already, sending him back here straight off the operating table six months ago. But, then, that was no surprise. George and the President were good at bending to pressure. That was why their supporters put them in office.

So, round one, they'd tried firing him. That was what the Deana Hanks affair had been.

Round two, Deana had tried to build her own power base among atevi by (against all carefully considered law and State Department regulation) contacting atevi opposed to Tabini.

Her ignominious return to the island had left George and the President in rather an embarrassing mess, because while they *had* to talk to atevi to keep the industrial raw goods flowing, there was no paidhi-successor but Deana who wasn't either older and rooted to Mospheira, or so junior as to be collegiate. A replacement for him even if completely qualified would be no more acceptable to the atevi than Deana Hanks had been, because *he* was the one Tabini insisted on having. And if the atevi bounced their choice back at them again, it just wouldn't inspire confidence among the Mospheiran electorate that the Mospheiran government was in control of things.

The President of Mospheira, elected with the support of various business interests, including Gaylord Hanks, father of Deana Hanks, got his advice from his advisor George Barrulin and the Secretary of State, Hampton Durant.

The Foreign Office, why, that was a mere bureau within the Department of State. It always *had* been a mere bureau, run by the Foreign Secretary, presently Shawn Tyers, who couldn't get a phone call through to his officer in the field.

So his was the only advice that might come to the President from anyone talking to the atevi. And good old George wouldn't pass it on to the President if it didn't serve the interests of George.

Well, lord Geigi at least had ceased to think that he ought to be shot. And lord Geigi had far more class than to allude to that old business.

The paidhi, for all his other grief, won a point, occasionally. He had to be content with that.

"If only you had another day here," lord Geigi remarked on a deep sigh, "one might arrange a day of fishing. The yellowtail are running at this season, or will. Absolutely a thrill, when they begin jumping. I had one land on the deck of the boat. It was a *very* exciting moment."

"One doesn't doubt so," Bren said, and laughed. "A

grown one?" It was his impression they were a large species.

"The deck crew couldn't decide whether they wanted the beast in the water or in the locker. He escaped through the rail and probably to this day laughs at us as he swims past. I think he would have been a record. But I wasn't measuring, nand' paidhi, I assure you."

"Oh, you do tempt me." It had been an eight-day series of cities and plants and labs. He hadn't rested in Guild-sanctioned hotels anywhere as well as he'd slept last night, not even on the luxury-equipped plane. And possibly Tabini could spare him a day. Possibly, too, it wasn't a peninsular plot to fling him overboard. Possibly he could convince Tano and Algini that their protection of him during a day's actual vacation was much easier if he was surrounded by all that wonderful blue water.

But most probably he should fly back to the capital this afternoon, and work on the plane while he did so. He had a towering lot of notes to enter, some export lists to glance over and approve, and a handful of quality control questions which had to be translated for the lab technicians in the last two facilities.

"Yellowtail," lord Geigi said wickedly, "cooked over the coals. Nothing finer."

"Lord Geigi, if you go on you will surely corrupt me, and I *have* to be back in the capital tomorrow. If I don't get my work done the stack of paper may reach orbital height before our ship does. I so wish I could accept."

He took a chance—he hadn't even realized he'd taken it. It was absolutely against Departmental policy to make a joke with strangers of rank, the language was that chancy even for him. But he did it with his guards and he did it routinely with Tabini, of all people: the aiji of Shejidan, whose displeasure was far more to fear.

Still, a lord in his province, touchy about his dignity, facing a human representative of the aiji of Shejidan, who had status of very indeterminate sort, was worthy of fear, too.

Geigi was amused. Geigi seemed mollified at the turn-down, even seemed pleased at the paidhi's assumption of intimacy.

So he had done exactly correctly when Geigi had made his rather stunning overture of a local and rustic pleasure to a human guest and a guest of state at that. It was yet one more of those small moments of triumph that the paidhi treasured unto himself, as part of his job—and a part he couldn't report nowadays, to a State Department convinced he was a fool as well as a turncoat.

And he couldn't explain to anyone else in the world, not even the man from the ship who shared his quarters, why it pleased him. Except it was the real job he'd signed on to do, and it was occasionally nice to have those little operational checks to prove to himself that yes, the larger civilization-threatening decisions he was taking routinely on himself were possibly founded on a more microscopic-level understanding of the people.

"Well, well," Geigi said, "the sun waits not even for the aiji, so I suppose it won't wait for us. We should be on our way."

That signaled that the breakfast was done. Security and servants moved in about their separate business. As Geigi rose from the table, Bren did, and accepted the formal, many-buttoned coat from the junior security (his own) who had had custody of it. He allowed the young woman to hold it for him to put on, and let her deftly adjust his braid to the outside of the fashionable stiff collar as he did so. He hadn't realized he'd been chilled through the shirt, but it was the case. Spring had offered the chance to sit on the balcony, had offered sea air and that marvelous view, and he'd said yes in an instant, never thinking that atevi called brisk what humans called bitter.

He bowed, Geigi inclined his head. Everyone was relaxed and polite. He had to visit his room on the way out and gather up his papers, in the custody of yet another junior security agent, also of the Guild. The luggage would make its way separately to the plane and be waiting for him.

But in all maneuvers of this sort, Tano and Algini never took their eyes off him, and insisted on having a car provided by the Assassins' Guild (oddly enough it was the one way, just as the Guild certified certain hotels, to be absolutely certain a vehicle was safe) to transport him while he was in the province and outside the ordinary security precautions that surrounded the aiji's household in Shejidan.

It was an official visit designed not just to showcase Patinandi Aerospace, the most important industrial complex in Sarini Province, but to allow the paidhi to talk directly to the engineers at this and at other facilities in recent days. He had allotted the morning to the former aircraft assembly plant, not enough time, but he would exit with a load of paper notes and a wallet full of computer files.

And *that* would go to the staff in Shejidan, the paidhi's now quite extensive clerical and technical staff. He had to go over his notes for the event, which he should be able to do in the car. Lord Geigi was coming too, but he had his own entourage. Once at the plant, he had a briefing and, he was sure, a similar set of pamphlets and papers would come from the company officials, even including personal requests just to be *carried* to the capital and left with the aiji's staff, a courtesy which official visitors had performed on trips to the capital from ages ago when the mails didn't come in at all reliably.

The collection of data and the succession of meetings and presentations was down to a foreseeable routine. He had, among the security personnel, one hard-pressed member of his secretarial staff who on receiving the news that he was going with the paidhi on this tour had acted as if he were being offered a government-paid holiday.

Possibly the young man *was* having the time of his young life just seeing the interiors of the Guild-approved hotels, usually luxurious, and the views from the Guild-escorted tours, and even just looking out over the land from the windows of the airplane; but the last he'd seen of him, the young man was collating the papers from the last stop on the tour and trying to bring sense out of them, with *his* breakfast a cold roll and a cup of tea in the downstairs of Geigi's stately home.

He did trust the papers would be in order before the next set was added to the stack: the young man—Surieji was his name—hadn't let him down yet. And as late as this morning was still cheerful.

2

The structures didn't look much like a spacecraft yet, either from the ground floor of the immense hangar or from the ladders of the catwalk that ascended to a dizzy height above, in a building with very small windows and spotlights high in the rafters. The structural elements which were the very beginnings of the spaceframe were cradled in supports, there, and there, and there. Some elements were forms on which the fuselage would take shape, in composites and ceramics. He saw elements of the wings which he was told were real and ready for their control surfaces. Atevi workers moved among such shapes, dwarfed by the scale.

One could grow dangerously hypnotized by the shifting sizes, and by the heights. A human did grow accustomed to a slightly larger scale of things, living on the mainland and among atevi, whose steps and chairs and door-handles were always a little off a human's estimation of where steps and chair seats and door handles reasonably ought to be. He was tall, on Mospheira, but he stood about the height of an atevi nine-year-old, and he wisely and constantly minded his step when he clambered about an atevi-designed catwalk, or as he paused for an atevi official to point out the huge autoclave that was a major step in the composite technology.

"Unique to this plant," the man said proudly, a statement which might as well have been, The only one in the world, although the atevi supervisor might not have been aware that Mospheira's prototype autoclave had died the death of No Replacement Seals a decade ago.

It was more than the pitch of the steps he watched. He walked cautiously for other reasons, moving through this crowd of black-skinned, golden-eyed gods, expressionless and implacable in manner, all with local and some with national agendas, men and women all distinguished by colors of rank, of post, of heritage and association.

His security disliked this part of the tours. On invitation of the Director he climbed to a catwalk exposed to the view of no less than seven hundred strangers below, any one of whom—or their relatives admitted to the plant for the occasion—could turn out to be a threat to his life. Such would be unregistered and unlicensed operators, of course, of which the Assassins' Guild and the law took a dim, equally lethal view; but still there was a threat, and he chose to put it at the back of his mind.

One of the lords constantly near him was, of course, lord Geigi, who outranked the lot, and who had already had his chance to do the paidhi harm; but there were lesser lords, and provincial elected representatives, and various secretaries and aides, all of whom had their small window of opportunity for whatever reason, including a deranged mind, to try to sabotage the atevi chance at space.

He was (while watching the crowd, the lords, the directors, and his step) negotiating dark, unfamiliar ladders above increasingly dizzy heights, occasionally with spotlights glaring in his eyes. He kept his hand at all times on the rail and refused to be hurried until, in this largest of all assembly buildings, he had a view of the whole floor.

He had no fear of heights. He skied. Or, well, he had skied, before the trips home had become an impossibility for him; and he lacked opportunity to reach the snowy Bergid, where atevi attempted the sport on new and chancily maintained runs. During this winter, he had grown accustomed instead to such catwalks and ladders, to echoing machine plants and clean-suited laboratories, to small spaces of structural elements that were diagrams on his desk back in the atevi capital of Shejidan.

This—*this* was the first sight of pieces that would become a spacecraft, pieces that were real, solid, tangible, pieces bound someday for space, the dream he'd studied so long, worked so hard, hoped so much, to have happen—in the generation after him.

The paidhi all this particular morning had been listening to the detailed problems of atevi engineers, technical matters and problems arisen from a rushed schedule and translated designs, plans and manuals and measurement standards in an alien language. That meant for several moderately pleasant hours he'd been doing the paidhi's old, original job, patching up dictionaries.

Atevi engineers adopted or made up a word for something hitherto unknown to atevi, and the paidhi dutifully wrote it down and passed it to other engineers via the official dictionary on the computer links that went to all the plants now. Science and engineering were creating their own words for things for which atevi had had no word, no *concept*, a year ago. The atevi language as a whole had never hesitated to assume technical terms into its grammar—the word *arispesa* was a hybrid of which he was entirely innocent.

He had his case full of reports, besides, on what worked, what didn't work well, and what the legislature, the Space Committee, or the laboratories and manufacturing plants upstream of the technological waters needed to improve. But, God, there wasn't all that much to complain of. At the beginning of last fall he'd toured mines.

Records from the abandoned station, the library which had come along to this star with what had been intended as a colonial space-based establishment—the sort of thing the paidhi had used to turn over to the mainland a piece at a time—had in the past gone for trade goods. But now there was a new source of ideas in the skies, pouring them down for free. Primary among those gifts was the design *this* spacecraft was using.

Whether Mospheira had already owned any of the records involved in this free transaction was an answer he still hadn't gotten past Mospheira's official silence, but he strongly doubted it. For one thing, the humans who had abandoned the space station to come down to the planet had done so in two waves. The first humans had landed by parachuting capsules into the planetary atmosphere, because the station officials had refused the would-be colonists the resources *and the designs* to build a reusable landing craft.

The second wave of the Landing had come down to the planet only after the ship had left, as they claimed, to find their way home; and after the station, increasingly undermanned, had begun to fail. Station officials at that time had lacked the resources and the manpower to build a reusable craft, so with what records they had, the last hold-outs and members of management had parachuted in, too, with no landing craft ever built. The station officials might have brought the library with them; or they might not. The craft described in the design sent down from the ship wasn't heavy-lift like the chemical rockets of the Mospheiran pro-spacers. In the plans of the ship, the heavy-lift aspect didn't matter. Raw material, the ship either had or could get in orbit the way their ancestors had gotten it, so the ship captain said. The essential thing was workers to use it. So Jason Graham said.

History also held certain troubling details of worker fatalities Jase had never alluded to, the very thing that had driven the colonists down to the planet—but once up there, *up* there, dammit, atevi had a voice; and atevi would outnumber the ship crew, a matter *he* didn't allude to with Jase, either.

And the library might have had records of how to build such a craft; or it might not.

Or the atevi shell that had blown up Alpha Base during the War might have gotten more of the salvaged library than human authorities had ever admitted it had.

At the very least a lot of bitter politics had come between then and now. He'd never had the security clearance even as paidhi—*particularly* as paidhi—to get into Mospheira's highly classified library archive files to find out. He thought it even possible that somebody during the station-versus-colonists-versus-ship dispute had deliberately wiped them out of station records and left the only copy in the ship's possession, to prevent the colonists getting off the planet without improving the industrial base.

But irony of ironies, *Jase* had still had to parachute in, wave three, because the sad truth was that the wondrous starship couldn't build the landing craft to which it had the design because it lacked the necessary manpower, and even if they somehow surmounted that difficulty, they still couldn't fly the craft down, because no space-bound pilot had the skill to fly in an atmosphere.

So for all those reasons, and even though Ms. Yolanda Mercheson, the starship's representative to Mospheira, was supposed to be arranging the building of a human-made ship identical to this one, he was increasingly sure that the ship that would first carry personnel and cargo up off the planet was the one he was looking down upon this very moment.

Even with the plans, humans on Mospheira no longer had the capacity to mount the construction effort he had in front of him. A lively aircraft manufacturing industry was a real asset to an accelerated space program. So were the skilled workers to reconfigure those molds and handle the composites.

Unfortunately humans on Mospheira didn't have that resource, either. Oh, there *was* an aircraft plant on Mospheira, but it had stopped manufacturing large jets, due to competition from the atevi industry on the mainland. Government subsidies necessary to sustain a virtually customerless Mospheiran aeronautics industry had been cut by the legislature in a general protest against taxes two presidential elections back, and the human aerospace workers had gone to other jobs.

Meanwhile the Mospheiran composites manufacturing

facility, despite pleas by the pro-spacers, had lacked the spare parts to keep it functioning, because it couldn't find customers outside the now defunct aircraft plant. Atevi-human relations had been peaceful for decades, and the defense implications of buying the few commercial jets Mospheira needed for domestic service from Patinandi Aeronautics on the atevi mainland just hadn't figured with the legislature against the public frustration with high taxes. Even the humans at the top of the campaign for a human return to orbit had promoted chemical rockets as the way to go, because that was the way humans historically had done it, those were the plans they apparently did have, and because it was easier to sell a *historical* concept to the dim lights of the Human Heritage Party who had fallen into bed with them, politically speaking, than it was to sell the technologically more complex reusable vehicle that depended on the composites manufacturing facility they didn't want to fund.

So *that* political bedfellowship had concentrated their lobbying efforts and the scarce tax money on their rocket program, for, supposedly, as the Treaty of Mospheira provided should happen, the simultaneous development of a human and an atevi space program. For decades after slow decades, through the paidhiin, the Mospheiran Defense Department had released only the minimal data that the Mospheiran government had to release to atevi to get the industry going that was ultimately going to feed both raw materials and finished goods to the human space effort on Mospheira—and in the way Mospheira liked to have such militarily dangerous exchanges, raw materials were going to get into Mospheiran hands sufficiently early to give Mospheira a running start.

He should know; some of it had already happened on his watch, brief as it had been. And on his predecessor, Wilson's, before Wilson retired.

On the other hand, from what Jase said, the ship had questioned Mospheira very closely on that matter and discovered a truth Mospheira had no way to deny:

Mospheira couldn't immediately or foreseeably launch a damn thing, manned or unmanned.

Probably the Mospheiran president in recent negotiations had told the truth to Jase's captain and there had never been a secret rocket launch site even contemplated.

So there they were: atevi had been bothering no one when the petal sails of legend dropped humans in their midst and they'd built their way up from steam engines.

Atevi had barely been contemplating satellites and manned space last year, sure that the station was unmanned and the only humans were on Mospheira, when a new thunderbolt of human presence in the skies had fallen on the world; and when blueprints guaranteed to work without experimentation had descended electronically from the heavens.

In the last six months it had become a national mandate to get the pieces of the atevi space program reconfigured—that was the word that echoed through all departments—*reconfigured*. Tabini-aiji was in a race, a race to show results to his own uneasy people, a race to get a foothold in the heavens where atevi could maintain their say over the future of *their* planet—and this particular aircraft manufacturing facility was critical.

Manufacture of a spacecraft that had much the same materials base and much the same configuration as the planes this facility had built commercially was far faster than invention of a rocket-driven heavy launch system from scratch.

Testing was on a materials-specifications basis, straight out of very clear records.

Training programs were already shaping up to teach a hand-picked set of atevi pilots the handling characteristics of the craft they were building.

As he understood the situation on the island, *human* scientists were running to catch up to the technological dataflood pouring down from the heavens.

He'd personally discovered the information gap in the university physics and chemistry programs: Defense had kept some things sequestered—FTL was only one example of it. The University hadn't taught him or his predecessors what it didn't have access to, and, wondrous to say, the people in Defense who'd understood the data had died, and their successors had just guarded the file drawers without knowing what they were sitting on . . . until the downloads from the ship in a matter of seconds had obsolesced the secrets the Defense Department was keeping.

So now the executive branch of the Mospheiran government had no cards to play. Atevi, holding the principle continent, held most of the developed mineral resources. Humans, on the large, mountain-centered island, had to trade fish for aluminum and copper. And human orders for those supplies hadn't yet increased, possibly because the human legislature hadn't moved to authorize the trade; but the aiji had with one pen stroke authorized atevi mines to produce what this ship needed.

Ceramics and plastics as well as aircraft were all mainland items that Mospheira imported. *Oil* was an import from the mainland. There was oil to the north of the island, offshore, but that had lain right near the highest priced real estate on the island and that development had stalled because the oil supply from the mainland had never been threatened since that discovery.

The atevi head of state was no fool. The atevi head of state had sold aircraft and oil to the island at very good prices—just as his father before him had done. Aviation guided by the paidhi's reports and the human desire for trade had run out of domestic market and diverted its ambitions toward satellites. It needed a launch vehicle which it planned to build on the island, but to achieve that it had to bring atevi industry up to such a capability itself in order to supply the components. So even before the arrival of the ship was a suspicion in the skies, rockets of Mospheiran design were on the negotiating table, and Patinandi Aeronautics on the mainland had become Patinandi Aerospace.

The ship arrived: the heavy lift rockets Mospheira envisioned were a dead issue. Plans for a reusable spaceplane arrived from the heavens and in one *day* after accepting the concept as viable the aiji in Shejidan had ordered Patinandi to shift its production of parts sufficient for the commercial air fleet to a somewhat older but still viable facility during the building of an auxiliary aircraft plant.

Consequent to that pen stroke in Shejidan, and literally before another sun set, Patinandi in Sarini Province had begun packing up the dies and essential equipment for that production for freighting to a province other than Geigi's, a province which was about to profit handsomely.

And with no one being cast out of a job, the aiji instantaneously and by decree converted the largest aircraft manufacturing and assembly plant in the world to a round-the-clock effort to build a spacecraft, no debates, no committees, no dithering. *Amazing* how fast the whole atevi system could move now, considering that the space program had once been hung up on a committee debate on the design of chemical rocket slosh baffles for three months.

Half a year ago none of this had existed.

And depending on the technical accuracy of the paidhi's trans-species interpretation and translation of what were in effect historical documents, that ship down there was going to fly sooner than he was supposed to admit even to Jase. The frame design was by no means innovative; the dual engines, the zero-g systems, the heat shield, and the interactive computers were the revolutionary items.

And as to *why* atevi accepted this design without the usual debate on the numbers that had previously absorbed atevi attention and slowed projects down to a crawl, why, the numbers of this craft were clearly felicitous and beyond debate, even its engines and computers. Down to the tires it landed on, it was an historical replica of an actual earth-to-orbit craft named *Pegasus* which had plied the skies of the human Earth for two decades at a similar gravity and on a similar mission, which had never suffered disaster or infelicity of any kind, and which had existed in harmony with the skies and the numbers of infinite space until its retirement, a craft thereby proven to have been in harmony with the universe and to have brought good fortune to its designers and its users.

On that simple assurance—and only the atevi gods knew how Tabini's canny numerologists had gotten *that* agreed upon—the debate which might have killed the project was done. The numerologists, still stunned by FTL, were all satisfied—or at least they retired to study the numbers of its design and to determine what had *made* it felicitous, so that atevi science might benefit.

That kind of rapid agreement had never accelerated any *other* program on record. No one had made anything of that fact in his hearing, but in his view it was a revolution in atevi philosophy as extreme as FTL, and almost as scary. One almost guessed that lives had been threatened or that somewhere in secret meetings the usual people who stood up and objected to the numbers had been urgently hushed. Tabini *wanted* this project and if atevi didn't have it, then the numbers of atevi fortunes might turn against them, indeed.

They'd lightened and widened the seats to accommodate atevi bodies, but to keep, as atevi put it, the harmony of successful numbers, they'd varied no other parameter, and the sum of mass was the same, figuring in that atevi simply weighed more than humans. Atevi would simply have to duck their heads, sit closer, and deal with the comfort factor once they'd become comfortable with spaceframe design.

There was even (to the absolute consternation of certain elements on Mospheira, he was sure) smug discussion of selling passenger slots to humans, if the diplomatic details could be worked out. Some human factions, it had been reported, *liked* that idea, as a way to have spaceflight without a sudden increase in taxes.

Others, Shawn had said in his last conversation, liked it because it so enraged the conservatives of the Human Heritage Society. The Foreign Affairs office had probably sent up balloons and blown horns when, eight weeks ago, he'd translated to the President the aiji's offer of selling seats; and George Barrulin's phones had probably melted on his desk.

The catwalk quaked as lord Geigi, having been delayed momentarily in conversation on the level below, came up the steps, followed by the rest of the lords and officials. Their respective security personnel took up watchful and precautionary positions and kept the paidhi slightly back from the rail. Black skin and golden eyes were the standard not only of the locals but of the whole atevi world, and he was all too aware that a fairish-haired human dressed generally in house-neutral colors stood out. There was no other way to say it.

Stood out, child-sized, against the silver-studded black leather of Tano and Algini, who represented the power of the atevi head of state.

Stood out, in the many-buttoned and knee-length coat of court fashion, and in the distinctive white ribbon incorporated in his braid: the paidhi's color, the man of no house. Tabini had told him he should choose colors, as he had to have something recognizable for formal presentations; and Ilisidi herself had said white would do very well with his fair hair, show his independence from the black and red of the aiji's house—and offend no one.

He glowed, he was well aware, like a pale neon sign to any sniper in the recesses behind those floodlights.

But count on it: there'd been a thorough security search before he entered the building and one last night, a search not only by his security, with an interest in keeping him alive; but also by lord Geigi's, interested in keeping their lord alive and in keeping any of lord Geigi's enemies from embarrassing him in an attack on the paidhi.

He knew for that reason that he was an inconvenience to the plant workers, who'd had to pass meticulous security to get to work this morning.

But the paidhi, personally sent by the aiji in Shejidan, was making a gesture of public support such as atevi politics absolutely demanded. The workers would see it. Atevi interested in Geigi's fortunes would witness another indication of Geigi's rescue from economic ruin and his subsequent rise to prominence and economic power in his region.

And standing where he was the paidhi only hoped all Geigi's people were loyal. Tano and Algini might well have been drinking antacids by the bottleful since he'd set down at the airport, and declared he'd sleep in Geigi's house, and now at the plant manager's urging he'd agreed to walk up on this exposed platform. Even they, however, had to admit that the odds of treachery from Geigi were practically nil and that the odds that Geigi would have loyalty from his own people were high. From the atevi point of view Geigi's numbers were still in active increase and therefore a problem in the atevi version of calculus.

Besides, no one had tried to file Intent on the paidhi's life in, oh, at least a month.

That was what the analysts in the aiji's court called *acceptable risk* in making this stop on his tour in the first place. The professionals guarding him while he was in the district making such spontaneous gestures he was sure had other words for it.

"Splendid effort," he declared to lord Geigi. "I'm truly amazed at the progress. I'm absolutely amazed. So will the aiji be."

"Nand' Borujiri," lord Geigi said, "has worked very hard."

"Nand' Borujiri." He inclined his head to acknowledge that worthy gentleman, director of Patinandi Aerospace, who despite physical frailty had accompanied him up to the highest catwalk, followed by the lords of townships within lord Geigi's association in Sarini Province. "I shall convey your recommendations to the aiji. Absolutely splendid organization. One would wish to render appreciation to all the persons responsible."

"Nand' paidhi," Borujiri said, moving slowly, not only because of age but also a long illness. "My monument, this work. I am determined it will be that. I have dedicated a portion of my estate to the recreation of the workers who will entitle themselves in this effort. And such an effort our people have made!"

"Everything here is in shifts," lord Geigi interposed. "Nothing stops for night. And quality control, nand' paidhi, meticulous quality control." A horn sounded several short bursts, a signal for attention; Bren and his trigger-ready security had been advised in advance, and lord Geigi rested hands on the catwalk rail looking out over the vast assembly area. "Nadiin-ji! The paidhi commends your work and your diligence! Attention, if you please, to the paidhi-aiji!"

He grew used to such addresses. But reporters dogged him: there were reporters below who would carry what he said to the news services, reporters who, because of the major transportation lines, were in greater abundance here than in his last two, more rural, stops.

"Nadiin," he called out to the upturned faces and himself leaned on the forbidden railing. "You have exceeded ambitious expectations and set high standards, *high* standards, in work on which brave atevi will rely for their lives in space. But more than that—" It was in truth a beautiful sight in front of him, those pieces. Though for the reporters' sakes, he tried to provide variety in his speeches and at the same time to keep them brief, he suddenly meant to say *something* different than he'd said before on such tours. In the presence of old Borujiri and lord Geigi, in this first time that he could allow himself to believe there *was* a spacecraft, and in the enthusiasm of engineers and ordinary workers who had foregone vacations and ignored quitting times to advance the work—he felt his inspiration.

"More than that, nadiin-nai, high standards in a work unprecedented in the history of the world. Plates of steel may make a sailing ship. But when it takes to the waves, when hands at work make that ship a living creature, then it binds all that ship's makers and all who ever sail aboard that ship in an association that reaches to every shore that ship touches. Your hands and your efforts are building a ship to carry the hopes of all the world, nadiin! The work of your hands, the vision of your director, the wisdom of your lords, and

the courage of atevi who will ride this ship will reach
out to new things in the heavens, and draw the heavens
and all their possibilities into your arms. The aiji in
Shejidan will receive my report of you as extraordinary
and dedicated workers, and I do not doubt you will
remain in his mind at the next seasonal audience, at
which lord Geigi and nand' Borujiri inform me and
permit me to inform you they will sponsor a representative from each shift at their own expense. My con-
gratulations, nadiin, I need not offer you! You have
distinguished yourselves and brought credit to your
province, your district, your endeavor! Hundreds of
years from now atevi will tell the story, how willing
hands and the skill of such builders carried atevi into
space on their own terms and in their own right!"

He expected nothing but the polite attention atevi
paid a speaker, followed by the formal, measured
applause.

"Nand' paidhi!" he heard instead, and then a
shouting from throughout the facility. "Nand' Bren!"

That less than formal title had gotten started in the
less reputable press. He blushed and waved, and
stepped away from the rail, at which point Tano
and Algini closed between him and the crowd, a living wall.

"Nand' paidhi," lord Geigi said, and wished him
with a gesture to go down.

"A wonderful expression." Nand' Borujiri was
clearly moved. "I shall have it engraved, nand' paidhi.
A marvelous gift!"

"You are very kind, nand' director."

"A passionate speech," lord Geigi said, and kept
close by him as they descended. "If the aiji can spare
you, nadi, *please* accept my personal hospitality and
extend your visit to a few days at Dalaigi, at a far
slower pace, in, I assure you, the most wonderful cli-
mate in the country. The yellowtail will not wait. The
paperwork will always be there. And if you provide my
cook the fish and a day to prepare it, nand' paidhi, I do
assure you the result will be an exquisite, very pas-

sionate offering. He so approves your taste in your brief experience of his art last evening."

It was partly, he was sure, formality and a desire not to have Borujiri suggest the same; it was likely, also, a truly honest offer, repeated, now, and he understood from Algini that the cook was extremely pleased in his requests for a local specialty last evening. The man *was* an excellent cook: Geigi's relationship with food was unabashed and the cuisine of the household was deservedly renowned.

He was weakening. He was about to request his security to inquire of his office whether he could possibly manage one more day.

But he felt a sharp vibration from his pocket-com as they started down the third tier of steps, and that flutter signaled him his security was wanting his attention or advising him to the negative—the latter, he decided, when Tano cast him a direct look and no encouraging *if the paidhi would prefer* regarding that invitation to a change in flight schedules and a return to the lord's residence.

"I fear, nandi," Bren sighed, "that my schedule back in the capital precludes it." He had no warning in that small vibration of imminent danger. He took it for his staff's warning against lingering in public view or a simple advisement he was, with more urgency than anyone had yet communicated to him, expected elsewhere. "But if the invitation were extended again through your kindness, perhaps for some other seasonal game, I would be more than pleased, nand' Geigi, very truthfully."

God, he *wanted* that holiday, and he *liked-liked-liked* lord Geigi against all common sense governing use of that deceptive and deadly word, and he *didn't* want to hear from his security that lord Geigi had changed sides again.

He set foot on the floor of the assembly area and the battalion of reporters tried to reach him. But the frontal assault of cameras failed to breach his security, as Tano and Algini directed him and his entire party aside through the plant manager's office and up against the earnest good wishes of a woman who, like Borujiri, saw fortune and good repute in his visit.

"Nand' paidhi!" She bowed, and proffered a card with a ribbon, white, for the paidhi, a card which the thoughtful staff had handed out to certain key people. There was the smell of heated wax, a wax-jack waiting in the office for that operation, and immediately lord Geigi and nand' Borujiri, and a number of other officials came pouring through the door with the news services clamoring outside.

He signed and affixed his seal in wax to cards which would make a proud display on a wall somewhere for not only this generation, but subsequent ones, while his security fumed and clearly wished a quick exit. But there were moments at which haste seemed to create worse problems than apparent lack of it; and they hadn't yet flung him to the floor and drawn guns, so he supposed it wasn't critical.

"The car is waiting, nand' paidhi," Tano said, the moment the last card was stamped.

Escape lay out the door: the news services hadn't yet out-flanked them. Algini went out first, surveying the Guild-provided car which procedure had dictated would never leave the personal surveillance of the paidhi's own security. Tano held the door for him, a living shield against what he had no idea.

For two seconds in that position they were without any locals at all in earshot. "Lord Saigimi is dead," Tano said to him, low and urgently. "Unknown who did it."

So *that* was the emergency. Bren took in his breath, and in the next firing of a neuron thought it likely that lord Geigi, stalled on the other side of the same door, was getting exactly the same news from *his* security.

The lord of the Tasigin Marid, the circle of seacoast at the bottom of the peninsula, was dead, *not* of natural causes.

The lord of the Tasigin Marid, an Edi, was the one interest in the peninsula most violently opposed to the space program. When Geigi had sided with the space program, and when Deana Hanks had provided the bombshell that weakened him politically, lord Saigimi had immediately insisted that lord Geigi pay his personal debts in oil investment in full, which lord Saigimi expected would ruin lord Geigi and force him from power in Dalaigi.

That had *not* been the case, thanks to Grigiji the astronomer.

Geigi came out the door, sober, dead sober in the manner of an ateva when expression might offend someone. Not displeased by the news, Bren would wager. Possibly—the thought hit him like a thunderbolt—Geigi was even directly involved in the assassination.

No. Geigi *wouldn't*. Surely not. Not with the aiji's representative literally under his roof and apt by that to be thought associated with the event.

"News," Bren said, resolved on his own instant judgment to ignore suspicion and treat the man as a cohort—as in the following instant he asked himself was *Tabini* involved—while Tabini's representative was a guest under lord Geigi's roof. "Nandi, lord Saigimi has just been assassinated. I'm immediately concerned for your safety; and I *must* make my flight on schedule. I fear events have left me no choice but to attend to business, and place myself where I can interpret to the ship in case *they* have questions. But will you honor me and ride to the airport with me, in my car?"

Geigi's face bore that slight pallor that an ateva could achieve. Indeed, perhaps Geigi—not involved, and fearing he might be blamed—had been about to cancel the proposed fishing trip as inappropriate under the circumstances, and to offer the use of *his* car for security reasons.

He had, however, just placed the shoe on the other foot.

Offered the man dessert, as the atevi saying went. Meaning the next dish *after* the fatal revelation at dinner.

"Nand' paidhi," Geigi said with a decisive nod of his head, "I shall gladly ride with you, and be honored by your company."

It also was, most definitely, a commitment mutually to be seen in such company: Geigi was casting his lot with the aiji in Shejidan, in case the neighbor lords of the interlaced peninsular association should think of annoying the aiji by striking at the aiji's prize piece in this province.

Geigi walked with him down the concrete path to the car, a quiet progress of themselves and their respective security personnel. "Do," Bren said, almost embarrassed to say, "look to nand' Borujiri's safety as well, Tano-ji."

"We have passed that advice to building security," Tano said as they approached the cars, the centermost of which was his, with others close about it. Tano would in no wise leave him. And somehow Tano had advised building security indeed, probably through Geigi's security, Gesirimu, while he was signing cards, without him ever noticing. *That* was how they'd forestalled the news services getting to the outside door.

"Distressing," lord Geigi said. "I assure the paidhi that no event will threaten his safety. I should be greatly embarrassed if such were the case."

"I would never wish," he said to lord Geigi, "to put my host at risk, and please, lord Geigi, never underestimate the value you represent to the aiji. I know that Tabini-aiji would take strong measures in any action against you or yours."

It was courtly. It was also true. Geigi was getting that ship built. Geigi was the source of stability and employment in the region.

Then as they came close to the road, well-wishers watching from the plant spied them and their company. The plant doors opened, and a crowd came pouring out toward them, waving and offering flowers, accompanied by the news services and the cameras, at which security, his and Geigi's, definitely looked askance.

But the plant workers seemed to have no inkling that there was a security alert in operation, and atevi polite, expressionless silence during a speech didn't at all mean restraint once good will was established. There were cheers, there were bouquets tossed at the handheld rope perimeter which hastily moving plant security established. That the flowers landed on the grass and couldn't be retrieved in no way daunted the well-wishers. The offering was enough, and atevi were used to tight security: the higher the lord, the tighter and more reactive the guard around him.

Bren darted a few meters from the walk to the lawn, stooped and picked up a bouquet himself, as a lord of the Association couldn't possibly do, but he, the human, he of the white ribbon, he had no such reservations and no great requirement of lordly dignity. He held the bouquet of flowers aloft and waved it at the cheering crowd as Algini and Tano urged him toward the open car door.

But the good will of the commons was his defense as well, and taking such gambles was in some measure his job. The crowd was delighted with his gesture. They shouted and waved the more. It satisfied the news services, who had a good clip of more than people walking to the cars.

Defending him from the consequences of such gestures was of course Tano's and Algini's job, and as he and lord Geigi entered the car from opposite sides, Tano entered to assume *his* back-facing seat in the capacious rear of the car and Algini took the front seat by the driver. Cars full of security staff preceded them as they pulled out; and more cars would come behind.

"One still extends the invitation," lord Geigi said. "I know that fish is laughing at us."

"I look forward," Bren said, "to the hunt for this fish. I hope for an invitation in the next passage of this reckless creature. I *wish* I might have had a try this season. I hope you will remember me in the next."

"One indeed will. Beyond a doubt."

Clearly Tano and Algini weren't going to relax until he was out of the province.

But he trusted they had heard the news of the assassination before the news services had heard, unless reporters of the same news services had happened to surround lord Saigimi at the very moment of his death—and then only if they had the kind of communications

the Guild had. His security had heard as fast as they had
because the agency responsible (or Saigimi's guard) was
electronically plugged into the Assassins' Guild, which
was able to get direct messages to Guild members faster
than the aiji's personal representatives, who weren't
always told what was going on.

And it *was* a Guild assassination, or there'd be real
trouble. The Guild was a fair broker and a peace-
keeper. It might authorize a contract for an assassination to be carried out by one member but it didn't
withdraw resources from other members in good
standing who might be defending the intended target. It
most severely frowned upon collateral damage—
biichi'ji, finesse, was a point of pride of the Guild in
authorizing and legally notifying targets as well as in
carrying out contracts—and the Assassins' Guild did
pass warnings where warnings were due in order to
prevent such damage.

So, of course, did Tabini-aiji pass warnings of his
own intent to his own security, who might not be
informed by their Guild—even the aiji filed Intent, as
he had seen once upon a time. But lords and lunatics,
as Tano had once said, didn't always file, and defense
didn't always know in advance. If Tabini had taken
lord Saigimi down, Tano and Algini might possibly
know it from Tabini's sources.

Unless it was Geigi who had done it. He was very
conscious of the rather plump and pleasant ateva
weighing down the seat cushion beside him, in this car
that held the pleasant musky scent of atevi, the size and
mass of atevi. It would certainly make sense. Geigi was
not the complacent man he'd seemed, and Geigi had
shifted loyalties last year *away* from lord Saigimi's
plots against the aiji.

It made thorough sense that Geigi, with his new
resources, had placed Guild members as near Saigimi
as he could get them; it was an easy bet that Saigimi
had done exactly the same thing in lord Geigi's district.

So there was very good reason, in the direct involvement of lord Geigi with past events, for the paidhi's
security to be very anxious about that gesture of stop-

ping and picking up the flowers. Sometimes, Bren thought, he had an amazing self-destructive streak.

Geigi leaving his own security to other cars, to sit beside him surrounded by Tabini's agents, was a declaration of strong reliance on the paidhi and on the aiji in Shejidan; but it also tainted the paidhi and the aiji with collusion if Geigi had done it.

Damn. Surely not. *Tabini* knew where he was and what was going on. Tabini's security wouldn't let him make that mistake.

Meanwhile all those reporters who had gathered to cover the plant tour were back there to report his inviting lord Geigi under his protection the length and breadth of the peninsula, not to mention reporting the gesture to all the lords of the Association.

Among them, in the Padi Valley to north, was the lady Direiso of the Kadigidi house, who truly did wish the paidhi dead, and who was alive herself only because the power vacuum her death would create could be more troublesome to the aiji than her living presence.

Direiso. *That* was an interesting question.

3

The cars of the escort passed like toys under the right-hand wing as the private jet made the turn toward home. A bright clot of flowers, more bouquets and wreaths, showed on the concrete where the plane had stood. Now they surrounded a cluster of black car roofs.

So lord Geigi hadn't driven off once the plane's doors had closed, nor even during the long wait while the plane had taxied far across to the east-west runway. Geigi had waited to see it in the air.

Even now, a small number of atevi were standing beside the cars, watching the plane, extravagant gesture from a lord of the Association, in a politics in which all such gestures had meaning.

No word for love in the Ragi language, and no word for friend, even a friend of casual sort. Among the operational ironies of the language, or the atevi mind, it rendered it very hard for an ateva in lord Geigi's situation to make his personal position clear, once there were logical reasons to suspect his associations—because associations colored everything, demanded everything, slanted everything.

Bren found himself quite—humanly speaking—*touched* by the display now vanishing below his window, not doubting the plant workers and the common people of the white-plaster township that came up in his view. They were the offerers of those flowers.

But from this perspective of altitude and distance, he was no longer blindly trusting.

Not even of lord Geigi, except as Geigi's known and unknown associations currently tended toward the same political focus as his own: toward Tabini, aiji of the Western Association, Tabini, who owned this plane, and the security, and the loyalties of lords and commons all across the continent.

Man'chi. Instinctual, not consciously chosen, loyalty. Identical man'chi made allies. There was no other meaningful reckoning.

You couldn't say that human word 'border,' either, to limit off the land passing under them. An atevi map didn't really have boundaries. It had land ownership—sort of. It had townships, but their edges were fuzzy. You said 'province,' and that was *close* to lines on a map, and it definitely *had* a geographical context, but it didn't mean what you thought it did if you were a hard-headed human official trying to force mainland terms into Mospheiran boxes. So whatever he had experienced down there, it didn't have edges, as the land didn't have edges, as overlapping associations didn't have edges.

A thought like that could, if analyzed, give one solitary human a lonely longing for *something* he touched to mean something human and ordinary and touch him back, and for something to satisfy the stirrings of affection that good actions made in a human heart.

But *if* something did, was it real? Was affection real because one side of the transaction felt it, if the other side in responding always felt something different?

The sound of one hand clapping. Was that what he heard?

The plane leveled out to pursue its course to the northeast. Outside the window now were the hills of the southern peninsula, Talidi Province, a geographical distinction, again without firm edges. Beyond that hazy range of hills to the south sat the Marid Tasigin, the coastal communities where lord Saigimi had had greatest influence, which would be in turmoil just now as the word of their lord's assassination spread.

Out the other window, across the working space on this modest-sized executive jet, he saw only blue sky. He knew what he would see if he got up and took a look: the same shining, wave-wrinkled sea he had seen from Geigi's balcony, and the same haze on the horizon that was the southern shore of Mospheira.

He didn't want to get up and look in that direction this afternoon. He'd done too much looking and too much thinking this morning, until, without even thinking about it, he'd rubbed raw a small spot in his sensibilities that he'd thought was effectively numb.

Thinking about *it,* like a fool, he began to think about Barb, and his mother and his brother, and wondered what the weather was like and whether his brother, ignoring the death threats for an hour or two, was tinkering with his boat again, the way he did on spring evenings.

That part of his life he just had to seal off. Let it alone, quit scratching the scab. He'd just come too close to Mospheira this leg of the trip, had it too visible to him out the plane window, had sat there on that balcony with too much time to think.

The other part, his job, his duty, whatever he wanted to call it—

Well, at least *that* was going far better than he'd hoped.

Every cheering success like that in the town and factory dropping away in jet-spanned distance behind them was another direct challenge to contrary atevi powers only uneasily restrained within the Association: if they didn't get rid of Tabini fast, the dullest of them could see that the change they were fighting was going to become a fact of atevi life so deeply rooted in the economy it would survive Tabini. Life, even if Tabini died this minute, would never be what it would have been had Tabini never lived.

Numerous lords among the atevi were hostile to human cultural influence—hell, one could about say *every* lord of the Association including Tabini himself had misgivings about human culture, although even Tabini was weakening on the issue of television and lengthening the hours the stations were permitted to transmit, a relaxation the paidhi had begun to worry about.

Other lords and representatives were amenable to human technology as far as it benefited their districts but hostile to Tabini as an overlord for historic and ethnic reasons.

And there were a handful of atevi both lordly and common who were bitterly opposed to both.

In all, it was an uneasy pedestal for a government that had generally kept its equilibrium only by Tabini's skill at balancing threat and reward. Geigi was a good instance: Geigi had very possibly started in the camp of the lords hostile to Tabini for reasons that had nothing to do with technology and everything to do with ethnic divisions among atevi.

But when Geigi had gotten himself in over his head, financially, politically, and by association, Tabini had not only refrained from removing him or humiliating him, Tabini had acknowledged that the peninsula had been on the short end of government appointments and contracts for some time (no accident, counting the presence of Tabini's bitterest enemies in control of the peninsula) and agreed that Geigi, honest, honorable lord Geigi, was justified in his complaints.

Now Geigi, who'd had the only large aircraft manufacturing plant in the world in his province, which *could* have been replaced, out-competed, even moved out of the district by order of the aiji, owed his very life and the prosperity of his local association to his joining Tabini's side.

So now director Borujiri was firmly on Tabini's side, and so were those workers. If atevi were going to space faster than planned, it was a windfall for Patinandi Aerospace, the chance of a lifetime for Borujiri, prosperity for a locally depressed job market, and a dazzling rise to prominence for a quiet, honest lord who'd invested his money in the Tasigin Marid oilfields and lost nearly everything—no help from Saigimi, whose chiseling relatives were in charge of the platforms that failed.

What promises Saigimi might have obtained from Geigi and then called due in the attempt last year to replace the paidhi with the paidhi-successor, he could only guess. Geigi had never alluded to that part of the story.

And how dismayed Geigi and Saigimi alike had been when the paidhi-successor rewarded her atevi supporters by dropping information on them that had as well have been a nuclear device—all of that was likely lost in Geigi's immaculate discretion and now in Saigimi's demise. No one might ever know the whole tale of that adventure.

And, damn, but he wished he did, for purely vulgar curiosity, if nothing else.

But clearly the Saigimi matter had either stayed hotter longer than he would have believed that last year's assassination attempt could remain an issue with Tabini—or it had heated up again very suddenly and for reasons that he'd failed to detect in planning this trip.

That was granting Tabini had in fact done in Saigimi.

In the convoluted logic he'd learned to tread in atevi motivations, if Tabini *had* done it, perhaps Saigimi's assassination had been timed *precisely* for the hour he was with Geigi on public view and thereby reassuring Geigi of the aiji's good will: if the news had come in the middle of the night and on any ordinary day, Geigi might have concluded the aiji was beginning a purge of enemies.

Then Geigi might have done something disastrous, like running to lady Direiso, far more dangerous an enemy than Saigimi, and that might have led to Geigi's death—if Geigi misread Direiso. Or, potentially, though he himself doubted it, it could have led to Direiso rallying the rest of her band of conspirators, drawing Geigi back to her man'chi, and setting him against Tabini, a realignment that would hold that ship back there hostage to all kinds of demands.

Tabini preferred not to provoke terror. In atevi terms, only a fool made his enemies nervous; and a far, far greater fool frightened his potential allies. Tabini rarely resorted to such an extreme measure as assassination, preferring to leave old and well-known problems holding power in certain places rather than elevating unknown successors who might be up to God knew what without such good and detailed reports coming back to him. That tendency to let a situation float if he had good intelligence coming back to him was a consideration which ought to disturb lady Direiso's sleep.

And in that consideration, either something had happened sufficient to top Saigimi's last offenses, demanding his removal or, it was even possible—the assassination of Saigimi had in fact been simply a warning aimed at Direiso, who was the principal opposition to Tabini.

Certainly it was possible that Direiso was the real target.

He certainly hadn't been moved to discuss that question with Geigi; and as for Tano and Algini, in the one careful question he had put to them as they boarded: "Is this something you know about, nadiin, and is the aiji well?" they had professed not to know the agency that had done it, but had assured him with what sounded like certain knowledge that Tabini was safe.

They were usually more forthcoming.

And now that he began thinking about it—neglecting the business of collating his notes, the paidhi's proper job—the news of Saigimi's death was eerily like a letter from an absent—

Friend.

Oh, a *bad* mental slip, that was.

But Banichi was infallibly Banichi as Jago was Jago, his own security for part of the last year, as close to him as any atevi had ever been. And of the very few assassins of the Guild to whom Tabini might entrust something so delicate as the removal of a high lord of the Association, Banichi and his partner surely topped the list.

Banichi and Jago, both of whom he regarded in that spot humans kept soft and warm and vulnerable in their hearts; and both of whom had been on assignment somewhere, absent from Shejidan, unlocatable to his troubled inquiries for months.

Tano and Algini, fellow members of the Guild, had assured him all winter that Banichi and Jago were well and busy about something. He sent letters to them. He thought they were sent, at least. But nothing came back.

And, no, neither Tano nor Algini knew whether or not Banichi and Jago might return. He'd asked them whenever something came up that provided a remotely plausible excuse for his asking: Banichi and Jago both outranked Tano and Algini, and he never, ever wanted to make Tano and Algini doubt his appreciation of their service to him—but—he wondered. He worried about the pair of them.

Dammit, he missed them.

And that wasn't fair to the staff he did have, who were skilled, and very devoted, and who offered him all the support and protection and devotion that atevi of their Guild could possibly offer, including a roster of Tano's relatives, one of whom headed the paidhi's clerical staff and some of whom, technical writers in offices across the mainland, sent him messages through Tano, whose clan seemed prolific, all very good and very solid people.

And Algini, God, Algini, who seemed to come solo except for his long attachment to his partner. Algini had been much longer unbending and had been far more standoffish than Tano had ever been, but Algini was a quiet, good man, who could throw a knife with truly uncanny accuracy, who had gotten (Tano hinted) two very bad assignments from which he had suffered great personal distress; and who had, Tano had said, been so quiet within the Guild they'd lost track of him for two years and dropped him from the rolls as dead until Tano had pointed out he'd been voting consistently and that he could vouch for his identity—they'd been partners for two years on the same assignments—and it was the aiji's request for them as personal security that had pulled up the information that Algini was listed as dead. Algini thought it a joke quite as funny as Tano did, but the paidhi understood it was a joke that had never gotten beyond the very clandestine walls of their Guild, and it was an embarrassment to the Guild never, ever meant for public knowledge.

It was indicative, however, of how very good Algini was at melding with the walls of a place. After nearly a year with the man, he'd finally gotten Algini to unzip his jacket, prop his feet up in complete informality, and smile, shyly so, but an approach to a grin, over one of Tano's pieces of irreverence.

Right now Algini was on his feet, zipped up to the chin and all business, up at the forward bulkhead, talking to Tano, who was also sober, while junior staff kept their distance, all frustrating his desire for information. He supposed that his staff was trying to get accurate reports on the situation in the Marid before they told him anything, or possibly reports were coming in from various other affected places, some of which they had to route over, and one of which might even be a touchy situation in the capital. There were times to talk to one's security and there were times to stay out of their way and let them work.

And right now he had notes to work over, a job to do. Possibly there were deaths happening. Possibly—

Hell, no, he couldn't do anything about it. And they didn't need his advice. He'd been long enough on the mainland to know certain things intellectually, and to understand the atevi way of doing things as part of a wider fabric that actually saved lives.

But he'd made the decision some time ago that he never wanted to get so acclimated that he didn't think about it. It still *had* to bother him. It was necessary to his job that it continue to bother him: he was supposed to translate, not transit into the culture, and no matter how emotionally he was tempted to damn Saigimi to hell for the decent people whose lives Saigimi had cost, he had to remember he *didn't* know what the reason was, not at the bone-deep and instinctual level at which atevi knew what they were doing to each other. He had to stay out of it.

He opened his computer as the plane reached cruising altitude, and called up dictionary files that held hundreds of such distinctions as man'chi unresolved.

Loyalty wasn't man'chi; man'chi wasn't loyalty. Man'chi responded to the order of the universe, a harmony which in some indefinable way dictated man'chi, and didn't.

Man'chi, he had learned, was emotional. Association was logical. And to figure how some other ateva saw them, atevi were mathematicians par excellence. One constantly added the numbers of one's life, some of more traditional philosophy believing literally that the date of one's birth and the felicitous or infelicitous numbers of one's intimate associates or the flowers in a bouquet mattered to the harmony of the cosmos, and dictated the direction one moved. Logically.

Tabini was a skeptic in such matters and regularly mocked the purists. Tabini would say, half facetiously, that Saigimi hadn't added his own numbers correctly, and had been unaware what the sum was in the aiji's mind.

Best for a human to stay right in the guessable center of a man'chi directed to a very powerful ateva, best that he listen to his security personnel, and never, never, never tread the edges with unapproved persons.

Deana Hanks had started out her tenure by courting the edges, and now had more blood on her hands than she would ever comprehend. Saigimi's, for instance. The circles of the stone she'd so recklessly cast into the waters, in her seeking out atevi who could give her an opinion opposed to the aiji (every dissident she could find), had associated a number of atevi who might never have been encouraged to associate. Hanks might *well* have killed Saigimi.

In the human sense of responsibility, that was.

Atevi would just say she'd brought infelicitous numbers into Saigimi's situation and Saigimi had done nothing ever since but make them worse.

"Fruit juice, nand' paidhi?" the juniormost of the guards asked, and Bren surfaced from the electronic sea of data to accept the offered drink.

It was about a two hour trip from the peninsula to Shejidan, factoring in the devious routing that took this particular flight into Shejidan Airport as if it originated from the east instead of the west. The detour wasn't much out of their way, but the plane had turned about half an hour ago, and that told Bren fairly well where they were.

He feared he would meet security delays due to the assassination in the south. He almost wished the food offering were something more than fruit juice, but he'd wait for food until he reached secure territory—they'd been to three towns and made four courtesy stops without taking on security-approved food service, they'd crossed boundaries that held the appropriate meat for the season to be something different than the last had. It was one of those little matters that didn't matter to every ateva, but that had to matter to the aiji's private plane, and he truly didn't think he could stomach another fish salad or egg salad sandwich, the items that were almost always *kabiu,* proper, and almost always the fallback for any plane with a security problem and a lot of seasonal zones to cross.

The sandwiches had seemed quite good, on the first three days of this eight day tour.

"Any news?" he asked the guard, meaning the Saigimi situation, which was bound to be general knowledge by now throughout the country as the news hit the television networks, and the guard said, "Shall I ask, nand' paidhi?"

There was, he understood by that offer, official news; and the junior guard wasn't going to inform the paidhi's serious need to know with his limited knowledge: the junior guard was, by that question, offering to advise his officer that the paidhi was asking.

"Do," he said, and before he'd downed the second sip of the glass Tano was there, slipping into the seat facing his.

"By your leave, nand' paidhi, the situation in the Bujavid is calm and the capital itself is quiet. We thought of routing you instead to Taiben, but there seems no need. Given your agreement, we'll proceed on to the airport."

"What do *you* think, Tano-ji?" It hadn't been his intention at all to question the security arrangements. "Absolutely I trust your judgment."

"I think we should go in as quickly as possible, nand' paidhi. I'm assured we'll be met by very adequate security, and the longer we delay the harder it may be to guarantee that, at least for the next few hours. Celebration is more likely than opposition to this event, as I would gather will be the case behind us in Sarini province; and that will discourage fools from unFiled retaliations. Professionals, however, may still be acting under legal contract against persons other than yourself, nand' paidhi, and I would advise discretion."

"I'm sure." Things were stiffly formal when Tano and Algini had the staff present, or he'd invite Tano and Algini both to sit down, share a drink, and tell him the *real* goings-on. The plane flew serenely between a human-occupied heaven and an atevi earth in turmoil. And his security, licensed assassins of the Guild, declared it safe to go into the capital city airport, but there were elements loose and still in motion that had them worried. That was what he heard in Tano's statement: knowledge of a threat not precisely aimed at him but through which he might have to pass. Guild members contracted to Saigimi were professionals who would not waste themselves or their colleagues' lives in a lost cause, but there would be moves for power within the clan and around it. Aftershocks were not over.

Trust these two, and leave Geigi, who owed him

his intercession and thereby his survival? Absolutely. Tano's and Algini's man'chi was to Tabini, and if Tabini ever wanted him dead, these were the very ones who would see to it. If Tabini wanted him alive, these were the ones who would fling their bodies between him and a bullet without a second thought. Man'chi was very simple until one approached the hazy ground between households, which was where Geigi's grew too indistinct to trust in a crisis like this. Man'chi went upward to the leader but not *down* from him. It was instinct. It was mathematics as atevi added matters. And these two advised him to move quickly and not to divert to any other destination.

So he simply began to fold up his work and to shut down his computer as Tano got up again to order something regarding their landing.

The plane banked sharply and dived, sending dignified atevi careening against the seats and up. Bren clamped his fingers to hold onto his precious computer as the smooth plastic case slid inexorably through his grip, aimed by centrifugal force at the window.

Fruit juice had hit the same window and wall and stood in orange beads.

The plane leveled out.

"Nand' paidhi," the copilot said over the speakers, *"forgive us. That was a plane in our path."*

Tano and Algini and the rest of the staff were sorting themselves out. The juniormost, Audiri, came immediately with a towel, retrieved the glass, which had not broken, and mopped the fruit juice off various surfaces.

He had not let the computer escape his grasp. His fingers felt bruised. His heart hadn't had time to speed up. Now, belatedly, it wondered whether it might have license to do that, but the conscious brain advised it to forget it, it was much too late.

"Nadiin," Algini was saying to the crew via the intercom, "kindly determine origin and advise air traffic control that the aiji's staff requests names and identifications of the aircraft in this matter."

"Probably it's nothing," Bren muttered, allowing Tano custody of the precious computer. The air traffic

control system was relatively new. Planes were not.
Certain individuals considered themselves immune to
ATC regulations.

If on a given day, and by their numerology, certain
individuals of the Absolutist persuasion considered the
system gave them infelicitous numbers, they would
change those numbers on their own and change their
course, their altitude, or their arrival time so as to have
their important business in the capital blessed by better
fortune.

And the assassination to the south had *changed* the
numbers.

Tabini and the ATC authority had fought that battle
for years, particularly trying to impress the facts of
physics on lords used to being immune to lawsuit.
There were laws. There were ATC regulations. There
was the aiji's express displeasure at such violations,
and there was the outstanding example of the Weinathi
Bridge disaster for a cautionary tale.

Security today had been very careful to move the
aiji's private plane onto a flight path usually followed
by slower-moving commercial air . . . for the paidhi's
safety.

His security was understandably worried about the
incident. But whatever the closeness of the other aircraft had been, the emergency was over. The plane did
some small maneuvering as the nose pitched gently
down and it resumed its landing approach.

Tano and Algini came to sit opposite him for the
landing, and belted in.

"Likely it was someone *else* worried by the Saigimi
business," Bren said. "And likewise taking precautions
about their routing. Or their numbers. I doubt it was
intentional."

"The aiji will not take chances with you, nadi Bren,"
Tano said.

"I'm sure not, Tano."

The Bergid showed in the window, hazy mountains,
still white with winter, the continental divide.

Forest showed, blue-green and likewise hazed—
but that haze was pollen and spores, as a lowland

spring broke into bloom and the endless forests of atevi hunting preserves, like the creatures that lived within that haze, reproduced themselves with wild abandon.

The fields came clear, the little agricultural land that developers had left around burgeoning Shejidan. And there were the stubbornly held garden plots clinging to hillsides—always the gardens: the Ragi atevi were keen diggers and planters, even the aristocrats among them. Gardens, but no livestock for food: atevi considered it cruel and uncivilized to eat tame animals.

Came then the geometries of tiled roofs, marching in numerically significant orders up and down the hills—little roofs, bigger roofs, and the cluster of hotels and modern buildings that snuggled as close as possible to the governmental center, the ancient Bu-javid, the aiji's residence. It was daylight. One saw no neon lights.

The plane banked and turned and leveled again, swooping in over the flat roofs of industry that had grown up around the airport.

Patinandi Aerospace was one: that large building he well knew was a maintenance facility. The aiji had spread the bounty of space industry wide throughout the provinces, and the push to get into space had wrought changes this year that wouldn't be stopped. Ever.

There was a new computer manufacturing plant, and atevi designers were fully capable of making critical adjustments in what humans had long regarded as one of the final secrets, the one that would adjust atevi society into a more and more comprehensible mold.

Not necessarily so.

Faster and faster the pavement rushed under the wings.

Wheels touched dry pavement, squealed arrival.

The paidhi-aiji was as close to home as he was likely to come. This was it. Shejidan.

And hearing the wheels thump and roll and hearing the engines brake and feeling the reality of ground under him again, he let go a freer breath and knew, first, he was in the safest place in the world for him, and second, that he was among the people in the world most interested in his welfare.

Delusion, perhaps, but he'd grown to rely on it.

4

The van transfer to the subway in the airport terminal was thankfully without extravagant welcome, media, or official inquiry. The paidhi-aiji was home. The paidhi-aiji *and* his luggage, this time together and without misdirection, actually reached the appropriate subway car, and without incident the car set into motion on its trip toward the Bu-javid, on its lofty and historic hill on the edge of Shejidan.

Then, while he leaned back in comfort and velvet splendor, there arrived, via his security's com link, a radioed communication from the airport authorities requesting an interview with the aiji's pilot and copilot, and reporting the identity of the pilot of the strayed prop plane: the son of the lord of the island of Dur, one Rejiri of the Niliini of Dur-wajran, whose affiliations Tano and Algini were ordering researched by grim and secret agencies which, God help them, the lords of Dur-wajran had probably never encountered in their wildest imaginations.

Figure that the owner of such a private plane was affluent. Figure that on the small island of Dur opposing traffic wasn't a problem the pilot, possibly of the only plane on the island of Dur, had ever met.

But as an accident, or near accident, it wasn't the paidhi's business to investigate or to deal with. Someone else had to explain the air traffic regulations to the lord's son. He sat back in the soft red seats of Tabini's private subway car and had a glass of fruit juice, confident his second try at a drink would stay in the glass. He timed the last sip nicely for the arrival at the station.

He let a junior security staffer carry the computer as he rose and left the car. He let others, very junior, carry the baggage while the clerical, Surieji, carried the voluminous physical notes. He let Tano and Algini deal with the details of routing himself and his entourage together down the concrete and tile walk in the very security-conscious Bu-javid station. The whole apparatus of government as well as the seasonal residences of various lords was above their heads in this echoing cavern, and he walked entirely at his ease to the lift that would carry him, Tano, and Algini to the third floor of the residences.

His apartment, on loan from the Atageini, was next door to Tabini's own residence, a location he could hardly complain of for security or comfort; but getting to and from it was a matter of armed and high-clearance security. There was no forgetting something at the office, for damn certain, and dashing solo back after it.

But long gone were the days when he could go anywhere unguarded, anyway.

"Tabini-aiji wishes to see you personally," Algini reported to him as they activated the lift, information doubtless from the device he had set in his ear. "But nand' Eidi says that the aiji is occupied with briefings at the moment. He says further that you may rely on him that the aiji will, contrary to his expectations, be occupied all evening, and Eidi-nai will take the responsibility of saying so. He hopes that the paidhi will rest comfortably, quite likely for the night, although I myself would never promise that that will be the case. The aiji does as the aiji will do."

Eidi was Tabini's chief of household staff, an elderly man, whose good will and private counsel one wisely kept.

"I have no regrets for a night of rest, nadi-ji, I assure you." The business with the stray plane had taken the spare adrenaline out of him. He felt bone tired, and a quiet dinner *and* a night of sleep in a familiar bed before dealing with any political matters, especially the very far-reaching politics afoot at the moment in the aiji's residence, came very welcome. He'd regretted the day's vacation he couldn't get, but now he wondered where he'd have gotten the energy to go out on the boat, let alone fight a fish of record proportions.

He wondered, with the comfort of familiar things, what Jason Graham had been doing in his absence, and how Jase had fared, left alone with the staff who spoke nothing but Ragi.

And he wondered whether or not the workmen repairing the historic Atageini lilies in the breakfast room (a casualty of a security incident) had gotten the painting done. They'd proposed to do that during the dry weather that had been forecast—accurately, as happened; he'd followed the weather reports as one touch he could maintain with Shejidan.

He'd imagined the tiled roofs of Shejidan under sunshine, under twilight—security might change the view on him, moving him here and there within the Bujavid, and he knew that one of these days the Atageini clan who really owned the apartment he was using had to repossess it, but for the while it was home to him; and the weather on the television in his hotel room had linked him with this place, and with what had become home.

And, oh, he was glad to be back, now. If there was a piece of hardwiring atevi and humans must share, he thought in that wandering way of a mind unwinding its tensions, it had to be the instinct that needed that anchor of a place to come back to. He felt vast relief as the lift let the three of them out upstairs, in the most secure area in the Bu-javid, a familiar hall lined with extravagant porcelain bouquets in glass cases, marble floor hushed by a broad carpet runner, gold-colored, hand-loomed and elaborately figured.

They reached the door of the apartment, a short walk from the lift, which would bring up more of the party, and items of luggage. Instead of using the key he was sure Tano had, Tano quietly rang for attention.

The lift opened again. Their luggage was catching

up. The door in front of them opened, the deadly devices deactivated, one sincerely trusted, which would have been the delay, and a servant let them in, as a half dozen other servants (they were all female in this household, which had been lady Damiri's before she scandalized the whole Atageini clan by moving next door and residing openly with Tabini) converged to take custody of the paidhi and his coat and his luggage.

"Nand' paidhi." Saidin, major domo of the lady Damiri, came from the inner halls to meet them in the foyer. She was a genteel and gentle household administrator who took her human guest's comfort and safety very seriously—and who probably rendered reports to lady Damiri on a regular basis. "One is very glad to see you safely arrived, nand' paidhi."

"Thank you." He'd bet any amount of his uncollectible wages that Saidin was well-briefed on the reason for the just slightly early arrival, maybe even on the ATC incident; and he knew by experience that everything he could possibly need would appear like magic.

"Bath and dinner, do we correctly apprehend your wishes?"

"Nand' Saidin, very correctly."

He was hungry, and in no mood to deal with the message bowl which sat on the small ornate table by the entryway, but he could see there a number of waiting cylinders. The only such that reached his apartment nowadays were messages his clerical staff couldn't handle without advice. And there was a fair collection of them, about twenty, most in metal message cases; but one—one was a caseless vellum scroll characteristic of a telegram from the wire service. It could be from some department across the country, some place he'd visited. The rest could wait. He picked that one up, cracked the seal with his thumbnail, scanned the content, because there was the remotest chance it *might* be from Barb, who had sent him a couple of messages on island gossip since her marriage; or it might be from his mother; or even from official channels in Foreign Affairs.

It was from his brother. From Toby. Dated two days ago.

Mother's been in the hospital. I've asked her to come and stay with me. If you can bring any influence to bear, it might help. She says her doctor's there and she won't leave the city. I'll write you a longer letter later. Don't worry about it, but I think we need to bring some pressure to bear to get her to move. I want your backing in this.

Damn, he thought. *Just* what their mother needed. Pressure.

Damn, again.

He supposed he'd stopped quite still, when in standard procedure he ought to have left the foyer and let his staff get to work on his behalf. They were all standing there. The door was shut. There came a rap from outside.

"That will be the luggage, nadi," Tano said, and took a look outside to be absolutely sure before he opened the door.

Bren pocketed the message. *Write you a letter later.* Hell and double hell. He didn't think Toby had anything pleasant to say in his next message. Toby never had made the obvious complaint to him: Give me some help, get home, brother, do something to reason with the government—it's not fair what you're doing to us. It's not fair what you're doing to Mother.

He couldn't go home and fix things for his younger brother. There wasn't a way in hell.

And their mother had been headed for this crisis for some time. Maybe her doctors would finally sit on her this time and make her take her medication and watch her diet.

Phone calls at three in the morning didn't help. Knowing her grandchildren were being followed on their way to school didn't help. He wasn't sure it would be better for her to move to the north shore, where the police and the phone company seemed to ignore Toby's complaints for what *he* feared were political reasons.

Damn, damn, damn, and *damn*. He'd been in a good

mood until he met that, which wasn't the first time their mother's health had been a concern. It wasn't even an acute crisis with their mother's health. It was just an ongoing situation. It was the first time for her checking into the hospital, but the doctor had been saying all along if their mother didn't get some rest and mend her ways, she'd have to go in, and it was probably good news in its way. They needed to get her to slow down, calm down, stop yelling at the fools that called at three in the morning: it only inspired them.

And for God's sake, she needed to stop arguing with the newscasters. Toby had already reported she'd called a national program and accused the head of the Human Heritage Association of harassing her with obscene phone calls.

Then she'd said, also on the air, that she didn't like her son living on the mainland with a lot of godless aliens.

He didn't know what to do about that. He really didn't. He'd written her letters. He'd gotten one furious letter back. She'd said he was ruining his brother's life.

The servants had opened the doors: the rest of the luggage had made it in, a considerable pile which they'd apparently waited to accumulate outside until it was all there before the security personnel handling it asked that the apartment door be opened. Maids valiantly seized cases and carried them off to deal with laundry and unpacking. His security was getting and giving information via their own pocket communications and the larger array in the security station just off the foyer, where several black-uniformed Guild members clustered.

Madam Saidin, chief of domestic staff, was still waiting.

He expected one other person to have come out to meet him, and stood, a little dazed and battered, looking toward that vacant hall that led to the private rooms.

"Where's Jason?" he asked Saidin. Jase was shy, still struggling with fluency, and for that reason generally avoided mass gatherings of servants, but he'd have expected Jase to be standing in that hallway by now, at least. The hauling about of a large amount of luggage had to advise Jason he was home early.

"Dressing, I believe, nand' paidhi."

Dressing? Dressing, at this hour. That was very odd for Jason, who kept a meticulous schedule and always bathed precisely at the same time every morning, and wanted breakfast precisely at the same hour every morning.

More, there'd been just a little hesitation on Saidin's answer. Has he been ill? he almost asked her. Perhaps he'd been studying late?

If he asked that question, he might get an answer.

Before his shower.

Before dinner.

Hell, no, he didn't ask. They had a deal. The day started on Jase's schedule, like clockwork. The day ended on *his,* when he managed to find time to eat. Jase would show up for supper. Whatever was going on to have thrown Jase off his meticulous schedule, he was bound to hear the details. He had faith in Jase that if the foyer looked intact and the servants were still alive, it wasn't catastrophic. He had faith in Saidin that if it were outrageous or against the dignity of the Atageini, he would have heard it implied much more strongly than that.

The hot water in the Atageini residence was, to Bren's experience, inexhaustible. The force of the spray, set at atevi height, could drown a man of human stature, and after traipsing about all day up and down steep atevi-scale steps and after having been spattered with sticky fruit juice at 5000 meters Bren was oh, so willing to melt against the shower wall and stand there unmoving in one of the few places of utter, total privacy available to him. He breathed a froth of water and air and let the spray hammer a knot of muscles in the back of his neck he'd forgotten to unclench.

He *trusted* Tano and Algini. He'd had no hesitation at all to put himself in their hands during the trip.

But he grew just a little anxious when unscheduled

planes veered into his path. It probably was exactly as security said, an island pilot not used to the concept of air *traffic,* let alone *control.* The son of the lord of Dur was not a likely sophisticate, much less a plotter in high places.

He shut his eyes and was *there* again, in the same plane seat where he'd spent so many hours this last, long, meandering trip. He could all but feel the cool surface of the juice glass in his fingers, a contrast to the heat of the water that pounded down on him.

He could if he thought about it look again out that aircraft window onto the vast mineral-blessed south, Talidi province just off the wingtip, misty blue-green hills, grass with that slightly younger green of springtime, well advanced in the south, and all that pollen, hazy clouds of it.

Talidi province and the Tasigin Marid.

He couldn't say he blamed atevi for asking themselves at least now and again what the paidhi-aiji *or* their esteemed aiji had in mind for the nation, in moving the paidhi into such prominence and now having *two* paidhiin in residence under the same roof, when the very essence of the Treaty was emphatically *one* paidhi. Some lords of the Western Association had indeed been more than a little suspicious of human motives even before the ship had shown up.

While a handful of truly devout conspiracy-theorists believed Tabini had known the ship was coming back and that he'd been in collusion with the human president on Mospheira from the day of his accession: a more unlikely combination one couldn't imagine.

But since the events of today, *everything* in that equation had to be re-reckoned.

Not that one expected immediate capitulation in the fall of a major player in the opposition to Tabini today: atevi lords weren't so graceless or quick to desert former allies. But they might sidle gracefully and as unobtrusively as possible closer to center, and closer to Geigi, who would thus undergo the most dangerous period of his rise in importance, because the neighbors would try him, now. They would test Geigi's cleverness, his finesse, his business acumen and his personal dignity. It was almost a sure bet that no less than Direiso would, directly or indirectly, test Geigi's security.

But no one had to tell an atevi lord *that*.

And since, with the lord of the Tasigin Marid dead, Talidi province, in which the villages of the Marid lay, now found its best customer for industrial supplies in lord Geigi's province, *that* would surely give the pro-Tabini dissidents and the worker associations within Talidi province the encouragement to turn toward Tabini and the central authority, not toward the coalition that had been trying to form in the Marid.

It was typical of Tabini's politics. A river would be flowing in one direction, and Tabini would place a charge to divert it so suddenly into another channel the fish swimming in it had no warning.

As Direiso up in the Padi Valley (she was not a peninsular lord) had to be doubling her security this evening, perhaps not even yet believing the degree of danger she was in if she didn't change course fast: she was clever and quick—she was alive because of that. But she was self-confident, meaning she *had* no man'chi, meaning she *felt* no man'chi, as aijiin of highest rank had and felt none, and was not a follower of anyone, but attracted man'chi: *that* meant she was dangerous in a way other atevi weren't psychologically armed to be.

Her followers were scattered, and *would* act after her death, breaking up into smaller associations difficult to track and possibly attracting others due to the different chemistry of the sub-associations. That was the protection high lords always had against assassination: kill them and you had not one large problem but twenty smaller ones, harder to track.

But so did Tabini have that defense. More so. Direiso only *thought* she could ride the waves Tabini's fall would generate. It was a time when atevi, threatened from the skies, could least afford to be indecisive, and most of the lords of the Western Association knew that Tabini was the only leader saving them from civil chaos.

He truly wished the Direiso matter were settled. He *didn't* trust any stated changes of direction or belief on her part. Even if atevi emotion *and* politics made it instinctually natural for her to make such changes, he wouldn't believe them. He'd never met the woman but he knew he didn't *like* her or any one of her followers.

Another psychological warning flag. *He* couldn't feel it as natural, *he* couldn't judge in his own blood and bone what was natural for any atevi to do, and he couldn't help but think how very, very delicately poised the whole of human and atevi survival was right now.

Lose Tabini? There'd be a bloodbath the like of which the world had never seen.

Let the conservatives on Mospheira get out of hand? Same result.

He was just outright shaken by today's events. He admitted it to himself finally. He'd been riding a fierce downhill course, and leaping from point to point to point until it was damn well no good mapping out where he'd been: where he'd been didn't exist any more. There was no going back to the atevi state that had existed, once upon a time. There was no dealing with the government on Mospheira that had sent him. The people he was loyal to hardly had any power left.

The plane was a pure, unheralded, no-damn-reason accident. Near accident. He was safe. So was a very chastened teenager.

His fingers were wrinkling. He had to go out and breathe air again. Problems were not his problems tonight. Supper was waiting. A very fine supper, prepared by a cook who accommodated his needs quite expertly.

He shut the water down and exited into the cooler air outside, wrapped instantly in a thick towel, a comfort and luxury of having servants which he did enjoy; and which by his order to this all-female staff was the job of one of the older, more—motherly—women.

But a blink of water-hazed eyes showed him not a

maid who had flung it about him, but Tano, continuing the personal attendance Tano had given him on the trip. He told himself he should decline Tano's attendance: the man had worked harder today than he had by twice.

On the other hand, since it was Tano, he was able to ask him—

But no, dammit, no. He wasn't going to ask about the content of the other messages that might be disasters awaiting his return. He'd been near a radio, and within reach of security communications, and his staff (forty-seven secretaries and a skilled supervisor devoted to such problems) would have known how to call him if there were anything amiss, including unreadable foreign language telegrams or phone calls. The one bombshell he'd picked out of the basket he'd chosen precisely because it was a telegram, and by that criterion urgent and newly arrived.

There couldn't be any more surprises. Peaceful dinner. Quiet sleep. Back to routine. It was all he wanted. Parsing verbs at Jase. A walk in the gardens— suitably guarded.

He let Tano wrap him in more warmed thick towels, a human vice grown harmlessly popular among atevi, although some still used the traditional sheeting. He accepted an informal and human-sized pair of draw-string trousers, a shirt, and a short, wide-sleeved lounging-robe which was adequate for an intimate dinner in the private dining room. He let his hair, toweled to a residual dampness, rest on his shoulders, as a gentleman or a lady could, in private and before a trusted staff.

A shadow turned up in the tiled doorway, along a row of several such showers.

Jase, coatless, dressed in a dark shirt. His dark hair just barely, in half a year, grown long enough to braid, was tied back and still falling loose around his face. The servants would not have let him out of his room without a coat. Or he'd been—troublesome thought— ignoring the servants.

"There you are," Bren said cheerfully, trying to

ignore the glum look Jase gave him. "One wondered about your whereabouts, nadi."

"I don't know where else I'd be." Jase hadn't spoken in the Ragi language. There was no cheerfulness on his face. But it was a homecoming. One supposed. "How was the trip?"

"Fine," he said, persisting in Ragi and in cheerfulness. Jase *wasn't* supposed to speak the human language. Jase had agreed to follow the regimen by which *he'd* learned: no Mosphei' at all. "How have you been, nadi-ji?"

"Fine." Jase switched to Ragi. "I hear there was trouble in the peninsula."

"Saigimi. Yes. Correct noun choice, by the way. —So you did hear."

"Not that much," Jase said. "But the staff was worried."

"Security was in a little hurry to bring me home. But nothing serious. —And you, nadi-ji? Nothing wrong, I hope."

A hesitation. And in the human language: "Welcome home."

Welcome *home.*

A little edge to that, perhaps. A little irony. Or friendliness. He wasn't sure. It was a term they'd had to discuss in Mosphei'. Jase hadn't understood what *home* was in relation to *this* planet, one of the myriad of little human concepts that had somehow not made it back from the stars unchanged. *Home* to Jase's original thinking was a world. *Home* was Earth. *Home* was, equally, an atevi star neither Jase nor his parents had ever seen, to which they'd returned from wherever they'd gone for nearly two hundred years.

And whatever *home* meant, Jase had never in his life been out of the steel world he'd been born to, until he'd entered a tiny pod and plunged into this world's atmosphere.

"Home, yes, nadi." Bren gave the ends of his hair, which reached the middle of his back when it was loose from its braid, a final squeeze of the towel. Tano was still standing there, along with two of the female servants. Jase had been practicing disconnecting the face and the tones of voice from the content, but it wasn't appropriate here. Or there were other interpretations. Jase had a temper. He'd seen that proved. But he wasn't going to light into Jase with lectures. "Relax. It's staff. Is there a problem?"

"No."

Which meant Yes, in that leaden tone of voice.

Fine. Disasters. He saw it coming. There'd been a crisis in the household.

But it didn't need to preface supper. Dammit, he refused to have it before supper. Not unless there'd been bloodshed.

"Can it wait until after dinner, nadi?"

Jase didn't answer him. It was a sulk. It was aimed at him.

He was in the witness of atevi, both servants and security. He was under a noble roof. He was getting angry—as Jase could make him angry, with a human precision no ateva quite managed. And, dammit, he wasn't going to argue. He made his tone smooth and his expression bland. "All right, if it can't wait, let's go to the library."

"All right," Jase said in that same dead tone.

He led the way. Jase walked with him quietly down the short curving hall from the baths to the main hallway and back to the isolation of the lady Damiri's private library, mostly of antique, fragile books.

Tano followed. Tano, having it unshakably in his atevi mind that Jase *was* of a different leader's man'chi, would *not* allow him alone in Jase's presence, or at least not far alone in Jase's presence when Jase was acting like this. It was well possible that, species aside, Tano picked up some of the same signals he did, of *his* anger, and that he wasn't damned patient at the moment for one of Jase's tempests in an atevi teapot.

Tano took up a post outside the door when he followed Jase inside and shut the door.

"So what is it?" Bren said.

"Just—" Jase lapsed into his own dialect. "Dammit, you could have phoned, that's all."

"For what?"

"It doesn't matter! I waited. I waited every evening. I couldn't even get the damn security to say what city you were in!"

Tano and Algini outranked the security he'd left guarding Jase, that was why. But it was petty business. *Not* the real issue. Jase began arguments by diversion—he'd learned that, and all right, Bren thought, he could chase diversion, if that was where Jase wanted to take this conversation at the moment; and they'd pretend to talk, and pretend to reach a conclusion and have the real issue for dessert.

In the meanwhile, and *in* Ragi:

"Security is security is security, Jasi-ji. They're not an information service. Don't swear about them. They *do* know that word. —And I'm sorry. I couldn't phone and, frankly, risk what you'd say without your knowing you were compromising my security. I'm sorry. I warned you I'd be impossible to reach. I called you four days ago—"

"For 'Hello, I'm fine, how are you?' Thanks!"

"I told you I wouldn't have a secure phone and I didn't. This afternoon, with the situation what it was, radio traffic had to be at a minimum. *What* the hell are we arguing about? —Is something wrong?"

Words didn't come easily in moments of fracture, and the paidhi-aiji knew, hell, yes, he knew, he'd expected it. Jase was close to nonverbal at the moment, too frustrated to find a word in Ragi or otherwise— and he himself, years of study, he'd been through it, too, the moments of sheer disorientation across the cultural interface. Jase's ship didn't remotely comprehend what they'd sent Jase into, without the years of training, without the killer selection process in a University that weeded out candidates with any faults in self-control, and Jase had made heroic efforts at holding back his temper—so much so that atevi had begun to realize they had two very different personalities under this roof and occasionally to observe the fact.

Jasi-ji, madam Saidin had put it to him, is rather

more excitable, is he not, nand' paidhi? Is this a correct observation? Or have we offended him?

By no means is it your fault: he'd said that to Saidin in early winter.

Consequently it was *his* job to cover for Jase's failures in composure now in spite of the fact that he himself was too tired to reason. Atevi outside the staff weren't going to understand Jase's difficulties, and wouldn't, and didn't quite give a damn.

He gave it a few seconds while he watched Jase fight for composure, careful breaths, a deep, difficult calm. Improving, he said to himself, while his own blood pressure, even with evidence of that improvement, exceeded his recent altitude.

"Bad day," Jase said finally, and then, having won his approval, had to add, "I can see you're not in the mood to discuss it."

"I'll discuss it." He *hated* himself when he agreed to suffer.

"We have cook waiting. I don't want to stand between you and supper."

"Control your temper, nadi." Jase had spoken in Ragi. Bren changed languages. Fast. While he had his temper in both hands. The atevi language reminded him of calm. It *exerted* calm, force of habit. *"Face."*

There was a scowl on Jase's face at the moment. It vanished. Jase became perfectly calm.

"Is there a danger?" Bren felt constrained to ask, now that reason was with them both. "Is there something I can imminently do something about? Or answer? Or help?"

Jase had been locked in this apartment for six months trying to learn the language, and there'd been moments of frustration at which the monolingual staff, without the experience Jase was going through, could only stare in confusion. There were moments lately when not only the right word wouldn't come, *no* word would come, in any language. There were moments when, helpless as an infant's brain, the adult mind lost all organization of images and association of words simultaneously, and the mental process became less than three years of age. Deep fluency started by spurts and moments.

Jase seemed, this day, this hour, to have reached saturation point definitively and universally.

"I'm back for a while," Bren said gently, and, which one didn't do with atevi, patted Jase's shoulder. "I understand. We'll talk."

"Yes," Jase said, in Ragi, and seemed calmer. "Let's go to dinner."

5

Jase sat at one end of the small formal table and Bren sat at the other as the staff served a five course supper with strict adherence to the forms. The staff might easily have kept less formality with the paidhi nowadays, though he was generally careful of proprieties, but he wanted Jase to *learn* the formal and correct set of manners, the correct utensil, the correct grip, the correct posture, the correct communication with the server: he had left orders, and the staff had mercilessly followed them, even today, when he would as gladly have omitted them.

Jase was in effect a child, as far as communication went, and in some regards as far as expectations of the planet went. Bren had said that to Saidin, too, and she perhaps put Jase's fits of temper in that basket along with her observation and with his recent declaration that the staff were all rain clouds—*ghidari'sai uchi'sama*—when Jase had wished to tell Saidin he'd possibly offended members of the staff—*jidari'sai uchi'sa-ma*.

Rain clouds had instantly become the running joke in the household the day before Bren had left. The staff had been accustomed to believe Jase couldn't understand.

And before he'd left he'd had delicately to explain to Saidin that, yes, Jasi-ji did understand the joke; and yes, Jasi-ji had been embarrassed, and, no, Jasi-ji would not pursue the matter of the staff's laughter to anyone's detriment, so they need not worry, but it was time not to laugh any longer.

Possibly that was what had blown up while he was gone. Jase might be a child in size to the atevi, and might use the children's language, which didn't have the rigid expectation of correct numbers, but Jase was *not* a child, and Jase had been on edge since before he left on the trip.

The staff brought in the third round of trays and served the seasonal game.

"I've been battling the irregular verbs," Jase said conversationally. "The staff has been very helpful. No more rain clouds. *Get.* I've been working on *get.* Indivisible plurals."

"Common verb. Defective verb?"

"Defective verb?"

"Old verb. Lot of use. They break."

Jase gave him an odd look.

"True," Bren said. "The common verbs wear out. They lose pieces over the centuries. People patch them. People abuse them. Everyone uses *get*." It was only half facetious, and having led Jase on a small chase that tested his command of unusual forms, he thought it time for explanation: "If only professors use a verb, it remains unchanged forever. Fossils. *Get* isn't such a verb. It's been used by the common man."

"It's a difficult verb."

"It certainly is. But your accent's vastly improved. Very good. —Listen: master *get* and you've got the irregular indivisibles of *shikira, makkiura,* and *shis'urna.* Any three quarters of any verb in the *-irei* class: they rhyme with the *-ra* plurals, at least in the past tenses."

"You're sure. You swear."

"In formal Ragi, there are, I swear to you, three hundred forty-six key words. Learn those, and most everything that rhymes with them follows their paradigm."

"You said there were a hundred and twelve!"

"I'm speaking of the court language. You're getting far beyond the children's forms."

"Not very damn fast, I'm not."

"It does go faster from here. Trust me."

"That's what you said when I landed."

The conversation had gone to banter. To high spirits. "What *could* I say? I couldn't discourage you."

But Jase didn't take up the conversation. Jase ducked his head and had a piece of fish, no longer engaging with him, and the mood crashed.

He looked down the length of a table set with dishes not native even to him, knowing he couldn't *imagine* the mind of a man who'd never seen a horizon with a negative curve, who'd never seen a blue sky, never seen the rain clouds he mistakenly invoked. Jase had never even met a stranger until he'd fallen down from the sky and met a world full of strangers and unguess-able customs. Jase's world had consisted of the crew of his ship—*his* ship, not *the* ship.

Jase had somehow acquired curiosity about things outside his steel world. That adventurousness, the ship's captain had declared, was why he'd sent Jase, who was (he and Jase had worked it out on the computer) two planetary years younger than his twenty-seven-almost-eight; and it was why they'd sent Yolanda Mercheson, who was a little older, a little steadier, perhaps. He'd never gotten a chance to know her when she landed with Jase—they'd rapidly packed her off to her job on the island—but he thought she might be a match for some of the harder heads on Mospheira. In his brief experience of her, Yolanda Mercheson would watch anything, no matter how odd, completely deadpan and without reaction—and remark it was certainly different than they did things on the ship.

Considering Jase's volatility, Jase's uneasiness at strange things, and his tendency to let his expressions slip his control, Bren asked himself if the ship-folk hadn't mistaken their envoys. Atevi would have accepted Yolanda's dry and deadpan humor, though mistakenly; it was *too* atevi without being atevi. But Jase didn't keep himself in the kind of shell his own predecessor, Wilson-paidhi, had built around himself. Say that for him: he was willing to risk everything, was willing to risk emotional and psychological hurt, get-ting close to the atevi.

Jase had come armed with curiosity and a history of the atevi-human conflict that not-well-disposed humans on Mospheira had fired at the ship; and, coming from a steel-walled ship-culture which he'd hinted had distinctions of rank but not of diversity, he'd gone into the business more blind and more ignorant as to what he was getting into than a native of the world could possibly imagine.

The personal recklessness it had taken for both Jase and Yolanda to come down here would have washed both of them out of the Foreign Studies program. Jase had been willing, intelligent, and had no essential duties aboard the ship, a computer tech, but in cold, blunt terms, the ship could risk him: low-level and ignorant. Exactly what Mospheira's government had thought *it* was sending into the field when it sent one Bren Cameron.

But paidhiin had a tendency to mutate on duty. It remained to be seen what the job would do to Jase, but the ship wouldn't get back the bright-eyed and curious young man it had sent down to the world, if that man had ever really existed. *He* hadn't seen that side of Jase, the Jase that had existed in the voice transmissions from the ship, not since the capsule had landed; and he was, he admitted it, disappointed in the transaction. Stress and communication problems and the need for one of them who knew all the answers to tell the other when to hold that frustration in and how long to hold it all took their toll. It had certainly undermined the relationship they might have had.

"So are there any messages in?" he asked Jase, meaning messages from the ship, via the big dish at Mogari-nai.

"The regular call from Yolanda."

"So how is she, nadi?"

"Fine."

They spoke the atevi language in the exchange. Madam Saidin dropped by to put a note beside his plate.

Join me after breakfast, it said. It bore Tabini's signature, was entirely in Tabini's hand, a rarity. *Unless*

*there's urgency about your report. I shall expect you at
the usual time.*

"No," he said with a glance up to Saidin. "Thank
you, nadi. I can leave matters at that. I don't need to
reply. This is a confirmation only."

"News, nadi?" Jase asked.

"An appointment tomorrow, with the aiji. Routine
matters. —Although nothing's routine at the moment."
He saw expression on Jase's face. Or had seen it.
"Jase?"

"No," Jase said. And drew a breath. "Glad to see a
human face."

Meaning *he* had an appointment and was bound out
of the apartment and Jase was alone. Again.

"The mirror gets old," he said to Jase with all sympathy, "doesn't it?"

"You said I'd get past it. I frankly don't see how
you've stood it alone."

It wasn't the time to lecture Jase again about reliance
on one's native tongue. Like it or not, one had to give
up one's native tongue at least for a while if one
wished to make that mental jump to full fluency. Jase
couldn't give it up, because Jase was their source of
technical words: Jase had to stay connected to the
human language because Jase's *job* was to take concepts in shipboard engineering terms and teach *him*
enough engineering and enough of the ship's slightly
skewed-from-Mosphei' way of speaking to get it translated accurately enough for atevi engineers. *He* was
having to deal far more in the human language than he
ordinarily ever would on this side of the strait, and the
back-and-forth was keeping him off his stride, too.

But tonight everything he was picking up from Jase
said that something major was wrong with that situation—or with some situation. Jase wasn't talking after
that last glum statement. Jase took a sip of guaranteed-
safe tea and dipped bits of seasonally appropriate meat
into sauce one after another with studied mannerliness,
not engaging with him on the issues.

Damn, he was so tired. It wasn't just today. It was all
the sequence of days before. It was the months before.

It was Saigimi. It was the meeting tomorrow. He *knew* Jase had reasons. He *knew* Jase had been through his own kind of hell in isolation, and he felt sorry for his situation, he truly did, but he was suffering his own post-travel adrenaline drop, and had no mental agility left. He wasn't going to come across as sympathetic, humane, or even human, if Jase wanted to push him, and he didn't know whether he could postpone their business until the morning without offending Jase, but that was what he should do.

Next course, the last course: Jase asked one servant for two bowls, baffling the young woman considerably.

"*Asso* shi *madihiin*-sa," Bren said quietly. "*Mai, nadi.*"

"*Mai, nadi, saijuri.*" Jase echoed him and made a courteous patch on the utterance, with good grace. Maybe, Bren thought, Jase was working through his mood and getting a grip on his emotions: he chose to encourage it.

"Difficult forms," Bren said in Ragi. The conditional request and the irregular courtesy plurals, six of them, were to create felicitous and infelicitous numbers in the sentence. "You were never infelicitous."

"One is pleased to hear so." The courteous answer. The flatly correct answer.

The courtesy plurals weren't the easiest aspect of the language. Jase had tottered along thus far using the ath-mai'in, commonly, the children's forms, which advised any hearer that here was an impaired speaker and no one should take offense at his language. Damn some influential person to hell in Mosphei' and it was, situationally at least, polite conversation. Speak to an atevi of like degree in an infelicitous mode and you'd ill-wished him in far stronger, far more offensive terms and might find yourself filed on with the Guild unless someone could patch the situation.

"I just can't get the distinctions," Jase said bitterly. "I'm guessing. You understand me?"

"It's like the captain," Bren said, drawing his inspiration from sailing-ships and human legend. "Never call the captain mister. Right? And the more important the person, the greater the politeness-number: just err on the side of compliment."

"I know it's a melon!" was the approximation of what Jase retorted.

Jase clearly wasn't in a mood for mild corrections. A servant was fighting laughter.

"You know it's *important,*" Bren corrected him, deadpan, deciding on confrontation.

"Damn," Jase said, and pushed his plate back in the beginnings of what could become an outburst. Bren thought, having grown tolerably cold-blooded over the course of several months of Jase's temper-fits, thank goodness he'd gotten almost to dessert. He'd been hungry. And damn Jase anyway.

"Jase." He attempted diplomacy. "This is the rough part. This is really the roughest part. I swear to you. The language comes to you pretty quickly after this. You've done a marvelous job. You've done in six months what takes much more than that on Mospheira. You've done a brilliant job."

"I don't see how you do it! I can't add that fast!"

"It develops."

"Not for me!"

"It will come. Maybe you'd better let me do the translations for a few days and let me muddle along with the engineering and develop the questions I really need to ask. Going back and forth is confusing. There comes a time you should be totally inside the language. You seem to have reached it."

Jase looked aside. "Not all I've reached."

"Well, I'm back for a while," Bren said. "And if you can just get the courtesy forms down, maybe we can go together on the next trip out. Would you rather?"

"I'd rather be on my ship, nadi!"

"It won't *ever* happen if you break down, nadi. And you know that."

"Maybe," Jase said, with a slump to the shoulders and a sadness he'd not heard. It was defeat. He'd not seen Jase defeated. Jase turned quietly back to the table, drew a deep breath, squared his shoulders, and said: "I apologize, nand' Bren."

The servants served the next course, a light fruit ice. Jase had two spoonfuls and wanted a drink to go with it.

"Serve us the liqueur, nadiin-ji," Bren said quietly, "in the sitting room. We can open the windows and sit and breathe the fine spring air. The workmen are through for the day, are they not? We can tolerate the paint."

"Indeed, nand' paidhi," the response was. "And the paint smell is much abated. One will advise nand' Saidin, nandiin-ji."

He rose from table, waited for Jase and walked with him to the formal sitting room where other servants appeared, opening the jalousies and letting the night air waft through.

It was on the verge of cold air that billowed the gauze curtains wide. But their chairs were near a comfortable gas-fired stove, wasteful notion, and the maids gave them lap robes and glasses of a liqueur like brandy.

"Do you want to talk?" Bren asked. "Jasi-ji?"

"I'm having trouble-with-a-neighbor," Jase said.

"You mean trouble-in-the-house," he guessed.

They were alone now in the room. "I am a fool," Jase began. Possibly he meant *awkward.* The words sounded alike. But Bren forbore to suggest so or to correct him further: he'd *been* through sessions like that, and had sympathy for someone trying to collect his thoughts in another language. "May we speak Mosphei', please?"

"If you wish." He spoke in that language. "What's the matter?"

There was silence. A long moment of silence in which Jase breathed as if air had gone short in the room. "I'm not *like* you. I don't know if I can take this."

"Only two other people on Mospheira are *like* me," Bren said mildly, "and the staff completely sympathizes with your mistakes. They admire your tenacity. They shouldn't laugh, but it's very well-intentioned. If they didn't laugh, you should worry."

"You mean it's all right if they think I'm a fool."

"If you were not a member of the household they wouldn't laugh. They call you Jasi-ji. They wish to please you. That's progress. You've worked very hard and come a long way. They respect that. Dealing with complete aliens to their way of life is comparatively new for this staff. It's not something nature or their culture equipped them very well to do. They've never met strangers, either."

"Can I be blunt? Can I be terribly blunt? I don't care. I don't want to live here. I want off the planet. I want to go back to my ship. If I have to stay here I'll die. I don't *like* it. I know I'm not supposed to use that word, but I can't take it here. I *do* like. I *do* dislike. I'm cold half the time. I'm hot the rest. The light hurts my eyes. The smells bother me. The food upsets my stomach. And I'm sorry if it's funny among the staff, there was a flying thing in my room—I didn't know it wasn't poisonous."

"This morning?"

"It doesn't matter."

"It's spring. Flying things do come to the lights. That's informational, not a criticism. If they laughed, it *was* funny, Jasi-ji. And probably your reaction was. They do not mean you ill."

"You say. I made a fool of myself!"

"And I'm sorry to state the obvious, but you have no choice—you have no viable choice but to smile and be pleasant. You knew when you came down here with no return that it wouldn't be easy. I know the exhaustion that sets in when *nothing* you touch or deal with is the same. I know what you're going through."

"You can't know! You were at least born to a planet! I wasn't! I don't *like* this, and I don't care that the language can't accommodate *like* and *dislike,* it's what I feel!"

"Possibly I can't imagine." He thought, and didn't say, and then did: "But I can't go home either, Jase, as I'm sure you've overheard at some time in your stay here, so be a little easy on *me,* if you can find it in you. I can't go home, and if we get this ship flying some time this next couple of years, you *can* go back. And you'll be a hero and I won't, not among the people that I was born with. So don't say I don't know at least something about how you feel."

Jase wasn't prepared to grant that point. He saw that in Jase's angry expression, and didn't push the point.

It was training. He was always professional, always rational, and when good reasons made him want to get up, drag Jase out of the chair and pound Jase's head against the wall, he didn't. This was, he reminded himself, a man capable of gentle humor and lightning wit, though neither was in evidence tonight.

"I'm telling you," Jase said, "I don't know if I can take it. I don't know that any more, Bren."

"And you know that it's not only you in danger if you cave in. So you won't. That's all. You won't."

"I can't exist here and not talk to human beings except on a radio!"

That stung. That really rather stung, right in the area of his own self-doubts. Bren sat there quite still and told himself there was nothing emotionally significant to him in Jase's unthought remark.

But to the diplomat, it was significant information regarding Jase's view of him.

And being the diplomat, he didn't bring that slip to Jase's attention. Pointing out that Jase might have a bias against the natives, including humans on Mospheira, was an egg which, the atevi proverb had it, once cracked, had to be eaten.

And, in truth, it was possible he himself didn't wholly trust the Pilots' Guild, the old human distinction between crew and passengers on the ship. The crew had once maintained the passengers didn't have a vote, until the descendants of the crew needed the descendants of the passengers for dangerous and vital work.

There was a lot of history between the long-ago passengers and the crew; and a lot at stake for the ship in that interface. The Pilots' Guild had never wanted the Landing, and had given in on the issue only grudgingly and in the confidence the project would have no support from the station management. The ship had surely expected to return to a spacefaring civilization with a well-maintained station, maybe with the original landing party dead; but not what they'd met—no station presence, no launch capacity, and a thriving planetary colony with very touchy relations with the native atevi.

"I understand your frustration," he said finally, and maybe Jase never realized his slip, but damn sure if Jase were taking the tests to enter the Foreign Studies program over on Mospheira, he'd have washed out, right there, first for making the slip, and then for not realizing it.

Though, again, maybe Jase did realize. Once you learned, atevi-style, to disconnect your face from your thoughts, you grew harder and harder to track in human terms.

And old friends in the human world grew harder and harder to keep.

"I know," Jase said. "I know that you do, Bren. But—"

Jase left that statement unfinished.

"You may never *be* what I am," Bren said. "I say that with no arrogance at all. You may not want to be. But your way to space has to go through atevi construction workers, to whom the paidhiin must be polite and infallibly encouraging, and it has to go through Tabini-aiji, to whom the paidhiin must be useful, and we can never, ever forget either fact."

"I try. God, I'm trying."

"I know you are."

"Bren—Bren, tell me the truth. Tell me the honest truth. When that spacecraft goes up, am I really going to go with it?"

What in hell brought that on? he asked himself. "Who said otherwise?" he asked.

"I just want to hear it."

"There'll be test flights. But when it's proven safe, you'll go."

"Dependent on the aiji's permission, of course."

"He'll let you go."

"How do I know that?"

"Well, outside of the fact he said so—which is considerable assurance—he's investing quite a lot in your education. This place. The training. Why shouldn't he want you on the job translating to the ship?"

"I might be a hostage."

"It's not the aiji's style. It wouldn't be dignified."

"He did with Hanks."

"Say he knows the Mospheiran government. It's *different*. He chose not to shoot her."

"I don't see the difference. What about when he wants something from *my* people?"

"Have you had a hint he does?"

"Don't be naïve, Bren."

"Whatever brought *this* up?"

"I just want to know there's going to be an end to this!"

"It doesn't seem to me you're being reasonable. Why do you think he wouldn't let you go?"

"Look—I want to get out of this apartment. Who do you have to ask?"

Maybe Jase wouldn't have washed out of the program. The paidhi, experienced in diplomacy, nearly fell into that little pitfall.

"I can take you wherever I like."

"Then why *not* on this last trip? Why not on the next?"

Because it wasn't that simple. But Jase wasn't in a reasoning mood. "You go nowhere until you learn the verb forms." That set it at some distance. "And until you don't make statements as rash as that you just made about our hosts."

"The hell with the verb forms!"

First the disorientation, then the anger. He'd been there, too. At least Jase wasn't fool enough to damn Tabini. "You can die of old age on this planet if we mistranslate a design spec and the program fails. You could die sooner if you don't understand culturally where you're likely to find security wires. You can die if your insults to the aiji disturb the peace of this country. Or you can sit idle and become a ward of the state while I do your work. These are serious choices. It is *not* 'to hell with the verb forms.' Your choices otherwise are all unpalatable. "

He'd made Jase mad. Real mad. But Jase didn't get up from his chair and stalk from the room as he'd done once last autumn.

"You do it even in human language," Jase said, "don't you?"

"What?"

"Nadi," Jase said in measured tones, in Ragi, and with no expression whatever, "one understands my options to be balanced with a felicitous fifth choice."

"That being?"

"The one you wish: my compliance, nadi."

He *had* posed it in a foursome, infelicitous four, when three, the human cultural choice, was felicitous. And Jase had at least *felt* it. "Good. Very good. You're catching on."

"Nand' Saidin has assigned a servant to assist me. And I have worked, nadi. I work very long hours because I hope for a release from this confinement and a sexual assignation with my job."

He didn't laugh. He didn't let his face twitch. "An opportunity."

Jase's face went red.

"Yes, nadi. An opportunity."

"I'm encouraged, nadi-ji, none the less. And I shall make every effort to include you in the next itinerary. Jase, it will get easier."

"How *do* you stand it?"

A deep breath. A sip of the liquor. "Stubbornness. I had alternatives early on. Now there aren't any. You do what you have to."

"You could quit. You could go back."

"I'd have Deana Hanks for my successor."

"Does that *matter?* Ultimately you're one man. After you, things will be what they'll be. Does that matter?"

"Yes, it damn well matters. This is my job."

The conversation was depressing him. He didn't want to discuss his own situation. He didn't think it would help.

"You have people harassing your family," Jase said. "Where did you hear *that?*"

Jase had a troubled look. "I'm not deaf. And, as you say, I *do* pick up things from the staff now."

"My family's situation isn't the official situation. There *is* a difference, Jase, and the ship needs to know that. Theoretically—" Theoretically the government was looking for the perpetrators. But it never found them. The police never caught anyone. And he had to ask himself how long before he had to hold international politics hostage to the threats against his family and get Tabini to demand something be done.

It was what the perpetrators wanted. It was *exactly* what they wanted. It would give *them* the leverage to threaten the government and become noisier than they were. And he tried to deaden his nerves and not react when he got news that upset him.

"Theoretically—" Jase said. Possibly Jase didn't know that word.

He'd not wanted, for one other thing, to lose his credibility in a descent into name-calling and accusations. He'd never wanted to bring the whole of the stresses on him into question in the household here: it would raise concerns even with the staff. But maybe Jase *was* able to understand the complexity of the constraints on him. Maybe he'd been around atevi long enough not to draw wrong conclusions and maybe it *was* time to lay some of the truth on the table, if Jase was listening behind doors. He changed to Mosphei'.

"More than theoretically, Jase, the sons of bitches are calling my mother at three in the morning. She's got a heart condition. —But they're freelance operators so far as I know. Isolationists. Pro-spacers. Anti-spacers. The whole damn gamut, Jase. It's the radical fringe that wants another war. Or an end to building on the north shore. I'm sure Ms. Mercheson has had lunch with them, though I haven't wanted to act as if I were trying to affect *her* independent judgment. They'll be perfectly polite to her. They'll be dressed in their Sunday best and telling her atevi can't be trusted." He knew he'd wandered further than he'd intended, into areas he probably shouldn't discuss with Jase, politically speaking. But if he didn't find a starting point to include Jase on the inside of the information flow, Jase couldn't understand the atevi's chosen isolation, either.

The hell with it, he thought. It *was* time to talk, seriously, about the con job the Mospheiran government was bound to be trying on Yolanda Mercheson; and he'd tried to take the high ground rather than have his own side sound like a con job. But that strategy could backfire, if Jase had gotten some report from Yolanda that painted the other side of the strait as flawless and cooperative; and he wasn't sorry to have hit Jase with the nastier truths of Mospheira's underside.

"There's a lot of humans," he said, in Ragi again, and more calmly, "who don't want atevi to go to space. And among those, some are crazy. Some are honest, law-abiding citizens."

"An infelicity of two: you mean—some are neither."

That was a first. He *was* pleased. If Jase had gotten that far, they *could* talk, and he was ready to do so. "Just so, nadi. Better and better. Another such improvement and I might well present you at court."

"Not—quite ready for that, I think."

"But very much better. I don't know if information helps the digestion, but that's the truth from my side. What's yours?"

A slight hesitation. Then: "My father's dead."

For a moment he didn't even hear it. Or didn't believe he could have heard what he thought he had.

"God, Jase. —When?" He couldn't figure out how Jase would learn such a thing. Whenever the ship called, it created a stir in the household; and he hadn't heard of it.

"Four days ago. —I got it from *Yolanda*. I haven't even been able to call my mother. Security wouldn't let me call the ship because you hadn't left instructions and I couldn't reach you."

That was the distress over the period out of contact. That was the aborted conversation before supper.

"Damn. *Damn*, Jase, what do I say? —I'm sorry."

"It's one of those things, you know. Just one of those

things. He just—just was working—" The glass trembled in Jase's fingers, and he lifted it and drank. "An accident. Yolanda had talked to the ship. She heard. She thought I already had. She offered condolences— All right?" The glass met the small table. Click. "But I haven't been able to call *her* back. I found out four days ago and I haven't been able to get hold of you. I haven't been able to call the ship."

He had to revise a great many estimations of Jase, with this performance, both cool-headed and confrontational, recklessly so: *Here's what I know, be damned to you, I want off this planet.*

No *wonder* Jase had been bearing down on the lessons in the last several days. To the point of hysteria, alternated with cold, clear, bloody-minded function. He was speaking now in Ragi and doing it with steady self-control.

"Jase. *I* didn't hear. I don't know why I didn't hear. And I don't know why you didn't get a call from the ship. I'll ask official questions. I'm extremely sorry."

The facial nerves were *very* well under control, as perhaps his were. He forgot, he feared, to adjust between languages. Between mindsets, he forgot to respond in the human sense. He *forgot* to use human expressions.

"Jase." He switched to Mosphei' and, like an actor assuming a role, brought expression consciously to his face. "I didn't know. I'm going to find out why I didn't know. I know that atevi will be concerned that you didn't learn this in any proper way."

"Can we use the word 'care' here? Are we finally permitted?"

"In this, Jase, I assure you the staff would care."

"Shed tears, I'm sure."

"No." He refused to back up from the attack, and equally refused to attack back. "But making demands like that serves no one. —I'm *sorry.* I'm extremely sorry. I put you off and I'm sorry. I wish I'd been here. I am here now. Can I do anything?"

"No. I've been keeping up with my studies." Jase's tone was light, his eyes distracted by something across the room. The wall, perhaps. Or a blowing curtain. "It's the only choice I have, isn't it?"

"Is your mother all right?"

Slight pause. Restrainedly, then: "I have no idea."

"Damn. Damn, Jase. I *will* straighten out the phone situation."

"I'd like to talk to my mother. Privately. If you can arrange that."

He didn't know what to say. "I'll arrange something. As soon as I can. Do you want to speak to her tonight?"

"If she's gotten to sleep, I'd rather not disturb her this late." The ship-folk had sensibly adjusted their day-night schedule to the Mospheira-Shejidan time zone. And it was still evening up there on the ship, as it was evening here, but he didn't argue that fine point with Jase, either.

Excuse, he thought. And asked himself why, and with what motive, and didn't come up with charitable answers, a reaction he didn't trust in himself. *He* was angry. He didn't know why that was, either. He didn't think he was angry at Jase. Or the staff. Having just talked about his own home situation, he knew why he *might* be angry.

He wasn't sure, though, why he *was* angry, or at what he could even be angry, and was far less certain that his anger would do any possible good to anyone.

The servant came in, hesitated, and at a slight lifting of his hand, poured two more drinks.

But Jase said, after the young woman had left, "I'll take mine to my room, if you don't mind, nadi. I'm feeling unsteady."

Jase rose. Bren did. One part of him said in spite of Jase's evasions and in spite of his anger he should go over to Jase and put his arm around his shoulders. He should offer—something of an emotional support.

But he didn't. As Jase never quite addressed him with the intimate form in Ragi, though he did it toward Jase.

Jase had never made such gestures toward him in that interpersonally sensitive language. Maybe Jase didn't think he was of status to do it. Maybe there was another reason.

Whatever it was, they'd never made such gestures toward one another, certainly not intruded so far as an embrace, between the only two humans on the mainland. He'd held out a hand to welcome Jase when he'd pulled him from the capsule and into the world. Jase had accepted that hand, but hadn't met him with the enthusiasm or the openness the transmissions from the ship had prepared him to expect.

The one gesture, nothing more, from either side. And somehow they'd found no way to begin again. Not in six months.

It seemed impossible to try in this situation, when sensibilities were raw-edged and, he admitted it, when he wasn't sure he'd mean any such move toward a greater closeness with Jase, because of an anger the causes of which he wasn't himself right now sure of.

He stood there as Jase walked away and out the door.

6

Maybe he should have made the try. Maybe, Bren thought, he should go after Jase all the same and make the gesture and try to sort out exactly why and at what he was angry, and why (he detected so, at least) Jase was so deeply angry, too.

But at such a juncture, what he did could intrude on sensibilities and shove the situation beyond all reason. He might instead do something he could bring to Jase as a peace offering. He might take measures to calm the situation. He might try to ease the strain on Jase and then talk to him, once the anger had settled. In both of them.

He saw the servant standing at the door, hands folded, waiting for his order, aware, perhaps that something was wrong.

"Is nand' Saidin still on duty?"

"I believe she has retired, nand' paidhi, but I doubt very much she is asleep. Shall I call her?"

"No. Is nadi Tano awake? Or nad' Algini?"

"Both or either, nand' paidhi. Shall I call them?"

"Do," he said; and stood sipping his drink until a quiet step and a shadow in the doorway advised him of presence.

"Nadi?" Tano asked. Both of them had come, and entered the room at his implied invitation.

"Nadiin," he said, intensely aware how they would blame themselves for a failure in information. "Jase says his father has died. He had this news from Mospheira, he says, four days ago, and complains he was not able to contact his mother on the ship because security couldn't clear a call to the ship or contact me. Are we able to remedy this?"

"I will make immediate inquiry, nand' paidhi," Algini said, ever the proper, to-the-point one; and Tano, equally atop any business he was supposed to monitor: "The record shows the call from Mospheira. The staff has it on tape. It was in Mosphei'. Do you wish to hear it?"

"I do." It was his business to. Someone had better find out what was going on, and how much else that message had contained, and he was the one who admitted to speaking the language. He was sure that certain atevi did, even that certain atevi close to him were staying up nights increasing their fluency at Jase's expense, while Jase persisted in resorting to human language, but with what accuracy atevi were understanding the biology behind the vocabulary, he was far from certain. "Did nand' Jase seem upset?"

"That was not in the report, nadi. He stayed to his room a great deal, that was all. One phone call came to him from Mospheira, late in the evening, four days ago. No others are on the record."

He didn't have enough information to cue them to report information they might not know they had.

More, he had to be extremely careful. Everything at the interface of atevi responsibility and human emotions was difficult and subject to error. As long as he'd lived among atevi, he could guess one's man'chi toward a lord, and he knew the specific man'chi of Tano and Algini and others toward Tabini, but he knew very little of their family ties or how man'chi to a lord fit into man'chi toward a mother or a father. He'd *heard* Tano speak of his own father, and of a desire to have the man's good opinion, but he also knew that Tano had defied his father's wishes to pursue a Guild career. He'd had Tano recommend relatives for posts as 'reliable persons,' a reliability one could attribute to man'chi, and the fact that it wasn't biologically likely for treason to operate where man'chi existed.

He knew that Damiri had defied her clan to associate

herself romantically and politically (or should that be, politically and romantically) with Tabini, who was close to an ancestral enemy of her clan, a close neighbor in the Padi valley holdings, and certainly persona non grata with uncle Tatiseigi, the head of the Atageini clan. Antipathy on the part of a clan head (toward whom Damiri held man'chi) certainly hadn't daunted Damiri—but then, few things did.

The one wisdom about atevi family relations that two centuries of paidhiin had gathered was that the bonds of affection that held a human family together were not only not present, they weren't biologically possible.

Different hardwiring.

Different expectations.

Different familial relationships and different necessities.

One didn't know, for instance, what an atevi child expected of his parents. Food and shelter up to a certain point, yes. The point of separation seemed to be about seventeen years, maybe twenty. That was all the accumulated experience could say. Anything else was rated speculative, in the textbooks. He himself tentatively theorized that as humans had to mature beyond emotional dependency on their parents, atevi had somehow to get out of man'chi toward their parents or the family unit would never mature. There had to be a psychological break, somewhere, for the culture to function beyond the family.

"If this were an ateva who had heard this news," he asked the two closest of his companions and guards, persons who, if they were human, he would have called friends, "what would other atevi expect of him? Principally, what would other atevi expect him to feel, or do, under these circumstances?"

"If relations with his father were good," Tano said, "then one would expect sadness, nand' paidhi. He would go to his household. He would bury his father. He would confirm man'chi within his house and within his associations."

Confirm man'chi. *Confirm* man'chi. With atevi, it

was not only an overriding emotion. It was *the* overriding emotion. A homing instinct under fire. The place you'd go. The person you'd rescue from a burning building.

"In what manner can one *confirm* man'chi, nadi, if I may ask such a question? Please decline to answer if I cross some line of decency."

"An expression, nand' paidhi. It's an expression. One visits the household. One remembers. One assembles the living members of the household, for one thing, to know where their man'chi may lie now that this man'chi is put away. The household has to be rebuilt."

"The man'chi to the dead man is put away."

"Into the earth, nand' paidhi, or into the fire. One can only have man'chi to the living."

"Never to the dead?" He watched a lot of machimi plays, in the standard of which man'chi and its nuances was the pivot-point of treachery and action, double-crosses and last-moment decisions. "In the plays, nadi, this seems possible."

"If one believes in ghosts."

"Ah." It was a belief some atevi held.

And more had believed in them, as a matter of course, in the ancient world of the machimi plays. Such a belief in the supernatural didn't include the two men present with him, he was quite sure. But belief in ghosts of course would tie directly into whether or not the dead could still claim loyalty.

"Also," Algini said in his quiet way, "the living will exact a penalty from living persons who might have been responsible. This does *not* require a belief in ghosts. But in the old days, one might equally well exact a penalty of the dead."

He was curious. It went some distance toward explaining certain machimi, in which there seemed to be some actions of venerating or despising monuments and bones, heaving them into rivers and the like.

But it *wasn't* a solution for the problem he had. "Jase is upset," Bren said, "because he can't reach his home or assure himself his mother is well." One didn't phrase a question in the negative: atevi, if cued that one expected a negative, would helpfully agree it wasn't likely. "Would security be concerned for an ateva's actions under such a circumstance?"

"If this death was due to another person," Algini said, "one would expect to watch him carefully."

"Or if this death dissolved essential man'chi," Tano said, "A wife, for instance. Her clan would be free to act. A set of cousins ambitious to transfer man'chi to *their* line. The family could break apart."

"Would he—" He knew these men well enough to ask about very delicate, ordinarily undiscussed, matters. "Would an ateva under such circumstances *feel* such man'chi to the cousins, say, if they succeeded in transferring the clan's man'chi to themselves and away from his father's line?"

"Not necessarily," Algini said and, rare for him, a dark frown came to his face.

That warned him that perhaps he'd touched something more than theoretical with Algini. Or perhaps just inquired into too delicate an area of atevi emotion. So he asked no further.

And because it was necessary meticulously to inform the ones who guarded Jase: "Jase would like to go back to the ship to assure himself of his mother's welfare. This he of course can't do. *He* says he wished to call the ship and was prevented because, he says, he couldn't get through security to reach me to authorize it. I can only guess. He does follow rules and schedules meticulously. Perhaps this results from living on a ship in space. I don't know. And he may have been unwilling to face atevi with his emotions out of control—I've told him very emphatically not to do that. It may have prevented him from fully explaining his distress to security." It was a cold and an embarrassing thing, to try to dice human feelings so finely that another mindset could grasp logically what was going on. "I would guess that he was already exhausted, either emotionally upset since I left or trying to achieve a good result—even my approval—on my return; and suddenly an emotional blow has hit him when he was alone, immersed in a strange language, surrounded by strange faces, and under my instruction not to react emotionally with atevi."

"Ah," Tano said, and both atevi faces showed comprehension. Of what—God knew.

"Remember," he said, "that this is a human being, and that this is not *truly* man'chi he feels but something as central to his being. Understand that he is under very extreme stress, and he's trying not to react. But I have serious questions, nadiin, about the propriety of humans on that ship toward him, who may have slighted him in a major way. I want to know whether the ship tried to contact him, I want to know where that message went if someone attempted to contact him, and why he had to hear this bad news finally relayed from the island, from Yolanda Mercheson."

"To whom has he attributed this failure of information?" Tano asked.

"I would assume, perhaps unjustly, to Manasi himself." Manasi was one of Tabini's security, who'd moved in to run the security office when he had Tano and Algini off with him. "He suspects atevi have withheld it from him. This is much more palatable to him than the thought that his people did. But whatever the truth is, whether it leads to atevi or to his ship, I need to *know* the truth, no matter how much truth I later decide to tell him."

"Nadi Bren," Algini said, "we will find the answer. We received no call from staff regarding any such matter."

"Nadiin," he said, "I have every confidence in you. I have every confidence in nand' Dasibi and in nand' Manasi. Please express it in your inquiry—please accuse no one. I leave it all to your discretion."

Look not to his clerical staff for fault, and not to Manasi, he strongly felt, rather to the aiji's staff on the coast, at Mogari-nai, where the great dish drank down messages from space and relayed them supposedly without censorship to him and through him to Jase. There had been politics at Mogari-nai, somewhere in the administration of that facility, which had withheld information from him on prior occasions, even against Tabini's orders. It was a tangled matter of loyalties which one hoped, but not trusted, had been rectified last fall.

Look even—one could think it—to Tabini himself, who might have ordered the interception and withholding of that message for various reasons, including the reason that Bren-paidhi wasn't at hand to handle the matter and they couldn't know how Jase would react.

But *Tabini* would certainly have no difficulty reaching Tano and Algini if Manasi thought Jase was about to blow up.

Information stalled in the system? Some message lying on a desk awaiting action? Perhaps. He was sure that the messages at Mogari-nai were gone over meticulously by atevi who could translate—and any personal message to Jase, as opposed to the usual routines, would raise warning flags, and possibly go to higher security, which could appreciably slow down transmission.

"Nadiin," he said, because he knew the extreme good will of these two men, and the conflict it might pose them, "if this thread should go under the aiji's door, advise me but leave it untouched. It will be my concern."

"Bren-ji, one will immediately advise you if that should be the case."

That from Tano, with no demur from his partner. Their man'chi was to Tabini, to him only *through* Tabini, and what they said was with the understanding, unspoken, that he knew and that they knew that certain atevi damned well understood Mosphei' and the dialect of the ship.

He suspected most of all that troublesome elements existed somewhere within the defense organization that protected the coast; and that such might have interfered, again, at Mogari-nai—or here, within the walls of the Bu-javid.

Tabini himself understood more Mosphei' than he let on. Threads that went under the aiji's door—or the hypersecret establishment of Mogari-nai—might cross and recross multiple times.

But an information slowdown could allow a critical situation to become a disaster. It also could signal a situation of man'chi; and that had to be fixed.

"That's all I need," he said. "And don't scant your own rest, nadiin-ji. Have some junior person begin the inquiry tonight. Pursue it tomorrow."

"Yes," Tano said, accepting orders which Bren feared he would not follow, nor would Algini. They slept on questions no better than he did.

The question was always—*how* did atevi interpret what humans asked, and how well did they forecast human actions? The War of the Landing hadn't happened because both sides had *meant* to go to war.

So he sat, in the sitting room, in his robe, at a small, fragile desk, writing by hand in the formal court script, for Tabini:

Aiji-ma, Mercheson-daja has informed nand' Jase of his father's unexpected death, causes unknown.

Bearing in mind your other imminent concerns—

No, that wouldn't do. He struck that last line: one left the aiji to the aiji's concerns and didn't express opinions on paper regarding Saigimi's death being *any* concern to the aiji at all.

I have informed my staff regarding nand' Jase's normal behavior in such instances and inform you, aiji-ma, that I foresee a time of tension in the household. I am also concerned for meanings behind the failure of that message to get through to him or to me in a timely fashion. It seems to have come to Mercheson-paidhi first, which should not have happened, as Mercheson is not Jase's superior, as the ship authorities well know. It was embarrassing and distressing to him to have heard such news from a source who should have been less well-informed than he was. If this was the choice of the ship's officers, there may be implications in their behavior regarding this matter: this could have benign causes, in either too great a zeal to protect Jase from knowledge of his

*family's distress or knowledge that I was absent from
the premises and therefore that nand' Jase was alone.
Not benign, however, would be the determination of
the officers of the ship that nand' Mercheson should
obtain quicker and more up-to-date briefings than they
allow to nand' Jase. These negative implications are
certainly possible conclusions he might draw, and I am
concerned.*

*Seeing, however, a third choice, that the withholding
of information might be action emanating from your
office, I have set my staff to learn the facts so that I
may be accurate and prudent in assessments I present
to you.*

That, to pave the way for Algini and Tano.

Lest you concern yourself regarding nand' Jase,—

Beyond any doubt, Damiri's staff reported to her
regularly, and Damiri reported what seemed useful to
Tabini, right next door: so it was inconceivable she
didn't know by now everything the staff knew; Tabini
probably knew, and he was sure both Jase's behavior
and his plus the fact he had called his two chiefs of
security in for a conference had been amply reported.

*—his behavior considering the extreme stress and
my absence has been restrained and circumspect.
Laboring under what may be a serious blow, he has
nevertheless held himself for days from displaying feelings extremely difficult for a human to repress under
far less strenuous conditions, all to obey my order not
to display inexplicable emotion near atevi. I am greatly
distressed that I was absent at the time and unable to
provide advice or assistance to him, but he behaved
very well indeed.*

He disliked dissecting Jase's private feelings. He
truly disliked it. But he tried to be clinical, for the
information of the one man—and the woman—who
most needed to understand how well Jase had actually
performed: Jase had occasionally upset the serving
staff, who had witnessed prior explosions and must
wonder what was the difference in the paidhi they
knew and the one who came from the ship.

But staff storms settled, once staff was reassured that

it was not their fault. Even in that, Jase was doing a very good job. Atevi had never seen the temper-storms even the most well-trained paidhi-candidates threw when language-deprivation set in, back in the university on Mospheira; and they didn't see it in Jase— Jase's were mere verbal explosions, restrained perhaps because of Jase's own upbringing, or because the atevi world around him was so very quiet and void of anger.

But he did hope that Tabini's good opinion would affect Damiri's, and that Damiri's would in turn become the staff's judgment of Jason Graham. It would certainly make life easier in this apartment. He hoped, too, that it might ease the strain on Jase if he could, through Damiri, encourage the staff to understanding. He knew that information flowed in and out by the servants. And one wanted a good reputation.

Aiji-ma, I should add that he had exhausted himself in study to please me and to meet my schedule, unknowing to what extent news about to fall on him would challenge his self-control.

I should advise you of the normal course of human reaction to such a loss—first to think about past time and missed opportunities regarding his relative. In such a time the future has no map for him; his present is full of responsibilities to relatives which, in his situation, he cannot satisfy. Frustration may well manifest, which may lead to anger with himself or with me, or even with the dead. But this anger will in no wise threaten harm to me or to the staff. . . .

God save us if he threatens the premises, he thought. He had only to look up and about him to see the contents of a veritable museum, the possession and the heritage of the Atageini clan, one of the most critical and dangerous alliances Tabini had forged, expressed in needlepoint draperies, in priceless carvings and fragile porcelain, in carpets which servants cleaned on hands and knees with dust-cloths.

He wishes to visit familiar places. He does not believe in ghosts and he does not believe in their intervention as far as I understand his religious opinions. He is brave and strong-minded or he would not have come down here. I request and hope for answers to my inquiries so that I can provide him some measure of assurance and rapid contact with his mother and other relatives on the ship. I will monitor such conversations and be sure of the content of messages passed.

I stand ready to report to you far better news regarding progress on the ship. Lord Geigi, who treated me as a very honored guest, and the manager of Patinandi in his district have shown me very encouraging progress; and likewise the laboratory at Gioli is making progress on the design of the engines and likewise on the test site. I have some concerns on the recent change of management at Ladisiri.

That was the computer design. The Determinists and the Absolutists were all but going at each other with knives, and the two most talented designers had been literally having tea with each other as two of their aides met in the hall in a set-to that other aides had had to break up by main force.

I have personnel recommendations which may separate and isolate members of the development teams at two sites rather than having discordant persons within the same facility. I do suggest that you assign persons to look into the issues involved, which are beyond my grasp, but which seem bitter and divisive and which are not, by advisements I have received, following the design specifications.

Freely translated, intervene in Ladisiri, aiji-ma, before someone gets killed.

And considering the province was dualistic in philosophy, with no felicitous third, the aiji might threaten to move the research to a rival institution. *That* might get the attention of the two staffs. Certainly the two senior directors were oblivious to the quarrels, being lost in a probably productive debate on a design that, God save them, might be useful in advanced theory but was not going to fly on this ship.

I also urge, aiji-ma, that the needs of the aeronautical engineers should have precedence over further theoretical research at this time.

I consider this a matter of great delicacy and

great urgency, which I shall manage according to your orders or leave to more tactful persons at your discretion.

It was the one truly unmanageable problem they had with the project, give or take a few operational difficulties which were not at that level. This one—the aiji might have to straighten out by calling in the lord of the province and having an urgent discussion with him.

He was, however, finished with letters. He rolled the missive, slipped it into his message cylinder, and sealed it.

And chose to get up and walk the darkened hall to the lighted foyer and security station at the other end of that hall in search of a messenger rather than calling staff to carry it to security. He had no desire to have them disturb Tabini's evening with it, and he could advise the junior staff to advise Tabini's staff to that effect. As much as anything, he wanted to see whether the light was showing from under Jase's door, to know whether Jase was asleep or awake, and by that—

Well, he didn't know, entirely, but he wanted to know Jase's state of mind, whether he was still awake, which might indicate he was still debating matters with himself; and that might indicate he *should* try to speak to him.

He'd looked in that direction, seeing no light. He looked where he was going and found a towering pair of shadows between himself and the distant foyer light, one very broad-shouldered and *not* the willowy silhouette of one of his staff.

He spun and ran for his lighted bedroom and slammed his door. And shot the bolt.

And kept himself from standing in front of the door in doing so. He had a gun. He had it in the bureau drawer. He wasn't supposed to have it. Surely staff had heard the disturbance. If they were alive.

Came a footstep on the carpet outside. A gentle tap. "Bren-ji?"

A deep and resonant voice. A familiar voice. *"Banichi?"*

"One is impressed with all your actions, Bren-ji. If

you have the gun in hand, kindly put it back in the drawer."

He had no doubt then it was Banichi. And the other would be Jago.

"Have you been well, nadi?"

"My life has been dull and commonplace." He said it as a joke, while his heart resumed a normal rate. He thought in the next breath it was true. He was firmly convinced that the day's events in the peninsula and Banichi's return weren't without relationship. And here they were, back with him, and just in shooting the bolt back to let them in he found his hands trembling.

He wanted so much to throw his arms around both of them.

But that would appall Banichi and Jago would be puzzled, and the most wonderful sight in the world to him was as he looked up—considerably—at two atevi in the silver-studded black of the aiji's personal security.

"One hadn't meant to alarm the house," Jago said earnestly.

"Although it would have been better for you to call out an alarm," Banichi added, "since you were behind the wall—not, one trusts, against the paneled door, paidhi-ji."

Light had come on in the hall. Servants arrived in nightclothes and robes from the rear halls, along with Algini and a couple of the junior security staff from the other direction in far calmer, knew-about-it attitude. Tano arrived from the same direction as the recently sleeping servants, in a bath towel and carrying his pistol: Tano *hadn't* known.

Jase's door opened. Jase appeared in his robe, behind the line of servants, looking rumpled and confused.

"It's quite all right," Tano said to everyone. "It's quite all right. No alarm, Jasi-ji. Banichi and Jago are back."

"Have you had supper, nadiin-ji," Bren asked, instead of hugging both of them, "or should the staff make up something?"

"We ate on the plane, nadi," Jago said.

"But being off-duty now," Banichi said, "and being in the place where we will sleep tonight, one *might* sit and talk for a bit over a glass of shibei if the paidhi were so inclined."

7

Jase had gone back to bed and, one hoped, to sleep.
Tano and Algini said they had business to attend to.

Business, at this hour, Bren asked himself; and
couldn't decide whether they were occupied with his
request for the message trail on Jase's business,
heating up the phone lines to the earth station at
Mogari-nai, or whether it was some new duty Banichi
had handed them as he came in, but whatever the case,
Tano and Algini kept to the duty station.

That left him Banichi and Jago alone for company,
and oh, he was glad to see them. Banichi made him feel
safe; and Jago—Jago, so proper and so formal—she
was the one who *would* talk to him with utter disregard
of protocols, the one who'd try anything at least once,
including intimacy with a human. It hadn't happened:
the time had never been right; but it *could* have happened, that was what he didn't forget.

Tonight was like picking back up as if they'd never
left—and yet he had to realize, truthfully, for all the
difference they'd made in his life, they'd been with
him just that few weeks of the crisis preceding Jase's
landing. Then they'd been gone again, a reassignment,
he'd been told, a fact which had saddened him
immensely, and put him in a very hard place with Tano
and Algini, who were wonderful people—but who
weren't the two he most—

Loved.

Too valuable to the aiji, he'd said to himself: he'd no
right to assume he could keep them in his service. He

was damned lucky to have Tano and Algini, whom he also—

Liked very well.

Maybe it was just a visit, maybe just a temporary protection to him during the latest crisis. Maybe they wouldn't stay. He was halfway afraid to ask them. He wanted to, as he wanted to ask Tabini whether he could have them with him permanently, but he felt as if he would be asking for something the worth of a province, and to which Tabini would have to give a state answer, and think the paidhi had gotten just a little forward in recent months.

They sat, they shared a nightcap in the sitting-room—that, and the warm stove with the window open wide to the spring breezes—the extravagance of the rich and powerful, a waste of fuel with which Bren had never reconciled himself morally, and which in prior and simpler days, he would have reported and protested to the aiji.

But there was so much he had never reconciled with himself—morally.

"Dare I ask," he began with them, "where you've been?"

"One might ask, but we can't say," Jago said. "Regretfully, nand' paidhi."

He'd come very, very close to going to bed with Jago—well, technically, they'd been *in* it, sort of—a fact that had crossed his mind no few times in the last half year, in the lonely small hours of the winter nights. She'd *been* there, in his imagination, at least.

She'd either be offended—or she'd laugh. He thought she'd laugh, and dared a direct look.

He got nothing back. Atevi reserve, he said to himself. Guild discipline, and just—that she was atevi.

Forget *that* for a starting point and, God, couldn't one get in a great deal of trouble?

She probably wasn't even interested any longer. Probably had a new hobby.

"One hears," Banichi said, "that Jase-paidhi has had unhappy news given him by improper channels."

"True," he said. Banichi had a very incisive way of

summing things up. And, summoning up the fragments of his wits at this hour, dismissing the question of Jago's reactions, and meanwhile trying to be as concise: "I'm concerned for three things, one, his human feelings, two, his isolation, three, the way atevi minds might expect him to act. I asked Tano and Algini what was ordinary reaction for an ateva, and it didn't seem far off the way humans react." He let that echo in the back of his mind two seconds, added, recollected, revised, definitely under the influence of the shibei, and said: "Four, sometimes when the difference between ship-humans and Mospheira isn't that apparent, it surprises me. And, felicitous five, complicating things, Jase is trying to restrain his reactions in front of atevi."

"How is his fluency lately?" Banichi asked.

"Improved just enough that he can get out of the children's language and into serious trouble. He's learned the words that pertain to this apartment and to the space program and engineering. His vocabulary is quite good for 'where is?', 'bring me food' and 'open the window,' and for 'machining tolerance' and 'autoclave.' Still not much beyond that—but acquiring felicitous nuance."

"One would be hard pressed to join these items in conversation," Banichi said dryly. "Even with nuance."

"One would." He was amused, and felt the unwinding of something from about his heart. Tano didn't tend to catch him up on the daily illogics of his trade, but Banichi would jab him, mercilessly. So would Jago. He had to revise the rules of his life and go on his guard all the time, or be the butt of their humor. And he enjoyed it. He fired back. "So what *did* befall lord Saigimi?"

"One hears," Banichi said, "someone simply and uncreatively shot him."

"So. Doubtless, though, it was professional."

"Doubtless," Jago said. "Though late."

So Tabini didn't trouble to make it look accidental, was his private thought: more dramatic effect, more fear on the part of those who should be afraid.

"Is it quiet in the south?"

"The south. Oh, much more so. But quiet often goes between storm fronts."

A warning. A definite warning, from Jago. "Is there anything you wish to tell me, nadiin-ji?"

"Much that I would *wish* to inform you," Banichi said, with the contrary-to-fact *wish,* "but essentially, and until we know the outcome of yesterday's events, please take no unnecessary chances. The situation is quite volatile. Lord Saigimi of the Hagrani had acquired allies, more timorous or more prudent than he, but should any of *those* lords fall within their houses, and some more radical members within those same houses rise—times might become interesting. In most instances, understand, the replacements for any of those persons would not lead with Saigimi's force of will; but one of the lot is worth watching, Saigimi's daughter Cosadi—a bit of a fool, and an associate of Direiso—*female* conspiracy, entirely impenetrable."

Jago made a face and shot her senior partner a look. And knowing these two, Bren recognized a tossed topic when it sailed by him. "A woman may be more in Direiso's confidence. Naturally."

"I don't think the junior member of the Hagrani clan is on Direiso's intellectual level," Banichi muttered. "And she will see herself eaten without salt."

Quickly, that idiom meant. The two had fallen to discussion in front of him, but played it out *for* him, quite knowledgeably so.

"But considers herself to be Direiso's intellectual heir-apparent," Jago said.

"Oh, small chance."

"An earnest student—capable of flattery."

"I thought discerning women saw through such frivolity."

Clearly it was a jibe. Bren failed to know where. But Jago wasn't daunted.

"They receive *that* kind of flattery so rarely, nadi."

Banichi's brow lifted. "What, praise? Admiration? I pay it when due."

Banichi evidently scored. Or came out even.

Jago shot him a sidelong look, and was otherwise expressionless.

"Jago believes she saved my life," Banichi said. "And will *not* decently forget it."

"Is *that* it?" Bren asked. "I at least am grateful, Jago-ji, that you saved his life. I would have been very sad if you hadn't."

"I did raise that point," Jago said, still straight-faced. "He of course was in no danger."

"None," Banichi said with an airy wave.

"Guild etiquette does not permit me to state he is a fool, Bren-ji, but he risked himself attempting to pre-empt *me* in a position of better vantage. —And I did *not* require help, nandi!"

A wise human sat very still. And ducked his head and bit his lip, because he knew it was a performance for his benefit.

He was appalled to think, then, like a lightning-stroke, that he was hearing details from this morning, regarding a death for which, dammit, yes, these two were directly responsible.

So who had fired? At whom?

Jago? To save Banichi? Jago had killed someone? Lord Saigimi?

Or his security? That would lack finesse. Banichi would never joke about such an event as that. And did Tabini want such matters communicated to him?

Banichi took a casual pose, legs extended, and had a sip of the liqueur.

"Bren-ji, just take care."

"I am very glad you're both safe."

"So are we," Banichi said, and gave a quiet smile. "We only said to ourselves, 'What does it lack now?' And Jago said, 'Our lives are too quiet. Let's find nadi Bren.' So we climbed back over the wall and took the first plane to Shejidan."

Not from the Marid airport, Bren was willing to bet.

"One is very glad," Bren said, "to have you both back. One hopes you'll stay a while."

"One hopes." Banichi kicked a footstool into reach

and propped his feet toward the fire, then leaned back, glass in hand.

"They won't—come after you here, will they?"

A totally innocent look, from golden atevi eyes. "Who?"

"The—" One was being stupid, even to ask. "The owners of the wall."

"Ah, that."

"No," Jago said primly. "One cannot file Intent on the Guild, Bren-ji. Certain privileges the Guild reserves for itself."

"Needless to say, however," Banichi added, "if one *is* one of those points of stability on which other stability rests, it's always well to take precautions."

Him, Banichi meant. Or Tabini.

"The project." He could only think of those remote, scattered facilities. "Has one accounted the safety of that? Even my eyes see possible vulnerabilities in the small plants."

"Oh, yes," Banichi said. "Carefully. Constantly. Although it hasn't been *our* direct concern."

"But it is at risk." He had cold chills even thinking of a flaw—deliberately induced. "Nadiin-ji, we have so very much at risk in that project. I don't know—I don't know if I can explain enough to the Guild how small a problem can be fatal. I'm the translator. And some things I know by being from the island and having the history humans have—but it's so important. It's *so* important, nadiin-ji, and I haven't succeeded in making enough people understand. All the lives of all the paidhiin before me come down to two things: the peace, and this project. This is what we were always aiming at, in everything we did, in all the advice we gave to atevi—the peace, and this project, was all to give us all the capacity that we lost in the War and in the failure of the station up there. And one act of sabotage, one well-concealed piece of bad work—and the ship we build is gone, lost, perhaps not to be built again. The humans aloft—they can't build your future, nadiin-ji. They *won't.* Atevi could lose everything."

There was something a little less relaxed in Banichi's pose. In Jago's.

"At least," Banichi said, "one perceives distress. *Why,* nand' paidhi? Why are you concerned? Is it a specific threat? Is it a general one?"

"Because if this spaceship fails, Banichi, I can't call that chance back again. There's so much at stake. Your governance over your own future is at risk. This is why I stayed and why I wouldn't go back to Mospheira when my government wished me recalled. I won't go even for my family's sake." He realized he'd reprised at least the feeling of his speech to the workers—that fear was working at the back of his brain, and it had been there since before he'd heard of the assassination of lord Saigimi. Perhaps—perhaps it had been there since he'd seen the ship lying in pieces at his feet, and seen all that devoted effort in those upturned faces.

There was so much good will, and so much desire in so many people; and it was so vulnerable to the vicissitudes of fortune—and a few ill-wishers.

Baji-naji. Chance and Fortune, the interlocked design in the carpet outside the dining room, the demon and the force that overwhelmed the best of numbers and improved the worst.

"Have you some specific reason to fear?" Jago asked: Jago, who would fling her body between any of her charges and harm; but who was trained to do things far more lethally useful for those within her man'chi.

"Just—nadiin-ji, a single act of sabotage, undetected, might set the program so far behind Mospheira we'd never catch up. And I saw so many plants where people from the towns came in without security checks, where lords' families had access. And shouldn't. Not that I want to be rude to these honest people—things are going so well. I think it makes me irrationally fearful."

"Not irrationally." Banichi let go an easier breath. "We *are* aware of the hazards—trust me in this. This is an immensely complex project, with many exposures. But without being specific, let me reassure the paidhi, we are not off our guard."

Banichi would *not* say Guild. This was, again, the man who hadn't known the sun was a star—nor cared. But what he did care about, he knew about in greater detail and with more forethought than most men could keep up with.

"And," Jago said with a quirk of the mouth, "lord Geigi has the number-counters contained. Or occupied."

"One hopes."

The decanter was on the small table near Banichi. Banichi reached over and poured a finger more; and one for Jago, who leaned forward to present her glass. "Nadi?" Banichi said, offering to him next.

He considered. He'd had one with Jase. But if Banichi was offering information, and it came on such skids, he'd have another: he let Banichi add a bit.

"Did I do foolishly to take lord Geigi's hospitality?" he asked them.

"Evidently not."

"I didn't ask was I lucky? I asked—"

Banichi grinned. "Far more wary, these days, our Bren."

"Lord Geigi's philosophical persuasion is one of the most rigorous," Jago said. "Most, understand, follow less rigorous systems, saying that there is no assurance that anyone has yet come up with right answers. But here are Geigi and his Determinist numerologists actually matching up answers with the universe *as* human numbers also perceive it, and the Rational Absolutists are prowling around this new set of ideas trying to find a problem it doesn't solve. This folded space business has acquired great credibility, Bren-ji. The numerologists are still gnawing the bone of the faster-than-light idea Deana-ji threw them—" That *Deana-ji* was certainly barbed. "But no one dares challenge folded space until they've posed certain classic problems— which keeps the 'counters and the Absolutists both out of mischief, at least until they've worked out their numbers. A challenge to folded space will be hard, by what I hear."

"I leave such deep questions to my partner," Banichi said, and took a sip of shibei. "Geigi's good will is secure. That secures the numbers of the northern reach of the peninsula, which are the numbers that concern me, pragmatically. Geigi's penchant for honesty— that and his penchant for inviting guests inside his security—that worries me. Tano says you bade Geigi take precautions."

"It seemed prudent to say. Possibly excessive."

Banichi gave a short laugh. "He'll naturally believe you have special inside information from your security, and he'll listen to you far more than to any advice his security gives him. I've no doubt he will lose sleep over it. A good stroke, nand' paidhi!"

"What *will* happen in the peninsula? Who do you think will take over the Marid?"

"Oh, difficult question. Very difficult, Saigimi's daughter, Cosadi, being a passionate follower of Direiso and all that lot—and a fool."

"On the other hand," Jago said, "Saigimi's younger brother, Ajresi, who is not resident in the house, and who absolutely can't *tolerate* Saigimi's Samiusi-clan wife, is much more forward to defend himself than he is to involve the house in adventurous actions. As a leader of his house he's both more and less dangerous. He let Saigimi take the risks. But for want of aggression, to allow himself to be pushed aside in the succession by a willful niece who might take the house even further down the path Saigimi took—I think not, myself."

"Wise conclusion," Banichi said. "*That* house will have internal difficulties. The wife, too, Tiburi, may take refuge with Direiso; Tiburi is, by the way, related to lord Geigi. That was the plan in driving Geigi into poverty, to slip her into that inheritance."

"Was *that* it?"

"Oh, yes. So thanks to her try at dispossessing Geigi, wife Tiburi of the Samiusi is not only no longer welcome with Hagrani clan—she's no longer welcome with her distant cousin Geigi. Nor will her daughter Cosadi be welcome any longer with Saigimi's brother Ajresi, *especially* since Geigi's fortunes are more and more linked to Tabini's, and the direction of Cosadi's man'chi becomes more and more unpredictable. She may claim the Hagrani estate with at least equal right, and certain of Saigimi's household more loyal to the wife might try to prevent the lordship drifting to the brother's line, in fear he will toss them out the door. Some say Cosadi has assassins belonging to the Hagrani clan poised to take out Saigimi's brother and make her the Hagrani lord. Certainly Ajresi also has Guild poised to remove her."

At this point a man wanted to grab a notepad and tell them to repeat it while he took notes. But it was too late. His head was buzzing. He at least had the critical names to ask them.

"And," Jago said, "certain of the Guild who have served Saigimi may now find man'chi lying elsewhere, rather than serve the daughter, who is suspected by some to be a fool and by others to be a mere figurehead for Tiburi, who is *not* even Hagrani and who cannot go back to her own clan."

"It should be an interesting summer in the peninsula," Banichi said.

"Direiso may attract those Guild members," Jago added. "And lose a few of her own, who will begin to think it towering folly to have so many targets move in under one roof."

Bren's ears pricked up. He wanted to ask, Can one *choose* man'chi logically? He had thought it, like love, to be unaffected by common sense considerations of survival during such machimi play sort-outs. Not evidently so.

But if he interrupted the flow of information, he could lose what they were trying, in their bewildering way, to tell him.

"One thinks," Jago had gone on, "that the Kadigidi themselves—" That was Direiso's house. "—will spend some time in rearranging loyalties. The son and likeliest heir to Direiso herself is an Atageini on his maternal grandfather's side—"

"Direiso's father never sitting as house-head," Banichi interjected, "due to a dish of infelicitous berries."

Berries. The paidhi, feeling the effects of alcohol, all but lost the threads.

"Last fall," Jago continued unflapped, "Direiso's son, Murini, was a guest in the Atageini house at the same time we have reason to believe Deana Hanks was a guest in Direiso's house. Mark *that,* Bren-ji."

Tag and point. Definitely in Direiso's house, then. It certainly deserved remembrance. He hadn't known *that* detail, either, that this son of Direiso's had been— what, hiding among Atageini *with* Tatiseigi, for fear of his mother's rash actions? Or had he been go-between, in Atageini complicity in the Deana Hanks affair?

That would mean aiming at overthrowing Tabini, while Tabini was sleeping with lady Damiri, heir of the Atageini.

If there were clear proof of that, he was sure Banichi or Jago would have told him.

It was only certain in what he did know that the Padi Valley nobles, of whom Tabini himself was one, had old, old and very tangled associations. It was the central association of the Ragi, which had produced all the aijiin ever to rule from Shejidan; a little nest of occasionally warring rivals, in plain fact.

None other than lord Geigi and Tabini's hard-riding grandmother had walked into a house the identity of which was clearly now the Kadigidi house, and taken Deana Hanks away with them, apparently to Direiso's vast discomfiture and no little breakage of fragile objects in Direiso's parlor, by what he had later heard about a fracas and the overturning of a cabinet of antiques wherever the event had taken place.

Add to that now the knowledge that Direiso's son had been in that very moment at the Atageini home, while the Atageini daughter was in bed with Tabini.

Definitely headache-producing. But among atevi, things could be very simple, too.

To find out who was the most likely person to start trouble, and the one toward whom all other atevi players would gravitate, look for the strongest.

Yesterday he might have said, regarding Tabini's known opposition, that the strongest players were

Tatiseigi of the Atageini, Saigimi of the Marid Tasigin, and Direiso of the Kadigidi.

Now with Saigimi dead, he would say it was up in the air between Direiso of the Kadigidi and Tatiseigi of the Atageini, and, hardly thinking about it, that Direiso was more likely to act against Tabini—he didn't know why he thought so, but Tatiseigi had dropped back from threatening Tabini the moment Saigimi, remote from him geographically, had dropped out of the picture.

Why did he think so? Tatiseigi's ancestral lands were in the Padi Valley, next door to the other survivor in that group, Direiso of the Kadigidi, his next door neighbor. Direiso had used *Saigimi* as front man for her rasher, more extreme moves.

But it wasn't loss of courage that would cause him to put Tatiseigi second to Direiso, in his bemused and shibei-overwhelmed subconscious, if Tatiseigi allied with that lady.

No, because Tatiseigi's niece Damiri was sleeping with Tabini, and might provide Tabini's heir. *If* Tatiseigi could recover his dignity as head of clan and *if* Tatiseigi's battered pride could be patched up—and bolstered instead of diminished by Damiri's alliance—that could make Tatiseigi very important in the Western Association, though not aiji, which due to her own ambitions Direiso would not let him become, anyway.

Ah. And ah-ha.

Direiso would see Tatiseigi at that point as threatening her bid to be aiji as much as helping her, because Tatiseigi would see the same set of facts: he would never be aiji; he was elderly; he had *not* produced an heir of his own line. That was why Damiri, Tatiseigi's sister's daughter, was the acknowledged heir; and Tatiseigi could not be thinking in terms of his own genetic or political continuance if he *were* aiji—that was what the subconscious was raking up. Tatiseigi had to reach a truce with Damiri, since he was less and less likely to bring her into line by replacing her. And Damiri was likelier and likelier to produce the next aiji.

Right now, a thorn in Tatiseigi's flesh, Tatiseigi's ancestral apartment in the Bu-javid was tainted by unwanted humans, his niece was, to all public perception defying him in bedding down with Tabini—and last year some excessive fool in attempting to state opposition to humans *or* to embarrass the Atageini had sprayed bullets across the breakfast room and taken out a frieze of elegant porcelain lilies . . .

Lilies which even now were being restored, angrily, defiantly, by Atageini-hired workmen: the breakfast room secured off from the rest of the apartment by a steel wall installed with screw-bolts, a barrier that let those workmen come and go without compromising the aiji's security.

The lilies had been broken by someone who'd authorized an attack on the paidhi.

By someone, he was relatively sure, who'd had no idea what he was shooting at, someone blindly bent on shooting up premises which held a human, and possibly bent on compelling an Atageini break with Tabini.

It was an unthinkable botch-up of a job if some Atageini had done it, because those bullets were not just sprayed into *an* apartment favored by the Atageini, they'd been sent into an apartment filled with priceless Atageini art treasures, and had hit the lilies which were the *symbol* of the Atageini.

The fact was public. The shame was public. And no Atageini would have been so stupid. Tabini wouldn't have done it—he had Damiri already and nothing to gain. No, an Atageini ally had done it—someone either wanting to push Tatiseigi into action *or* (the whisper was) chastise him for inaction in the matter of human influence.

But the result had embarrassed him instead of angering him.

One *hell* of a dangerous situation was what was left. Either Saigimi had attacked the lilies—or Direiso had, the two likeliest suspects.

And if Saigimi had, and was dead, Tabini had removed a man Tatiseigi now could not get vengeance from. Now, in the aftermath of Saigimi's assassination, Direiso would have to move against Tabini soon—or die next.

That left the highly embarrassed Tatiseigi with no vengeance available, standing eyeball to eyeball with Direiso, who herself wanted to be aiji of Shejidan at the expense of Damiri, who could weld the Atageini onto Tabini's line and unite *two* Padi Valley lines in a way that might alter the hitherto several-way contest in the Padi Valley forever.

Damn, a man could get a headache, but he was beginning to see through this set of moves of Tabini's. Diminish *all* other prospects: it was Direiso that the Saigimi affair was setting up for a fatal fall, and if Tabini could only recover Tatiseigi's dignity in such a grand gesture as Tabini had made to salvage lord Geigi's finances, then Tabini had the man and a *very* valuable alliance with the Atageini in his pocket and the potential mother of his heir with her man'chi secure and solid as a rock.

"Are we secure here?" he asked his security, with a notion how very, very much was at stake in the apartment he was occupying. "I mean—staying here. Under the circumstances."

"One simply watches. Say only that you're as safe as the aiji himself."

Ironic double meaning. If lady Damiri betrayed Tabini at this juncture—or if the Tatiseigi matter blew up into violence—they were in real trouble.

If Tabini's grandmother Ilisidi didn't take over. Which Ilisidi might do—*longed* to do, at least, by some reports. God—one *wouldn't* suppose *she'd* blasted the lilies?

She *was* an Atageini ally. And a major power among the Eastern lords around Malguri. It was why Tabini's grandfather had married her: to hold the East in the Association.

On the other hand—he was running out of hands—considering grandmother—Ilisidi—you couldn't say she was disposed unfavorably to the paidhi or to humans. If she hadn't wintered at Taiben, in the open land she preferred, he himself would have passed no little of his scarce free time this winter in Ilisidi's company.

He *liked* Ilisidi. As he *liked* Geigi. Human judgment. Which wasn't, dammit, automatically invalid. No ... Ilisidi would not destroy the lilies, the way Ilisidi wouldn't destroy what was historic, and beautiful. He could never believe such a gross act of her. It was a human judgment, but it *was* accurate.

"Nadiin," he said, head aching from all this circular thinking, "one has to get to bed, nadiin-ji. I've a meeting with Tabini after breakfast. You're not obliged to be up at that hour—I'm sure Tano or Algini can manage and you can sleep late."

"This house sets a memorable breakfast," Banichi said. "Jago may be unconscious and immoveable when the sun rises, but I at least intend to be there."

"Those who didn't spend the night on a roof in a rainshower may be drawn out for breakfast," Jago said. "I may be there, nadi Bren. I may not."

"It's so good to see you two." He rose, took the decanter and poured Banichi another helping, and one for Jago.

"You will corrupt us, nadi," Banichi said.

"Take it, take it. People who do and who don't spend the night on a roof are alike due some comforts when they reach a safe place, aren't they?"

"One is willing to be corrupted," Jago said, lifting her glass. "At least tonight, Bren-ji."

So the two of them went out with refilled glasses and, he was sure, headed to the two bedrooms that had been waiting half a year for them, next door to Jase's.

It had been a long day, Bren thought as he stripped off clothes and prepared for bed. A fine day, a disastrous day—a good day again, in finding Banichi and Jago.

Not a good day for the lord Saigimi. He *could* feel sorry for everyone in Saigimi's man'chi. He watched the machimi plays on television, in professional curiosity, as paidhiin had watched for years, trying to decipher the codes of atevi behavior. The Saigimi mess was absolutely high classic—the unknown loyalties, man'chi shifting unpredictably even for those most intimately involved with the dead lord.

There was even a chance that Cosadi, the daughter, wasn't sure where her man'chi rested from hour to hour, self-doubt which was real emotional upheaval, as he began to perceive it, a fundamental uncertainty for the young woman as to which elements in her blood, to use a human expression, were going to pull her which direction, and whether she'd survive the shake-out as the same uncertainty resolved itself for a dozen characters at once.

A new lord, probably Ajresi, meanwhile took control, driving out the Samiusi-clan wife, Tiburi, *Geigi's* relative, along with Cosadi, to a household (Direiso's) involved to the hilt in the dead lord's conspiracy against the aiji.

Classic machimi, indeed. He'd been fascinated by the color, the banners, the movement of troops, the texture of ancient atevi fortresses.

He was acquainted with one such fortress, at Malguri, on an intimate basis, right down to the classic bathroom plumbing. He'd told himself that as a human he had no business there.

And still he loved the place, and the *feel* of the windy height and the age of the stones tugged at something ancestral in him. He'd come to grips with what was essentially atevi there. He'd learned lessons he, whose business was words, couldn't put in words; he'd seen things that sent a lump into his throat and a quickness into his pulse.

Ilisidi had shown him.

Proving, perhaps, that human instincts and atevi man'chi did have something in common, before they diverged and became what they were in the higher branches of evolution.

Or just that—their species both came from planets. Something in both species loved the earth, the stones, the touch of what was alive.

Off went the shirt. It slid from his fingers before he had a chance to turn and deliver it to the servants.

Atageini servants. Who were, one sincerely hoped, loyal to lady Damiri next door, and not to uncle Tatiseigi.

Machimi.

Whose man'chi came first? Which man'chi had become clear to the servants, when they met their human guest—or dealt with Jase, who was having trouble with the earth and dirt and stone aspect of things, and who really, now in a family tragedy, had a profound justification for his winter-long distress.

He'd long since gotten beyond embarrassment in this lady's household, about this servantly insistence a man couldn't undress himself or deal with his own laundry. Tano had been stand-in for the staff during the last number of days, Tano and he taking the opportunity to exchange information in that little space of privacy: what they'd done for the day, what they expected on the morrow. And he'd felt *far* more comfortable in that arrangement, and closer to Tano than he'd ever otherwise been.

But they were definitely back in Shejidan, and Tano was no longer accessible. Give or take the one nightcap too many, he found his nerves still buzzing with the information he'd gotten, buzzing so he wasn't sure he'd sleep easily at all.

Still, bed was calling to him with a promise of satin sheets and soft pillows. The television was over in the corner, his panacea for sleeplessness on the road, and a concession, in this antique bedroom, to the paidhi's necessity to keep up with the news; and occasionally just to have entertainment or noise to fill the silence.

But he had his *staff* back with him. He had Banichi and Jago. He had them again.

It was Sasi into whose hands he shed the clothes: she was an older servant with, Sasi had informed him proudly, along with the requisite photos, four grand-children.

An apostate, far-from-his-culture human chose to believe that made Sasi absolutely professional at seeing people into bed and tucked in, and that she was a decent and sobering influence on the two young maids who stood by and offered and received the exchange of garments, the lounging robe for the sleeping robe, in which one didn't ordinarily sleep, but there it was, nonetheless, the requisite robe. One just did wear appropriate garments, that was the explanation, even if said robe was immediately, fifteen paces away, to be taken off to go to bed.

It was polite. It was expected. It was what was done. The paidhi had rank in the court, therefore the paidhi's closet overflowed with appropriate garments which were the pride and the care of his staff on display.

And the paidhi couldn't, God, no, dress or undress himself, without showing lack of confidence in his Atageini staff.

The paidhi *had* gotten the message of the staff over the last year of his life, and had ceased to frustrate the servants in their zeal to please him.

"How *are* the repairs?" he asked as Sasi applied a cursory brush to his hair, towering over him the while. The faint aroma of paint and new plaster had been constant. But it seemed fainter this evening. "Nadi Sasi? One heard the painting might be over."

"All the work is most nearly complete, nand' paidhi. The tiles are all in place, so we hear. The painters have been at work almost constantly, and now they seem finished."

And the young servant by the door: "The artisans think—perhaps in a day, nand' paidhi. So nand' Saidin says."

"I believe, nand' paidhi," Sasi said, "that they have told the lady so."

Damiri, in other words. The crews that had been scraping and pounding away down the hall were Atageini workmen, or at least workmen intensely scrutinized by the Atageini lord.

In the thoughts of a few moments ago, one worried.

"Nadi." One maid produced a scroll from his robe's pocket, and offered it to Sasi, who gave it to him.

Toby's telegram. Damn. He hadn't gotten to answering it.

But he couldn't do anything about answering it, or about his mother's condition. She had medical care. He couldn't help. When they talked on the phone, she grew upset and got onto topics that upset her, like his job, her getting hate calls. It was better he didn't call.

He laid the scroll on the night table. Then he took off the satin robe and surrendered it to Sasi before he lay down on the sheets of the historic Atageini bed—in which an Atageini had been murdered, oh, some centuries ago, under a coverlet which was a duplicate of that coverlet.

As the lilies down the hall would be exact duplicates of the lilies destroyed by whatever agency.

The Atageini were stubborn about their decor. Their power. Their autonomy. The hospitality shown their guests.

Damiri had had resources to check out the workmen. He'd told himself so for months. That special steel expansion barrier, an ingenious affair with screw-braces that extended and bolted with lock bolts in all directions, had occasioned a fuss over the woodwork; but the security barrier had gone in; and that meant workmen and artisans had to come and go by a scaffolding let down from the roof, under the supervision of Tabini's guards. So the nearby residents had sealed *their* windows with similar precautions.

"Shall I leave the windows open, nand' paidhi? Or open the vents?"

"I think just the vents, thank you, Sasi-ji." He trusted no one was going to make a foray into the apartments from the construction. But the scraping and hammering and the smell of paint and plaster had gone on all winter; and now that it was spring, when neighboring apartments as well as his own had the desire to take advantage of their lofty estate well above the city and the general safety that let these apartments open their windows to the breezes, it had certainly put a matter of haste into the repair job—a need to get the smelly part done, before, as Tabini said, someone declared feud on the Atageini over the repairs.

They were nearing an end of that situation, as it seemed—an end of bumps and thumps that made the guards get up in haste and go investigate, and an end of a major eyesore in the apartment. 'A few more days' had gotten to be the household joke, long predating 'rain clouds,' but it did sound encouraging.

So they were going to be rid of the barrier, the workmen, the casting and solvent smells wafting in through the balcony windows, and he would have back a room of exquisite beauty, which happened to be *his* favorite place in the apartments, whether for study or breakfast or just sitting and relaxing.

God. Oh, God. The date.

He was supposed to do a television interview on the 14th. Tomorrow. Was it tomorrow? The 14th?

It *was* the 14th. He hadn't even thought about it since he'd left. He hadn't remotely considered it when he'd thought about extending his visit with Geigi.

He had no wish whatsoever to tie the business of the space program to the assassination of lord Saigimi in the public mind; he didn't want to answer questions regarding lord Saigimi, which might possibly come up—the news services, generally well behaved, still occasionally blundered into something in a live interview—live, because some atevi believed that television that regarded politics had to be live for the numbers not to be deliberately misleading.

But he couldn't, at this date and at this hour, even by coming down with an attack of poisoning, *cancel* the news conference, not without having people draw the very conclusion he didn't want.

He had to get his wits together and face it tomorrow—do it with dispatch and in full control of his faculties. He'd set the interview up fifteen days ago when it had sounded perfectly fine and within his control. He'd had it on his calendar as just after the factory tour. He'd made sure it missed the trip dates. They'd added two days and three labs onto his tour at the last moment and he'd totally forgotten about the damn interview as significant, just one of those myriad things his staff steered him to and out of and on to the next thing on the list, and that Tano would have advised him of the very moment he proposed to them accepting lord Geigi's offered day on the boat. They'd have been able to do it: they'd have just shunted the event to Sarini Province and set up in Geigi's front hall, cameras, lights, and baggage, and *he* wouldn't have been put out by it except as it affected the fishing schedule.

But, given a choice now, he wouldn't have done it tomorrow.

Damn! He wouldn't. But he supposed that nobody, including people who had or had not been atop certain buildings in the rain, had considered the paidhi's interview schedule when carrying out the assassination of a lord of the Association.

8

Banichi and Jago came to the dining room in the morning, cheerful and clearly anticipating the breakfast that was loading down the two service carts that were waiting along the wall outside.

Jase remained shut in his room. Jase was getting some sleep, madam Saidin said. Staff had quietly looked in on him to be sure that he was resting; and that he was safe; and they would be sure that he ate when he did wake.

"I think that sleep is more important for him," Bren agreed as he sat down at the table. "Thank you, Saidin-ji."

Tano and Algini came in for breakfast. And Tano, with a little bow, placed two objects beside his plate as he went to his chair, one a piece of vellum paper folded double, not scrolled as one did with formal messages; and the other a scroll in a gold (but very scarred) case.

In the inquiry regarding Jase-paidhi's message, the simple folded note said, Tano's writing, *no message was received at Mogari-nai directed to him during your absence. I have verified this by electronic record as provided by Mogari-nai.*

Indeed, while he'd been sitting talking with Banichi and Jago last night, others of his staff had been querying the Mogari-nai earth station via levels of the Bu-javid staff that could obtain valid and reliable answers.

So Jase's ship hadn't informed him of something that personal and urgent. The question was *why* they hadn't informed Jase; and *why* they'd told Yolanda without telling her Jase didn't know and consequently let her blurt out a piece of news like that. It was stupid, to have set up two agents in the field to be in that situation, and stupidity did not accord with other actions the ship had taken.

Nor did Manasi nor any member of the staff receive any request from nand' Jase to call the ship, although this would not have been granted. He wished to speak to you personally and this request was denied. Nand' Jase expressed extreme emotion at this denial and requested no call be made to you on his behalf. Nand' Manasi expresses his distress at the situation, but he passed the tape of the Mospheira contact to the aiji's staff with no knowledge it was out of the ordinary and the aiji's staff has issued no report as yet on the content of that tape. Investigation is proceeding on the matter of timely report.

Meaning the aiji's staff, probably busy Mospheira-watching on other topics, had the tape of the phone call but hadn't interpreted it against the background of what else was going on, meaning matters in the peninsula, with which it might have been preoccupied. Manasi, watching Jase, hadn't known what was going on. Jase had given Manasi a request against his orders and then told Manasi to let the matter drop.

Jase also had that tendency to assume a rule could be neither questioned nor broken, a trait that came of the ship-culture Jase had come from, Bren very much suspected, one of those little points of difference between the ship and Mospheira. He and Jase *almost* shared a language, and met towering problems centered in wrong assumptions. On one level this had all the irrational feel of one of those.

But the misunderstanding wasn't trivial, this time.

And it still didn't answer the question why Jase hadn't been informed by the ship via Mogari-nai. And it didn't answer the possibility the aiji's staff had realized something was wrong and hadn't informed him. He wasn't sure Manasi had erred; he wasn't sure, either, that the staff had held anything back from him, but his instincts for trouble were awake.

Tano's note went on to a second item of the business he'd laid on his staff last night: *I forwarded your note to nand' Eidi. The aiji asks we advise his staff as soon as you've finished breakfast. He said he cannot be precise as to the time the aiji will have available to meet, nor should you be kept from your business* (it was the lordly *you;* Tano never seemed to know what to do with their familiarity on paper.) *One may have to wait and that will be arranged.*

Also, do you recall that there is a live television interview scheduled today at noon? I asked nand' Eidi yesterday should it be postponed or taken on tape, and nand' Eidi says the aiji believes any deviation in your schedule would be interpreted by the public at large not as your legitimate wish for rest but as the Bu-javid security staff's reaction to the general security alert, an intimation of concern the aiji does not wish to convey.

It is therefore the aiji's wish that you conduct the interview on schedule. I state the aiji's words. If we may be of service, we will carry another message.

"Thank you, nadiin-ji," he said, in the plural, figuring that both Tano and Algini had shared duty last night and lost sleep over the Jase matter; the message to the aiji had been much the simpler case, but pursued before he had even thought of it, thank God for Tano's keeping his schedule straight.

Then there was the second message cylinder, which staff, presumably, had already opened: the seal was cracked. The scarred gold case had a seal he didn't recognize, but evidently it was a message the clerical staff as well as his household thought he should see, on a priority evidently equal to the Jase matter.

The message he unrolled, as Saidin was serving the muffins and another servant was pouring tea, bore the written heading of the lord of Dur-wajran. That was the unknown seal.

That matter, he said to himself: the pilot who'd nearly collided with their jet.

Nand' paidhi, it read in a less than elegant hand, *one wishes most earnestly for your good will. The unfortunate circumstance* (misspelled) *of the encounter was unwished by me because of error and I wish to take all responsibility personally. Please do not take offense at my household. I did not mean to hit your plane. I am solely* (misspelled) *to blame and offer profoundest regrets at my stupidity.*

It was signed by one Rejiri, with a clan heraldry he took for the seal of Dur-wajran.

"This was the pilot? How old is he?"

"Young," Tano said. "I'd be surprised if he's twenty. He brought the message to the residential security post with flowers. On policy, they declined the flowers and sent them to the public display area but accepted the message." Tano added, then, in the manner of a thoroughly ridiculous proposition. "He wanted to come upstairs."

"What are we talking about?" Banichi asked.

"A pilot brought his plane very close to ours yesterday," Bren said. "I take it he's not still downstairs."

"I wouldn't think so," Tano said. "They say, however, he was insistent."

"Young," Algini said. "One thinks some of his distress may be the impoundment of the aircraft, which may bring his parents to Shejidan. He may wish to ask you to clear the record. I would *not* advise you meet with him or to grant that request."

"He," Tano added, "has a record of small aerial incidents around the coast near his home. He had no business bringing the plane to the largest airport in the world."

"True." He had campaigned for stricter enforcement of the ATC rules. He passed the note to Jago, as the most forgiving member of his security. "I hope they won't deal too harshly with him." One could get into a great deal of trouble coming too close to the aiji's residence during a security alert. "Please have someone advise him I take no personal offense and that the Bujavid staff has more urgent business."

"The staff has tried to impress the gravity of matters

on him," Tano said, "and to make clear to him that he should pay closer attention to public events. —One does take the impression that this young man lacks seriousness of purpose."

"Why is the paidhi involved with this person, nadi?" Banichi wanted to know, and the potential rebuke to junior security was implied in that 'nadi.' "And what, in full, happened?"

"An ATC violation," Tano said. The note went from Jago on to Banichi. "We *are* treating it seriously, nandi, at least to be sure there was nothing more than seems. It seems to be a young island pilot—the lord of Dur's son."

"Ah," Banichi said, as if that explained any folly in the world. Banichi reached for more toast and, so supplied, perused the note and looked at the seal.

"A minor thing," Algini said. "The authorities will advise the parents. —I would advise, nadi Bren, against accepting the boy's apology. Apology to a person of your rank should come from the lord of Dur first, then the boy."

"I understand," Bren said as nand' Saidin offered him curdled eggs and pastry. Considering the necessity of meeting with Tabini, it might be one of those days mostly marked by waiting. Tabini's day looked to be one of those unpredictable ones, with various emergencies coming in. "Thank you, nadi. The paidhi would have offended half the world by now, and all the noble houses would have filed on him, if he didn't have staff to keep him in order."

"This *is* a young fool," Banichi said, laying the note aside. "Don't concern yourself with him, Bren-ji. This is for other agencies to pursue. Meanwhile we will be trying to solve the other questions you posed."

The other questions, meaning the situation among the lords, post-Saigimi: atevi politics.

Meanwhile he had a computer and a briefcase full of plain, unadorned work he had to do for the space program.

And he had to deal with Jase personally. His staff said there was no impediment they could locate at

Mogari-nai with messages to which they could gain access, which ought to be everything; and they did indicate that Jase hadn't pushed Manasi to carry his request through channels. The request *still* might not have been granted.

But primarily he had to unravel what in bloody hell was going on inside the ship and why Jase had gotten a message that personal from a source who had apparently been notified by the ship in preference to Jase.

That just damn well wouldn't do, he thought, not in that personal matter, not, by any stretch of that policy, in other matters regarding the business on which Yolanda and Jason had come down to earth. *There* was the center of the matter, not Jase's father, however tragic it was on a personal level.

Meanwhile Banichi and Tano and Algini had fallen to discussing the state of building security and whether they were going to need to establish a service alert on the third floor (a decision which rested in the hands of Tabini's staff, and not their own) regarding the scaffold, which rumor on the staff held was going to be dismantled tomorrow.

Tomorrow, Bren thought, pricking up his ears. What a glorious piece of news. The workmen finished. No more scaffolding.

"No more barrier to the breakfast room?" he asked. "They're going to take that ugly door down?"

"One hopes, paidhi-ji," Tano said.

"But," Jago said, "there's a Marid lord arriving today to press a claim with the aiji."

"Or," Banichi said, "he wishes to escape the politics of his district. Note he *hasn't* applied for an audience."

"Who is this?" Bren asked.

"Badissuni, by name," Algini interjected. "And one wonders, nand' paidhi, whether it's an honest request."

"One hardly thinks so," Jago said. "I vastly distrust it. I would protest that door being removed."

Banichi had a very sober expression. So, Bren trusted, did he.

"The press says," Tano said, "that lord Badissuni is

escaping the politics of his district. *I* think the press was handed that information."

"A fair guess," Banichi said, and tapped the table with a sharp egg-knife balanced delicately over his thumb. "My bet? He wants the press to say so. But he wants them following the story so if Tabini-aiji tosses him out of his ancestral apartments in the Bu-javid he can make politics at home."

"So will Tabini do it?" Bren asked. "Pitch him out, I mean?"

"The Hagrani of the Marid have an apartment on the floor below, at the corner," Algini said. "Quite close, nand' paidhi. One hopes he doesn't ask to take up residence. But we fear he will. The balcony is standing open for the paint to dry and the room to air. This is not a good security condition. If they take down the security panel we have the same condition as before, glass doors, a balcony, no difficulty if all residents of this wing are reliable. But it's not alone these glass doors. It's the *aiji's* apartment next door. This is a serious exposure. Saigimi did not use the apartment. He let it to lord Geigi, who is *not* in residence, nor will be."

"The aiji *should* forbid his opening that apartment," Jago said under her breath. "This man is dangerous. He should be sent home unheard. We'll have official functions here in the building, we'll doubtless have windows open. This is an invitation perhaps the aiji is consciously extending. But I protest it when it comes near you, Bren-ji."

It was sensitively close to this apartment, and close to the aiji, was what Jago was saying. And the glass doors of the breakfast room had already proved a flimsy shield against bullets. That was why they were repairing the lily frieze.

"I'm here to rest," was Banichi's pronouncement on the situation, meaning, Bren supposed, and agreed, that they could leave that to others to decide, and enjoy their time in safety.

So Banichi had another helping. And with Banichi, Tano, and Algini at the table, all of them in their uniform black, all in shirt-sleeves so as not to scar the delicate chairs with the silver-studded coats, the paid-hi had his favorite breakfast, thought over *his* unavoidable problems, and, while the very large bowl of curdled eggs vanished, along with half jars of marmalade and various muffins, listened to his staff discuss in their cryptic way. He pricked up his ears again as the conversation made him absolutely *certain* the Saigimi business had come as a complete shock to Tano and Algini and that the orders which had caused it had not come at all unexpected to Banichi or Jago. Banichi wouldn't have let that much slip, he well knew, if Banichi didn't trust the entire company, and that had to include madam Saidin.

Or they were setting something up.

Since—he realized at that instant—Saidin herself was doing all the serving.

He was sitting in a room totally occupied by the Assassins' Guild, including madam Saidin, as shop talk went on about this and that, involving Guild policy on the recent assassination, the configuration of the apartments, and the aiji's schedule, on the security of which the paidhi's as well as the aiji's life and safety depended.

Tiburi, the wife of Saigimi, *and* her daughter Cosadi, one also learned, had bolted for Direiso's estate as Saigimi's brother Ajresi seized power in the Tasigin Marid.

"Don't count that as the final skirmish," was Jago's observation.

"Badissuni," Banichi said, "may be a messenger from Ajresi to Tabini."

Queasy thought to have with the breakfast eggs—uncommon discussion to have flowing around him, but he took his own internal temperature and decided he wasn't nearly as shocked as he ought to be about the recent assassination.

And he'd just thought—maybe it would be a lot better if an accident befell several more people associated with Saigimi.

He *was* slipping toward a certain callous view of these things; and did he *lose* something by that change

in himself, or *gain* something, when he envisioned the
fear Tabini could strike *if* he decided to kill the first
messenger of peace and by that action to signal (as in
the machimi) his wish for Saigimi's Hagrani clan to
remove its own new leadership in order to have peace
with the aiji? Clans apparently had done it in the past.

But Tabini wouldn't make that demand. At least the
paidhi didn't think so. Tabini continually asked the
filers of Intent to choose recourse to the courts instead.
It would say something very unusual for the aiji who
backed judicial resort as policy to choose a second
assassination.

Possibly Tabini's own moderate position on this
issue had placed him in a bind and threatened more
bloodshed.

And Tabini was dealing with an Edi lord. That was
another consideration: the ethnic division. The fact that
Tabini *was* Ragi, and the majority of the peninsula, the
most industrialized section of the nation, *was* Edi.

There were reasons for moderation, then, rather than
touching off ethnic jealousies; and Tabini knew what
he was doing first in taking out Saigimi and then in
leaving alive a man Jago in her own judgment called
dangerous.

Jago clearly wanted the assignment in Badissuni's
case, should Tabini decide to take the harder line.

Don't count that as the final skirmish, Jago had just
said, regarding Ajresi's seizure of power. Meaning
Badissuni was going to take out Ajresi? Banichi
said Badissuni was here as Ajresi's messenger—while
the other heir to the Edi lordship of the Marid, Cosadi,
the daughter, was currently sheltering in *Direiso's*
household.

Ajresi might not like Tabini, but he'd definitely take
alarm at Cosadi running to Direiso. He'd be watching
his doors and windows for certain, since Direiso could
give Cosadi a springboard to try to take the Marid *and*
the peninsula from Ajresi.

So damn right Ajresi might send someone to hold
talks with Tabini. Jago believed Badissuni was unreliable and didn't want him near; but Banichi said a)

the heirship wasn't settled yet and b) Badissuni was a
messenger.

If Ajresi claimed the clan by force of arms and sat as
lord in the Hagrani household, he had *no* percentage at
all in dealing with Direiso so long as she was sheltering the other Hagrani heir from Ajresi's assassins,
bet on it. Ajresi had, at least for public consumption,
detested Saigimi's previous adventurous dealings with
Direiso—the attempt against the paidhiin, which had
cost the clan so dearly.

And as a result of Damiri's association with Tabini,
which had gone public in that attack, now Direiso's
association—the Kadigidi, the Atageini, the Tasigin
Marid and the lords of Wingin in the peninsula and
Wiigin in the northern reach—was threatened. *Damiri*
was the Atageini heir as well as Direiso's neighbor,
and the day Damiri succeeded her uncle as head of the
Atageini clan, Direiso's days were numbered.

Tabini's removing Saigimi, whose heir, if it was
Ajresi, would take the Marid and Wingin *out* of her
association, meant Direiso was twice threatened. If
Ajresi once secured an understanding with Tabini, the
two holdings, the Marid and Wingin, wouldn't become
independent from Tabini—they'd never get that—but
possibly they'd be held with a far lighter grip. They'd
win rights, even economic consideration. Ajresi could
win an immense advantage by talking to Tabini early
and very politely in his rise to power.

Ajresi might well be talking to Geigi politely, too,
and mending fences with another Edi lord increasingly
important in the peninsula and high in Tabini's favor.

He very much hoped so. That could be immensely
important to the space program.

As for why Banichi might have been selected for an
assignment in the peninsula, Banichi *was* from Talidi
Province, right next to the Marid. His house, whatever
it was (and Banichi had never said) was at least well-
acquainted with the situation.

"What do you think?" he asked Banichi. "Are we
under threat from the south now?"

"Not from the Marid," Banichi said. "Ajresi isn't that crazy."

"If he relies on Badissuni he is," Jago said.

"Make the man commit in public to serve Ajresi as lord?" Banichi returned. "Badissuni had as soon eat glass. But he *has* no choice but represent Ajresi; and he'll be dead by fall."

"Do you know that?" Bren was so startled he forgot the softening *nadi* and spoke intimately and into Guild business at the same time.

Banichi didn't give a flicker of offense. "Of course Ajresi might be dead by fall, instead, if *he* doesn't move first. So everything Badissuni negotiates with Tabini is also for himself, if he gets Ajresi before Ajresi gets him. I don't think he will, though. I know who's working for Ajresi."

"Simpler for us to do it," Jago said glumly. "And make Ajresi come in person and beg for himself."

"I don't think he'll beg," Banichi said. "But a message may already have come from Ajresi signaling Tabini that a public agreement would secure private alliance."

"Do you know so?" Jago asked, echoing the former query.

"Say that messages have flown thick and fast between Ajresi and Tatiseigi of the Atageini, and I think that Badissuni is the topic." Banichi finished off his tea. "Dead, I say. Before the snow falls, if Tatiseigi doesn't join Direiso—and Tabini-aiji is too wise to provoke that."

Saidin was in the doorway, and Banichi said that. Bren's heart gave a thump.

But it did tell him—Saidin was Damiri's; and Damiri was Tabini's; as Banichi and Jago were. Conspiracy was thick around them. Warfare was going on. One just didn't see lines of cavalry and blazing buildings.

And hoped one wouldn't.

The first order of business after breakfast was, Bren decided, to deal with Jase. The staff said Jase was sleeping; and sleeping through breakfast he accepted.

Jase waking after he'd left and receiving still more information through the staff was a different problem, very like the situation Jase had been presented by Yolanda Mercheson, in point of fact; and that could only add to his distress.

He knocked on Jase's door. And had no answer.

He walked in, found Jase abed. "Jase," he said, and stood there until Jase opened his eyes and frowned at him.

Then Jase looked both startled and upset to find him there.

"The phone lines are clear," Bren said calmly, gently. "At your wish, at any time, call the ship. The staff will assist you, nadi."

"With or without recordings made?" Jase asked.

"Everything we do is recorded," Bren said. "I've told you that. Never expect differently. There are no exceptions, nadi."

Jase flung off the covers, got out of bed and reached for his dressing-robe. "I need to talk in private!"

"For your own protection, nadi. If some unscrupulous person should accuse you of wrongdoing—and in this society it can happen—there's proof of your honesty."

"Damn this society!" The latter in his language. He shoved his arms into the robe and tied it.

They'd been down this path about the recordings before. And Jase challenged him on it one more time. But the manners were a step too far.

"In this culture—" Bren said patiently.

"Bren, just give me some room. I don't want to talk about it. I just want privacy to talk to my mother, dammit."

"I can't guarantee that. If you'd use your head you'd know if *I* guaranteed it you couldn't trust the people *I* can't trust, and that's a long list, none of them with your or my welfare at heart, so you wouldn't know; they could edit it. So let's be sure our own people are listening and making a record."

"Heart, is it? Affection? Are we talking about hearts, here?"

He hadn't meant to provoke Jase. But Jase was working hard to get a reaction, and it was one thing, with him; it was quite another with the Atageini staff, starting with Saidin, and he hoped to hell Jase hadn't taken that pose with Saidin while he was gone.

"I can't trust *you*," he retorted. "Is that what you're saying? Jase, just—for your information, for what it's worth: no one had any idea, and if you'd told Manasi what was going on, the message might have reached me."

There was dead silence. No response. No change of expression.

He tried again. Looking for reaction, a fracture, any way past that reserve and into the truth. "Not that I could have found a secure phone immediately. But if I knew there was an emergency here, I'd have found one."

"Well. I'll call her. Thanks for checking for me."

"I'm sorry, Jase. I'm really sorry."

Jase had his back turned. His bedroom had no exterior windows, just a decorated screen, gilt, beautiful work. In the center was a painting of a mountain, no specific mountain that he knew. Jase stared at that as if it offered escape.

"Yeah," Jase said. "I know."

"I have a meeting to go to. With Tabini. I'll have to go when he calls. But we need to talk, Jase. We need to talk—personally." He wished to hell he hadn't come in here for this interview on a fast, in-and-gone-again basis. Assassins talked about a broken-legged contract, where the object wasn't to kill someone, just to keep them out of action. And, God, such desperate measures did flash through his mind where it regarded Jase's crisis and the one racketing through atevi affairs right now. "I don't want you to have to track things second-hand again. I'm sorry. I really am. Please, just take it easy. The staff *doesn't* entirely understand. They're trying to, in all good will toward you."

"I'll manage. I'll call. I'll talk to you later."

He couldn't expect Jase to be cheerful *or* balanced, considering the situation; and he tried to desensitize his own nerves to Jase's jangled reactions with all the professional detachment he owned. Jase had some consideration coming.

Like time to talk, when he could spare it. If he could patch the gulf that had already grown between them. He hadn't been able to talk. Now he wanted to, and didn't dare open up the things he had to explain until Jase had weathered this crisis.

But he'd delivered his message. And there *wasn't* time right now. "See you, probably at noon," he said, and left and shut the door, wishing there were something he could do, and trying to hang on to his own nerves.

Depression, he thought, was very easy from Jase's present situation. Human psych was part of the course of study that led to his job; he knew all the warnings and all the ways one fought back against isolation, bad news, lack of intelligible information from one's hosts or one's surroundings.

Depression: general tendency to want to sleep, general tendency to believe the worst in a situation rather than the better possibilities, general tendency to believe one couldn't rather than that one could.

And maybe his accepting being told that the phone lines were inaccessible to him without his even objecting to Manasi that it was a legitimate emergency wasn't just some ship-culture unwillingness to question a rule. Maybe it was a growing depression.

But, dammit, he had problems, too, and didn't, again, dammit, have time to worry about it right now.

Though he did note, now that he questioned his perceptions, that Jase hadn't asked him the other critical and obvious question: hadn't asked if he'd discovered why the ship hadn't called him first with news of his father's accident.

Jase hadn't asked him, second, whether the ship *could* have reached him directly with the information he'd ended up hearing from Yolanda Mercheson via Mospheiran channels—or whether there'd been some communications crash around that critical time.

Jase hadn't asked, and he realized as he walked away

that he hadn't exactly ended up volunteering the information he had from Tano, either, that Mogari-nai maintained there was *no* call to Jase.

Maybe, Bren thought, he should go back and raise the issue. Or maybe the situation would find some rational explanation once Jase had had the chance to talk to his mother at some length and find out what had happened—and he did trust that Jase's call would get through. It was reasonable that Jase's mother herself might have asked that the news be withheld from Jase, perhaps wanting to get her own emotions under control before she broke the news to him, perhaps not wanting to distress Jase over something he couldn't help at a time when she might just possibly know that Jase was alone with only atevi around him. He hoped that that would turn out to be the answer. Maybe that was what Jase was hoping.

"Nand' paidhi," he heard from a servant as he trekked back through the area of the dining room, "the aiji wishes you to come meet with him now, please."

"Thank you, nadi," he said, and shifted mental gears again, this time for Ragi in all the grand complexity of the court language: a session with Tabini was nothing to enter bemused or with the mind slightly occupied, and he would need to go straight over next door.

Tons of stuff to deliver next door, documents, various things for the aiji's staff, but he'd sent those ahead. Unlike the situation in the past, when he'd resided still within the Bu-javid governmental complex, but far down the hill in his little garden apartment (and far down the list of Bu-javid officers responsible for anything critical.) He had nothing personally to carry when he spoke with Tabini nowadays. He didn't appear in audience and wait his turn among other petitioners any longer. When the paidhi was scheduled to meet with the aiji in this last half year, he waited comfortably in his borrowed apartment, on a good day with his feet up and with a cup of tea in hand, while the aiji's staff and the paidhi's staff (another convenience he had not formerly had) worked out the schedule over

the phone and found or created a hole in the aiji's
schedule.

Today the aiji had passed orders, one suspected, to
make a hole where none existed. Tabini was squeezing
him into his schedule and he would have understood if
Tabini had postponed their meeting a second time or a
third or fourth, counting what else was going on. If the
ship in Sarini Province hadn't blown up, Tabini had to
reckon him and it at a lower priority.

But that Tabini wanted to see him, of that he had no
doubt. He and Tabini on good days made meetings
long enough to accommodate their private as well as
their official conversation. He and Tabini, two men
who had come to office young and who shared young
men's interests, often ranged into casual converse
about politics, women, philosophy, and the outdoors
activities they both missed. Sometimes Tabini would
choose simply to discuss the management of game, not
the paidhi's direct concern. Or the merits of a particular invention some ateva had sent up the appropriate channels—which *was* the paidhi's concern, but it
wasn't the aiji's, except by curiosity.

He had the feeling that sometimes they had meetings
simply because Tabini wanted someone to talk to about
something completely extraneous to his other problems.

But definitely not today. There was the interview
at noon.

And meanwhile he had a distraught and grieving
human roommate whose conversation with his mother
might for all he could predict blow up into God
knew what.

He went immediately to the foyer, stopped by the
duty station to advise Tano they should go now, and
was mildly disorganized in his expectations to find
Banichi and Jago, both of whom he'd gotten out of the
habit of expecting to see. They'd been very much who
he expected to see there, once upon a time.

"I'll escort the paidhi myself," Banichi said cheerfully, like old times, and left Jago and Tano and Algini
to do whatever had involved a group of Guild close
together and voices lower than ordinary.

Curious, Bren thought of that little gathering, not curious that they were talking, but that it had fallen so uncharacteristically quickly silent. If their job was to protect him, it did seem appropriate for them to advise him what they were protecting him *from*.

But no one had volunteered anything. And it was probable that Banichi and Jago were relaying things pertinent to things the paidhi's conscience truly didn't want to know about, down in the peninsula.

Besides, once the aiji had found a hole in his schedule, other mortals moved and didn't delay for questions.

9

The meeting was evidently set not for the little salon, but for the formal salon of Tabini-aiji's apartments with, in the many wide windows, the Bergid Range floating hazily above the city's tiled roofs. The morning overcast had burned off. The air had warmed. It was a pleasant and sensual breeze flowing through the apartment—untainted with the smell of paint, Bren noticed.

Banichi had dropped to the side as they passed the security station in the foyer of the aiji's apartment, and as the paidhi acquired nand' Eidi for a guide. Banichi had settled into the security station with Tabini's security. The lot of them, Bren suspected, would trade information of a sensitive sort, so Banichi was about to spend a profitable few moments, maybe more informative on the real goings-on in the Western Alliance than his own meeting was about to be.

Elderly Eidi (undoubtedly of the Guild as the formerly näive paidhi began to suspect *all* high lords' close attendants were of the Guild) poured tea and handed it to him while he stood waiting. "The aiji will be here at any moment," Eidi said. "He's been on the telephone, nand' paidhi, an unexpected call."

One of those days, Bren thought, thinking of the Badissuni matter, wondering whether it would divert Tabini's attention completely away from the report he had to give.

But he stood waiting, exercising due caution with the teacup and the priceless rugs underfoot—he had once

managed to drop a cup, to his intense embarrassment—
and gazing out at the mountains at a view very like the
one from his apartment.

Out there, unseen from this range, forest swept up
the mountain flanks. Forest reserves and hunting
villages existed, an entire way of life remote from
the city.

Closer in, the tiled roofs of Shejidan advanced along
the hills in their significant geometries, neighborhood
associations which defined atevi life. You could belong
to several at once; you could belong to two that hated
each other and hold man'chi, he had learned, to both
in varying degrees. He was looking at associations economic, residential, political, and, he guessed, but could
not prove, marital.

And there were those walls that separated a few houses
off together in private unity. Those were associations by
trade or by kinship within the other associations. The
relationships were defined even in the orientation and the
age-faded colors of the tiles.

Once the eye knew what it was looking for, it could
find information laid out to simple observation in Shejidan. Atevi had never hidden those most intimate
secrets from humans. One supposed they took for
granted they hadn't hidden them. But humans had
looked right at this view for decades and never grasped
what they were seeing. The paidhiin before him had
failed precisely to explain the nuances of those faded
colors and, no different than his predecessors, he made
his own guesses and bet the peace on them.

It damn sure wasn't a Mospheiran city. You couldn't
forget that, either.

You stood under the same sky, you looked at the
same stars, the same clouds, the same sea ... but it
wasn't Mospheira where you were standing.

It wasn't the ship, either. It certainly wasn't the ship.
He felt sorry for Jase. He really did. In the moments he
most wanted to strangle Jase, and there had been some,
he still knew what a strain Jase was under. And this last
stress, the blow to his family, the safe home one left

behind and imagined was always inviolate—was extreme.

God, he knew.

"No, no, and *no!*"

That was Tabini in the hall outside.

"Light of my life, you will not, you will *not* have your uncle in the apartment, it will not happen!"

"It's *our* ancestral residence!" he heard: lady Damiri's voice. "What can one do?"

"I *know* it's your ancestral residence! It's Bren's *life,* gods less fortunate! You *know* your uncle! He's dealing with that damned Hagrani!"

It didn't sound good. It didn't sound at all good.

The door opened. Tabini walked in, the aiji of the aishidi'tat, the Western Association, the most powerful man on the planet—far overshadowing the President of Mospheira, who couldn't rule his own staff, and who didn't, additionally, command an Assassins' Guild.

—For which, Bren often thought, thank God.

Damiri came in second, and the respective guards, third through sixth, as servants hurried to catch up. Bren bowed and maneuvered toward the appropriate chair by the window, as Tabini chose one of the pair facing the view.

Tabini and Damiri settled comfortably side by side, the image of felicity and domestic tranquility in a flurry of servants in red and guards in black.

"So," Tabini said. "Good trip, nand' paidhi? I received your preliminary report. Gods felicitous, you have stamina."

"A productive trip, aiji-ma. I've left the small data with nand' Eidi, if you will. As busy as this season may be, I would be happy to expand the account to details in writing—"

Tabini lifted his fingers. "I by no means doubt the accuracy of your general estimations. Damned nuisance that your trip home had to be so hasty. I trust it curtailed nothing of moment."

"No, aiji-ma." There was no indication the stray pilot rated the aiji's notice, and he left the matter silent. "Everything of moment is in the files I've made available. And there's nothing critical. I would claim your generous attention, aiji-ma, to honor certain promises I've made."

A wave of the fingers. "Data for the experts and the sifters of numbers. News of yourself. News of nand' Jase. What is this about an accident—about the death of Jase-paidhi's father?"

Atevi had so many delicate words for death. Tabini chose the bluntest, least felicitous. And note that Tabini *did* know. At what hour Tabini had known— the paidhi was perhaps wise not to ask.

"I've advised him to contact his mother for information," Bren said, "and that he should by all means use official channels in such emergencies. Apparently the information came to him by Mercheson-paidhi, instead of directly from his mother or his captain, as would have been more appropriate to his relationship and his rank."

"My spies report the fact of the phone contact between Mercheson and Jase." Atevi had the devil's own time with the combinations of consonants in *Yolanda* and preferred *Mercheson,* never quite making sense of the protocols of human names. "There was a set of messages from the earth station on Mospheira to the ship and the ship to Mospheira preceding and following the contact between Mercheson and Jase-paidhi."

"Possibly," Bren suggested softly, with the definite impression that, yes, Tabini had held this particular piece of distressing news from the paidhi until the paidhi was home to handle Jase, perhaps for fear the paidhi might breach security, alter his schedule, or call the ship himself. "Perhaps this communication between Mercheson and the authorities on the ship was because she realized she'd let out something, aiji-ma, or it might have a less felicitous interpretation. I would imagine, but not swear, that she was distressed to have broken the news and had no idea he didn't know. But *before* Jase's contact with Mercheson—clearly there was one prior call, but several—would be somewhat unusual."

"The name Deana Hanks has floated to the surface of such messages in the last four days. Deana Hanks has advised. Deana Hanks has said. . . ."

Damn, was the word that floated to the surface of his mind, but one didn't curse in the aiji's presence.

"One is far from pleased to hear so, aiji-ma, but I have no means to curtail her activities. I'll certainly review the transcript of those contacts."

"I have provided one. My informants say that Jase Graham has taken to his room in high and angry emotion. But that you estimate no danger in him."

The informants were the entire staff over there, via lady Damiri, who said not a thing.

"He wishes to return to the ship," Bren said, "—and he knows the way—the only way—lies through his performing his job. I do worry for him. But I believe he already shows signs of recovery from a very profound shock." That was stretching it a bit. But one never wanted atevi to grow too quick-fingered about their defensive instincts. "Jase is not a dangerous man, aiji-ma. In terms of his knowledge, perhaps, but in terms of deliberate harm to the premises or to any individual, no, my human judgment says no."

"On your judgment, Bren-paidhi. Do as you see fit regarding security, only so you protect yourself, the staff, the premises. You may have heard—" He slid a glance at Damiri. "There will be an inspection."

"The lilies," Damiri-daja said quietly.

"Lord Tatiseigi," Tabini said, "will tour the restored breakfast room. And there will be cameras—official cameras. Do you think you can keep nadi Jase proper and *kabiu* for the duration? This is unavoidable timing. And highly unfortunate. But it might be an excuse, if Jase-paidhi were to take to mourning. Perhaps some human custom of retreat. Would it be appropriate for him to take ill?"

God, he wished he could say yes. He felt sick at his stomach, from sheer imagination of the Atageini lord visiting the apartment, ahead of television cameras. A formal reception. Jase, distracted as he was apt to be, in the mood he was bound to be in. He felt *very* sick at his stomach.

A broken-legged assassination? Dared he?

Maybe they could just slip Jase a sedative. A dose of mildly poisonous tea.

But no, no, then the press would blame the lord of the Atageini. The headlines would banner an assassination attempt.

Perhaps *he* should take a double cup of the tea himself, and not have to face this lordly inspection tour.

But that would leave everything in Jase's hands and *that* was impossible.

"I'll decide," he said to Tabini, "based on what I hear from him after he's talked to his mother. But, in all honesty, aiji-ma, I fear I can't offer a method. Unless we claimed some custom on the ship. Which—could answer to most anything, I suppose. If it were necessary."

"I would have avoided this timing," Tabini said. "But trying to delay it could make a worse problem."

"One can't tell my uncle no," Damiri said, hands folded in her lap, very proper, very demure. "He wishes to see *you,* nand' paidhi. And one believes this business on the peninsula has made him that much more aggressively determined."

Bren drew a quiet breath, getting the full picture: Saigimi's wife and daughter, relatives to Geigi, had fled to the Atageini's neighbor, Direiso.

And Tabini entertaining lord Badissuni, the one Banichi said would be dead by fall.

"Not," Damiri went on to say, "that my uncle will grieve for Saigimi. Nor that he will be displeased to see Direiso discomfited—but he will set great store on *being* here, nand' paidhi, and in public, and— One relies on your discretion."

Tabini shifted in his chair and propped his elbow on the arm, his forefinger across his lips as if, unrestrained, he would say something incredibly indiscreet.

The paidhi could well imagine. Tatiseigi would rather double-cross lady Direiso only *after* she'd knifed Tabini.

Failing that, was Tatiseigi's move a public display calculated to annoy hell out of Direiso *and* to promote Tatiseigi's importance in the aiji's court—as uncle to the aiji's now publicly revealed lover, and unwilling host to two humans?

There was the sticking point.

But meanwhile they'd be civilized. That was the essence of things: civilization. They were the lords of the Padi Valley: Tabini's house, the Atageini, Direiso's Kadigidi, and a handful else.

Tatiseigi of the Atageini and Direiso both had encouraged the peninsular lords to rash actions, which Saigimi had undertaken most rashly of all. Saigimi's death was the means by which the aiji pulled the chain—hard—and reminded them all where authority and force rested.

Hell, it did beat war as a solution.

What he thought of saying was, It's rather brave of Tatiseigi to walk in next door, considering he's a logical target.

What he also thought was, God, what kind of Guild members is the old man going to have with him, and what if they break out guns, and shoot at Tabini?

What he did say was, "Would it be wise of me and nand' Jase both to relocate permanently and allow your uncle possession of the apartment, Damiri-daja? Would that solve the problem? Or we might move for a few days—"

"No such thing!" Tabini said. "Let him be resourceful in his lodging!"

"I'd by no means wish—"

"No, nadi, let my uncle be resourceful," Damiri said more quietly. "Nadi-ji, he will manage. With the aiji-dowager's good grace, perhaps he will lodge directly downstairs: he is no stranger to her premises."

"Is she here? I thought she was bound for Malguri."

"Oh, grandmother *is* returning here," Tabini said. "She will arrive tomorrow. I'm *sure* she stayed on in the western provinces for exactly this show—I mean the matter of the lily porcelains, not lord Saigimi and that nonsense. She'll amuse herself with the party.

Then she'll be off to the east in all haste, mechieti and staff and all. So she promises me." Tabini had settled back in the chair and folded his hands across his stomach, both elbows on the chair arms, feet out in front of him. "If you have wondered, nand' paidhi, *yes,* regarding lord Saigimi. That is all I will say on the matter. And all you should reasonably ask. Grandmother will of course be furious with the affair in the peninsula and *very* busy with phone calls all about the Padi Valley. But you have such a marvelous capacity to soothe her tempers, Bren-ji. —And I do trust you to do so."

"Aiji-ma, I have no such influence, I assure you—"

"Oh, don't be modest. She dotes on you. You're *civilized.* That's her word. *Civilized.* And you have, she says, such lovely hair."

He tried not to flinch or to blush. Tabini was amused and Damiri's mouth courted dimples one after the other. "So my security tells me," he returned dryly, and was immediately aghast at himself. He'd twice now gotten direly reckless with atevi lords, but he drew a laugh from Tabini, who'd, in point of fact, challenged him.

In truth, the paidhi sat outside the system of lords and inheritance, and couldn't possibly challenge Tabini in any sense that mattered.

"My uncle will not lodge with *you,* nand' paidhi, be assured so." That from Damiri-daja, and quite soberly. "Only be very careful. *I* ask you, be careful of him. He is in some ways delicate in constitution and more delicate in sensibilities."

"He's in all ways an unreasonable old man," Tabini muttered. "It would be indecorous to file Intent on him, but, gods less felicitous! He does try me. —How, by the by, *is* the peninsular society this season? I hear you took advantage of lord Geigi's hospitality."

"He was a very good host and wishes you well, aiji-ma."

"Well he should. Well, well, I'll have your report of him. I trust you have it in preparation."

"My staff does, yes, aiji-ma."

"The plague of Uncle descends tomorrow—"

Tomorrow! he thought, and did not say.

"—barring rain," Tabini said, "which I am told prevents the paint from drying completely enough. And the weather report is clear. —If you charm this impossible man, Bren, I do swear I'll make you a ministerial department."

"I doubt that I can do so much." The relationship between the Atageini and the aiji's house was already such that the aiji himself couldn't stall the man or his questions, and probably many of those questions (except the peninsular assassination) involved two humans guesting on the property.

He'd enlist the staff to keep Jase and Tatiseigi separated. Saidin might do it. Saidin might have far more luck than the aiji of Shejidan, in that matter.

No one, it seemed, could tell uncle Tatiseigi no—and, technically speaking, he supposed no one could do so legally in the matter of the impending visit. What he had heard of the shouting in the hall indicated something truly beyond Tabini's control, unless Tabini wished to take extreme action.

The old man was going to push that situation. And Tabini. Which was one thing considering inter*personal* relations. But this was two clans involved. And Damiri.

Wonderful place for two humans to be standing. And impeccable timing. Jase wasn't up to this.

"One can still wish for rain," Tabini said. "So. Bren. —What *about* Geigi?"

Now it came down to the matter on which the aiji wished to be informed—officially speaking. It came down to Geigi's good reputation and the reputation of all the workers in that plant and in all the other labs and plants he'd visited, who relied on him to represent their work, their good will, and all the things they'd tried to demonstrate to him. He tried to collect his scattered wits and represent them well.

"So when will it fly?" Tabini asked him bluntly. Early on, it had been, *Will* it fly?

"Ahead of schedule, by some few months, aiji-ma, I still maintain so, until and unless we find some problem that delays us the months we allowed for such events."

"But as yet no such problem exists." Tabini rested his chin again on his hand and looked satisfied. "It might have arisen, understand. Now such an interruption is far less likely."

He was so busy thinking of engineering details he didn't take Tabini's meaning immediately.

Then he did.

"Saigimi did not want that ship to fly," Tabini said. "He viewed it as a means to bring down the government. He was wrong. His assassins did not reach Geigi and they did not reach the director of Patinandi Aerospace. So you had a very quiet trip."

"Yes, aiji-ma."

"You noticed nothing untoward."

"No, aiji-ma."

"Good," Tabini said. "As it should have been."

10

The interview with Tabini had gone relatively quickly, and on a day interrupted by phone calls and upsetting news of the Atageini visit—to *his* apartment—Bren was hardly surprised.

That left him time to go back to the apartment before the television interview, or, on the other hand, time to visit the office down in the legislative wing and to pay a courtesy call on his staff.

He might, he decided, accidentally interrupt Jase's phone call if he went back to the apartment: Jase had to make his call either from the library or from the security station, and the library venue had been so hard to predict regarding noise from the reconstruction (hammering would begin at the damnedest times, and the staff would go running, trying to silence the culprits) that he rather imagined Jase would use the security office phone near the front hall out of force of habit.

Which didn't need the confusion of the front door opening and closing and the servant staff running about.

So he opted for the office downstairs, where his clerical staff maintained a dike against the flood of correspondence. It was a rare honor, the dedication of one of the three available offices inside the Bu-javid, 'for security reasons,' as he'd heard, meaning that he tended to visit the clerical office often and that his security and Tabini's didn't want the paidhi going to the building that was the other option, down the hill to what was officially called the Maganuri Annex

Building. It had been built in haste among the hotels
at the foot of the historic real estate, and it probably
forecast the trend: the governmental complex was
starting to sprawl, and the last rank of intruders, the
hotels, were, only since last year, starting to crowd the
residential areas, which the Planning Commission
wouldn't have.

So there was to be a new subway link to a hotel district being built on the city outskirts. Tabini's enemies
pointed to the growth of government.

But those same enemies supported the creation of
various commissions and agencies that kept the aiji
from making autocratic decisions, which was the alternative. And they required more offices and more
hotels. He'd warned Tabini against more committees.
Tabini had been willing to let the power go last year,
saying that certain things needed more study than his
staff could give it.

But now Tabini was looking with a very suspicious
eye at some of the commercial interests that had crept
in with agendas which had no place in the traditional
structure, agendas being backed by some of the lords.
That office building out there, the Maganuri Building,
built to house the study committees proposed by the
legislators opposed to the growth of government, was
beginning to be plagued by sewer and electrical problems. The opposition blamed sabotage by Tabini's
agents, or by the old aristocracy, a *wide* range of conspiracy indeed, and no few of the commons avoided it
and wouldn't attend committee meetings there because
of the reputed bad numbers.

Others said it was built on a battlefield (it was) and
that the dead troubled it. Oddly enough, the surrounding hotels and businesses had never had such difficulties.

So the paidhi was quite glad to be honored by the
office he had, and not to have to take the subway down
the hill, or to the edge of town—where according to the
latest rumors, the construction, since the folded space
controversy had set certain numerologists playing with

an expanded deck, was also plagued by bad numbers, which might even halt construction.

Certain numerologists were suggesting that the number of state offices be shrunk, and the whole thing be cast back to the system whence it had blossomed, tossing the responsibility for information-gathering back into the hands of lords and representatives, who, in the old days, might suffer personal disgrace if they handed in bad information. The names of lords authoring reports previously had been permanently attached to the measures they proposed and the results, good or bad, had remained *their* responsibility.

Some said the fact that Maganuri had died and that the three local lords (who had been very forward to hire construction agencies within their associations) failed to affix their names to the building ought to be a warning.

Some said that old Maganuri himself haunted the office building on stormy nights, looking for Shimaji, Sonsini, and Burati, the contractors in question, to put them to haunting the building in his place.

So the paidhi was definitely glad not to be down there, in a building some were seriously talking about demolishing before it was fully occupied. As it was, he needed only go to the lower tiers of the Bu-javid complex and, via the security access, walk into his premises, never having broken a sweat.

Secretaries scrambled out of their chairs, rose and bowed as he and Banichi walked in, and nand' Dasibi, the chief of his clerical staff, came hurrying from his office to bow and receive the paidhi's personal inquiry into office affairs.

While he was listening to Dasibi's running commentary, Dasibi walking beside him with his notebook the while, the paidhi took his usual tour down the aisles of the clerical desks, pausing here and there for a word to the clericals who answered his mail, the first line of defense between the paidhi and his more interesting correspondence.

He routinely scanned that, too, or at least the prize pieces. Nand' Dasibi had established a board on the south wall in which the staff delighted. It recorded, Bren had discovered, the tally of death threats versus marriage proposals, choice crank letters, some proposing how to protect the earth's atmosphere against pollution from passing spacecraft and one, his favorite, from a husband and wife in the East, regarding the invention of a ray that would convert the ether of space into breathable atmosphere so that airplanes could fly to the station.

The paidhi through his staff had suggested that the proposed spacecraft did have wings for atmospheric operation, so that, if the gentleman and his wife could perfect the conversion ray, it would be perfectly compatible with the current design.

So far there was no news from that province of such a development.

And there was the board devoted to children's letters: the staff tallied those, too, mostly sweet, occasionally clever, sometimes fearful of half-heard adult conversations. The staff passed on to him the best of the children's letters and the letters which seemed to represent a trend, and occasionally gave him copies of the really good crank letters and marriage proposals. His security handled the death threats.

But mostly these clericals dealt with the flood of general correspondence, which would have inundated him and taken all his time. They also transcribed his tapes and cleaned up his rough and informal notes into the language most appropriate for the occasion. That small service alone saved him an immense amount of dictionary-searching—not that he didn't know the words, but he was never sure there wasn't a better one and never, on an important report, dared trust that the word that popped into his head didn't have infelicitous connotations that he had no wish to set onto paper. A written mistake might fall into the hands of news services interested in catching the paidhi in such an infelicity. The press daren't take on the aiji, mustn't, in fact; but a lord of the Association was a fair target; and in less than a year he'd become such a person—

protected, still, in certain ways, but increasingly fair game if he made a blunder that saw print.

Besides, his dictionary was one humans had compiled, of necessity, to equate human words—and sometimes one could make an unthinking glitch on the numbers because counting *didn't* come naturally and even atevi made mistakes. These experienced governmental clericals would, like his experienced governmental security, fling their knowledge between the paidhi and the dedicated number-counters who sometimes sent letters specifically designed to entrap the paidhi into numerically infelicitous statements, which *they,* in the perverse self-importance of such experts, could then term significant.

As a minor court official, again, he'd been immune from such public relations assassinations. As a major player in affairs of state, he, like the aiji, *was* a target of such manipulators, and his strike in return was a standing order for commendations to any clerical who by handwriting, postal mark, or other clues, identified one of these nuisances by name, handwriting, and residence and posted them to others in the pool. The staff shared information with the aiji's staff and, in a considerable network, with various lords' staffs: 'counters could be a plague and a pest, and the clericals detested and hunted them as zealously as the Guild hunted armed lunatics.

It made him feel a certain disconnection from the job he'd used to do himself, however, and he feared that he was in danger of losing touch with ordinary atevi as fast as his increased notoriety and importance had gained him the ability to know them. He *liked* the atevi he'd met, the elderly couple at Malguri, his former servants in the Bu-javid, the astronomy students at Saigiadi—most of all, people of various staffs he'd dealt with.

And he couldn't. stay in touch with them, and couldn't allow himself the human softness, either, to reserve a spot for them in that inner limbo where lost and strayed acquaintances dwelled. They were outside his man'chi. They weren't *his*. He couldn't expect them to become *his*.

And in that one simple example he saw why humans could become so disruptive of atevi society in so short a time, just by existing, and dragging into their *liking* persons who really, never, ever should be *associated* with them in the atevi sense.

Humans had created havoc without knowing the social destruction they were wreaking on the foundations of society where people could be badly bent out of their comfortable associations, in that region where man'chi could become totally complex.

In some wisdom the aiji had set *him* up in the rarified air where man'chi could flow safely *up* to him—but sometimes he looked with great trepidation at the day when, their mutual goal, atevi might be working side by side with humans on the space station they were diverting the economy of a nation to reach.

In such moments he asked himself what potentially disastrous and crazy idea he'd given his life to serve.

He deliberately didn't think too deeply into the changes in his personal status he'd encouraged or accepted—or a part of his brain was working on it, but it wasn't a part that worked well if someone turned on the lights in that dark closet.

Stupid choice, Bren, he sometimes said to himself, when he realized how high he'd climbed and how he'd set himself up as a target. Deadly stupid, Bren Cameron, he'd say, on cold and lonely nights—or standing as he was in the middle of the atevi clerical establishment that, with great dedication to him, for emotional reasons he couldn't reciprocate, continually and routinely saved him from making a fool of himself.

He could afford at least the question of what in hell was he doing and what did it all mean and where was he leading these people who approached him with the kind of devotion they ordinarily spent on the aiji, who *was* worth their devotion.

How did he dare? he asked himself; and *Chance and George Barrulin,* the answer echoed out of the haunted basement of his suspicions, one of whom, Chance, was the demon in the design of the atevi universe and the other of whom, the President's chief advisor, was the devil in the design of Mospheiran politics.

Neither of them was fit to be in charge of as many lives as they controlled.

But Tabini, he strongly believed, *was* fit: fit by biological processes he couldn't feel and political processes purely atevi.

To his continual wonderment, Tabini accepted what the paidhi did, double-questioned him on his choices, and threw his authority behind the concept of atevi rights in space, when human authority said atevi might be destroyed by the concept of microchips and nuclear energy.

What atevi did after they were up there in space, that was another matter.

He asked himself, on lonely nights, whether he'd live, himself, to see that ship fly. He could envision himself standing at the side of the runway. But in his imagination he never could see the ship. He'd become superstitious about that image in his mind, even gloomy and desperate, and he wasn't ready to dig too deeply and learn what exactly his subconscious thought he was doing. He didn't have a choice; he didn't currently have a better idea, and what he was doing had to be done before the next stage of worrying.

He came down here when he was scared. As the interview had him scared. He faced that fact now. He'd had it easy in the provinces, on tour. He'd been traveling in the aiji's plane, under the aiji's guard, and everybody was glad to see him because he might bring trade and funds.

Here, in the Bu-javid, the predators gathered, and snarled and swarmed after scraps in ways that reminded him very uncomfortably of the situation back home.

He'd discussed it with Tabini.

Now a man was dead, who'd been part of the drive to take the power back to the provinces. It wasn't just that Saigimi was a disagreeable man with bad numbers: it was that Saigimi was a peninsular lord who'd represented a policy and a movement that didn't like the influence of the paidhi—that didn't like the paidhi's acquisition of this office, this prominence, this kind of loyalty. Or Tabini's appetite for technology and power.

It was remotely possible that Saigimi had had a point. A rotten way of expressing it, but a point.

And that was one of those items that was going to be seething under the surface of the questions various news services wanted to ask him. The conference was supposed to be about the space program, which he desperately wanted to talk about. But atevi knew there was something very significant going on in the *way* the space program was being built, and in the way prosperity was being handed out to one lord and assassination used against another.

The answers whether it was a good or bad change in atevi affairs were in those baskets of letters—ordinary atevi expressing their opinions.

"There are a few items difficult of disposition, nand' paidhi," nand' Dasibi informed him. "One understands there was an untoward incident in the skies on your return. Might one inquire, will the paidhi wish this incident acknowledged if the public inquires?"

"The matter," Banichi said, his shadow as he had walked through the room, among the desks, and now as they stopped at the head of it, "is still under staff investigation. It was minor."

"Say," Bren added, "that I was not hurt and never alarmed. The skill of the aiji's pilots prevented harm. It underscores the importance of pilots observing air traffic control regulations and filing flight plans . . . and so forth. You know my opinions on that."

"One does, yes, nand' paidhi."

"There will also be an announcement shortly of a tour of the residence by lord Tatiseigi."

Brows went up. Dasibi said not a thing.

"I'm sure," Bren said quietly, "that there'll be inquiries, and the event will not be open to the public. Don't comment on the situation in the peninsula unless it's cleared through the aiji's staff. The official answer and the real one is that I had a successful tour, enjoyed fine hospitality, and was never threatened by the events to the south. I will forewarn you however that one should not schedule very many staff leaves of absence during the next week or so."

"We do hope nothing is amiss."

"One likewise hopes, nand' Dasibi. Very sadly, one member of my household has received bad news from the ship." Short guess who *that* was. "A death in his family. But he knew his choice to come down here to serve would separate him from his family as well as his people. Please limit public questions on this matter and assure inquirers that the ship-paidhi is a young man of great courage and resolve who shares my purpose in seeing the atevi ship built."

"One will do so, nand' paidhi. Please convey to him our good will."

"With all appreciation, nadi."

"There is—another message from lord Caratho. With maps."

Lord Caratho saw no reason if Geigi was prospering why a space industry plant couldn't be built in his district. That was the crux of the matter.

The problem was, neither did numerous other lords see why they shouldn't have the same advantage. Caratho, and four others, had inundated the Economic Commission's office with figures and proposals. But Caratho alone figured, since various regular channels had turned him down, to deluge the paidhi's staff with maps and reports promoting such a plant.

Oh, damn, was the thought. Here it comes.

"If the paidhi will allow me to frame a reply," Dasibi said, "I believe I can create a list of honored supporters of the space program which one might send to the aiji for his information, a list which others may wish to join and include among their honors—providing a disposition for all these reports and offers of resources to the effort. I have consulted the aiji's staff and they concur. Meanwhile—lord Caratho has no need of such a plant, in the determination of the Economic Commission. He has ample revenues. He has fourteen hundred and fifty-four persons he's had to write onto his staff because of unemployment in the district, which is not unusual for a lord of his wealth, and these are persons who used to be employed in railway construction, when the spur was being built. Let me apply finesse, if you will trust my discretion."

Finesse was the same word Banichi would use—biichi'ji—in a strike without side damage.

"I have all confidence in you, Dasibi-ji. Please do what you can. I am *not* concerned so much for lord Caratho, but by the persons unemployed. Find out the history on that, via the staff, if you can."

"Taking a little liberty, nandi, I have, and they are persons who would not be employed by the plant he proposes."

"Ah. He's seeking to diminish his obligations."

"One believes he is *collecting* them into his employ, nand' paidhi, particularly to present appearances and make those rolls larger. I am concerned, nand' paidhi, that he may have done so with disregard of the welfare of the individuals he claims as dependents."

"Do you, nandi, believe this is a situation to pass to the aiji's staff?"

"I would say so, nand' paidhi." This last the old man offered with downcast eyes and some trepidation: he was accusing a lord in the reach of a person of rank sufficient to do him harm.

"I would concur," Banichi said in a low voice, and the old man looked much happier. "And *I* know the rascal's reputation: you will not surprise the aiji, nadi."

"One is very glad to think so." The old man let go a heavy breath. "And there are two messages from one Rejiri, the son of the lord of Dur, wishing your good will. We have no idea why he sent twice—he mentions a meeting. We are unaware of any meeting with him on your schedule, nand' paidhi."

"The pilot of the plane. And I accept his good will. Assure him so. I have no time for a meeting."

"If not the front door, the back," Banichi muttered. "He *is* young, nadi."

"Should I not accept his good will?" he asked.

"Young," Banichi said. "And a fool. But, yes. Accept it. Nand' Dasibi advises you very well in everything."

"And," Dasibi said, clearly pleased, "a message from the aiji-dowager's staff, saying there is no need for a response, but that she will conclude her winter season with a brief visit to the capital, and that she will see you, nand' paidhi, at your convenience."

"Delighted," he said, and was, from the time he'd heard it from Tabini, whose protestations about the dowager as a force in politics were frequent, half in jest and half not.

Himself, he'd been very sorry to think of Ilisidi going back to Malguri and particularly of his having no chance at all to see her, perhaps for a very long time, once she settled into the estate she best loved and once she settled deep into the local politics. The most recent turmoil around Malguri had been the dropping of bombs and the launching of shells. They were provincial lords of the eastern end of the Western Association, lords neighboring Ilisidi's mother's home—lords whose tangled thesis was that the paidhi, the aiji in Shejidan, *and* the human President were all involved in conspiracy to deprive atevi of their rights.

They were the same nuisances who had it that Tabini and everyone involved had known the ship was about to appear.

And some diehard theorists *still* maintained there was not only a spaceship secretly already built on the island of Mospheira, but that it was constantly coming and going—which wasn't true, but nothing including showing the lords in question the output of the radar dishes that guarded the whole maritime coast would dissuade them from their belief in conspiracy against them. First, they weren't capable of reading the data; second, they would declare it was being falsified by some technical system so elaborate it would have made building a spaceship all but superfluous; and third, they were *determined* to believe it was conspiracy, and therefore it was conspiracy even if they had to invoke secret bases on the moon or mind-warping rays sent down from the station at night. The point was, they wanted to believe in conspiracy and their own political situation was a lot better and easier to maintain if there were one.

The fact that Ilisidi, whom these lords knew well and generally believed had the education to read the data, also had the brains to read the situation in Shejidan and the experience to read the truth in the paidhi had not persuaded the diehards. It had only persuaded Ilisidi, so she'd said to him, that the lords she led were not going to follow her further if she didn't convince them by the force of her presence. *Her* politics revolved relatively simply on the wish to retain some areas of the world untouched by industry and some aspects of atevi culture untouched by human influence.

Oddly enough she'd found the paidhi an ally in that agenda.

So the woman, Tabini's grandmother, who'd almost been aiji of Shejidan on several occasions, must, as she'd put it to him at their parting last fall, go pour water into the ocean: meaning she wouldn't enjoy the work of politics in Malguri. But it was, she'd said, work which needed doing, and it aimed at mending attitudes and regional prejudices which had sadly cost lives and threatened livelihoods. It was work that she could do—uniquely, could do—though he had a great personal regret for seeing Ilisidi spend her efforts on provinces when they needed her as Tabini's unadmitted right hand on a national level.

Even if Tabini complained of her interference.

"Tell her—" he began, completely undaunted by the statement no reply was requested. Then he changed his mind a second time. "Pen and paper, nadi, please."

He had one of his message cylinders in his pocket. He traveled with one. He sat down at a table and wrote, in his own hand,

I am delighted by the prospect you present and would gladly scandalize your neighbors, though I fear by now they have fled the paint and the hammering. Please find the occasion in your busy schedule of admirers to receive me or, at any time you will, please do not hesitate to call upon me.

That would remove any doubt of Ilisidi's welcome to walk into the apartment at her will, and if uncle Tatiseigi was going to pay a call on him, damn, *she* knew the man, and could judge better than he could what might constitute a rescue. She might even intervene: as Tabini had said, she and he did get along, and her presence at any formal viewing might be an asset. *He* couldn't choose the guests for an Atageini soiree, but let Tatiseigi try to keep Ilisidi from doing as she pleased—as soon try to stop a river in its course.

He had his seal, too, and the office provided the wax. He put the finished message into nand' Dasibi's hands, spoke his usual few words to the staff.

"Nand' paidhi," Banichi said, attracting his attention. "The news services."

He had, in some measure, rather deal with Uncle.

But the mere *thought* of Ilisidi had waked up his wits in sheer self-defense, and that was, considering where he was going, all to the good.

It was down the corridor then, and into that area near the great halls of the two houses of the legislature, the commons, which was the hasdrawad, and the house of lords, which was the tashrid. Last year, for the first time on atevi television, a human face had brought into atevi homes a presence which atevi children had once feared and now wrote letters to in the thousands. Last year he'd appeared on tape. This year his press conferences went live. A room across from the tashrid was set up as an interview center—that crowd of microphones and cameras was another accoutrement of notoriety, and of life close to the place where decisions were made. Lines snaked into the little room so that one had to walk very gingerly. The place bristled with microphones surrounding the seat he would take.

He allowed all the paraphernalia he had collected, the computer (which rarely left him) and the notes and the various small items with which he had become burdened in the clerical office, into the hands of junior security, and let Banichi see him to his place and stand near him.

He settled in, blinded by the lights. He waited, hands folded on the table that supported the microphones, until the signal.

"Nand' paidhi," the first reporter began, and wended through the convolute honors and courtesies before the question, a circuitous approach calculated, he sometimes thought, to let the paidhi fall asleep or start witwandering.

The question when it finally emerged from the forest of titles, was: "Having just returned from touring the plants and facilities supporting the space program, are you confident that atevi and human construction are of equal importance and on equal footing with the ship?"

"I am very confident," was his automatic answer. It gave him a running start toward: "But not just that we are on an equal basis with Mospheira, nadiin: atevi are well-advanced toward the goal of space flight and may actually be in the lead in the race for space. It's not a position in which one dares slacken one's effort. We don't know what delays may arise. But I am encouraged that we have made vast progress." He was very glad to report nationally that the aiji's monumental risk of capital was producing results: success bred stability—and complacency—he had to avoid that extreme, too. "I am very encouraged about the future of the program."

"On what account, nand' paidhi, if you would elucidate."

"I am encouraged by the people, nadi. I have seen the actual elements of what will become the first spacecraft to be launched from this planet. They now exist. I have met atevi workers dedicated to their work, whose care will safeguard the economic prosperity of generations of atevi."

"What do you say, nand' paidhi," this came from a southern service, "to the objections regarding the cost?"

Lord Saigimi's platform. *Not* an innocent question. Provocative. It identified the source of trouble. He hoped not to have another question from that quarter, and could not gracefully look to the staff officer controlling who stood up to ask, not without exposing that glance on live national television.

"The rail system on which all commerce now moves was vastly expensive to build," he said calmly. "Look at the jobs, nadiin, look at the industry. Were we to back away from this chance to lift the people of this planet into authority over their own future, someone else would exercise that authority. By the Treaty, I look out for the peace. And I *see* no peace if such an imbalance develops in the relationship that now exists between atevi and humans. That would be more than expensive, nadiin, it would be unthinkable. The program *must* give atevi the power to direct their own lives."

"Is this within the man'chi of the paidhiin?"

"Indisputably. Indisputably. By the Treaty, it is." The question had come from the same source. The man did not sit down. And from all his worries about changes in atevi life, he was reminded now of Saigimi's *other* qualities. The same whose associates built shoddy office buildings and who personally tried to ruin lord Geigi in order to own his vote in some very critical measures.

"Did the paidhi feel at all that his safety was threatened in the peninsula?"

That was *not* a permitted question, by the ground rules that governed all news conferences. He knew that Tabini was going to hit the rafters over that one, and other reporters were disturbed, but he lifted a hand in token that he would answer the direct provocation.

"The paidhi," he said calmly, and in meticulous Ragi, "has the greatest confidence in the good will expressed to him by honest people." The news service this reporter represented, whether by one of Deana's little legacies or a new inspiration of Tabini's enemies, was attempting to politicize itself—implying (because a retaliatory strike by Guild members would have to follow a line of direct involvement) that the paidhi or lord Geigi had a connection to the assassination. He had no compunction whatsoever about derailing the effort in a rambling, time-using account. Two could play the games of a live, limited-time broadcast.

"Let me recount to you the scene as I left the plant, nadiin, as the goodheartedness of the workers brought a crowd out the doors, brought them carrying flowers toward the cars. When my plane dipped its wing and came about toward Shejidan I saw, beside the cars of my local escort, flowers of the springtime of the peninsula pass beneath us. So, so much generosity of the people, so much care of the vastly important task under their hands and so generous an expression of their belief in their task. Their hope for the future is visible now. Tangible." They'd edit when bits of this replayed, and after what had been asked, he was careful to give them only positive, felicitously numbered statements. The paidhi did *not* intervene in atevi internal affairs. That was what they were trying to get him to do, so he played the uninvolved innocent. "I was greatly impressed, nadiin. I tell you, I was impressed so much that I believe as they believe, in the felicity of this project, in the felicity of this nation, in the felicity of the aiji who has been foresighted in making this reach toward space at a moment when all these fortunate things coincide."

A second reporter rose. "Have you authorized, nand' paidhi, the direct exchange of messages between the island and the ship-paidhi, in your absence?"

What in hell *was* this? A second out-of-line question?

"I have not forbidden it, nadi."

"Can you, nand' paidhi, confirm a death in the ship-paidhi's house?"

There was a leak. There was a serious leak. It smelled of Deana. If he could figure how—and methods including radio did occur to him.

Damn it, he thought. He'd meant to report it, because with servants aware of something, informational accidents could happen, and he didn't want speculation getting ahead of all the facts he had. But he'd meant to report it *after* Jase had talked to his mother. The death on the ship implied infelicity.

And he could either shut down the interview right now on these two rude and unauthorized questions on the very plain point that they violated protocol—he could signal his security to create a diversion; or he could handle the problem they'd posed and then loose security on the matter of who'd put them up to it.

"I can," he said, "confirm, nadiin, that there is such a sad report; as best I am informed, an accident of some nature. I will try to obtain that information for you. But that is not officially announced, and the release of that information could cause great pain to Jase-paidhi, who has borne the effort and worked honestly to bring good fortune to atevi as well as humans. I'm certain that isn't your intent."

Sometimes his own callous response to situations appalled him. Atevi would wish to know. Number-counters would wish to know. All sorts of people would wish to know for good and sensible reasons, for superstitious reasons, and just because they were justifiably curious about human behavior.

The next two questions, which he took from the major news services, were routine and without devious intent. How was the space program meeting the engineers' expectations and was the design translation without apparent error?

"We are developing a set of equivalencies between the two languages which render translation of diagrams much easier. We're dealing with a scale of measurements which has a scale of directly comparable numbers"—Atevi ears always pricked up at that word—"which renders the operation of translation much faster. Atevi engineers are actually able to read human documents where the matter involves written numbers, and to perform calculations which render these numbers into atevi numbers with all the ordinary checks that these skilled persons perform."

Not of significance for a human audience, but for an atevi audience a real bombshell of religious and philosophical significance. If the universe was rational and numerical, numbers were a direct reflection of its mathematical dependability; numbers could predict, safeguard, direct, and govern. No project would succeed without good numbers; the ship on which the design was based *had* flown, the human numbers were therefore good numbers, felicitous numbers, more to the point—since numbers could be felicitous or infelicitous, leading to success or disaster—and to have the news that atevi engineers could make clear sense of human engineering diagrams was the sort of thing that would actually fight with the peninsular assassination and the death on the ship for space on the news, at least briefly. He'd meant to drop that later, but it was capable of knocking Jase's tragedy right out of the headlines, and that was, coldbloodedly, what he intended.

He answered four or five questions at the limits of his own mathematical ability, and took his leave of the reporters, with the (he said to himself) not unreasonable notion of the leisure to go back to his apartment and work through the translations he had to have ready before—the next duty he had on his agenda—he briefed the aiji's aides, who had to go to the various departments to present the paidhi's arguments before—step after that—the paidhi had to go before the off-session legislative aides to answer questions so that when, step three, the legislatures reconvened, they did it with good information before them.

But there was a far more immediate item on his agenda.

"We have a problem," he said to Banichi as they walked toward the lift, and as the junior security held the curious at bay, out of ordinary hearing. "I don't know how that information on Jase's private business got to them, I don't know whether there's a leak somewhere, but my own thought was that either there's a leak on the aiji's staff—or ours—or that they're broadcasting that on the news on Mospheira and somebody on the mainland follows enough of the language to pick it out."

"Such persons who know Mosphei' that fluently are all official," Banichi said under his breath, informing him of something he'd wanted to know, and now did.

"There is," Banichi added, "nand' Deana." One was respectful in a public venue, and accorded a name its honorifics, even when one proposed cutting the individual into fish-bait. "And I can tell you, Bren-ji, there has been illicit radio traffic."

They'd reached the lift. He gave Banichi a sharp, alarmed look.

"How much else don't I know?"

"Oh, much," Banichi said. The door opened. "The names of my remote cousins, the—"

"Banichi, my salad, the truth."

Banichi escorted him inside and delivered an advisement to hall security above that they were coming up. And Banichi grinned, not looking at him after the salad remark.

"The paidhi is still alive," Banichi said, "and we keep him that way. But the details are his security's concern."

"Not where it regards Hanks!"

"Ah. Humans *do* proceed to feud."

"With this woman? Damned right." The door spat them out into the upper corridor, that with the porcelain bouquets. "Unfortunately the Guild has no offices on Mospheira. —And I need to know this, Banichi-ji."

"It seemed at the time to involve only atevi, on this side of the strait," Banichi said, "and Tano and Algini didn't know. Had Jago and I been here, our rank would have obtained that information for you. Yes, there has been such traffic between Mospheira and the coast, in Ragi, definitively her voice."

"Nand' Deana." Deana, who had had such widespread contact with all the wrong people, until someone had kidnapped her from Shejidan, someone whose identity both Ilisidi and lord Geigi had to this day declined to reveal, nor had he ventured to ask his own staff too closely. The embarrassments of the great houses were a volatile subject.

And when a rival paidhi was at issue, perhaps, he'd decided last of all, they were uncertain how he'd react and whether he'd be able to, in human shorthand, *forgive* the atevi responsible.

"Where *was* my female colleague lodged when she was not in the Bu-javid?" he asked Banichi as they walked. "May we now ask officially, and for the record?"

"With lady Direiso."

He was not utterly surprised. To say the least. "And Geigi simply walked in there?"

"Guns were involved, but not seriously. Direiso-daja had launched her greater hope without guns, simply in her acquisition of Hanks-paidhi."

"*She* took her away."

"Without serious resistance."

"One thought so. And getting Deana back—was there bloodshed?" That defined a level of seriousness in most quarrels. Not in this, he thought. "Did Direiso resist?"

"No bloodshed," Banichi said. "Against fear of her own harm, she saw there was nothing left but graceful acquiescence to the aiji-dowager and the hope that Tabini would soon be a dead man. And that you would be. That would leave Deana Hanks as paidhi. And if Direiso's wishes had proved to have stronger legs, it would have led to *her* in possession of the ship-paidhiin—which again would have made her powerful. Hence her easy capitulation on the day in question."

That was a plateful of information. Direiso had folded when Ilisidi, whom Direiso had regarded perhaps as rival *and* as ally, had walked in at gunpoint and demanded Hanks be turned over to her. Direiso had still hoped to reach the descending capsule and get her hands on Jase and Mercheson-paidhi.

But she hadn't won that race. *They* had.

So Direiso had lost Ilisidi's support (realizing perhaps at the last that Ilisidi would have cheerfully put a dagger in her back, perhaps not even figuratively, rather than see her as aiji.) And now it was possible Direiso was courting the Atageini after an assault on Atageini pride last year, which had destroyed the lilies, perhaps by accident or perhaps not.

"Was not Direiso's son *with* Tatiseigi of the Atageini

at that moment?" he asked Banichi. He recalled hearing that.

"That he was, Bren-ji."

"You exceed my human imagination. Why?"

"If I knew that for certain, Bren-ji, Damiri might be lord of the Atageini at this hour."

Serious news. Banichi suspected Tatiseigi of existing on the fringes of Direiso's conspiracy, and the son's presence there as not without Direiso's approval. "You suspect Tatiseigi was *with* Direiso, at least in the attack against us in Jase's landing?"

"We suspect everything." They had reached the doors. "We act on what we know."

"And she's still plotting against the aiji. Hence the business in the peninsula."

"True."

"And its timing?"

"One can only guess, Bren-ji."

He was talking to the entity both best and least informed on the matter, the one who'd most likely carried out the strike against Direiso's ally Saigimi.

While *he* guested with lord Geigi, who'd seemed Direiso's ally and then Tabini's.

One needed a flow-chart. One truly did.

But probably the atevi thought that about humans.

There were things they had never admitted to one another. Radios belonging to the atevi government listening to transmissions. Jamming. On both sides of the strait. Phone lines that went down every time a stray cloud appeared. Banichi had said it once: an old man in a rowboat could invade the island. Or the mainland.

If Hanks had been transmitting to Direiso, there were atevi working for Tabini who would intercept those messages—and Deana and those behind her were just clever enough to plant what they wanted planted: poison, no matter the recipient, poison, whether in the hands of Tabini's people or Direiso's.

"Damn," he said, envisioning listening posts up and down the coast, on which atevi could pick up whatever short-range transmissions the conservative faction on Mospheira wanted to send. It wasn't just Direiso's cause such hateful broadcasts might incite, if Deana and her supporters wanted to see bloodshed.

The fact that such conservative humans hated atevi was in no way skin off Direiso's nose. The fact that Direiso hated her was no skin off Deana's. Both the conservative atevi that wanted Tabini dead and human technology restricted—and the conservative humans whose varied agendas just wanted humans to stay technologically superior to atevi—shared the same agenda: restrict technology getting to Tabini. Tabini *in* power and Bren Cameron *in* office meant a rapid flow of tech into atevi hands. So get rid of one or both.

The door opened. The servants received them. Junior security, having used the same lift on its return trip, overtook them before the doors shut and rearmed. He wasn't acutely aware of his surroundings.

That Banichi told him what he did was indicative at least that he was being told truth on a high level. Atevi no longer kept the paidhi, who was acting in their interests, more ignorant than other humans, who were working against those interests.

That was useful. It was one step deeper into the situation he was already in.

It didn't, however, stop Deana Hanks, whose agenda he didn't believe he entirely guessed—and he couldn't act upon his suspicions until he could hear exactly what she was saying and what she hoped to provoke.

And there'd been no atevi offer yet to provide him that information.

Damn, again.

11

"The matter we were discussing," Bren said to Banichi as they entered the apartment, as servants converged and he began to undo the buttons of his coat. "Can you prepare me a more extensive report on the problem, Banichi-ji? *And* report to the aiji regarding the reason for my question, regarding the interview? I want the text of what she's been saying."

"Yes," Banichi said in that abrupt Ragi style, which was an enthusiastic yes, and went immediately to the security station, where, Bren said to himself, there was about to be a very intense, very serious session that might well extend feelers next door, and might end in a reporter finding himself in serious dialogue with the aiji's security. Reporters on Mospheira questioned government agencies with a great deal of freedom and were lied to routinely. But on the atevi mainland, the concept of instant news was under current consideration by the government, the way the inclusion or non-inclusion of a highway system had gone under consideration by the government—and been rejected as socially destructive. Similar airy assumptions that what had worked for humans was good and right for atevi had started the War and killed tens of thousands of people.

In that consideration Bren didn't like what had happened down in that interview. He saw interests at work that didn't lead in productive directions for atevi—atevi interests that wanted Tabini dead and someone else installed as aiji.

But the implications of a person like Deana Hanks, a person trained to deal with atevi, working by radio purposely to destabilize the atevi government—that was against every law, every principle of the office. He was on shaky moral ground with the State Department because of the decisions he'd taken, but dammit, he was trying to *keep* the stability of Tabini's regime. His way was sanctioned by the people that had sent him here; and sent him *back* here by means so desperate Shawn had secreted the new computer codes under the cast on his arm and hadn't even told *him* he was doing it.

He wanted a Mospheiran newspaper, dammit.

He wanted to know what was happening on the island in details on which the government *couldn't* lie.

But in an atmosphere where people were afraid for their lives, as some clearly were on Mospheira, including his mother and his brother and his former fiancee, he wasn't sure of getting the truth even if he got such a newspaper, or the unrestricted datafeed. So much for Mospheira's supposedly free press.

The situation scared him, deep down scared him—for his family, for atevi, for everyone on the planet.

And he himself had argued with Tabini-aiji *not* to detain Deana Hanks on the mainland: to ship her home, safe and sound, mad, and dangerous. If things had gone that wrong, he had fault to bear. He could muster excuses when atevi politics were at fault. In this one, he could by no means blame the atevi government.

He smiled for the benefit of the servants who put away his coat, and he accepted their polite questions soberly: he didn't lie to his staff, who had to handle touchy situations, and who had to fend away importunate and unauthorized persons of sometimes ill intent. "There was a difficulty at the interview, nadi," he replied to the question of how it had gone. "A subject which should not have been brought up: nand' Jase. We know the staff here didn't release the information, but it is out."

"One will inform nand' Saidin, paidhi-ji. One is distressed to hear so."

"Thank you, Sasi-ji. —How *is* he doing?"

"He's speaking to his mother now, nand' paidhi."

"*Thank* you, Sasi-ji." He went aside immediately to the security station, into the usually open doorway and straight into the monitoring station which lay just inside.

Tano was there with an ear-set, as were Banichi, Jago, and a junior security operator, all listening.

Tano didn't say a thing, just surrendered his earpiece to him, and Bren tucked the device in his ear.

"—don't know what else I can do," he heard, Jase's voice, speaking the language of the ship, and a long pause followed, where a reply should be.

"I know," a woman's voice said finally, sad-sounding. *"I have no way to help you. I can't. And you can't. Except to get back as soon as you can."*

"They say it's making progress. That's all I can say."

"Can you call again?"

"I just don't know. I'll try. I will try."

"I love you."

A long pause, while that human expression hung thin and potent in the air. Then: "I love you, too, mama. I'm fine. Don't *worry* about me."

Another pause. *"I'd better shut down now."*

"Yeah. —It's good to hear your voice."

"Good to hear yours, Jase. Take care. Please take care."

"I will, mama."

There was silence, then. Bren looked at the occupants of the room, tall, black, a collection of alien faces one of whom was a woman he'd almost gone to bed with, all looking to him for reaction.

Some of whom understood enough of what had been said and some of whom trusted him enough to have expression on their faces.

Banichi did. And Jago.

"There's nothing out of the ordinary in the exchange," he said. "A son talking to his mother in—" There was no word for affection. There was just no concept. There was no possibility in the faces that stared at him with such good will and acceptance—

and worry. "In terms ordinary for that relationship. Jase is concerned for his mother. He fears she is concerned about his mental well-being. She asked whether he could call again. He replied that he wasn't certain, but he'd try. —He *will* have access, will he not, nadiin-ji?"

"There's no reason to the contrary," Banichi said.

"The death of his father is attributed to accident," Jago said. "We do not follow the precise cause."

It was an offering of good faith in itself, that the most security-conscious atevi he knew let him know how much they understood. The faces came back into ordinary perspective for him. His heart was beating hard in sheer terror and he thought it was because he'd *been* somewhere else for a moment, he'd been in human territory, and seeing two people he loved very much—

—not through a distortion, but as the atevi they were, incapable of returning that emotion. Seeing them as incapable of saying, as Jase's mother said, I *love* you.

Seeing them as incapable of understanding, as Jase had said to a woman orbiting above them, *I love you, mama.*

Atevi children clung to their parents. But it wasn't love that made them do that.

Go to the leader. Always go to the leader when the bullets start to fly: rally to the leader.

Could a human *feel* the emotional satisfaction atevi got when they responded to that urge and were responded to? No more than atevi could *feel* what Jase meant when a mother and son said, at such uncrossable distance, I *love* you.

But they knew that, held at such distance from the chief of their association, *their* profoundest instinct would find no satisfaction. And on that side of the gulf, one face of the lot was deeply troubled.

Jago said, quietly, "As if she were on the moon, isn't it?"

It was a proverb for the unattainable.

"Even the moon," Banichi said, ever the pragmatic

one, "will have railroads and television if this ship flies."

"That it will," Bren said, with that hollow spot still cold inside him. "And Jase knows it logically. —I'd better talk to him."

They seemed relieved then, whether to think he could deal with the trouble, or simply to close off the presence of alienness they couldn't grasp without analogy.

He left them to their discussion of whatever they might discuss—the oddness of humans was his guess. He walked across the foyer and down the hall that led to the heart of the apartment, and to the library, where the phone was, where Jase had to be.

But so were the servants—all the servants, who weren't standing in knots talking, as his first glance informed him, but arrayed somewhat in a line, and holding each a flower, whence obtained he had no idea; maybe one of the cut arrangements which appeared every few days. They bowed as he walked past in mild confusion, his attention on the same destination, past the dining rooms, past the bedrooms and the baths, alongside the grim steel barrier of the construction and on to the private office where the lady Damiri's personal phone was.

Jase stood outside, his hands already holding a few blossoms, as one by one the servants came, each solemnly presenting him a single flower, bowing her head and walking away in silence.

Jase didn't seem to know what to do. He stood there accepting the flowers, one after the other, and Bren stopped, just stopped and stood, as madam Saidin came up beside him, and also waited.

Jase stood there with his arms increasingly loaded, with the load greater and greater on his soul, by the look of him, until his arms were full, and the last servant had passed, given him a flower, and bowed and gone her way.

"If you please, nand' Saidin," Jase said with meticulous courtesy, and offered the mass of flowers toward her. "What is proper to do?"

"You may give them to me, if you wish," Saidin said, and carefully took them, all forty-nine, as Bren guessed there were in that armful of assorted flowers. The whole hall smelled of them. "Shall I personally cast them on the garden pond, nand' paidhi?" It was Jase she addressed. "That would be appropriate."

"Please do," Jase said, looking and sounding very much at the end of his self-restraint. But he bowed correctly. "Nandi. Thank you."

"We are all sad," Saidin said, and took the flowers away.

Bren expected to speak to him, and waited.

But as soon as Saidin had gone, Jase violently shoved past him and went toward the front of the apartment, headed, as Bren guessed, for his room.

The opening and slam of a heavy, well-hung door said that he guessed right.

Well, he thought, Jase had done everything in an exemplary fine manner, right down to the shove at him and the door. Which he, personally, would forgive, though his nerves *felt* that door shut.

And he could ignore the gesture, and forgive it, and let it pass. It wasn't the task he wanted when he was still exercised over the news conference: adrenaline started flowing and he couldn't use it here, no matter what.

But *they* had uncle Tatiseigi visiting tomorrow night, and Jase had to get his reactions either done with or under control, whichever came first.

He was going to have to do something.

Jase hadn't *locked* the door. That was good—Jase was not sealing himself in. Or that was bad—Jase was in such a state he didn't think of such things. He pushed the latch and walked into Jase's bedroom.

Jase was lying on the made bed, hands behind his head, staring at the ceiling. Jase *had* taken the shoes off, in consideration of passionate atevi feelings of propriety in that regard. Jase was improving, and Jase had stopped to think.

And starting a conversation with a positive statement seemed a good thing.

"That was very well done, Jase."

Tightjawed, and in Mosphei': "Did you listen in?"

"I came in late. I heard the close. I'm very sorry, Jase."

"Thanks."

"Can I help you?"

"Not unless you fly."

"I know. I know that part of it. I'm sorry. That's all I can say. How's your mother?"

"She's fine." A fragile, angry voice. "I'd rather you got the rest of it from the tape. I'm not up to questions right now."

"Jase." He was inclined to sit down on the other side of the bed. Jase wasn't looking at him. And he had seen Jase's temper boiling to the surface. He didn't risk sitting. But he risked walking directly into Jase's field of view. "Jase, this is someone talking who at least knows what you're going through. Don't wall me out. Tell me what happened, so two of us know it. Tell me how you're doing. Tell me if there's any risk to the ship or station up there."

"Is that what you're after? It's fine."

"Jase. I'm sorry. I'm sorry. I'm sorry. I can't make it better. But tell me what happened and tell me what's going on as a result of it."

"It's not your damn business!"

"It *is* my business! I'm in charge of this mission."

"Who said? My captain? I don't think so."

"Sure, fine, you're in charge of yourself and you can't speak the language or get across town on the subway. No, Jase. You did all right out there. You did extremely well. And I know it's your private business, but the paidhiin don't *have* private business when it affects the safety of everybody else."

"What if I *wanted* to get across town on the subway?"

"What's that to do with anything?"

"I'm a prisoner here. I'm a prisoner under guard. Is that the way it is?"

"You're a fragile entity in this culture. You're not qualified to be out on your own: an atevi six-year-old might get where he was going solo, but I wouldn't lay odds on your making it *to* the subway, let alone elsewhere. —So where do you want to go, or what do you want to do? —Can I help you?"

"I'd like to see the ocean."

Occasionally conversations with Jase turned right angles. This one went three-sixty degrees.

"The ocean."

"I'd like to see the ocean. The sea. Whatever the word is. I'd like to stand on the edge of the water and look at it. Is that safe? Is it a stupid request?"

"It's not a stupid request." He was no better informed, and understood Jase no better. The question had to be asked, if only to know there was nothing more ominous going on in the heavens. "—Jase, what happened to your father? Staff says it *was* an accident that killed him."

There was a long pause. Several breaths. Jase never varied his position otherwise. "Old seals on the station. Dangerous place. That's all. Hard vacuum. My father"—several more breaths, eyes fixed on the ceiling—"was blown out into space. That's all. He was working, and the seal went."

"It was fast."

"Yeah. It was."

"So how's your mother taking it?"

"Oh—all right. —I mean, she's upset, what do you expect? And I can't do anything."

"I can understand that well enough."

Jase still lay with his hands under his head, looking at the ceiling.

"So—is your mother off work, nadi, or working, or what?"

"Working."

"No trouble your reaching her this time? I hope there was no trouble."

"I had no trouble." Jase moved his arms, slowly got to his feet. The hair he professed drove him to distraction fell around his face. He shook it out of his way and raked it back. It fell around his ears, on its way to respectable atevi length, but not there yet. "Stupid accident, that's all. You can't stop something like that. Can't plan."

"Yes," he said. "That's true."

"Can you arrange—for me to visit the sea, nadi?"

He didn't want to point it out, but Jase had had trouble walking when he'd first landed. Jase had had trouble with orientation, particularly with peripheral vision. He wouldn't see an atevi doctor. He said the world had no edges.

And described, later, a world of only corridors, and small rooms.

"I know a place," Bren said, thinking that lord Geigi would be surprised to have two guests.

But he didn't think Jase was ready for a boat. Not quite.

"When? Soon?"

"Soon." But the world came crashing in. In all its complexity. "Yes. —But there's something first. Something we have to do. Something you have to do for me. Please."

"What?"

"There's a visitor coming. A very important visitor—to see the apartment."

"Why?" Jase asked. "What?"

"One night. He'll look at the place. And go. He's very strict. Very *kabiu*. The lord who owns this place, understand? It's important we impress him as proper people."

"And you want me not to make a mistake."

"Simply put, yes."

"Do I get my ocean?"

"If you do that, I'm pretty sure about the ocean."

"I'll do it. For that."

Maybe, Bren thought, it was just something he'd said to himself up in the heavens that he wanted to see. Maybe it was something his father had said he'd like to see. Jase gave him no clue at all.

But Jase was being reasonable, at cost, he could see that. Jase's color wasn't good. Jase's hands shook when he went to the bureau and tried to put his own hair in order.

"Shall I call for tea," Bren said, "and we can sit and talk and I can explain about the visitor, and the situation?"

"Yes." Jase transited back to Ragi, and secured his hair, as best it could be without elaborate effort, braiding it from high up and fastening it in a simple clip. "Please do, nadi."

Impeccable manners. Impeccable, almost, accent. Jase had been practicing.

Bren went to the hall, found madam Saidin *and* Tano not far away, and said, "Tea, please, nadiin-ji," trusting it would arrive quickly.

The conversation went amazingly easily—at least, Jase listened soberly, objected to nothing, questioned for understanding, and called nothing unreasonable.

In some measure it was sad to see Jase attempting to follow all of it, knowing the load he was under, and knowing how his tendency was to look for absolute orders. In some measure, Bren thought without saying so, he did provide a framework for Jase's expectations: how to dress, what to say.

But now it had to be dealing with an atevi lord and a lady who was that lord's chief rival; and how to deal in public and formally with the aiji of Shejidan, whom Jase had met in far less formality, among the first people on earth he had met, with a wildfire burning across the horizon, water pouring into his descent capsule, and the whole world in upheaval.

But Jase brightened when he turned the talk then toward lord Geigi's balcony—seemed a little taken aback by the description of battling a fish and then eating it; and of a fish big enough to chase lord Geigi's boat crew across the deck.

But Jase said then he wanted to look at the map in the office, and they walked back to that room, at the rear of the apartment and next to the steel security barrier, to see where they were, and where the sea was, and Mospheira, and where the South Range of Taiben was: the South Range, one of the vast hunting reserves, was where his capsule had come down, and Jase was able to point out that spot on the wall map. He could find that.

Then he wanted books on the sea. Bren took him to the lady Damiri's library.

"How is he?" Banichi asked him at one point when he was outside and Jase was in the library pulling down books and going through references. "What is he looking for?"

Bren drew a deep breath, having understood, somewhat, this redirection of emotions, but finding it difficult to render into Ragi, particularly for Banichi, who tended to shoot down air castles, even as atevi defined them.

"It's a human reaction," he said to Banichi quietly. "He's suffered a great blow. His emotions are unreliable. Possibly he's looking for something to distract his thoughts toward something without emotional context, perhaps something approved by the deceased person, perhaps only a personal ambition."

"To view the ocean."

"From space, the ocean-land boundaries and the polar caps would be the only easily visible features. I suppose he might have wondered about it."

"And clouds," Banichi said. Space photography had made its way into atevi hands even before the War of the Landing. All sorts of space photography had come out of the files prior to the release of the first rocket technology, preparing, the paidhiin had said, the expectation of space travel, never the concept of the rockets in war, directing the psychology of a species toward the sky, not toward armament. It had been a narrow thing for the human race, historically, so the records said; and atevi so readily converted technology to self-defense.

"Many clouds," Bren agreed.

"So he wishes to go to visit lord Geigi?"

"Something like," Bren said. "I think he might be ready to make such a venture."

"He became ill from looking at the sky, Bren-ji. Will it not afflict him again once he goes into the open?"

"I think it's important to him to prove to himself he won't be ill."

"Ah," Banichi said.

"I'm not sure I understand, myself, Banichi. Please don't believe I have a perfect idea what's passing through his mind. But it might mark a place of new beginnings for him, new resolve to do his job. —And it might be time for him to try something difficult. If he's to be a paidhi in fact, and interpret atevi to the ship-folk, I think it important for him to understand the way atevi look at the world. If security can accommodate it. I *promised* him, Banichi. I *assumed* security could accommodate it."

"Certainly a consideration. But there are places of safety, well within perimeters we can guarantee. I think one could find such safety. But Geigi—I am less sure."

"Would you find that out, nadi-ji, what might be safe?"

"One will do so. —Meanwhile, the other matter—"

Deana. He'd been so rattled he'd forgotten what he'd asked Banichi to do.

"We are producing a transcript, paidhi-ji, of this woman. Tano wishes you to understand, he had no idea that this was going on. —Nor did Jago, nor I, Bren-ji. *We* were of a level to be informed, once we returned, that was one critical matter. Certain agencies between us and the aiji did *not* wish to distract us with your staff matters. This is not to dismiss the matter of their failure to inform *you*. And their failure to inform Tano."

"I have great confidence in all my staff, Banichi. I *do* not doubt you."

Banichi seemed to weigh telling him something. Then: "The aiji, nadi-ji, has detected a slight lack of forwardness among certain Guild members to pass along information to higher levels, both times regarding those who monitor transmissions, which are a Guild unto themselves; and both times regarding a transmission of information from that Guild to the house Guard. The aiji is making clear to both services that my absences, whenever they may be necessary, should not constitute a dead end for information. He is, the paidhi may imagine, making this point very forcefully with the Messengers' Guild, which is the one at issue at Mogari-nai."

"I accept that as *very* definitive, nadi," he said, and did. He would not care to be the Guild officer or the Guard whø twice thwarted the aiji, either because of a political view opposed to Tabini or simply due to ruffled protocols—some touchy insistence on rules, and routings of requests that were being run over by the needs of a human office placed by the aiji on the list of persons to whom the Guild traditionally gave information.

Definitely he'd just heard more than his predecessors had known about Guild and Guard conflicts.

And bet on it that, one, Banichi told him what he did with Tabini's full knowledge, and, two, that it was a very necessary warning to him where gaps in necessary information flow had occurred in the past and might occur in some similar crisis in the future: don't believe that you've heard everything from the ship, was what it boiled down to. Don't trust that all communications *are* getting through: there's a serious, quirky roadblock.

That was as serious as it could get. A Guild not once but twice now had ill-served the aiji. If that was not a fatal offense in Tabini's book, he feared it was hedging very close on one, that was one thing, and he didn't want to see a contest of power inside the administration, or Tabini using the Assassins against the Messengers.

But equally serious, that particular information flow, from the ship through Mogari-nai and on to Shejidan—was usually diagrams, data, and handbooks. There were, however, other kinds of information: Jase's message. God knew what.

He knew there was somebody, at least one person, that was not the ordinary ateva, and probably at Mogari-nai, sitting there and reading what came down. It struck him like a lightning stroke that it *would* make sense that that person be one of the Messengers' Guild,

not the Assassins' Guild that regularly guarded the aiji.
It was not in his knowledge to whom the Messengers'
Guild reported.

But having delivered that bit of information, Banichi
went off about his business.

And Jase, when he went back to check on him,
seemed to have focused himself on the library and was
working, so he supposed Jase had reached some point
of stability.

12

The paidhi had, however, after trying to deal with Jase, an actual routine working day to begin, it being toward afternoon. He had to deal with the records and reports to his own office that he'd brought back from the plant tour, those that hadn't gone to Tabini's staff.

He had letters to write, fulfilling promises he'd made in more cities and townships than he could conveniently recall.

He had a computer full of files with unresolved requests, some of which he could perhaps put into other hands, but first he had to sort those things out, at his classified level, to discover what he *could* move on to other desks.

And he had a stack of raw notes he had tried to keep in a notebook, but which had ended up on small pieces of paper borrowed from various sources, a shaggy affair he would have to turn over to the clericals in his office for what they could do for him, once he had been through it to be sure there was nothing tucked into that notebook that didn't belong to that level of security. He thought he'd retrieved everything, but regarding that particular notebook, which had followed him closely through various sensitive laboratories, he wasn't sure.

So. The Jase matter was, thank God, at rest. Not settled. But at rest. He'd done what he could; he humanly *wished* he could do more. He wished in the first place that he'd been able to get personally closer to Jase. Jase wanted to keep his own observations and reports to his superiors clear and objective, he was sure, and Jase always held him at arms' length—so he didn't have that kind of closeness that would have let him step in and offer . . . whatever people offered one another at such a time. He was sad about Jase being sad; he was disturbed about it; it made him think uncomfortable thoughts about mortality and his own scattered family; and he was, considering Jase's temper, uneasy about Jase's ability to deal with the isolation and the sense of loss together.

Hell of a homecoming, in short. A household in disarray. If he started worrying about it—and about security lapses, information gaps—well, that wouldn't persist.

Banichi and Jago hadn't been here. Good as Tano and Algini were, they weren't *as* good, and problems had crept in. People hadn't told them things they should have known.

Banichi and Jago were on it. Things would *get* right.

Meanwhile there wasn't anything more he could do than he'd done, there wasn't any more he could learn about Jase's situation than he'd learned, nothing more he could feel than he'd felt, and at this point, if Jase had settled on dealing with it alone, he could just retreat to a distance and be sure Jase *was* really all right, that was all.

Chasing down the other problems that might impinge on Jase's situation was Banichi's business. The files—

—were his.

So he settled into the sitting room, asked the servants to have one of the junior security staff bring his computer and his notes to him, and spread out his traveling office for the first uninterrupted work he'd gotten done since the plane flight.

The simple, mind-massaging routine of translation had its pleasures. There were days on which he *liked* pushing the keys on the computer as long as it produced known, predictable results.

A servant came in to ask what sort of supper he'd wish. He asked them to consult Jase about what *he* wanted and to go by that if Jase wanted anything formal, but by his preference he wanted a very light supper: he'd been on the banquet circuit, and he'd gone back to a sedentary life in which he preferred a lighter diet, thank you. Jase, he was relatively sure, was not in a mood for a heavy meal.

To his mild surprise Jase came to the door and said the staff was asking about supper and what would *he* prefer. He really hadn't expected Jase to surface at all; but Jase came voluntarily to him, being sociable, and seemed to be holding onto things fairly well, considering.

"I'll join you, if you like," Bren said.

"That would be fine," Jase said, "nadi. Shall I arrange it with the staff?"

"Do, please, nadi-ji." He had a lap full of carefully arranged computer and notes. He considered a *how are you?* and settled on "Thank you."

"I'll do that," Jase said, and went away to the depths of the apartment where one could ordinarily find the staff.

So it was a supper with him and Jase alone, the security staff otherwise occupied. Jase was somber, but in better spirits, even offering a little shaky, unfeigned laughter in recounting things that had gone on during his absence, chiefly the matter of a security alert when the lily workmen's scaffold had jammed and they'd had to get the Bu-javid fire rescue service to get the workmen back to the roof.

"We couldn't get the security expansion panel down," madam Saidin added to the account, herself serving the main dish, "because Guild security wouldn't permit that. So there they were: the workmen had two of the porcelains with them on the scaffold, so they wouldn't risk those. And the artist came down to the garden below and began shouting at them that they shouldn't put the lilies in a bucket, which was what the firemen proposed—"

"God."

"The hill is tilted there," Jase ventured. He meant the

hill was steep: but he was close to the meaning. "And the ladder wouldn't go there."

"They ended up letting firemen down on ropes to take the porcelains," madam Saidin said, "so they could get the porcelains to safety. But meanwhile the artist was locked out of the building and stranded herself on the hill in the garden—she is an elderly lady—and *she* had to be rescued, which took more permissions to bring someone *through* the doors below from the outside."

"Bu-javid security," Jase said, "was not happy."

Bren could laugh at that—it was not, he was certain, a story which had amused lord Tatiseigi, whose sense of humor was likely wearing thin; but if an Atageini such as madam Saidin could laugh, then they all could, and he could imagine Damiri involved—from her balcony next door, if security had let her past the door.

But Jase seemed worn and tired, and declared at the end of the meal that he had rather spend his evening studying and turn in early.

"Are you all right?" Bren asked in Mosphei'.

"Fine," Jase said. "But I didn't sleep much last night."

"Or the nights before, I'd imagine."

"Nor the nights before," Jase agreed. "But I will tonight."

"Good," he said. "Good. If you need anything, don't hesitate to wake me."

"I'll be fine," Jase said. "Good night."

They'd occasionally talked in the evenings, but mostly it was lessons. Sometimes they watched television, for the news, or maybe a machimi play, which was a good language lesson. He'd expected, with supper, to need to keep Jase busy, and had asked after the television schedule, which did have a play worth watching this evening.

But there was no shortage of work for either of them, and without work there was worry: Bren understood that much very well. If Jase felt better sitting in the library and chasing references and doing a little translation, he could understand that.

Himself, he went back to the sitting room, deciding that he would deal with the correspondence, finally, now that he'd dulled his mind with a larger supper than he'd intended, and now that his brain had grown too tired to deal with new things.

Top of the correspondence list was the request from the pilots, who were trying to form a Guild. The Assassins, the Messengers, the Physicians, and the Mathematicians were Guilds. There *were* no other professions, since the Astronomers were discredited nearly two hundred years ago. And now the pilots, who had heard of such a guild among humans, were applying to the legislatures for that status on the ground that atevi could not deal with humans at disadvantage—but they were meeting opposition from the Guilds and from traditionalists in the legislature who thought they weren't professional. The pilots, who had never enjoyed Guild status, were incensed at the tone of the reply.

On the other side, the legislature wanted justification for the sacrosanctity and autonomy that a Guild enjoyed, when they did nothing that regarded confidentiality, which was the essence of a Guild.

That was one problem. Tossing into it Banichi's information, there were interface problems with other Guilds, and the question of how such a Guild would relate to, say, the Messengers—who argued at length that the pilots in question might fit within *their* Guild structure since they traveled and carried messages.

Like hell, was the succinct version of the pilots' opinion, as it came to his ears.

To add to the mix, a fact which he knew and others might not, there was serious talk this winter of the Astronomers attempting to regain their position as a Guild, but as Tabini put it, their Guild status had originally been based on their predictive ability, and getting into *that* now-antiquated forecasting function would touch off a storm of controversy among several atevi philosophies, which on one level was ludicrous, but which to believers was very serious and which, to politicians, signaled real trouble.

The pilots wanted him to write a recommendation to the aiji and to the legislature—and there was, additionally, a letter from the head of the Pilots' Association stating that they accepted the use of computers on his recommendation that they would prove necessary (this had been a *very* difficult matter) and hoping again, since he had supported the paidhi in that situation, that the paidhi would grant his support in their cause.

The fact was, he did take the Guild status seriously—for reasons he didn't quite want to make clear to the pilots involved.

Yet.

They were, assuredly, going to enjoy a certain importance once the earth-to-orbit craft was flying; and once the coming and going became frequent; but more than that—more than that, he began to think, the computer programs the pilots right now disdained were ultimately going to be run by atevi computer programs, using atevi grasp of mathematics.

And in that respect he could see where it was going to go over a horizon he couldn't see past, into mathematical constructs where a lot of atevi couldn't follow, arcane mysteries that might *totally* confound a set of philosophies built on mathematical systems. And responsible handling of *that* might be far more important to atevi than any reason these men and women yet saw.

Aiji-ma, he wrote somberly, *these pilots will in years to come work closely with the Mathematicians' Guild and with the Astronomers in whatever capacity the Astronomers enjoy at that time. I believe in due consideration that there will be reasons to facilitate exchange of information at Guild level. I know that I, being human, only imperfectly comprehend the advantages and disadvantages of a change from professional Association to Guild, but there may be special circumstances which will place these persons in possession of sensitive information which I think your greater wisdom and atevi sensibilities alone can decide.*

Let me add, however, that the term Guild as atevi apply it is not the human model; and this should be considered: it came to be among the most divisive issues of the human-against-human quarrel that sent humans down to the planet.

There was a human named Taylor once, when the ship was lost in deepest space and far from any planet. Taylor's crew gave their lives to fuel the ship and get it to a safer harbor. The sons and daughters of the heroes, as I was taught was the case, gained privilege above all other humans, used their privilege and special knowledge ruthlessly, and attempted to hold other humans to the service of their ship, a matter of very bitter division.

He stopped writing—appalled at the drift of what he was admitting to atevi eyes, to an ateva who was working to his own people's advantage far above any theoretical interest he held in humans—an ateva whose *feelings* about the matter he couldn't begin to judge, no more than he could expect Tabini or even himself accurately to judge the feelings of humans dead two hundred and more years ago.

He was appalled at how far he'd forgotten the most basic rules in dealing with atevi. He security-deleted what he'd just written, wiped every possible copy, and then grew so insecure about his fate and that of the computer he wasn't sure humans had told him the truth about a security-delete.

The room after that was quiet. There was the dark outside the windows. There was the hush in a household trying not to disturb those doing work they generally couldn't discuss. There was the burden of knowing—and not being able to talk about things.

Never being able to talk. Or relax. Or go out of that mode of thought that continually analyzed, looked for source, looked for effect.

Looked for ulterior motive.

And he was on the verge of making stupid, stupid mistakes.

He needed a human voice, that was what. He badly needed to touch something familiar. He needed to *see* something familiar—just to know—that things he remembered were still there.

He folded up the computer, got up, walked back to the office, quietly so. Jase was still in the library, reading, but Jase didn't look up as he shut the office door.

And dammit, no, Jase wasn't the prop to lean on. A human born lightyears from the planet wasn't it. A man under Jase's level of stress wasn't it. He didn't need to dump all his concerns on anybody.

He just needed—he needed just to hear the voices, that was all. Just needed, occasionally, to hear the accents he knew, and the particular human voices he'd grown up with, and even—he could be quite brutally honest about it—to get mad enough at his family to want to hang up, if that was what it took to armor him for another three months of his job. He loved them. He was technically allowed to say the fatal word *love* in their instance, angry and desperate as they could make him.

Maybe, he thought, *that* was the part of his soul that needed exercising. Maybe it was hearing Jase talking to his mother. Maybe it was the self-chastisement that maybe he ought to make peace with his own family, and not carry on the war they'd been fighting.

Maybe it was the definite knowledge that his mother had justification for complaints against her son. It came to him with peculiar force that he'd been blaming her for her frustration when it was the same frustration and anger the whole island of Mospheira was likely feeling with him, and showing to his mother by harassing her sleep. *He* couldn't explain his position to her, hell, he couldn't explain it to himself on bad days, and now she had health problems the stresses of *his* job weren't helping at all.

Not mentioning the mess he'd put his brother and his family in.

At least he could call. At least he could make the gesture and try to plead again that he *couldn't* come back and turn over the job to Deana Hanks, which was his alternative.

Jase didn't look up. The hall was shadowed: possibly Jase didn't notice him at all. Or thought he was being

checked on by security or one of the servants—or by
him—and purposefully didn't notice.

He went to the little personal office instead, picked
up the phone and, through the Bu-javid operator, put
through a call into the Mospheiran phone network,
which got a special operator on the other side.
Checking the time, he put through a call to his brother
Toby's house.

*"This number is no longer a valid number. Please
contact the operator."*

"I'm sorry," the Mospheiran operator said coldly,
cutting in. *"There's a recording."*

I know there's a damn recording! was what he
wanted to say. Instead, he said, reasonably, "Call Bretano City Hospital. My mother's a patient there."

There wasn't even a courtesy Yes, Mr. Cameron.
The operator put the call through, got the desk, a clerk,
the supervisor:

"We have no Ms. Cameron listed as a patient."

"They say," the operator said, *"they have no Ms.
Cameron listed."*

He *didn't* want to call the Foreign Office. He had a
short list of permitted persons he *could* call as paidhi
without going *through* the Foreign Office or higher.
And he was down to the last ones. His mother's home
phone didn't work during the evening hours: the phone
company had blocked incoming service because of
phone threats. Toby *might* be there. His mother might
be. Possibly she'd come home from the hospital and
Toby might have taken his entire family there because
he didn't dare leave the kids or his wife alone back at
their house. *Damn* the crawling cowards that made it
necessary!

"All right. Get me Barbara Letterman," he said to the
operator. "She's married to Paul Saarinson."

*"I don't have authorization for a Paul Saarinson's
residence."*

"You have—" He made a conscious effort to keep
his language free of epithets. "—authorization for
Letterman. She is the same Barb Letterman. She has a

State Department clearance to talk to me. She hasn't changed her clearance. She just got married."

"I can only go by the list, sir. You'll have to contact the State Department. I can put you through to that number."

The operator *knew* that number wouldn't find anybody able to authorize anybody at that hour. He could try Shawn Tyers at home. But he didn't want to compromise Shawn, and he had sure knowledge that his calls were monitored at several points: in this apartment, with Tabini's security, with Mospheiran National Security and God knew, it was possible there were leaks with this particular operator. *George's* friends were gaining increasing access through appointments to various offices, just a quiet erosion of people he *used* to be able to reach.

And it did no good, no good at all to lose his temper. He wasn't out of names, if *that* old list was the one she was going by. There was one woman, one woman he'd dated in time past and who had gone on the list, before he and Barb had almost gotten to talking about a future together. Sandra Johnson was a *date,* for God's sake, not a resource for a Foreign Office field officer in trouble. But she was a contact—to prove he could get someone.

"Sandra Johnson."

"Yes, sir."

He shut his eyes and blocked out the atevi world. Imagined a pretty woman in an ivory satin jacket, candlelight, *Rococo's,* and a quiet chat in her apartment. Nice place. Plants everywhere. She named them. Clarence, and Louise. Clarence was a spider plant, one of those smuggled bits that the colonists weren't supposed to have taken, and some had, and spider plants were common, but no ecological threat. Louise was a *djossi* vine, and he'd said—he'd said she should set it on her balcony. They liked more light. The paidhi knew. They grew all over Shejidan.

The phone was ringing. And ringing.

Please, God, let someone pick it up.

"Hello?"

"Sandra? This is Bren. Don't hang up."

"Bren Cameron?" Justifiably she sounded a little shocked. *"Are you on the island?"*

"No. No, I'm calling from Shejidan. I apologize. Sandra. I—" Words were his stock in trade and he couldn't manage his tongue or his wits, or even think of the social, right words he wanted in Mosphei'. It was all engineering and diplomatese. "I've run out of resources, Sandra. I need your help. *Please* don't hang up. Listen to me."

"Is something wrong?"

God. Is something wrong? He suffered an impulse to laugh hysterically. And didn't. "I'm fine. But—" What did he say? They're harassing my family and threatening their lives? He'd just put Sandra Johnson on the list, just by calling her. "Sandra, how are you?"

"Fine. But—"

"But?"

"I just—was rather surprised, that's all."

"Sandra, my mother's in the hospital or she's home. I can't get the hospital to admit she's in there. Probably it's a security precaution, but the clerk's being an ass. I know—" God, he had no shame. Nor scruples. "I know I have no right to call up like this and hand you a problem, but I can't get through and I'm worried about her. Can you do some investigating?"

"Bren—I—"

"Go on."

"I know she's there. I know they've got police guards. It's in the news. Bren, a lot of people are mad at you."

"I imagine they are. But what in hell's it doing in the news about my mother and police guards?"

"Bren, they've thrown paint on the apartment building. Somebody shot out the big windows in the front of the State Department last week. You're why."

He felt a leaden lump in his stomach. "I don't get all the news."

"Bren, just—a lot's changed. A lot's changed."

The operator, he was sure, was still listening. The call was being recorded.

"Shouldn't have bothered you."

"Bren, I'm a little scared. What are you doing over there? What have you done?"

"My job," he said, and all defenses cut in.

"They say you're turning over everything to the atevi."

"Who says? Who *says*, Sandra?"

"Just—on the news, they say it. People call the television station. They say it."

"Has the President said anything?"

"Not that I know."

"Well, then, not everything's changed," he said bitterly. Eight days out of the information flow, maybe. But by what Banichi had said about things not getting to Tano's level, with Banichi gone for six months, God alone knew what hadn't gotten to him.

And common sense now and maybe instincts waked among security-conscious atevi told him he'd both made a grave mistake in getting on the phone and that he'd learned nothing in this phone call that he could do a damn thing about. "So now that I've called you, *you* could be in danger. How's your building security?"

"I don't know if we have any." It was half-laughing. Half-scared. Life on Mospheira didn't take crime into account. There wasn't much. There weren't threats. Or had never been, until the paidhi became a public enemy. *"What do I do?"*

"Get a pen. I'm going to give you instructions, Sandra."

"For what? What's going on?"

"Because they're threatening my family, they're threatening my brother and his wife and kids, and Barb got married to get an address they couldn't access. I shouldn't have called your number."

"You're serious. This isn't a joke you're making."

"Sandra, I was never more serious. Have you got a pen?"

"Yes."

"I want you to go to Shawn Tyers. You know who he is. His apartment is 36 Asbury Street."

"The Foreign Secretary."

"Yes." The line popped. His heart beat hard. He knew he was about to lose the connection and that it was not an accident. The window he had was closing, the operator had found someone of rank enough to terminate the phone call because they'd gotten into things they didn't want flowing across the strait, and he'd just put Sandra in real danger. "Leave Clarence and Louise on their own, go to a neighbor and get them to take you directly to Shawn. Wait in his lobby all night if you have to. Don't let them arrest you." This was a woman almost entirely without experience in subterfuge. And if they were monitoring, the people who would harm her were listening to what he was telling her to do. "This instant. I'm serious. You're in danger, *now*. They're listening on the line, Sandra. These people could send the taxi if you call one. Get help from people you know or don't know, but not taxis and not government. Get to Shawn. Now! Move fast! Don't go on the street alone—and don't trust the police!"

"Oh, my God, Bren. What's going on? What are you involved in? Why did you call me?"

It's not *me*, he started to say.

But the line went dead.

He stood leaning against the desk. He was gripping the phone so hard his hand was numb. He hung up the receiver knowing he commanded any security help he wanted on this side of the strait—and couldn't get through to his own mother on the other.

Deana Hanks was broadcasting messages to incite sedition on the mainland. That no one stopped her meant no one knew or that no one could get an order to stop her.

That no one in the atevi government including Tabini had told him about Deana meant that, Banichi's protestations aside, either no one had told Banichi or Banichi was covering something—Banichi ordinarily wouldn't lie to him, but there were circumstances in which Banichi *would* lie to him. Definitely.

He'd thrown in the bit about the damn houseplants to cue Sandra he was speaking on his own and now he didn't know but what she didn't take it as some joke.

The stakes had gotten higher, and higher.

And higher.

Maybe he was just so out of touch he was a paranoid fool. But what he could feel through the curtain of security that lay between Mospheira and the Western Association scared him, it truly scared him.

He straightened, met the grave face of an atevi servant who'd, probably passing in the hall, seen him in the office and seen his attitude and paused. Or his own security had sent her. God knew.

"Do you wish anything, nand' paidhi?"

He wished a great deal. He said, for want of anything he could do, "I'd like a glass of shibei, nadi. Would you bring it, please?"

"Yes, nand' paidhi."

Instant power. More than fifty people completely, full-time dedicated to his wants and needs.

And he couldn't safeguard Sandra Johnson and two stupid houseplants he'd put into grave danger.

God! Led by his weaknesses and not by his common sense, he'd made that phone call. Why the hell had he felt compelled to push the matter and try to get information he knew damned *well* was being withheld from him by the whole apparatus of the Mospheiran government and the rot inside it?

What did he *think* was going to respond when he kicked it to see whether, yes, it was malevolent, and widespread, and it had everything he loved in its grip.

The drink arrived in the hands of a tall, gentle, non-human woman, who gracefully offered it on a silver platter, and went away with a whisper of slippered footfalls and satin coat, and left a hint of *djossi* flower perfume in her wake.

He finished the drink and set down the glass. The spring breeze blew through the sitting room, chill with spring and fresh with scents of new things.

He'd had a nice, tame little single-room apartment down the hill, before he'd come to this borrowed, controversy-dominated palace.

He'd had glass doors that opened onto a pretty little

garden he'd shared with a Bu-javid cook and several clerks, trusted personnel, persons with immaculate security clearances. Never any noise, never any fuss. Two servants, a small office with no secretary at all.

But someone had broken into his little apartment one rainy night, whether a person of Tabini's staff setting him up, or whether truly an attempt on his life, he didn't know nor expected the persons who might have been responsible ever to say. He would never ask, for his part, since it seemed vaguely embarrassing to say it to persons who if they were human would be friends.

Persons whose turning against him would mean he'd have only duty left.

He was aware of a presence in the shadowed hall. He thought it was the servant spotting an empty glass. They were that good, sometimes seeming to have radar attuned to that very last sip, to whisk the glass away, perhaps zealous to restore the perfection of numbers in the room, perhaps that the night staff had to account for the historic crystal. He had no idea and had never asked.

He turned his head and saw Jago standing there.

"Are you well, Bren-ji?"

"Yes." It was perhaps a lie he told her. He wasn't even sure.

Perhaps Jago wasn't sure, either. She walked in and stood where he could see her without turning his head.

"Is there trouble?" he asked her.

"Only a foolish boy who tried to ride the subway to the hill. One can't reach the hill by the subway without appropriate passes, of course. But he carried identification. When he argued with the guards it rang alarms."

"The boy from Dur?"

"He's very persistent."

"He's not hurt, is he?"

"No, no, Bren-ji. But he *is* becoming a great nuisance. Three letters today—"

"Three?"

"Felicitous three." Jago held up three fingers. "Two would have been infelicitous. He was therefore compelled to send a third."

He had to smile. And to laugh.

"One did," Jago said slowly, "listen—to your phone call, Bren-ji."

It was an admission of many things. And she came to him with that as an implied question.

There was a word, *osi,* that had no clear etymology, no relationship to any other word. But when one said it, one wanted a teacup full or a piece of information amplified to its greatest possible extent. He said it now, and Jago said quietly:

"This woman. One doesn't recall her."

"Sandra Johnson? A woman I saw socially, before you came." There was no atevi word for *dated.* Or if there was, it was a set of words for social functions including bed-partners: he was definitely on shaky ground with that vocabulary.

And with Jago. They'd been—interested in each other. Curious, on one level. Aware—on another— that, being what they were, who they were, things being as they were, they couldn't trifle with one another.

The air was suddenly charged. He didn't know whether she felt it. He'd been celibate for almost a year, now, in a household full of women all of whom, including women he knew had grandchildren, acted as if they found him attractive. He'd met with too many memories tonight. He'd endangered a woman he'd slept with, trying to reestablish a connection he'd no business trying to activate. He might even have *killed* Sandra Johnson. He didn't think things had gone that far on Mospheira, on an island where in very many communities people didn't lock their doors—but he was afraid for Sandra, and felt a guilt for that phone call that wouldn't make an easy pillow tonight.

He wanted—

He wanted someone to fill the silence.

Someone like Barb. Sandra hadn't been that way for him. A fun evening. A light laughter. No talk about the job.

But to Barb, he'd told more than he should. And when it was clear he wasn't coming back any time soon, and when his actions had alienated a lot of the population of Mospheira, *she'd* married a government computer expert, whose clearances and whose indispensability to the State Department could assure her safety in ways he couldn't.

Jago walked closer to his chair. Was *there,* in the warmth and scent and solid blackness of an ateva close at hand.

"I should have shot Hanks-paidhi," Jago said, stating fact as she saw it.

"Possibly it was the right idea," he said, and Jago's hand rested on his on the arm of the antique chair.

"Nadi-ji."

His heart beat in panic. Sheer panic. He thought of moving his hand to signal no. But a sexual No wasn't what he wanted either, not forever.

"If a person associates with the powerful," Jago said in that rich, even voice, the low timbre only an ateva could achieve, "there are penalties."

"But they never expected the paidhi's job to be that, Jago-ji. I didn't. I *know* you think Barb failed me. But there *is* no Guild for her to appeal to. My family has no clan, no power. She went to a man whose connections in the government are more secure than mine."

"And will Barb-daja help you?"

"If I could get to her—"

"What would she have done?"

"Checked on my mother."

"And rescued her?"

"Barb *can't,* Jago-ji. She has nowhere to go. She has no one to call on. There is no Guild. There's none for Sandra Johnson. There *is* no help."

"I have heard of *po-lis.*"

"Some of *them* aren't reliable. And if you're not inside the system you don't know which ones."

Jago took back her hand. And pulled up a chair. "Is this Sandra John-son knowledgeable of such things?"

"Shawn might help her. The Foreign Secretary. He might put her under some sort of protection. I don't know."

"And his superior? What of the President?"

He was suddenly looking not into the face of an ateva he trusted, but an Assassin, a guard in the man'chi of the aiji of Shejidan, asking things he had never quite admitted, like the real inner workings of decision-making. God knew and Tabini knew the President was not quick; but a helpless figurehead, he hadn't quite admitted to.

Matters on the island had never been quite this desperate, either, unless he was a total fool and had scared himself into some paranoid fancy. *Shooting*—at the State Department windows.

"Jago-ji. I'm not sure. I don't *know* who's holding power. Hanks is using a radio transmitter, on an island. *Tell* me they can't find her and stop her. They *know* who's doing it. There *isn't* but one person on Mospheira who can speak fluent Ragi! They aren't that stupid, Jago-ji! Stupid, but not *that* stupid."

"If I see her I *will* shoot her, Bren-paidhi. This is a person doing harm to the aiji's interests and to you."

What did he say? Yes?

"I regard you highly," was what he found to say in Ragi. And what else could he say? Something that evaded moral connection to the ateva she was, and the plain truth and good sense she offered? "You were right, Jago-ji. You were right."

"Yes," she said quietly. "I think so." She rose and towered against the light, and walked to the door. "Banichi says go to bed and sleep."

"Does he?" He was surprised. Then amused at the source of it. At both sources.

"Good night, nand' paidhi."

"Jago-ji." He almost—almost—asked her to stay. No matter Banichi's admonition. But she wouldn't disobey that order, and he shouldn't pose that conflict to her moral sense.

"I am also," she added, "right about Barb-daja. The direction of her man'chi is not to you. She sought another place. —Shall I secure the computer?"

He turned it over to her, and walked out with her. But she went to the left, to the security station, and he went to the right, toward his bedroom, where servants converged and helped him to undress.

Jago's shots were generally on target. Even the man'chi business, which had no human application.

But it *was* true. He and Barb had done each other a lot of damage, the same as he'd done tonight to Sandra.

Barb hadn't—hadn't told him about things. Barb had carried all the load until she couldn't carry it any more. And he loved her for that.

But she'd acted at the last to save *herself*. Jago saw that part, too. Practical of Barb. Maybe even essential.

But—*dammit*—she could have just moved in with Paul. She didn't have to make it legal. *That* said something final to the man she'd been illegal with for years.

It said—a lot of what an ateva had just observed. The drift was in a direction other than toward him.

He sat down on the immaculate bed, and turned out the light and pulled the covers over himself.

He was more tired than he'd thought.

Worried about Sandra. Worried about his mother and his brother, but he'd *been* worried so long he'd worn out the nerves to worry. Things just were. Somebody had thrown paint on his mother's building and the landlord was no doubt mad; it was in the news it was so notorious and somehow the atevi of the Messengers' Guild who monitored such things hadn't told Tano who consequently hadn't told him.

But Banichi indicated they hadn't told Tabini certain things, too, and that heads were about to be, the atevi word, collected.

He couldn't help matters. He knew that now. He sank into that twilight state in which a hundred assassins could have poured through the windows and he'd have directed them sleepily to the staff quarters.

13

The television was on its way out. One servant dusted the table on which it had rested for more than half a year in the historic premises, another stood by with a gilt and porcelain vase which would replace it, and a third carried the incriminating modernism out to the kitchen where (rather than send the thing through the dissection of security when it had to come back again) it would hide in the rear of a cupboard of utensils that the Atageini lord would surely not inspect.

The cabinet that held the vegetables, especially the locker that held the seasonal meat, Bren would not lay odds on. Cook *had* illicit tomato sauce. Cook had by a miracle of persuasion gotten it through Mospheiran customs (let *Cook* talk to George Barrulin in the President's office, Bren thought glumly: Cook might fare better than he had) and now the offending cans of sauce from a human-imported vegetable had to hide somewhere. One simply didn't want to put anything through security examination if it could possibly be tucked away out of sight. Everything that went out of the apartment was a risk and a nuisance in its coming back in.

"I have the dread of Uncle opening a linen cabinet," Bren said to Jase as they stood watching, "and being crushed by falling contraband."

"They've even checked under the bed," Jase said. "Will *he?*"

"I don't think he'll go that far." He'd explained to Jase the importance, the deadly fragility of relations between Tatiseigi and Tabini, and the fact that on one level there was amusement in it; and on another, it was grimly, desperately serious, not only for the present, but for all the future of atevi and humans and Tabini's tenure as aiji. "Ready?"

"Hamatha ta resa Tatiseigi-dathasa."

"Impeccable."

It was. Jase had been working on that tongue-twisting *Felicitous greetings to your lordship*. Which wasn't easier because the name was *Tatiseigi*.

"So," Jase said. "Where *is* the tomato sauce?"

"Cook's bed."

Jase's nerves had been on all day, a skittish zigzag between panic and nervous humor. He laughed, and looked drawn thin and desperate. "I can't do this. Bren, I can't."

"You'll do fine."

Uncle Tatiseigi had asked to see *both* human residents, a point that had come to them by message from Damiri-daja this afternoon, and he had pointedly not told Jase that small fact, not wanting to alarm him. But either the old man was curious, or the old man was going to make at least a minor issue of the human presence, possibly to try to create an incident that would give him points against Damiri—or Tabini.

"Just, whatever he says to you, listen carefully and stick to the children's language. He won't attack you if you do that."

"What do you mean attack?"

"Just stay calm. You don't argue numbers with children or anyone speaking like a child. No matter if you know the adult version, stick to the athmai'in. *Believe* me and don't be reckless."

"I don't see how you do this."

"Practice, practice, practice." There was a commotion at the front door. He went and looked from the hall, Jase tagging him closely, and met an oncoming wall of atevi with cameras, cable, lights, and all the accouterments of television. The television *set* went out as not proper, not *kabiu,* in an observant household, while the television service for the Bu-javid Archives came *in* to record the reception and to (unprecedented) broadcast live pictures of the restored lily frieze, the emblem of the Atageini, which, damned right, Uncle wanted on national television.

Tabini had discovered how very useful television was: the world in a box, Tabini called it. The little box that makes people think the world and the screen are the same thing. Tabini used it, shamelessly, when he wished to create a reality in people's minds, and now Tatiseigi took to the medium, at least, no laggard to understand or to use *that* aspect of technology.

So there was an interview area being set up in the hallway near the historic dining room, so that for an evening the Atageini household would, hosting the aiji *and* the Atageini lady closely allied to him and possibly intended to bear Tabini's heir, be linked in the minds of the whole aishidi'tat, the whole Western Association, meaning the majority of the world.

And public interest? The rare chance to *see,* on live television, the residential floors of the Bu-javid, inside a historic residence, with all the numbers and balance of arrangements about the rich and famous apparent to the eye?

The national treasures on display? Museums on both sides of the strait could long for such treasures as filled this apartment, but no public tours such as frequented the downstairs legislative halls had *ever* reached this floor. Such photography of historic treasures the security staff had allowed was limited to fine detail of certain objects, or set against a background, to prevent any public knowledge of the geography and geometry of the—in truth—rather simple and austere corridors outside, and of these fabled, far more ornate rooms. It was a television first.

And a live reception in a premise of the Bu-javid where cameras had never been, with a guest list that included Tabini *and* his favored lady, who was contesting Uncle for supremacy in the Atageini clan?

Machimi plays couldn't possibly touch it.

All of a sudden *his* stomach knotted up in panic.

"Nadi," Banichi said, briskly coming from the same

direction as the camera crew. "It's all on schedule. The aiji's party is arriving in short order. Entry will be by precedence *and* tenancy. They just settled it: *simultaneously* lord Tatiseigi will arrive at this door and the aiji and Damiri-daja will arrive from next door."

The mind refused to grasp what convolutions of protocol and argument *that* statement had settled.

"I'm going to forget," Jase muttered under his breath. "I'm going to forget his name. I'm going to forget all the forms."

"You won't," Bren said. "You'll be brilliant. Just, if I have to go off with someone, stay with your security: Dureni will be with you—*he'll* do the talking."

Banichi was off down the hall talking to Saidin, who was keeping a stern eye on the camera crew and the gilt woodwork. Junior security was down there standing by with grim expressions. Dureni and his partner Ninicho had come from the security station, junior, very earnest, and they stood by, attaching themselves directly to the paidhiin at a time when Banichi and Jago were apt to have their hands full or be distracted to a critical duty at any given moment.

Jase was saying to himself, *"Hamatha ta resa Tatiseigi-dathasa. Hamatha ta resa Tatiseigi-dathasa. Hamatha ta resa Tatiseigi-dathasa."*

Madam Saidin was talking furiously with the cook. One of the maids ran—*ran,* to the rear hall. He didn't think he'd ever seen anyone run in the household.

The steel security barrier was gone. They'd taken that out while he was getting dressed for the occasion and he still hadn't seen the breakfast room, though he'd heard relief that the woodwork and the plaster was intact. Carts were coming from the kitchen, he heard them rattling. There was, for which he was infinitely grateful, no formal dinner, just a reception, at which guests, too many to seat, were going to be straying back and forth between the formal dining room and the breakfast room.

No one was stated to be a security risk except the lord who owned the apartment.

The rattle came closer. It and the maid must have

met and dodged. There was a momentary pause: then a
continued rattle.

Something evidently wasn't on schedule.

Jago passed them, coming *from* the breakfast room
and from a brisk pause for a word with Banichi. She
was resplendent in a black brocade coat with silver
edgings. He'd never seen her in formal dress. She was
beautiful, absolutely beautiful.

"They're coming," Jago said to them, and delayed
for one more word with a servant. "—To the foyer,
nadiin-ji, please!"

"Calmly," Bren said, and with Jase, walked to the
foyer, which smelled of the banks of springtime
flowers, and sparkled with crystal and gold and silver.
Mirrors multiplied the bouquets, and showed a pair of
pale, formally dressed humans. Saidin overtook them,
and so did Jago, and they made a small receiving line.

The door opened. Tabini and Damiri were there,
Tabini in a brilliant red evening-coat; Damiri in
Atageini pale green and pink, both escorting an elderly
gentleman with an inbuilt scowl and a dark green coat
with a pale green collar. Atageini green, like Damiri's.

Saidin bowed, Jago bowed, they bowed to the lordly
arrivals. Tabini wore his cast-iron smile, Damiri had
hers stitched in place, and Tatiseigi—Bren had no
doubt of the gentleman's identity—came forward with
jutting jaw, folded hands behind him, and looked down
at them with unconcealed belligerence as a black and
red and dark green wall of atevi security unfolded into
the foyer, transforming the place from bright floral
pastels to a metal-studded limiting darkness.

"Lord Tatiseigi," Bren said, as he had prepared to
say, "thank you for your"—he had meant to say *gracious,* and gravely edited it out—"presence on this
occasion."

Tatiseigi said, "Nand' paidhi," in glacial tones, and
turned an eye to Jase, who said with an absolutely
impeccable bow, "Felicitous greetings to your lordship."

Tatiseigi stood and stared. Jase stood his ground,
bowed his head a second time, briefly, a trick of

courtesy he had—thank God—correctly, but verging on impudence, recalled.

Miming *him,* dammit, Bren thought. It put the onus of courtesy on Tatiseigi.

"Nadi," Tatiseigi said. Not the rank: *nand' paidhi.* Not the respectful: *nand' Jase.* But the more familiar and in this case slightly supercilious *nadi,* as acknowledgement and finality on the matter.

And looked at Tabini and Damiri. "I'll see the room."

Tabini had an eyebrow that twitched occasionally. It never boded well. "That way," Tabini said with a negligent wave of his hand toward the hall, as if the lord of the Atageini didn't know the way under his own roof.

"Tati-ji," Damiri said, snagged the old man by the arm and whisked him off down the hall.

Tabini cast a look at them, drew a deep breath, and before there could be courtesies, followed as if he were going into combat.

Bren found himself with an intaken breath and a rise of temper he hadn't felt since he'd last dealt with the Mospheiran phone network. And he was still politely expressionless as he said to Jase, "You took a chance, Jase."

"What was I supposed to do?" There was a touch of panic in the half-voice. "He was staring at me!"

"Don't flinch. Don't stare back. You did the right thing. Just don't risk it again with his lordship. Wait for help."

"From who?"

"Whom."

"Dammit, *whom?*"

He had his own quirk of an eyebrow. He gave it to Jase, who shut up, shut down, and lowered his voice.

Just as the door let in the aiji-dowager.

And he couldn't—*couldn't* resist Tabini's grandmother. Ilisidi, diminutive and wrinkled with years, with her lean, graying chief of security, Cenedi, beside her, cast an eye about, leaned her stick on the polished stone of the floor, and snapped, in the face of *no* receiving line but him, Jase, Jago, and Saidin, "Well,

well, if my grandson won't stay to meet me, at least the paidhiin have manners. Good evening."

"Nand' dowager." Saidin bowed, Jago bowed, he bowed. And looked up with no need to mask his delight to see the old woman.

"Nand' dowager," Jase said. "I'm honored."

"He's improved," Ilisidi said with a nod at Jase. "Hair's grown. You can understand him."

"Yes, nand' dowager."

"So where's my damn grandson? Here to meet me? No? Lets his grandmother wander about without directions? Where are these fabled porcelains?"

"Nand' dowager, we would most willingly show you the restorations."

"Manners. Manners. You should teach my grandson. *And* his neighbor. *We* should have stayed at Taiben, for all the courtesy we have here."

Cenedi never cracked a smile. But, veteran of many, many such maneuvers, Cenedi caught Jago's eye and stayed, along with the rest of the abandoned security who had gone into the security station to talk, as Saidin and Jago stayed to greet the rest of the guests.

Ilisidi was bent on viewing the interior of the apartments. Bren offered his arm, and Jase walked on the other side, as the aiji-dowager went.

"I haven't been here in ages," Ilisidi said. "Gods felicitous, the old man hasn't moved a stick of furniture in twenty years, has he?"

"I'm only a recent guest, aiji-ji."

"Tatiseigi has no imagination. *No* imagination. I'd have thought young Damiri would at least be rid of that damn vase." This, with a wave of her cane narrowly missing the vase in question. A servant flinched. "The old woman hated that thing. Tatiseigi's *mother* hated it. But no, they shoot the lilies, never the damn vase. Next time someone tries to shoot you, Bren-ji, promise me, *have* that vase in the room."

"One will remember, aiji-ma."

They reached the back halls and the formerly walled-off doorway that let into the brightly lit breakfast room, where lordly guests and armed security, notably

Banichi and Algini, in formal knee-length coats, stood before buffet tables laden with fantastical food, Cook's supreme and sleepless effort since yesterday's notification of Uncle's chosen menu.

There *would* be a kitchen tour, Bren was quite sure.

"*There* you are!" Ilisidi said in the felicitous three mode. It was Tabini, Damiri, *and* Tatiseigi she headed for; and it was time for the paidhiin to beat a judicious retreat from potential in-law negotiations.

"Is there going to be trouble?" Jase asked as they ducked out and back toward the foyer.

"Only if they get in 'Sidi-ji's way," Bren said, in high spirits for the first time in two days. "And don't call her that! I don't. Certainly not here."

Jase had met her before. And knew, at least, the aiji-dowager's abrupt manner; but *last* time he hadn't been able to understand a word except *Felicitous greetings* and *My name is Jason. Don't shoot.*

They reached the foyer again, and enjoyed a few moments alone with Cenedi, Jago, Saidin, and the flowers, before another party turned up at the door, the lord of Berigai and his entourage, early, while Bren was sure the company in the breakfast room was still engaged in preliminary negotiation and had hardly gotten to the general walking tour the staff expected.

But he knew that Berigai, in whose province Grigiji the astronomer emeritus lived and taught, was well-disposed to him; and by extension, to Jase or whomever the paidhi wished to introduce him to—the Grigiji affair having brought good repute to the observatory and prosperity to the region. It was a very auspicious start to the party which would begin in the formal dining room with a few tidbits and a glass of spirits until it had gathered numbers.

And until the business in the family was settled.

More guests showed up. Jase was bright-eyed, and stayed with hot tea—they both did, as some of the guests also chose to do. There was nothing on the menu, Cook had promised them, except any dish with the red or the purple vegetable, that was harmful to humans. There were a couple of noble guests clearly in the Tatiseigi camp who spent a great deal of time in the corner looking toward them, and discussing matters in private behind the floral arrangement.

Then another arrival, who created some movement among the quiet security presence, and brought Cenedi to consult with Tano, quietly, just outside the dining room. Another lord walked in, unescorted.

Algini slipped to Bren's side.

"Nand' paidhi, Banichi wishes you to know that lord Badissuni is in the company this evening."

Badissuni, Bren thought, looking at the thin, grim-faced lord who broke into a pasted smile as a servant offered him a drink, then coasted up to the lords and ladies around the dining table. Conversation there staggered, took note, and lurched forward valiantly.

Algini had gone, doubtless on some business known only to security. The business in the Marid had just walked in, had a drink, and smiled its way around the table with the occasional flat, wary glance atevi gave to the novelty of humans.

"What's the trouble-in-the-house?" Jase asked in a low voice, and this time the noun was entirely appropriate.

"Badissuni, from the peninsula. Messenger to Tabini. *Don't* get involved with him." The doorway electronics, he was sure, contained a metal detector of some kind. His mind was busy adding up Badissuni as a guest while the relatives of the man Badissuni was serving (and wished to kill: dead before autumn, Banichi had said) were guesting in the house of the lady Direiso, who was Tatiseigi's ally last year when Tatiseigi was plotting against Tabini—who was back on the kitchen tour with Tatiseigi and Damiri looking for contraband in the vegetable bins, God save them.

Badissuni smiled at everyone but him and Jase: the smile was still there, but it went rigid and unpleasant when his gaze fell on either of them, and Bren avoided staring back. Jase was staring—and he moved between Jase and the view of trouble.

"Don't look at him, nadi. You invite trouble."

"He doesn't like us here."

"No," Bren said. "He doesn't like us *anywhere*."

Jago appeared from the doorway and definitely kept a watch on the situation. Cenedi had gone back to keep an eye on the dowager and no doubt to pass a message, but Jago tracked them, and eased up next to him.

"That is Badissuni, Bren-ji. Don't come close to him."

"Is he armed, nadi?"

"No one brings weapons past the door save the three authorized security present: the aiji's, the aiji-dowager's, and lord Tatiseigi's, one assures you, nadi."

Which counted his own among the aiji's and Saidin technically among Tatiseigi's, to be sure.

"Danger?" Jase asked.

"Be careful, nadi," Jago said to him. "Only be careful. He is an invited guest."

"Who invited him, nadi?" Bren asked.

"The aiji," Jago said—Jago who'd wished for the contract on that lordling's life, and who'd already occupied a rooftop vantage in the Hagrani estate. Jago was, he was sure, armed; and that coat surely concealed body armor. "Don't stand near him, nadiin-ji."

"Nadiin." Madam Saidin appeared and spoke in a clear voice. "The host suggests the party adjourn to the breakfast room."

They lingered with Jago, letting the lords and ladies exit, Badissuni among them. The party left a table of serving platters mostly down to crumbs by now, and a clutter of abandoned glasses which the servants hastened to gather up on trays.

"What's happening?" Jase asked.

"Just be calm," Bren said, and they drifted in the wake of the others toward the restored rooms, which rapidly filled shoulder to shoulder with guests admiring the lilies, praising the workmanship, gossiping about the event last year which had necessitated the repairs. There was applause, and lights glared as cameras pretended to be unobtrusive, creating the effect of sunlight across the lilies and the blinded guests. Security was tense in that moment, and Naidiri himself, chief of Tabini's security, set himself in their path and moved the traveling cameras definitively out of the room.

The camera lights went out. Music began, a simple duet of pipes played by two of the servants, who were quite good at it. Talk buzzed above the music and grew animated.

The two humans found refuge against the restored frieze and simply listened to the conversation, as Tatiseigi and two other provincial lords discussed the menu, and Tatiseigi looked at least marginally cheerful, except the looks he threw Badissuni.

"Doing all right?" Bren asked.

"I think," Jase said. He looked tired, and it *was* tiring to keep up with a high-speed translation problem. Jase had gone into it on the edge of his nerves.

"So tell me," Ilisidi said, coasting up, one of the few atevi present not too much taller than a human, "how do you find life on Earth? Different than the ship, nand' paidhi?"

Jase cast him a desperate look.

"Answer," Bren said. "Nand' dowager, I did tell him be careful with his language."

"Different," Jase said. "Thank you, nand' dowager."

"Vastly improved," Ilisidi said, leaning on her stick, creating a small space around them by her presence. "The last time I saw you, you and those two human women were boarding a plane for Shejidan, and they were bound for the island. How *are* they faring, nand' paidhi?"

"I hear from my companion from the ship, nand' dowager. She fares well, thank you."

"And nand' Hanks?"

Nand' Hanks, hell. Ilisidi *never* used honorifics for Deana Hanks. Bren's heart rate kicked up a notch and weariness with the noise went sailing on a sea of adrenaline.

"I don't hear from nand' Hanks, nand' dowager."

"Does your companion?"

"Aiji-ma." Bren took a deep breath. "How do you find the lilies?"

Ilisidi broke into a grin. "I was wondering how to get

you off to yourself, Bren-ji." She snagged his arm and drew him aside, and he could only go, trusting Jase to the security watching both of them.

"Neighbors will talk, aiji-ma."

"Become a scandal with me." She leaned on his arm and directed their steps toward the windows. "Ah, the city air. You should come back to Malguri."

"I wish that I could, aiji-ma."

"I think, if the schedule permits it, I shall invite the astronomer emeritus for a weekend at midsummer. *That* should prove interesting, don't you think?"

"The last I saw they were shooting at strangers, aiji-ma."

"They *need* new ideas. I would delight to have you at the gathering, nadi. Do consider it. Malguri in summer. Boating on the lake. —You should," the dowager added, with a wicked grin, "bring this nice young man. He has possibilities."

"Should I assist a rival to attain your interest, aiji-ma? I am devastated."

"Oh, but one hears that *you* have favored a certain member of your own household, nand' paidhi. Should I not take offense?"

He was appalled. Did she mean Barb, perhaps, or— God help him—Jago?

Dangerous territory. He was *never* certain whether Ilisidi's romantic fantasies were a joke, or just a hazardous degree serious.

"Aiji-ma. No one could possibly rival you. I've so missed our breakfasts together."

Ilisidi laughed and squeezed his arm. "Flatterer. I shall steal you away alone to Malguri in a lightning raid and simply not return you to my unappreciative grandson at all." Curtains billowed around them, and Ilisidi's face went grave. "So would Mospheira lock you away. *Beware* that woman."

"Hanks?"

"Hanks!" It had as well be an oath. "I warn you, beware her."

"I do. I do very much. —May I dare a question, aiji-ma? Should I also beware the lord of the Atageini?"

"Presumptuous, Bren-ji."

"I am very aware, aiji-ma. But I have never known you to lie to me."

"I've loaded your arms with lies, nadi! When in our dealings have there not been lies?"

"When I have relied on you for advice, aiji-ma. When I have truly cast myself on the truth inside your mazes you have *never* left me lost, aiji-ma."

"Oh, you thief of a woman's better sense! Flatterer, I say!"

"Wise woman, I say, aiji-ma, and cast myself utterly on your tolerance. Should I beware the lord of the Atageini?"

"Beware Direiso. As *he* must. As that scared fool Badissuni must."

"I entirely understand that."

"Wise *man*. Would that *Tatiseigi* did."

He almost threw into the mix a similar and equally urgent question about lord Geigi's current relations with Direiso, and with Tatiseigi, and instantly thought better of it. Geigi had ridden beside Ilisidi to the rescue, after Ilisidi had repeatedly and forcefully called Geigi a fool. He believed that in her riddling reply about Tatiseigi needing to beware of Direiso, Ilisidi had just told him the unriddling truth on three points: that something was going on, that Tatiseigi was still uncertain in his man'chi, that Direiso was very much a problem.

But regarding the matter of Geigi's relation to Ilisidi, Geigi might be a fish best left below the surface of that political water, where he could swim and conduct his affairs unseen.

It was Direiso on whose affairs Ilisidi might have information she was willing to share with him. In specific, she had signaled she would talk about Hanks, but he prepared a question, a simple, But what *of* Direiso and Tatiseigi—skirting around the fact of the departed Saigimi's wife's relationship to Geigi *and* to Direiso.

Badissuni and Tatiseigi were at the moment in converse, the topic of which seemed grim and urgent.

"Nand' paidhi," a servant came to him to say, and placed a note in his hand.

A male human on the phone, it said. Something wrong with his mother, was all he could think; and his face might have gone a shade paler. He might have looked as blank and stunned as he felt for a moment, blindsided out of a totally different universe.

14

"**D**ifficulty?" Ilisidi said to him.

"Forgive me. It's a phone call from Mospheira. It can wait." He was watching Badissuni and Tatiseigi as they spoke briefly, then moved apart, Tatiseigi instantly surrounded by the curious and less restrained, and people gazing in speculative curiosity at Badissuni, whom—God!—Tabini snagged for a small exchange.

And his mother—dammit, he needed to know.

"Go, go, go," Ilisidi said, "attend your phone call. Come back to me. I'll gather the gossip. Your mind is clearly distracted." Ilisidi's face betrayed no concern whatsoever. But her tone of command, sharp and absolute, told him he'd slipped his facial control and let things through he would rather not have allowed to the surface.

But he *wanted* the phone call. Ilisidi gave him leave. And might learn more than he could—or than she could with him attached.

He cast a worried look around for Jase, who was quietly in the corner, talking to his security and having no difficulty. Jago was watching him, and he coasted past Jago on the way to the door. "A phone call's come from the island," he said. "I'm going to the office. I'll be right back."

"Yes," Jago said, and tailed *him* as far as the door, when he'd been so bothered he hadn't even twigged to the possibility of a set-up to draw *him* to disaster. She stayed close, stationing herself in the hall as he went the short distance to the private office, at the door of which the servant stood.

He went in and picked up the phone. "Hello?" he said. "This is Bren Cameron."

"Bren, this is Toby." It was a tone of voice he almost didn't know. *"I thought I'd better call."*

"Damn right you'd better call. How are you? How's Mother?"

A pause that said far too much. *"Heart attack. Small one. How are you?"*

It was better than his worst fears. His knees weren't doing so well. He sat down. "I'm doing fine. Tell her that. Listen. I want you to call Barb and have her call me."

"No. No! You get yourself home, Bren. You want your damn business carried on, you come do it, and you come back and take care of the things you need to take care of! Stop asking your family to put up with this kind of crap! Mama's having surgery this week. She wants you, Bren. She wants you to be here."

"I can't."

"I can't be up here in the city, either, but I'm doing it! I can't leave my house and my business, but I'm doing it! Jill can't answer the phone without lunatics harassing her! We've had to leave home and all come up here, and I can't let my family go down the street to the park! You know what put mama in the hospital, Bren? You did. People throwing paint on her building, the landlord saying he wants her to move—"

He tried to think through the things he didn't want to hear to the things he *had* to hear—while remembering agencies on both sides of the water were recording everything. "Toby. Call my office. Ask Shawn—"

"I've done that! I can't get through! None of the numbers you've given me work any more, and I don't even know whether Shawn's in office this week, by what I'm hearing in the papers!"

"What's in the papers, Toby? They don't exactly—"

"No, no, no! I'm not doing your work for you! I'm your brother, *not a clerk in the State Department! And I want you back here, Bren. I want you back here for*

mama! *One week, one miserable* week, *that's all I want!"*

"I can't."

"The hell you can't! Tell the aiji your mother could die, dammit, *and she's asking for you!"*

"Toby—"

"Oh—hell, I forgot. You can't explain *feelings, can you? They're not wired for it. Well,* what about you, Bren? *Is it all the office, and* nothing *for your family?"*

"Toby."

"I don't want your excuses, Bren. I've covered for you and covered for you and not told you the truth because it'd upset you. Well, now I'm telling you the truth, and mama's in danger of her life and I can't take my family home, and I'm scared to death they're going to burn my house down while I'm gone!"

"Just hang on, Toby. Just a little longer."

"I can't! I'm not willing to, dammit! I'm tired of trying to explain what the hell you're doing! We can't explain it to ourselves *anymore—how in* hell *do we make it make sense to the neighbors!"*

"You know damn well what the score is, Toby. Don't hand me that. You *know* what's going on in the government and what game they're playing."

"What are you talking about? What are you talking about, Bren? That we're *the enemy, now?"*

"I'm saying call Shawn!"

"I'm saying Shawn's number doesn't work anymore and the police won't answer our emergency calls, Bren, try that one! You're not damn popular, and they're taking it out on my family and our mother!"

"Wrong. *Wrong,* Toby! It's not the whole island, it's a handful of crawling cowards that on a bright day—"

"These are our neighbors, *Bren. These are my* neighbors *that aren't speaking to me, people I've known for ten years!"*

"Then get yourself a new set of friends, Toby!"

"That doesn't work for mama, Bren, that doesn't work in the building she's lived in for all these years and now they don't want her any more. What does that do to her, Bren? What do you say to that?"

"It's a rotten lot of people you've fallen for."

"What are you talking about? What *are you talking about, Bren? I don't understand you."*

He grew accustomed to silence on his feelings. He was a translator, a technical translator, by necessity a diplomat, by cooption a lord of the atevi Association. And he spoke out of hurt and anger on the most childish possible level, maybe because that was the mental age this argument touched, the last time he and Toby *had* accessed what they felt. Toby had moved out to the coast. He'd thought then, and still thought, it was to put space between Toby and their mother. *He*'d gone into University, and aptitudes had steered him toward what the job was supposed to be, which hadn't been this.

"Tell mama I love her," he said, and hung up on his brother.

That little click of the receiver broke the vital connection, and he knew there wasn't a way to get it back. The training didn't let expression reach his face. The training didn't let him do anything overt. He just sat there a moment, with an atevi lady's office coming back into focus around him, and the sounds of the party going on above the silence that click had created, and with the knowledge he had to get up and function with very dangerous people and go be sure Jase was all right.

And he had to finish his talk with Ilisidi, somehow, get the wit organized to regain that mood and that moment and do his job.

If you couldn't do anything about a vital matter, you postponed it. You put it in a mental box and shut the lid on it and didn't think about it when there was a job to do.

And once he'd done that, damn it! He was mad at Toby, who *knew* things about the government Toby could have told him, critical things, and Toby hadn't, wouldn't, no matter whether peace or war could hinge on it. Toby's peace was unsettled, Toby's life was put out of joint, Toby came at him with *personal* grievances of a sort the family had once known to keep

away from him—which Toby could have been man
enough to hold to himself this week and handle,
dammit, since there wasn't and wouldn't be anything
he could do from where he was.

But it had been a succession of weeks. Toby was getting tired of holding it.

Jago appeared in the doorway. She had her com in
hand. Had been using it, he thought, maybe even following the conversation via a relay from the foyer-area
security station. Surveillance here, in these premises,
was always close, and lately it was overt, just one of
those jobs his staff did to be up on things without
having them explained.

Sometimes that was a good thing.

"The aiji is aware, nadi-ji."

Not Bren-ji, not the familiar; but the still-remote
formal combined with the personal address. Jago was
being official. He was grateful for the professional distance. It was a damn sight more consideration than his
brother managed.

"My man'chi," he said, going to the heart of what he
was sure would worry atevi, "is still to the office and
the aiji, nadi. You may tell him that."

"He wishes to speak to you, but cannot leave the
breakfast room without notice nor speak to you intimately there. He says, through your security, that
though he has said so before, now he urges your acceptance of his offer: at any time of your choosing, you
may bring your household to the mainland and he will
establish a place and lands for them, nadi-ji, as fits the
house of a man of your stature. If you ask, he will make
strong request to the Mospheiran government to secure
their immediate passage across the strait, with all their
goods and belongings. He is aware of the demands of
those of your house, and your difficult position, nadi-ji,
and is willing to take the strongest action to secure
their safety."

"Tell him—" The last time Tabini had moved to
secure something from the Mospheiran government, he
had threatened to shoot Deana Hanks if they didn't get
him back in twenty-four hours. Tabini's offer was not

without international consequences. And not without force behind it, though he didn't know what human official Tabini could tell them he'd shoot this time. "Tell him I am grateful. Tell him—I hold his regard as the most important, even—" He almost said—above my family's good opinion; and knew that circumstances and duty had made it true. Now anger and bitter hurt almost confirmed it. "Even above my life, nadi. Tell him that. And I will come back to the gathering when I have composed myself, which should be only a moment."

"I shall tell him that, nadi."

Jago was gone from the doorway, then, giving him the grace of privacy, but he was sure she'd gone no further than the hall outside to relay the message. And to achieve that composed manner he tried to widen his focus, to remind himself how very much was at issue, for three nations counting the ship Jase represented; and what a very extraordinary honor Tabini had offered him.

It was done for state reasons, he had to remind himself. For the same damn reasons of state that had put him in the position he was in.

He'd hung up on his brother.

And wouldn't be home.

Fact. Fact. Fact. There was nothing that could change it, nothing that would get the barrier between peoples down any faster than the things he was doing. So it was two deep breaths and back to work.

He got to his feet and walked out into the hall, where as he expected, Jago was waiting; and where, in the distance, the television interviews were going on, with a scatter of the guests down there in the bright lights. He walked with Jago back into the crowded breakfast room, in which alcohol and alkaloids as well as the sweets were beginning to be a factor and the simple noise of conversation was beginning to sound like the subway below the building. Jase was still safe where he'd left him; and, not willing at this moment to talk to Jase or answer human questions, he tended toward Tabini, who was with Damiri, with Banichi, too.

Tabini's regular security was at the moment hovering much closer to Tatiseigi, who was talking to Ilisidi.

"Aiji-ma," Bren said quietly with a slight bow. "I heard your generous offer. I will present it at my first opportunity, but—" His wits unraveled. "I don't know how to persuade them, aiji-ma. I wish that I could."

"It seems to me," Damiri said, "that this is a trap, nand' paidhi. They *wish* you to become concerned and to go there. This attack on your mother's residence is not unrelated to this pressure on the Association and the outrageous behavior of your government. I even suspect the death of Jase's father, but I know no design to make of it."

He felt himself increasingly in shock, and *willing* to make patterns where possibly none existed. He dealt with atevi. And to the atevi mind there were patterns he could see, too, dire and threatening patterns; but he dealt so deeply in the language now he feared his own suspicions. "I know none, either, daja-ma, but I shall certainly think deeply on it."

Another person moved up to speak to the aiji, a lord of the northwest coast, who was clearly waiting his turn, and he was, he decided, done with the things he could say. To be replaced was at the moment a relief from having to think in atevi complexity. He moved aside with the due and automatic courtesies—

And encountered lord Badissuni.

"Nandi," he said.

"Nand' paidhi." The thin, unhappy lord looked sternly down at him. "Your security, one wishes to say, is highly accurate."

What did one say? His heart was racing. "They *are* Guild, nandi."

"Two of you, now," the lord said. "Does Hanks speak for you?"

"By no means, nand' Badissuni. I disapprove of her adventures and she wishes me dead."

"So one hears," Badissuni said. "*Is* this faster-than-light a lie?"

"No, nandi."

"Will this ship fly?"

"I have no doubt, nandi. There is *no* deception."

"One was curious," Badissuni said, and strayed off without another word.

More than damned curious. People were staring at him. He had the feeling he'd been used for display. A political prop. Talk to the paidhi. Be seen to talk to the paidhi. As he'd been *seen* to talk with Tatiseigi and everyone else available. He didn't see Jago. He didn't think she'd approve his being used; and perhaps neither would Tabini, who'd nevertheless invited the man.

He retreated to the corner next to the doorway, next to a porcelain stand for abandoned drink glasses, where Jase, drink in hand, stood talking with his security, Dureni.

"What was *that?*" Jase asked. "Is anything wrong?"

A flash of dark and pale green advised him of someone of the house beside him, and he turned to find lord Tatiseigi himself under Ilisidi's relentless escort, bound past them, he was sure, toward the interview area just outside.

"Everything all right?" Jase asked, and in that sense, yes, he was relieved to think.

Then something popped.

Security moved. *Everyone* moved. Tatiseigi and Ilisidi were in the doorway and he didn't think—he just shoved Jase to the floor as Jase was diving toward lord Tatiseigi in the doorway.

Lord Tatiseigi continued to the floor along with others diving of their own volition—Bren was down, half sheltered by Dureni; everyone was low; and an apparently unarmed security around the aiji had turned into a crouched, gun-bearing battle-line.

"A lightbulb exploded!" someone shouted from the interview area beyond the door, where indeed a deep and startling shadow had fallen. The lily room burst into relieved laughter, and more laughter, amid a murmur of disgust from Dureni and an apology as Dureni hoped he hadn't hurt him.

"By no means," Bren said, accepting a hand up.

Jase, meanwhile, was in very intimate contact with a very offended lord Tatiseigi as lights flared in the doorway, and the television cameras, a live broadcast, swept over the confusion, Tatiseigi, struggling to rise—and Jase, who got to his feet with more agility.

"Nandi," Jase said faintly, edging backward, attempting to efface himself. But the camera tracked him relentlessly as the documentary reporter with a microphone turned up at Jase's shoulder.

"Nand' paidhi," the reporter said, "an exciting moment."

"I think dangerous," Jase answered quite correctly, and Bren reached him, seized his arm, and propelled him back out of the spotlight, as lord Tatiseigi also escaped the cameras. "He wishes to convey his apology, nand' Tatiseigi, and his profound concern." He didn't mention that the fall had happened partly because Tatiseigi had shown no reluctance to trample others underfoot reaching the door; and Jase had, indeed, tried to carry an adult ateva to the floor to protect him.

"Certainly it might have been more serious," Tabini said. In the tail of Bren's eye, Tabini came walking cheefully in among those who had hit the floor, including a wryly amused Ilisidi, whom Cenedi was helping to her feet. "Grandmother-ji?"

"Certainly an exciting party," Ilisidi said, and the cameras were still going in the doorway. "What for dessert, nandi?"

There was general laughter. And Tabini, never slower than his grandmother, as the camera's glaring eye carried it across the continent: "Nand' Tatiseigi! Good, good and fast! Our first line of defense, and damned well restrained, I say, of the lord of the Atageini, or there'd *be* no cameramen standing. My father used to call you the best shot in the valley, did he not, nandi?" Tabini waved his hand at the cameraman in the doorway. "Out, out, nadiin! You and your exploding lights! Take them out, *out!* You've seen the lilies! You've leaned over our shoulders long enough, you! Let us enjoy our evening!"

That was the aiji's word. The aiji's security intervened more directly, and the lights on which the cameras relied went out, all at once; someone had gotten the fuse. Lights died, cameras retreated.

Bren realized he had a death grip on Jase's arm and let go.

"It's all right," he said to Jase in Mosphei'.

But Jase retorted in Ragi, "I thought they were shopping."

There was an immediate and embarrassed silence. Then laughter from those in earshot.

"Shooting," Jase said, and went red. And fled out the door and hardly got out of sight before security bounced him back, angry and confused.

Lord Badissuni, disheveled and distraught, sat in a chair by a potted plant and looked overcome, possibly with premonition, or a recollection of gunfire.

"It's all right, Jase," Bren said. "You did all right."

"Toward the Atageini," someone near them had remarked. "Did you note that? Toward the Atageini, would you think so?"

Lord Tatiseigi himself was talking and joking, albeit shakily, with Ilisidi, and with Damiri. Tabini was talking with the Minister of Defense, in a very serious mode; and madam Saidin went over to the lord of the Atageini, as did others, to express their hopes that he was unhurt.

Likely the news service was embarrassed, too, and frightened. "Jago-ji," Bren said, "one wishes the news services to mention the matter in a good light. Tell nand' Saidin so."

"One understands," Jago said, and moved over to speak quietly with madam Saidin, who nodded, looked toward her lady's human guests, and then took herself outside, where he trusted Atageini diplomacy was well up to the task of reassuring the reporters. Jago went there, too, and then Cenedi, and Naidiri, of Tabini's personal guard.

Jase was very quiet. But Jago came back to say that the camera crew was greatly reassured. "We're putting junior security in charge and offering the camera crew the formal dining room. Nand' Saidin has ordered trays of food and drink and asked them not to cross the security perimeter. Nand' Naidiri has assured them of the aiji's good will and suggested an interview with the Atageini."

The adrenaline that had been running began to settle down. The television coverage had been scheduled to go on only another half hour. It was a consequence of the evening that the lord of the Atageini had not gone on television *in* the historic apartment, *in* his planned interview regarding the lilies, but there might have been worse consequences, and *no* one could be at fault for a bad bulb and the reaction in a roomful of hair-triggered Guild.

Lesser lords and dignitaries began to come to speak to the paidhiin, and one, Parigi of some western township, asked the delicate, the almost unaskable question, "One did remark, nand' paidhi, that the paidhiin moved to protect the house."

He'd moved because he thought Jase didn't know the danger; and Jase had dived for the Atageini probably because he'd had it dinned into him how important Tatiseigi was. Maybe it *did* say something to atevi how Jase had thought instantly to protect the Atageini lord. But it didn't say at all what atevi thought it did.

"He doesn't speak fluently, nand' Parigi, but I think it startled everyone. And Jase-paidhi knew lord Tatiseigi might be intended; remember we're human and draw no conclusions about man'chi—we often startle ourselves with man'chi, isn't that what they say in the machimi?"

"Certainly it startled me," lord Parigi laughed. "And my daughter, who's plagued me for a year to attend a court party, was quite sure we were *in* a machimi ourselves—perhaps a little more excitement than we country folk are used to."

He could almost relax with such people. And with the good will offered. "Is this your daughter?" She was at the gawky stage, all the height, not enough weight yet: all elbows and knees. But excited, oh, very. "I'm very greatly honored. Nand' Jase, this is the—eldest?

Is it the eldest? Daughter of lord Parigi. Caneso, do I remember correctly? From—"

"Laigin, lord paidhi." The young lady was delighted to be addressed by someone technically a lord, but not landed; and he chose not to notice the gaffe at all: refreshing that an ateva could mistake such a thing.

"And this is your first time in Shejidan?" Jase asked her.

If anything, spirits were higher, the alcohol went down faster, and when a (fortunately not historic) glass dropped and broke on the tiles, there was laughter. The teenager laughed when she saw others laughing, and her father found occasion to steer her away.

"For a party on this floor," Ilisidi said, coasting by, "this is riotous and unrestrained. It will *never* equal harvest dances in Malguri. —Ja-son-paidhi, Tatiseigi will survive the rescue."

"Is the lord angry?" Jase managed to ask for himself, and remembered to add, "Nandi?"

"He will recover, I say." One didn't—ever—press Ilisidi on first acquaintance, even if one did limp through the language, and Ilisidi's reply was curt and less delighted. "Come, Bren-paidhi, I will make you make amends for your importunate associate." The latter as she caught Bren by the arm and drew him, perforce, with her.

"I should keep Jase in sight, nand' dowager."

"Oh, he's there." Ilisidi took him, to his dismay, to Tatiseigi himself. "Indulge his lordship, who wishes to ask you direct questions."

"I do no such thing," Tatiseigi muttered, and it might have been time to beat a retreat, or it might be the worst time to do so. Ilisidi did not play pranks on this scale. And Ilisidi, damn her, was off and escaped from the confrontation.

"Nandi," Bren said, and bowed and searched the bottom of his resources for compliments. "Your quickness and your forbearance with a young and mistaken person were very apparent to everyone."

"His foolishness was *apparent,* nand' paidhi!"

"He cast himself between you and expected harm,

knowing your great importance to the aiji. Unfortunately—he lacks the grace and the mass of the Guild."

"Importance to the aiji, is it, nadi? With my niece in *bed* with the upstart of Taiben! And the dowager no better—attaching herself to humans and astronomers."

"I fear my regard in your eyes must be far less, then, since I regard the people you name with great respect and must defend them."

"Humans! Makers of machines! Polluters of the good air! Defilers of the land! The ether of space itself isn't safe from you!"

"Not defiled by *my* work, nandi. *Not* by my work." The lord of the Atageini had raised his voice to him. He came back in kind, which might be a misjudgment, but the dowager apparently got along with this man, and Ilisidi backed up for no one. "I hope for the good of atevi *and* humans to come from the work I do, lord Tatiseigi. So does Jase, who *wears* no bulletproof vest. Good *evening,* nandi."

Tatiseigi went so far as to seize his sleeve. Unprecedented, and commanding his attention at a disadvantage of size and strength. Atevi eyes reflected, catching the light just so, and Tatiseigi's shimmered gold.

"Defilers, I say."

"No, lord of the Atageini. And still bearing good will to you despite your attacks."

"Why? Are you a fool?"

"No, nandi. I do so because of the aiji-dowager, who has defended your interests to the aiji and to others and advised *me* to do so."

"Oh, the aiji-dowager, is it? Do her tastes run so *small?*"

No ateva in a polite setting had ever delivered him an insult of that kind, not on a personal level.

"I am devastated," he said with all the coldness he could muster. "She spoke well of *you.*"

"Impudence."

"Nadi." He had never envisioned addressing a lord of the Association in that style of hostile equals on the field, either. But he did. Nor had Tatiseigi once let go of his sleeve. "You will disappoint your niece."

"How?"

"Because *she* also has spoken well of you. I assure you the ship-paidhi thought only to rescue you. That the cameras caught it was either unfortunate *or* an opportunity. *I* being a representative of governments advise you, nandi, to take your security, visit the reporters, and conduct the interview in the dining room. Such a report will air as often as the other, it will still be within these perimeters, it will often be rebroadcast because it will show yet another room of this historic residence. And, *and,* I advise you speak well of nand' Jase in order to erase the memory of a mutual indignity before millions. Play the part instead of a lord protected by one of the paidhiin at risk of his life!"

There was utter silence. The music played. The conversation continued around them.

"Impudent, I say."

"For the dowager's sake, I give you my advice unasked."

"For her sake I consider it and not the source." Tatiseigi let him go and stared at him. He stared back, having to look up to do it.

Then he became aware, to his utter consternation, that Tabini was and had been behind him.

"I also counsel you do so, lord Tatiseigi," Tabini said. "Your niece will stand beside you. So will the ship-paidhi."

In support of her uncle. A thunderbolt. Perhaps made necessary by what Jase had done. But a solution, all the same.

He looked for Jase, who occupied the same corner beside the door as before, with his security, but with a small cluster of guests near him. He asked his leave, and went over to Jase and explained the situation.

Jase didn't say much, except, in Mosphei', "I thought he was in danger. What do they *want* from me?"

"A good appearance," he said. "The lord is willing."

"I can't do this," Jase said in a tone of panic.

"Yes, you will," Bren said. "You *will,* Jase. You have to."

"No," Jase said quietly, and at that moment *Jago* caught his attention.

"Nand' paidhi," Jago said, attracting his attention, and he went aside, next to the porcelain lilies' most extravagant display, the north wall, one of those sections that had remained largely untouched, and where a large potted plant afforded a buffer from the crowd and a quiet place for whispers. "Nand' paidhi, I dislike to bring another matter to you, but the boy from Dur has come a second time into the subway."

"Oh, *damn!*" He'd spoken in Mosphei', having done it with Jase, and for a moment went blank.

"The boy," Jago said, "is in very serious trouble with the Bu-javid guards. He was warned. He saw the news coverage, apparently from a hotel down the hill. He has checked into three."

"What, hotels?"

"His behavior, nand' paidhi, has been entirely suspicious. The boy has checked into three hotels to throw security off his track."

"A boy that young—"

"I have not met him. He is not Guild. The moves he is making are provocative of very serious consequences."

"How serious?"

"There was gunfire, nand' paidhi. He did stop when ordered, for which one is very grateful. I understand he was hit by a masonry chip and that blood was drawn. Damage was done to the ceramics in the station and to a subway car, for which he will be held accountable. I haven't been down there. But I have asked them not to charge him yet, knowing your involvement. What do you order us to do?"

"Am I qualified to judge? Have I *caused* this boy's reckless behavior, Jago-ji?"

"Nand' paidhi, *I* think the fault is, as Banichi is wont to say, *far* too much television. The boy is ashamed to go home without the plane and without your release from feud. To him, at his age, this is great tragedy. To his father, this latest incident will be a disgrace that *will* indeed harm him in his dealings. The boy is coming to realize this and, being young, is now *truly* desperate."

"If I write the boy a card, with a ribbon, will he go home?"

"I hesitate to reward such foolishness but, if you will write it, nand' paidhi, I will send it down with one of the juniors. I will not have this boy's death attached to your name, nadi-ji, and some of the guards imagine him as Guild. Three hotels, paidhi-ji."

"But you know definitively he isn't."

"Not in remotest possibility."

"I'll sign the card." The lady's office had the more traditional wax-jack. The security office had a high-speed device that didn't require live flame. He started toward the door.

And missed Jase. Who was not where he'd been.

"Has Jase gone to the interview area?" he asked Jago, who talked to her pocket com.

"The lady's office. He's attempted to use the phone, nadi."

He stopped cold, at a place where an ateva lady felt free to brush close and say, "Nand' paidhi, *such* an interesting party, isn't it? The paidhiin were *very* brave."

For a moment he couldn't think, not where he was, not where he was going, in a room otherwise filled with people all towering head and shoulders above his head, through a doorway blocked by such people. He wanted air and a sane space for thought, and knew that Jago was following him. He found a gap and went through it and out the door.

"Be careful, nadi-ji," Jago said, overtaking him in the quieter, cooler air of the hall; she had the pocket com in hand.

"Who is he talking *to,* Jago-ji?"

"To the station at Mogari-nai. To the ship. But the call didn't go through. Our office stopped it."

He was less alarmed. He could use the wax-jack in the little office. The device had a lighter. He could talk sense to Jase in private.

"He's hung up," Jago said before they reached the door.

And when they reached the door and walked in, there were blowing white curtains, past the tapestry and needlework side panels that curtained the balcony and the dark.

But no Jase.

Jago moved. He thrust out a hand and prevented her, knowing, he decided in the next heartbeat, that Jase was in a mood, and that atevi intervention might gain compliance, but not a lot of information.

"I'll get him in," he said to Jago, and approached the balcony carefully, as Jago would.

From that vantage he could see Jase, in the dark, hands on the balcony rim, gazing up at the sky. And he *knew* it wasn't a situation into which Jago should venture. He said to her, "Nadi-ji, please find the card I need," hoping that Jase would think their intrusion wasn't directed at him. And he ventured into the dark, knowing Jago wasn't liking his being near that window, or even near Jase.

Jase gave him only a scant glance, and looked again out over the city.

Jase, who hadn't done well under the daytime sky. It was, as far as he knew, the first time Jase had stood under the sky since he'd arrived.

The balcony where the party was spilled light and music into the night.

"No stars," Jase said after a moment of them standing there.

"City lights. It's getting worse in Shejidan."

"What is?"

"Haze of smoke. Lights burning at night. Neon lights. Light scatters in the atmosphere till it blots out the stars."

"You can't see them on the ship, either," Jase said.

"I suppose that's true." He'd never really reckoned it. He was vaguely disappointed.

"I just—know my ship is up there. And I can't see it."

"I have. But it was in the country. No lights out there."

"From the ocean can one see the stars?"

"I think one could."

"I want to go there."

"Come inside. You're in danger. You *know* you're in danger. Get inside, dammit."

There was a long silence. He expected Jase to say he didn't care, or some such emotional outburst. But Jase instead left the rail and walked with him back into the light of the office, where Jago had the wax-jack burning and the card ready.

"I have to make out a card," Bren said, and sat down at the desk. He welcomed the chance to do something extraneous to the worst problem, namely Jase's state of mind. He was glad to offer Jase and himself alike a chance to calm down before they did talk. He wrote, for the boy from Dur,

Please accept my assurances of good will toward you and your house, and my hopes that the paidhiin will enjoy yours. I will remember your earnest wishes for good relations to the aiji himself, with my recommendation for his consideration. From the hand of,

Bren Cameron, paidhi-aiji, under the seal of my office.

Cards were more commonly just the signature, the seal, the ribbon. This one, with a personal message, was calculated to be a face-saving note the boy could take to his father in lieu of the impounded airplane. He hinted that he might intercede, and that Tabini, who had the power to release the plane, might consider forgiveness for a parental request. He didn't know what more he could do. He folded it and stamped it with his seal, and gave it to Jago to pass on.

"Now," he said to Jase. "The interview."

"May I speak with you, nadi."

"Jago-ji, will you maintain position in the hall for a moment?"

"Yes," Jago said, and went.

Which left the two of them, him seated, Jase standing. There was a chair by the corner of the desk and Jase sank into it, pale and tense.

"Bren," he began, in Mosphei', and Bren kept his

mouth shut, figuring that confession was imminent. He waited, and Jase waited, and finally Jase took to hard breathing and helpless waves of the hand, wishing him to talk.

He didn't. He sat there. He let Jase work through his wordless, helpless phase.

Finally Jase was down to wiping his eyes surreptitiously and shaking like a leaf.

"Going to foul up?" Bren asked with conscious bluntness.

"Yes!" Jase said fiercely, and not another word for another few moments of hard breathing.

"Going to panic?" Bren asked, wary of an unwarned punch and the fragile antiques around them. He nipped out the wick on the wax-jack with his bare fingers, ignoring the sting of fire and hot wax.

Jase didn't answer him. He stood up, put the wax-jack in the cabinet where it belonged, and walked to the other side of the little space, psychologically to give Jase room.

"They worked quite a while to choose me," Bren said finally. "I warned you. I was picked out of a large population, because I *can* take it. Can't find a word, can you? Totally mute? Can't understand half I'm saying?"

Silence from Jase, desperate, helpless silence.

Jase had hit the immersion zero-point. *No* communication. Total mental disorganization, for the first time, not for the last.

"I want you," he said to Jase in Ragi, "to go to that interview, say, yes, lord Tatiseigi, no lord Tatiseigi, thank you lord Tatiseigi. That's a very simple thing. Do you understand?"

A faint nod. The very earliest words were coming back into focus, yes, no, thank you. Do you understand?

"I want you to go to that room. I want you to be polite. Do you understand?"

A nod. A second, more certain nod. Fear. Stark fear.

"I," Jase said very carefully. "Will. But—"

"But—"

For another moment Jase didn't—couldn't speak, just froze, wordless.

And *that* wasn't going to do the program, the aiji, or the interview any good. Jase had reached that point, that absolute white-out of communication students of the language tended to reach in which things didn't make sense to him, in which the brain—he had no other explanation—was undergoing a massive data reorganization and stringing new cable in the mental basement, God only knew.

He reached for a bribe. The best he had.

"I want you," he said, "to do this, and I swear I'll get you to the ocean. Trust me. I asked that before. I'm asking it now."

There was no answer. But it was more than a bribe. It was close to a necessity. He *knew* the state Jase was in, and he was going to sweat until he'd gotten Jase off the air.

"Yes," Jase said in a shuddery voice.

"Good." He didn't chatter. He didn't offer Jase big words at the moment. He just gestured, got Jase on his feet and to the door and out into the hall.

"Are they set up down there?" he asked Jago.

"Yes," Jago said, having her pocket com in evidence, and going with them. "As soon as they remove lord Badissuni. The man's taken ill."

He was startled. Dismayed. "*Is* he ill?" he asked.

"Quite honestly, nadi." There were tones Jago took that told him it was the real and reliable truth. "It seems to be stress. They're taking him to the hospital for the night."

Amazing what bedfellows politics had made. It made a sensible man careful of making any rash statements about anyone, sharp-edged words being so hard to digest.

Tatiseigi stood in the lights, reporting the absolutely ridiculous and totally true fact of a security alert downstairs, which had turned out to be explained, and somehow never mentioning that the culprit was a young boy from the islands.

Then Tatiseigi wended his way into a report that security had been on edge, and that all threats had been dealt with.

Tabini, who had used the newfangled airwaves quite shamelessly to justify his positions, could take notes from this performance. Tatiseigi, who publicly decried the deleterious effects of the national obsession with television and machimi actors, by what the paidhi had heard, who had spoken against extending television into new licenses, certainly knew the value of it.

"I will tell you," he began, traditional opening of a topic, and launched into the matter of his restorations, his programs, the history of the Atageini. It was an unprecedented chance for one of the houses. Tatiseigi went on into historic marriages, about the relations of the Atageini to the founders of the capital at She-jidan—and then, with Damiri standing beside him, as Jase also did, he talked about the Atageini "venturing into a future of great promise and adventurous prospect."

My God, Bren thought, listening to it, looking at the picture it presented to a watching world. It was almost a declaration of support for the space program.

It was damned near a declaration *for* Tabini and *against* Direiso and the Kadigidi and all their plots.

Certainly, long and soporific as the history had been, it had snapped to a sharp and dangerous point, right there, in three carefully chosen words: future, adventurous, and prospect, meaning the hitherto changeless and conservative Atageini were shifting into motion; and the so-named *prospect* was going to refer in some minds, with Damiri visible before them, to heirs and marriage and the final merger of two Padi Valley families of vast power, a merger that might firm up the political picture very suddenly.

Very frighteningly so for some interests, Direiso chief among them.

Not mentioning Ilisidi with her ties to the distant and often rebel East.

The old tyrant had intended this when he'd headed for that room and the lightbulb blew. He'd been wound up for the bitter necessity of peace with Tabini, consoled by the chance for public glory, and then embarrassed by a human.

Thank *God* he'd gotten this chance, this bit of theater. He could only imagine with what fervor the man *hadn't* wanted his niece *and* the aforesaid human on stage with him.

Bet that a speech of this magnitude had been set in the man's mind before he came up here and that the alternative was not to give it, and to keep balancing peace and war with Tabini and dancing a slow dance with Tabini's enemies. He'd suggested a change from the infelicitous venue down at the small dining room, for this area, and no matter how irreverent an ateva grew, there was still that cultural and public reluctance to accept a place or a set-up for an event if that place had been tainted by ill fortune.

Hence this set-up in the state dining room, still within the apartment, proving that *humans* were not the infelicitous item, with a human, emblematic of change, right there beside the conservative lord. And with Damiri, the tie to Tabini who might wish to supplant him, standing right there by him, the old man got to the fore of the rebellion in his own house and did it with style—on national television.

He didn't know whether he'd helped at all or whether Tabini had come to rescue a rash human or to propose exactly the same things; but Tabini would at least be glad *he* hadn't had to get into a verbal brawl with the old man.

Who might well wish the paidhi's head on the ancestral battlements. *Two* paidhiin, infelicitous two, might urge that as a solution.

He kept smiling. He kept smiling as he rescued Jase, who was practically wordless after the event, but who'd responded appropriately during it. He fed Jase a stiff shot of alcohol before putting him in the hands of his security, which gained *him* the silence and the window of opportunity to reach Ilisidi.

"Aiji-ma," he said with a deep bow to her and her chief of security, Cenedi, "aiji-ma, I have an urgent request, a very extravagant request, which I must make of you foremost of all; and also of your grandson. If I have *any* favors unclaimed, hear me at least. I know I am too extravagant. But I have no other resource—as your grandson, having no other resource, came to you under very similar circumstances."

Ilisidi's eyes were a record of years lived and intrigues survived. And her mouth quirked in amusement. "You've just murdered the lord of the Atageini in his own dining room and wish asylum?"

"Almost," he said. "Very close, aiji-ma."

15

"**N**and' paidhi," the Bu-javid operator said. "I can't establish the connection. One fears—there is some reason beyond a failure of equipment."

"Thank you, nadi. One believes the same." He set the receiver back in the cradle and heard distantly in the house the noise of steps on the stone floors of the foyer. Their household was gathering for their departure, unaware of the phone call he couldn't resist attempting and which he foreknew wouldn't get through, no more than the rest had.

Baji-naji, chance and fortune, the devils in the design: symbolically they existed somewhere in every atevi building as they did in every design for action. The random numbers of creativity, serendipity or destruction lurked within the rigid system of numbers, and once a design gave them leeway to work, the building tumbled down, a situation acquired additional possibilities, or the world tumbled into a new order of things.

He couldn't raise the island, let alone get a call through to Toby or his mother's house.

And that was no equipment failure. That was politics *keeping* him from making that call, and like a fool he'd hung up on Toby in their last conversation. Toby had been able to call him, but he couldn't get past the blockade in the other direction.

Or Toby couldn't reach him, either.

He'd resorted to sleeping pills since the conversation with the dowager, medications from the island, carefully hoarded since the repair to his shoulder. There'd been, after his brief talk with Ilisidi, a flurry of phone calling and rescheduling legislative meetings, which consumed an entire day.

But, good part of the operation, Jase grew more cheerful—as if the promise he'd been able to keep had gotten him past the depression and the despair. Jase was going to the ocean. He would see the sea. They'd talked last night of fishing, not from Geigi's port but from a more protected, governmentally owned site on the reserve across the same bay.

"Maybe we'll have a chance at the yellowtail," he'd said to Jase, although he was by no means certain the run of those fish would carry within the bay. Among the myriad other things he did keep up with, marine fish weren't within his field. Toby would have known.

But he couldn't ask the first question he'd had in years that Toby would have delighted in answering.

So with the appropriate baggage, just as a second dawn was breaking, they were gathering in the foyer for the promised trip—Banichi and Jago, Tano and Algini.

And himself with Jase.

"The baggage has gone, Bren-ji," Jago said. "The car is waiting."

Subway car, that was. His security was in a good mood: it lifted his spirits—shifted the world back into perspective. It was an emergency at home, yes; but, dammit, Toby could handle it—Toby was in the city, Toby was at their mother's apartment. Toby could deal with their mother and Toby didn't have to call him up and rage at him, when it was the first damn time *Toby* had showed up to handle one of their mother's crises, be it the divorce from their father, be it the lawsuit over the sale of the mountain cabin, be it aunt Gloria's husband's funeral, be it—God knew what. *This* time Toby was on duty and Toby could take care of their mother and the two of them could do the talking they should have done when Toby'd married to get away from the family and run off to live on the north shore having kids and making money hand over fist. Toby was the one she'd held up to him as the model son—well-married, stable, somebody to go visit.

Mother'd held Toby and Toby's familial situation up to him as the way *he* ought to be, but she'd damned sure phoned the University every time there was a crisis to get *Bren* across town. That was understandable, since it was in the same city; but even after he'd gone into the field and the strait had separated them, she'd not phoned the north shore for Toby to disturb his family, come home, and hire a lawyer for her. No, Toby'd had a *family* to consider, so she'd phoned the mainland and wanted *Bren-dear* to drop the governmental crisis and come home and fix things, which sometimes he could and sometimes he hadn't been able to. For a string of years every time he'd come home on vacation she'd had a crisis specifically designed to get him involved the second he stepped off the plane, to the point where he'd begun to think of marriage to Barb as an insulation.

It had gotten so his nerves were strung tight every time he knew his mother needed something, because *need* had gotten to be the relationship between them, and he'd already puzzled out that fact.

It had gotten to be the relationship between him and Barb, too, starting with *his* increasing need for her to meet that plane and shield him from his inability to say no. Someday he'd have married her so he'd have a wife to take precedence over what his mother needed. He'd puzzled that out, too.

Grim thought. Sobering thought. He could get aggravated with Barb, but the fact was that his cheerfulness once he'd arranged for Barb to meet the plane, the alternative being his mother arriving with a list of grievances and plans for his time, told him maybe—just maybe—his relationship to Barb breaking down in crisis wasn't just a case of Barb rushing to Paul Saarinson's soft life. Barb, being a healthy individual, had perhaps realized she wasn't up to being a support for a man who got off the plane every few months *needing* to be reassured and *needing* to be made happy and not to have troubles poured into his ears during his vacation.

The paidhi's home life and the paidhi's love life were neither one damn good and never had been, was the truth. The *I-need-you* business was no way for any two adults to have a relationship, not mother-son, not man-wife.

Not even brothers.

And it was about time their mother learned to call on Toby, because Toby was the one of her two sons she was going to have in reach; and it was about time Toby learned to define that relationship in a way he could live with. That was the plain truth. And they were all going to have to get used to it. She couldn't get Bren-dear home again.

Maybe duty to his family said he should resign his professional life, come home and live with it and do all those familial, loyal things, including suffer through a marital relationship that wouldn't work and a relationship with his mother that wasn't going to improve, and maybe it would improve his moral character to do that.

But it wasn't his job. It wasn't what other, equally important individuals relied on him doing for reasons a lot more important to the world than his personal problems. And he rather thought, as much trouble as it might make for the family, he should tip Toby off to the *need-you* business and the fact he was entitled to put his foot down and define his relationship with mama otherwise—early—before it ate Toby alive.

"Bren-ji?" Jago asked as he took his place in the elevator car.

"Tired," he said. "Tired, Jago-ji." He managed a cheerful face. "Time for a week on leave."

Banichi pressed the button. The elevator carried them down, down to the cavernous tile and concrete of the restricted subway station beneath the Bu-javid.

It was a short walk to the subway car, in a larger space than Jase had been in since he'd come into the Bu-javid by this same route.

"All right?" he asked Jase, seeing that little hesitation, that intake of breath.

"Fine," Jase said, and walked steadily beside him, Banichi and Jago in front, Tano and Algini behind, down past the train engine to the two cars which were waiting with the requisite House Guard and a Guild pair from the aiji's staff—Bren's eye picked them out.

"Nadi?" Banichi took up his post just inside, and they boarded, Tano and Algini going to the baggage car with junior security, Banichi and Jago staying with them.

"Rear seat's the most comfortable," he said to Jase—he recalled saying that the day he'd escorted Jase *to* the hill, in the same car, on his way to the confinement in which Jase had lived. They took their seats. Jago, on pocket com, standing by the door, talked to someone, probably intermediate to the Bu-javid station that governed use of the tracks, clearing their departure.

The door shut and the car got underway.

Jase sat with nervous anticipation evident as the shuttered private subway car rumbled and thumped along its course down the hill and across a city Jase had never seen except from the windows of the Bu-javid and once from the air.

"Nervous, nadi?"

"No, nadi." Jase was quick to say so. And sat, hands on knees, braced against the slightest movement of the car.

But a lot of strangeness, Bren could only guess, was surely impacting Jase's senses right now, from the shaking of the car, the smells, the noise.

Evidently some of them were alarming sensations from a spaceman's point of view, as were large open spaces: the echoes disoriented him, maybe. Maybe just the size did. Bren had no idea, but to reassure Jase he adopted an easy pose, legs extended, ankles crossed, and kept talk to a minimum while Jase's eyes darted frantically to every different rattle of the wheels on the switching-points, the least change in sound as they exited the tunnel and went in open air.

"We're on the surface again," Bren explained. "We've been in a tunnel."

Jase didn't look reassured. And probably Jase knew

he was overreacting, even suspected he looked foolish in his anxiety, but they had one more rule in effect, and Jase had agreed to it as Jase had agreed to every other condition: no matter what, Jase wasn't to speak anything but Ragi on this trip. If the car wrecked, he'd made the point with Jase, *scream* in Ragi. He might not be able to hold to it throughout, but if that was the ideal, maybe, Bren thought, it would encourage Jase to shift his thoughts into the language totally, the way Jase had existed while he was gone on the tour. If it didn't do everything he'd hoped, in terms of forcing Jase into Ragi, it might at least force Jase back into that mindset so that he had a chance of arguing with him.

Meanwhile the car thumped and rumbled its way toward the airport.

A happy family, on its way to the beach, Bren thought, surveying his complement of catatonic, well-dressed roommate and heavily armed security in black leather and silver studs, themselves in high spirits and having a good time.

"We were *due* a vacation," Banichi remarked cheerfully. They were not quite so vacation-bound that he or any of his fellow Guild members took advantage of the stocked breakfast juice bar in the aiji's own, red velvet-appointed subway car, but Banichi did sit down at his ease, stretch out his huge body and heave a sigh. And doubtless it *was* far better than a rooftop in the peninsula. "We're due rain, of course, but it's spring—what can one hope?"

"It should still be fine," Jago said from her vantage by the door, one hand loosely on a hanging strap. "The sea, the sand—"

"The cold fogs."

"Nadiin," Bren said, and roused himself to the same level of enthusiasm as his security, "we are safe, we are away, lord Tatiseigi is visiting his *own* apartment tonight, we are *not* there, and I believe they have gotten the illicit television downstairs."

"The Guard is guarding it, nand' paidhi," Banichi said, "with its usual zeal, of course."

There were grins. Probably Jase didn't follow the

joke. But security was in a high good mood and the car rocked and thundered on, swayed around the turn that meant the airport station was coming up. Junior security, who had their baggage under close watch, would get it all aboard the vans.

The subway train stopped, security rose to take routine positions as the doors opened and security went out first.

Bren collected Jase, left the details to his staff, and sure enough the vans were waiting, with Bu-javid security in charge from beginning to end, in this very highly securitied spur of the regular public subway.

"Careful," he said, fearing Jase's balance problems, but Jase made a clean step out of the car and onto the concrete.

Jase had no difficulty there, and none in boarding the waiting van. He flung himself into the seat, however, as if relieved to sit down; his face was a little pale, his eye-blinks grown rapid as they did when he was fighting problems in perspective. Bren sat down more slowly beside him, with Banichi and Jago immediately after while others were loading the luggage into the second van under Tano's supervision.

The van whisked them to the waiting plane and braked right by the ladder. Immediately, the second van was with them, bringing the luggage, which was not alone their clothes, but the clutter of weaponry and electronics that went with the paidhi wherever he and his security went.

It was Tabini's jet. And it was needful now, Banichi out first and Jago next, and Bren third, for Jase to climb down from the van into the noise of the jet engines, and walk, on a flat surface and under a sky with a few gray-bottomed clouds, from the roofed van to the ladder and up the ladder into the plane. Jase made the step, didn't look up (which he'd said especially bothered him), and crossed to the ladder, shaking off Jago's offered hand.

"Wait," Bren said to Banichi and Jago, because the metal ladder shook when that pair climbed it with their usual energy, and he didn't figure that would help Jase at all, whose knuckles were white on the rail as he climbed doggedly toward the boarding platform, his eyes on the steps, never on his surroundings.

Jase went inside, to be met by the co-pilot. Bren went up next and Jago and Banichi followed him; Tano and Algini stayed below to stand watch over the luggage-loading.

The computer, alone of their luggage, went in the cabin with them; Jago had it, and tucked it into a storage area, while outside the luggage-loading went so fast that the hatch thumped down while Jase was settling into his seat in the table-chair grouping and while Bren was saying hello to the pilot and co-pilot.

"One hopes for a quieter flight, nand' paidhi," the pilot said.

He'd actually *forgotten* about the boy from Dur during the last twenty hours, during which they'd accomplished the logistics and arrangements, and during which uncle Tatiseigi had lodged in Ilisidi's hospitality.

They were away and clear. The boy from Dur had his ribboned card which might save him from parental wrath, the apartment was still intact after the state reception, and the television was out of the pantry, entertaining the House Guard for the duration of uncle Tatiseigi's stay, which should about equal their days on the western shore near Saduri.

"I anticipate a quiet flight and a quiet ten days, nadi," Bren said to the pilot and co-pilot, "and I hope you and your associate have ample time for a little fishing yourselves. I've expressed the wish the staff could lodge you at some place that would allow it for however long you have at leisure."

"Nand' paidhi, they have done so, and we thank you, nand' Jase as well." This with a nod toward the seating where Jase had belted in.

"Nadi," Bren said in ending the conversation, and went back to sit beside Jase. He *did* feel better now that things were underway. His blood was moving faster with their stirring about, and the slight headache was diminishing: possibly the sleeping pill had worn off.

"It's excellent weather for flying. A smooth flight, nadi. Sun shining. Calm air."

"Yes," Jase said. It was a word. It was a response. Then: "Too close to the planet," Jase muttered, then grinned; and Bren obligingly laughed, in the understanding both that it was an uneasy joke and that Jase had, finally, just been able to get a few words assembled into an almost-sentence of Ragi this morning. After twenty-odd hours of intermittent wordless moments and frustration, losing all confidence in his ability to speak the Ragi language, Jase was showing signs of pulling out of it—phase two of his mental break, a tendency to suspect all his word choices and to blow his grammar—which, coupled with fears of insulting the atevi staff, wasn't improving his confidence. But it was textbook psychological reaction. Jase had been vastly embarrassed, humiliated, terrified of very real diplomatic consequences at the same moment he was put on national television—at his worst moment of personal crisis. It wasn't just the illusion of helplessness language students went through, it had been real helplessness, and real danger, and thank God, Bren thought, they'd had the dowager there, and an understanding security, and Damiri. Also thank God, Tatiseigi was no fool.

And meanwhile Jase, being around staff who'd forgive him his mistakes, was trying again, understanding again, and regaining a little shaky confidence in himself.

"Please belt in, nadiin," the co-pilot said over the intercom. The engines roared into action.

And as the plane began to taxi toward the runway, with security taking their seats and belting in around them, Jase's knuckles were white on the armrests.

Couldn't fault that reaction. He'd explained to Jase *and* Yolanda the physics by which planes stayed in the air during their initial flight to Shejidan, but there was so much new then and since that he wasn't sure how much had stayed with him. They'd come from a rough landing on the Taiben preserve, an overnight at Taiben only sufficient to catch their breaths, then a rail trip ending in a hasty boarding of the aiji's plane to fly them all to the international airport at Shejidan.

After they'd landed at Shejidan, there'd been no hesitation: the aiji's guards had packed Yolanda and Deana Hanks both onto a second, atevi-piloted commercial plane bound for Mospheira, and hastened him and Jase onto the van and then into the subway station on a fast trip to the Bu-javid, to enter the aiji's very careful security arrangements, all to assure—in a world seething with change and disturbance at that moment— that nothing befell the two paidhiin.

It hadn't afforded Jase much time to learn about the world. And Jase had been disoriented and more focused on the fact that he and Yolanda weren't going to find communication free or easy. Possibly they hadn't known it would be that way.

Possibly Deana Hanks, sitting near them on the plane, saying that he'd be a prisoner in Shejidan and that they'd deceive him, had set Jase up for far too much suspicion. He'd *told* Jase that Deana was a liar. But Jase might not have believed him that day.

And as he explained the full extent of what Deana had done and why, Jase's comment had been, Neither one of us will have it easy, either, will we?

Half a year ago.

Just about half a year ago. Yolanda had gone away in a van along with Deana, bound for a plane nearby; Jase had gone with him and Banichi and Jago in another one, bound for the subway, and that had been it, last contact, except the phone calls.

Jase had been so scared in those first days, so very scared—of the staff, of security, of the devices that guarded the doorway. Of the simple fact they found it necessary to lock the doors of the apartment.

Of the simpler fact of thunder crashing above the roof. He remembered.

The plane rushed down the runway, lifted, and a moment later Jase was trying to improve the plane's angle by leaning as it banked for the west.

Bren kept himself deadpan and didn't say a word about what was probably an instinctive reaction. One would think a man from weightless space would have overcome such tendencies. But Jase said his ship made itself gravity the same way the station did, so Bren supposed Jase wasn't used to being without it.

The plane retracted the trailing edge flaps. Jase was still white-knuckled and had looked askance thus far at every noise of the hydraulics working, from the wheels coming up to the slats coming back. This was the man who'd boarded a capsule and let a crew shove him into space in free fall toward a parachute drop into the planetary atmosphere.

On the other hand . . . Jase said very little about that trip down. Jase had waked now and again with nightmares, startling the staff, and he had once remarked that the parachute drop had perturbed him. He hoped the trip back into space once they had the ship, Jase had said to him very early on, would be a good deal more like the airplane ride to Shejidan.

"You know," he remarked to Jase, who, after ten minutes at least and almost up to cruising altitude, hadn't let go the seat arm, "planes don't often fall out of the sky. They tend to stay up. Airfoil. Remember?"

Jase took several deep breaths. "I'm fine," he said, in the manner of someone who'd just survived hell. "I'm fine."

Jase stared straight ahead. There was a lovely view of clouds out the window, but he didn't look, evidently not trusting the plane would stay level without his encouragement. Jase didn't look at him, either, and didn't seem inclined to think about anything but the plane.

Well, there was work he could do while Jase was helping the pilot.

He could unpack the computer. Or he could sit and worry about the situation on Mospheira with the State Department and its windows.

Or the situation in the capital, where shockwaves of the peninsular affair and Tatiseigi's apparent realignment were still ringing through the court and lords marginally aligned with Direiso were reconsidering their positions—disturbing thought, to have a continent-spanning war going on, and thus far the casualties amounting to one man, a lightbulb, a piece of glassware, and Badissuni of the Hagrani in the hospital for a stomach condition—so that one wondered *was* it stress that had sent him there, or had Jago been near his drink?

The ship and probably the man beside him were completely unaware of the struggle except insofar as Jase had had to deal with Tatiseigi.

Well, the island *would* become aware of it. With the illegal radio traffic going on, bet that Deana Hanks would become aware of it.

If she could translate *assassination* without mistaking it for *pregnant calendar*.

Banichi and Jago were meanwhile taking great care to have him apprised of what was going on, after, presumably, some shaking at high levels had gone on in the Messengers' Guild. The information delivered with their supper last evening had been an intercepted radio message on the north coast, up by Wiigin, where they were *not* going, a message which—laughably under less grim circumstances—purported to be between atevi, when clearly only one side was atevi even by the timbre of the voice, let alone the vocabulary and syntax errors.

The fluent side of the transmission had discussed at great length the situation with the assassination of lord Saigimi. It had claimed lord Tatiseigi had made the television interview under extreme threat and it claimed that only fear that the Atageini would be taken over by the aiji had weakened Tatiseigi's former—the message called it—*strong stand for traditional values*.

He knew why Tabini *had* let that radio traffic, ostensibly between small aircraft flying near the Association-Mospheiran boundary and a tower controller on the atevi mainland, go on without protest: it was deliberate provocation on someone's part on the mainland to be doing what they were doing, bold as brass on the airwaves. That they continued had nothing to do with rights of expression as they defined free speech on Mospheira. By the Treaty no Mospheiran had the right to use a radio to communicate across the strait. By allowing those radio messages to continue, Tabini was simply, in human parlance, giving the perpetrators enough rope to hang themselves and draw in others before he cracked down, definitely on Direiso, possibly on the perpetrators of the messages, and diplomatically on Hanks.

But the area where that was going on was (he had checked) well north of the area where they were going.

And, while he would be involved in the crisis those messages were bound to engender when the crackdown came, it wasn't his problem now. His job right now was simply making sure that Jase got his chance to relax and reach some sort of internal peace with the land and the people. He had great faith that a little exposure to problems more basic and more natural than living pent up in the pressured Bu-javid environment would help Jase immensely. And *he,* himself—

He needed to rest. He finally admitted that. He'd reached the stage when there just wasn't any more reserve. No more nerves, no more sense, no more flexibility of wit.

He'd had his last real leave—oh, much too long ago.

He'd stood on a ski slope, on Mt. Allen Thomas, in the very heart of the island, getting sunburn on his nose, coated in snow from a header. (He'd gotten a little slower, a little more cautious in his breakneck skiing.)

But, oh, the view from up there was glorious, when the sun turned the snow gold and the evergreens black in the evenings.

When the mists came up off the blue shadows and the wind whispered across the frozen surface in the morning—then he was alive.

It would have terrified Jase.

Ah, well, he said to himself, and propped one ankle on the other and asked junior security for a fruit juice.

"Would you care for one, Jasi-ji?"

"Yes, nadi, please," Jase said.

Definitely better.

The fruit juice arrived. "Pretty clouds," Bren

remarked, and Jase looked and agreed with relative calm that they were that.

Vacation would do them all good, he said to himself.

Because . . . he had a sip of fruit juice and stared at the empty seat across from him, the one Jago usually occupied . . . he was definitely reaching the fracture point himself, and seeing conspiracy under every porcelain lily petal.

Conspiracy that linked the various shattered major pieces of the last several days, from whatever had necessitated the assassination of Saigimi, to whatever Hanks had pursued, to Direiso, to a couple of radio operators up by Wiigin, and even to the paint flung at his mother's apartment building.

He just wished he hadn't hung up on Toby. Their mother's surgery was this week. And he wouldn't hear. He just wouldn't hear. He'd resigned himself to that.

Hard on the relatives, the job he'd taken, the job Jase had volunteered for, never having been out of the reach of family and familiarity in his life.

He sipped his fruit juice. Jase eventually remembered to drink his.

The plane took a turn toward the west. Jase braced himself and looked at the window as if he expected to see something.

"It's all right."

Jase took a deep breath. "Can you see the water as we come in, nadi?"

"We're starting descent. You should be able to see it. You should have a good view."

He didn't know why Jase had taken the ocean as his ambition. He was only glad that Jase had taken something that easy for his goal, something *he* could deliver.

He got up briefly and spoke to Banichi.

On the paidhi's request and the local tower's willingness, the plane made a very unusual approach, swinging low and slow over the water's edge, then flew out over the sea and the large resort island of Onondisi, which sat in the bay, affording the ship-paidhi a view. Bren stood up to see, with his hand on a safety-grip, mindful of island pilots, standing and looking over Jase's shoulder at a pleasant rock-centered island with bluffs to the north and sandy beach to the south, where the resorts clustered.

"Melted water," Jase said in a tone of awe. "All that melted water."

Now and again Jase could utterly surprise him.

"Melted it is."

"Is it warm?"

"About the temperature of a cold water tap." He reached past Jase to point at the hotels that clustered among trees on the heights of the island. "Vacation places. Hotels. You stay there and go down to the beaches."

"Ordinary people go there?" Jase asked.

"And lords, nadi. And whoever wants to. The ordinary consideration is security, for the lords, so usually the high lords stay on the south shore of the bay. A lot of private beaches over there, but not as fine as these."

"Other people, they don't have to worry?"

"No. —Except if they've made somebody very, very angry. And even then they know whether they have to worry."

"Are they scared with this assassination going on?"

"The Guild won't touch a common man without a Filing of Intent. Even then the Guild has to be convinced there's a strong and real grievance, so," he said, with an eye to all the tiny figures on the beaches, wading the surf, "unless someone's done something really outrageous enough to get a Filing approved— they're safe, down there."

"But not lords?"

"Lords have Guild in their households," Jago said, standing close. "And the Guild doesn't necessarily have to approve a greater lord moving against a lesser if right can be demonstrated later."

"And a lesser against a greater?" Jase asked.

"It must approve that. And with common folk, it must. And often," Jago said as an afterthought, "we mediate between common folk. Many times, a feud among folk like that doesn't draw blood. We see many, many situations that common folk think extraordinary. We can bring perspective to a matter."

One suspected (Tano had hinted as much, and he'd observed it on the daily news) a commoner-feud usually went quite slowly indeed if the Guild suspected mediation would result. Sometimes, the paidhi strongly suspected, the Guild did absolutely nothing for a few months, expecting its phone to ring with an offer to the opposing side, once the targeted party grew anxious.

Jago didn't volunteer such information, however; and the plane swept on over water, this time with the view of Mospheira a distant blue haze past the rolling hills.

"That's the island, nadi. *The* island. Mospheira."

The wing tipped up, hiding it, as they were obliged to veer off along the invisible boundary.

"I didn't see it," Jase said.

"It's just hazy out there. It *was* the haze."

"I didn't see it, all the same." Jase sounded disappointed.

"Well, I'll point it out to you when we're on the ground. I'm sure we'll be able to see it. —The hills closer to us, that was the height of Mogari-nai."

Behind them now lay the rocky coastal bluffs that photographers loved, along with those of Elijiri which were near Geigi's estate, further inland. Mogari-nai was set, one understood, on the aiji's land, well back from the scenic areas, in a zone dedicated once to firing cannon balls intended to fall on hostile wooden ships approaching the port at Saduri Township.

Now Mogari-nai faced a periodic barrage of electronic interference launched from Mospheira, and that opposing shore was lined with radar installations.

Ask about that interference in a protest to the Mospheiran government, and naturally the problem immediately spread to the phone lines.

"Will one wish another pass, nandiin?" That was the co-pilot. *"We have the sky to ourselves."*

"No, thank him, nadi," Bren said, and Tano, standing near the intercom, relayed that information.

"We will land, then, nandiin. Please seat yourselves comfortably and safely."

Bren sat down and belted in. Jase fastened the belt and drew a long breath.

"Routine landing," Bren said, and talked Jase a second time through the process of landing, and *why* planes stayed in the air and how they got onto the ground.

Jase seemed very much more relaxed, just three deep breaths as they were approaching touch-down, and a grin as they did so exactly when Bren predicted.

"A lot better than parachutes, nadi," Jase said. They'd begun with a scared, withdrawn passenger and ended with one smiling and joking—one who'd been able to look out his window even during a steep bank, only occasionally clinging to the seats.

This was a good idea, Bren thought, this trip was a very good idea.

The plane taxied to the terminal of what was, for defense and seasonal tourist reasons, a fair-sized airport. The transport vans were waiting.

"We're here, nadiin-ji!" Bren said cheerfully, and was not quite first on his feet, but close.

Vacation, he was thinking. It wasn't quite the hoped-for chase after yellowtail, but Banichi was right: Geigi's estate, just on the south shore of Onondisi Bay, was peninsular, and going there at this precise moment might send some unwanted signal and interfere with the aiji's politics with that region.

Taiben, the aiji's summer retreat, the other possibility—that was in the Padi Valley, and that was, again, politically sensitive right now, as well as dangerous, being in lady Direiso's own front yard.

There'd been Malguri, which he'd most wished, but that was three hours by air into a set of provinces seething with intrigue.

So the aiji's lands, meaning the public defense zone near Mogari-nai and the Historic Site near Saduri Township, that became the fallback. They couldn't use the public resorts. The good one got out of being an atevi lord was mostly limited to a lot of ancestral knick-knacks you didn't own, by his own observation; and the bad one got was that the more politically active you were and the more resolutely you did your job for the people you represented, the more true it became that you couldn't ride regular airlines or go into pretty public resorts like Onondisi or go into the tourist restaurants he'd dearly love to go to—if he weren't the paidhi-aiji, and a human to boot.

But, well, rank had other privileges. Supper tonight with Ilisidi could make up for the restaurants.

They didn't have to gather up baggage. That was another good part of being lords. They let their security handle it and the moment the ladder was in place and the moment Banichi had been down to make direct contact with Ilisidi's people, who were in charge of ground security, they could go.

"I'm fine!" Jase announced as they went out into the brisk, sea-charged wind. Bren went down first, to meet Banichi at the bottom and to catch Jase if he tripped. But he felt the ladder shake and looked back to find Jase had seized the safety rail in his accustomed death grip and watched Jase enthusiastically and adventurously come after him without waiting for the ladder to stop rocking.

Not to push the point by lingering in the open air, Bren went to the nearest van of the three as the driver, who was not commercial hire, but one of Ilisidi's 'young men,' as she called them, opened the door. Bren ushered Jase in, got in ahead of Banichi, and Jago brought up the rear and shut the door as she hit the seat.

The van started up immediately and whipped around a tire-squealing one-eighty turn toward the gate.

Like a van ride he'd taken once before to visit the dowager. He started to protest the driver's recklessness, but—they were in Ilisidi's territory now, and it was what he'd bargained for. The driver wouldn't kill them; he knew that now—having been through far worse; and Jase looked startled and apprehensive, but looked at him, too, for reassurance. So he grinned and Jase tried to mirror the expression.

Roads across the countryside weren't approved tech, except on a local basis. There was definitely rail service to Saduri Township, he'd checked that out, but it didn't serve the old fortress, as such service didn't serve, specifically, *two* of the aiji's estates, he'd learned; one of those two was Malguri, and the other was Saduri. No rail went up to the big dish at Mogarinai; and it didn't go to the Saduri Historical Site, either.

So he'd understood there'd be a drive to get there; and he could have expected the driver would do what this driver was doing.

The van left the maintenance road and whipped off on a gravel spur that led around a grassy hill, and around another, and generally up, at a ferocious pace.

Jase looked less reassured at the sound of gravel under the wheels and at the feel of the van skidding slightly on the turns. He grabbed at the handles and the window-frame.

"Is this dangerous?" Jase asked. "Is someone after us?"

"Oh—" Bren began to say lightly, and settled for the truth with Jase. "This driver is having a good time. Relax."

Banichi grinned broadly. "He's not lost a van this spring,"

Jase did know when he was being made fun of. He gave a sickly grin to that challenge to his composure and clung white-fingered to the handholds.

"I'd have thought someone from up there," Bren finally said over the noise of the van, "would be used to motion."

"I am!" Jase retorted. And freed a hand to gesture an erratic crooked course. "Not—this motion."

It did make sense. Jase's body didn't know what to expect and Jase's stomach kept trying to prepare for it, to no avail.

It was for the same reason, he supposed, that the subway made him anxious. And that the plane did. He watched Jase's facial reactions, the twitch as a swing of the road brought light onto his face and immediately after as a stand of young trees brought a ripple of shadow and a series of flinches and blinks, all exaggerated.

So what *would* it be like, Bren asked himself, to live in a building all his life, and have all the light controlled, the flow of air controlled, the temperature controlled, the humidity controlled, every person you *met* controlled; and the whole day scheduled, the horizons curving up and movement entirely imperceptible? He had as much to learn about Jase as Jase did about the world; Jase was the book he had to read to gain knowledge about the ship—which he needed to know, and his professional instincts had turned on in that regard, to such an extent he told himself he should abandon curiosity and track on his other job, to reassure Jase.

But Jase had reacted uncertainly to change in the apartment; he added up that maddening insistence on rising at exactly the same moment, on breakfast at the same time every morning, and reckoned that change, as an event, was *not* something Jase was used to meeting. He'd dealt with Jase and Yolanda both on their last exposure to the world when they were still in a state of shock from landing and when their passage under open sky to the safety of Taiben lodge had been brief, ending in the safe confines of the Bu-javid—at least Jase's had ended there.

And now, right before his eyes, that twitchiness was back: that extreme reaction to stimuli of all sorts, even when Jase was trying to joke about it. Randomness of light and sound had become a battering series of events to senses completely unused to interpreting the nuances.

He rated himself tolerably good at figuring out what went on in atevi, and he could make a guess, that the way a baby overreacted once it had started being startled, it must seem to Jase as if there *were* no order and no recognizable logic in the sensations that came at him. Jase had that look in his eyes and that grip on the edge of his seat that said here was a man waiting now for the whole world to dissolve under his feet.

But the logic inside the man said it wouldn't, so Jase

clung to his seat and kept his eyes wide open and tried with an adult and reasoning brain to make sense of it.

And an infant's brain, not yet reasoning, might have an advantage in programming. A grown man who from infancy had never had light flashed in his face, never had a floor go bump, never been slung about from one side to the other—what was he to do? Jase came from a steady, scheduled world, one without large spaces. If he'd lived in the equivalent of a set of small rooms, God, even *textures* must be new.

What had Jase said to him? The tastes, the smells, were all overwhelming to him?

It was possible he'd never seen bright color or different pattern. The ship Jase had come from began to seem a frighteningly *same* kind of place.

The beach, the waves, the rocks and hills, these things should, if Jase could meet them, be a very good cure for what ailed him. And if he could tolerate the environment, get a look at the natural processes that underlay the randomness of storm and weather that reached the capital at Shejidan, he would have far fewer fears. Jase was scared of thunder, and knew better than most now what it was, but still jumped when it thundered, and was embarrassed when the servants laughed. *They* thought it made him like them. He thought it made him foolish.

Let Jase see the historic origins of the atevi, let him experience the same sort of things that had opened the atevi world to *his* imagination. *That* was the plan.

It was, though he hadn't thought so then, the best thing that had ever happened to him in terms of his understanding of the world he lived in, a textured, full of smells and colors world that could fill up his senses and appeal to him on such a basic level that something in his human heart responded to this atevi place and taught him what the species had in common.

On the other hand, watching Jase flinch from sunlight and shadow, it might not happen to Jase. It at best might be a bit much to meet all in one day. Their spaceman was brave, but growing vastly disoriented just in the sounds and level of perceived threat constantly coming at him; fast-witted, but lost in the dataflow that had begun to wipe out the linkages in his brain and rearrange the priorities.

It wasn't just the language now that had overwhelmed Jase with its choices. It *wasn't* just the same linguistic shift that overwhelmed every student that came close to fluency—it was the whole physical, natural world that came down on Jase, stripping away all his means not only of expressing himself—that was the language part—but also of interpreting the sensations that came at him. Jase was hanging on to that part of his perceptions with his fingernails.

And that disorientation, coupled with what he guessed Ilisidi might provoke him to, would make it a very good idea to limit the breakable objects in Jase's reach.

He began to have misgivings. Jase *wasn't* planet-born. There might not be that common ground he hoped to have Jase find with atevi. For the first time he began to fear he'd made a mistake in bringing Jase out here and asking this of him.

It was a lot of input.

But it was fractal, soothing input if Jase's brain could just figure out it did repeat, and loop, and that it didn't threaten.

Ilisidi, however, *didn't* give you an inch.

And you had to go farther into atevi territory to meet Ilisidi than she was going to come onto human ground to meet you: that was a given.

"Pretty view," he said desperately as they rounded a turn, and it was, a glorious view into the distance of the plain. "Taiben is that way—a fair distance, though."

Jase faced that direction. He gave no indication his eyes even knew where to focus two seconds running or what was pretty or what he was supposed to look at.

Bren thought of asking the driver to stop and let Jase get out and have a steady, stable look and catch his breath; but he thought then that they weren't within a security perimeter, and that they were going to such a perimeter, within which they could stand and have such a view, presumably. And Jase could calm down.

It was a risk. Their whole lives were a risk. But you limited them where you could. It was different from the catwalk at Dalaigi.

There was no crowd watching them.

The trip went a good distance up and up, among rolling hills of greening grass spangled with wildflowers in yellow and purple and white, with no structures, no building in sight until, just around a steep turn in the rolling hills, they passed through a gate in a low stone wall and then, in the next turn, caught a brief view of a stone building.

That view steadied in the forward windows after the second turn, a pile of the local rocks with a number of high, solid walls, one slightly tumbled one, and a staff posed crazily on the battlement of a two, in places three and four floored fortification with a bright banner flying, on a staff slightly atilt, from the front arch.

Red and black, the aiji's colors.

The van pulled up to the door, under a sweep-edged roof, as the door opened and poured out the aiji-dowager's men, who opened the door of the van.

Jago was first out. Bren climbed down.

Jase stayed seated. Blocking Banichi's path to the door was never a good idea. Jase, however, was not doing so in panic. Jase was frowning darkly.

"Where's the beach?" he asked.

"Oh, it's here," Bren said. "Come on, Jase."

Jase stayed put. And belted in. His arms were folded. From that position, he spared a fast, angry gesture around him. "Grass. Rock. High rock. You promised me the beach, nadi."

Not trusting this, Bren thought. From overload to a final realization they were on a mountain. "Jasi-ji," he said reasonably, "you're preventing Banichi getting up." Not true, if Banichi weren't being polite. "There is a beach down the hill, where water tends to be and remain, as physics may tell you, and I promise you ample chance to see the ocean. One just doesn't build these kind of big houses down there. Too many people. And it's old. And it's the aiji's property. It's all *right,*

Jasi-ji. Get down, if you please, before Banichi moves you."

Jase moved then, carefully, ducking his head, and stepped down into the shadow of a building, clinging to the van and evading the offered help of the servants. He stood there a moment, then sighted on the door and started walking.

Bren walked with him, looking at the open, iron-bound doors; at the dim interior ahead of them and around them as they walked in.

Malguri was the oldest fortress still functioning, he knew that. This place had a dusty, deserted look as if it hadn't quite been maintained on the same level as Malguri. Like Mogari-nai, it was supposedly from the Age of Exploration, younger than Malguri: it had supported the fort at Mogari-nai, when atevi had started trading around the Southern Rim, when East and West had made contact, when they'd gotten out on the seas in wooden ships and rival associations had shot at each other with cannon.

But by what he was seeing he understood in a new light what Ilisidi had said to him when she proposed it, that Saduri wasn't on the regular tour circuit, and was not legally permitted to hikers—a security advantage, she said, which Malguri hadn't had.

This fortress might not be as old as Malguri, but he wouldn't lay odds on the plumbing. That banner on the roof, too, said something about the way things were put together. No regular bracket for the staff. No regular provision for such a thing—he could imagine one of the dowager's 'young men' climbing up there to do it, out of the reckless enthusiasm and the loyalty they showed for Ilisidi.

And for the sheer hell of it.

Malguri's hall had been lively and full of interesting banners. This one—

—had one of the ceiling beams lying crashed onto the floor at the rear of the hall. Workmen's scaffolding occupied that end, which, with no interior lighting and with only the light from the door, was brown with dust.

Even Banichi and Jago stopped in some dismay.

Where is the beach, indeed? Bren asked himself.

What have I let us in for?

"Nadi Bren." One of the dowager's servants came from a side hall, and said, with the usual calm of the dowager's servants, "Nadiin. One will guide you to your rooms."

16

Down a long hall to the side, dust everywhere—but the dust on the stone floor showed a clear track of feet having passed this way recently. Like bread crumbs in the wilderness, Bren thought to himself as he and Jase, behind Ilisidi's man, climbed a short flight of stairs where Banichi, following them, surely had to duck his head.

Jago had stayed behind in the downstairs, having something to do with Tano and Algini and the baggage in the second van, Bren thought.

The stone of the stair treads was bowed, worn by the use of atevi feet—old. Older than the use of cannon, perhaps. He wasn't sure how long it took to wear away stone. The floor above was stone, which he had learned from Malguri meant a barrel vault beneath, in this age predating structural steel.

The hall above had no windows, no light but what came from a lamp at the side of the stairs and what filtered up from the open door below. It was increasingly shadowy at the top of the stairs, pitch black down the hall, and the servant—if such he was: he looked very fit—opened the second door of a small row of doors, and showed them into a hole of a room, into which the thin stream of white daylight from a glassless window-slit showed the outlines of a bed and a table. The draft from that window was cool spring air. It moved languidly past them, doubtless to find the door downstairs.

The servant struck a match and light flared in a golden glow on an atevi face, atevi hands, a candle on a rough (but recently dusted) table. A small vase stood next the candle with three prickly-looking flowers that looked to be from the hillside. The wick took fire, and illumined a rubble stone wall, a deeply shadowed but smallish room, bare timbers helping the masonry hold up a doubtless weary roof.

"There are more candles," the servant said, and indicated a small wicker basket at the end of the same table. "And matches, nandiin. The dowager requests one have a caution of fire." The man presented him a small bundle of matches, neatly tied with ribbon. "One regrets that the inner halls are under restoration and not pleasant. Ordinarily, guests would be lodged there, but there are plenty of blankets. The accommodation is at the end of the hall and it does function. Please follow me."

The paidhi sensed intense unhappiness in Jase's silence and chose not to touch it off with a question. "Down the hall, then," he said, as cheerfully as he could. Banichi was waiting in the doorway, and one wondered whether *he* had had any warning.

Possibly Banichi was thinking, You fool, Bren-ji. But Banichi gave no hint at all in his mildly pleasant expression. It might be more comfortable than a rooftop in the much warmer peninsula. Might be. Marginally.

And *this* was the vacation spot he'd chosen.

The putative servant took several candles from the basket and lit the first from the lighted candle on the table, then carried it outside and lit another, which, as they all stood watching, doubtless with separate thoughts of the situation, the servant set in a wall-sconce.

"Nand' Banichi, your room, and nand' Jago's," the servant said, lit a candle and set it by *that* door to relieve the darkness of this tunnel; and so they went; the room for Tano and Algini was next.

On the other side of this hall, although there were doors, as best the paidhi could judge the geometry of the building he'd seen from outside there were no windows: the rooms they were not using must be little more than stone coffins with no source of light but the candle, rooms dependent on mortar imperfections or God knew what for ventilation. He supposed, since he had challenged Ilisidi to challenge Jase, they were lucky not to be lodged on that side of the hall.

And the euphemistically named accommodation? The servant opened the door on a room with cold spring daylight showing through a hole in the stone floor. With the stack of towels. And a dipper and bucket.

The servant explained, for Jase's benefit. The paidhi well understood. He wasn't sure Jase quite believed it was the toilet.

The one at Malguri had had indoor heat. This didn't. It had an updraft.

Malguri had had glass windows. Fireplaces in palatial suites, however old the plumbing. The distinction between Historical Site and Oldest Continuously Occupied Site began to come through to him with a great deal more clarity.

Jase hadn't said a word. He was probably in shock, and walked along tamely as they all retraced their steps, the supposed servant in the lead, back down the candle-lit hall toward their room—their—singular room.

Their—singular—room, which to his memory had one—singular—and not very wide—bed.

It was not polite for a guest to complain of accommodations. It was just not done. One assumed one's host knew exactly what her guests were being put into, and one smiled and made no complaint.

He'd said trustingly to Ilisidi, in a private meeting in her luxurious study, in the Bu-javid apartment she maintained, "Aiji-ma, Jase doesn't understand atevi. You taught *me*. And I daren't go so far from the capital as Malguri. Might I impose on you, aiji-ma, to linger a little at Taiben this season? Perhaps to go over to the seashore and show Jase-paidhi the land as it was? I've promised him the sea. I've undertaken to provide him that—and your help would be best of all, aiji-ma."

There'd been one of those silences.

"What happened to 'Sidi-ji?' " Ilisidi had asked with

a quirk of her age-seamed lips and a lift of a brow, meaning why didn't he use that familiar, intimate address he'd a number of times dared with her.

"I think," he'd said, knowing he was fencing with a very dangerous opponent, at a very unsettled time in the aiji's court, "I thought I should show some decency of address in such an outrageous request of your time, nand' dowager."

And Ilisidi had said, after an apparent moment of thought, one thin knuckle under a still-firm though wrinkled chin: "I think—I think that if you want the seashore, nadi, why, we should *go* to the seashore. Why not Saduri?"

He hadn't *thought* it was a site open to the public. He'd foolishly said so.

And: *"We* are not the public," Ilisidi had said, in that aristocratic mode that could move mountains.

So here they were. Tano, Jago, and Algini, with a number of putative servants, came up the steps at the end of the hall with a fairly light load of baggage.

"The rest of the baggage is going to be stored downstairs," Jago said cheerfully.

Bren didn't *feel* cheerful. Tano looked bewildered, and Bren didn't dare look at Jase, just depressed the iron latch on his door to let their personal luggage in.

"Is there a key for this door, nadi?" he asked Ilisidi's servant.

"No, nand' paidhi. That room has no lock. But one assures you, the entire perimeter of this site is very closely guarded, so one may be confident all the same."

Bren rather expected Banichi or Jago to say something caustic about that situation. But by that example, and their silence, he wondered whether *their* rooms had locks.

One servant took his and Jase's baggage in. Jago handed him his computer, which was *not* going to find a recharge socket in this building, but which he on no account allowed to remain outside his immediate guard, especially in a premises occupied by uncle Tatiseigi. That servant left. He walked in, Jase walked in, and he shut the door, leaving them in the white day-light from the window and the golden glow from the candle, which had by a whisper of a flame survived that gust from the closing door.

"Nadi," Jase began with, he thought, remarkable restraint, "what are they doing? Why are we here?"

"Well," he said, and tried to think of words Jase knew.

"I," Jase began again, this time in his own language. He was clearly now fighting for breath—and probably falling down that interlinguistic interface again.

Bren said sharply, "I'm sorry."

"Where is the *ocean,* nadi?"

"Clearly not here. Let me explain."

"In my language! Please!"

He'd said that in Ragi. Which said Jase was at least getting the reflexes under control.

"Five fast minutes, then, *in* Mosphei'. You remember how dangerous I said Tatiseigi was? —Well, the aiji-dowager is the *focus* of every anti-Tabini dissident in the country. *She* has the legitimacy Tatiseigi doesn't. Except for the legislature voting the other way after her husband died, she could have been aiji. Except for them voting for her grandson after her son died, she could have been aiji. She could step in tomorrow without the country falling apart, and she's the *only* one who'd avoid an unthinkable bloodbath, but she's also—" One was *never* sure a room lacked bugs. And was always playing for an audience. "She's also fair and honorable. She's been exceedingly moral in all her dealings with the welfare of the Association. It would have been a *lot* easier for her to have raised a civil war against her grandson. But she didn't, and I'm alive to say so. So keep objections to a minimum. And for God's sake don't make any objections to her. I asked her to show you atevi life as it was before humans came!"

"This is it, then, this falling-down ruin?"

"You listen to me, Jase."

Jase shoved him, hard, and he grabbed Jase's coat to prevent a swing at him.

"I've *been* listening to you," Jase said, trying to free himself, and shoved again.

"You're being stupid, *stupid* is what you're being! Stand still!"

Jase clawed at his hand and he let go. And they stood and stared at each other, Jase panting for breath, himself very much on the verge of hitting him, someone, anyone.

"All right," Jase said. "All right, I'll go along with this. I'll play your rules, your game, let's just keep smiling."

"Let me explain, before we switch languages again. If you insult this woman, you could have a war. If you insult this woman you could be killed. I am not exaggerating. We are dealing with cultural differences here. We are dealing with people who don't owe anything to whatever code of ethics lies in our mutual past. So whatever happens, you get a grip on that temper, Mr. Graham. You get a grip on it or I'll suggest to our staff they feed you some tea that'll have you throwing up your guts for three days and ship you back to the apartment before you say something to kill several million people! Do I make myself clear?"

"No guts yourself?"

"No *brains,* Mr. Graham? If I hit you, and I'm tempted, God! I'm tempted; they'll see the bruises— which I'd rather not, for your reputation and future—"

Jase swung. Bren didn't even think about doing it— he hit Jase hard. Jase grabbed his coat, Bren blocked a punch with one arm, hit Jase in the gut, and had to block another punch.

They hit the table together, holding on to each other. The candle fell, they both overbalanced and went down, and Bren writhed his way to his knees, blind, angry, and being hit by an idiot he wanted to kill. Before he got a grip on Jase, Jase got a grip on him, and they knelt there on the floor like two total fools, each with a deathgrip on the other's coat, sleeve, arm, shoulder, whatever.

"Get up," he said. "We've put the damn candle out. Are you trying to burn the building down?"

"Damn you."

He shook at Jase. Jase was braced. They were that way for several more breaths.

"Are they going to walk in and find us like this?" he asked Jase. "Get up!"

"Let go."

"No way in hell."

"Truce. Let go."

He didn't let go. He started to get up, Jase started to get up, and they got up leaning on each other, still holding on to each other, managing a slow, mistrustful disengagement.

Fool, he said to himself. He wasn't surprised. He wasn't happy, either, as he trusted Jase's common sense enough to pick up the candles, the extinguished one in the holder and the entire basket of them that had been overset.

He took a match, relit the candle. They'd delivered body blows, at least of those that had landed; and hadn't done each other visible damage, give or take dust on their clothes. The candle and the wan light from the window showed him Jase with hair flying loose, collar rumpled, a sullen look. He figured it had as well be a mirror of himself at the moment.

"We have to go to dinner tonight."

"In this wreckage?"

"*This* is a Historic Monument, Jasi-ji, and I suggest if she declares it's a palace on the moon you bow and agree that it's very fine and you're delighted to be here."

There was a long silence from the other side.

"Yes, sir," Jase said.

"I'm not *sir*."

"Oh, but I thought you'd taken that back. You are *sir* or you *aren't* in this business, so make up your mind!"

"Damn that talk. This is not your ship. You're supposed to be doing a job, you're not doing it, you damn near created a rift in the government and I brought you here to patch the holes, the *gaping* holes, in your knowledge of these people, *their* customs, *their* language, and *your* sensitivity to a vast, unmapped world of experience to which you're *blind,* Mr. Graham. I suggest you say thank you, put yourself back to rights, and don't expect *atevi* to do the job you volunteered for. They weren't born to understand *you,* they're on *their* planet, enjoying *their* lives quite nicely without your input, and I suggest if you approach atevi officials who owe *their* precious scant time to their own people, you do so politely, appreciate their efforts to understand you, *if* they choose to make such efforts, or I'll see you out of here."

"Thank you," Jase said coldly.

"Thank you for waiting to blow up."

"Don't push me. *Don't* push me. You need my good will."

"Do I? You could have an accident. They'd send me another."

There was a small, shocked silence. Then: "You're an atevi official. Is that the way you think of yourself?"

"You don't question me, mister. When it comes to relations *with* the atevi, I *am* sir, to you, and you do as you're told. You and your rules-following. This is the time for it, this is the time in your whole life you'd *better* follow the damn rules, and *now* you want to do things your own way! What do I need to diagram for you? Where did you get the notion *you* know what in hell's going on? Or did I miss a revelation from God?"

A long, long silence, this time. Jase didn't look him in the eye. He stared at the floor, or at dust on his clothing, which he brushed off, at the light from the window, at anything in the world but him.

"I think we should go back to Shejidan," Jase said to the window. "This isn't going to help."

"Well, it's not quite convenient at the moment to go back. You asked for this, and you've got it. So be grateful."

"The hell! You've lied to me."

"In what particular?"

A silence. A silence that went on and on while Jase stared off into nowhere and fought for composure.

There was a small rap at the door.

"Nadi?" Bren asked, wishing the interruption had

had better timing, to prevent the incident in the first place. He shouldn't have hit Jase. It hadn't helped. The man had lost his father. He was on a hair-trigger as it was. He'd chosen this particular time to bear down on the language, probably *because* of his father's death; and now he didn't know where he was: he was temporarily outside rational expression.

The door opened.

"Is there a difficulty, nadiin?" Banichi asked— Banichi, who was lodged next door, and, if there was anyone besides Ilisidi's chief of security, Cenedi, who was likely to have heard the entire episode, he'd about bet Banichi had the equipment in his baggage and would use it.

"No," he said. "Thank you, Banichi-ji. Is everyone settled? What's our schedule?"

"A light dinner at sunset. An early start, at sunrise."

"We'll be ready. Thank you, Banichi-ji."

"Nadi." The door closed.

"He heard us," Bren said quietly.

"I thought they took orders from *you,*" Jase said in a surly tone.

"No. They don't. One of a great many things you don't know, isn't it?"

Another small silence.

"You *need* to know, Jase. You'd better learn. I'm trying to help you, dammit."

"I'm sorry," Jase said then. "I'm just—"

Jase didn't finish it. Neither did he. He waited.

"I am sorry," Jase repeated, in Ragi. "Nadi, I was overturned."

"Upset," he said automatically and bit his lip. "Overturned, too, with reason. Jasi-ji. I know that. Can we recover our common sense?"

"Nadi," Jase said, "I wish to see the ocean. Will it be possible?"

"Nadi, you're very forward to keep asking me. If I were atevi I should be offended. Learn that."

A small hesitation. A breath. "Nadi, I take your information, but you are not atevi and I wish very much to know and not be surprised."

"I'll try to find out," Bren said. "There are things I don't understand." He hesitated to say so, but there were very quiet alarm bells ringing in the subconscious. "Observe a little caution. This is in excess of the conditions I expected. We *are* possibly in danger, nadi. One wonders if we have quite left behind the events in the city."

"Is this part of the lesson?"

Layers, upon layers, upon layers. "No," he said. "It isn't."

"Are you lying to me right now?"

"No," Bren said. "And of course, if I were, I would say I wasn't. But I'm not. I've turned us over to Tabini's grandmother, and I don't know what the truth is. The aiji thought us safe to be here. But I am, however mildly, concerned at the conditions. I can't say why I'm concerned. I just would expect—somewhat more comfort than we have here, more evidence that someone had some idea of the conditions here *before* the aiji-dowager took guests here." He wasn't sure Jase followed that. But there was something ticking over at the back of his brain now that he was no longer focusing on Jase's potential for explosion. That feeling of unease said that the dowager had security concerns, very reasonable security concerns, as did they. As did Mogari-nai, some distance away across the plain, which one would expect would be a very sensitive area; and they weren't seeing the security level at this place he had expected.

"Can you ask Banichi?"

"Within his man'chi, yes."

"Qualified yes."

"Always. It always is." It was the truth he gave Jase, and the answer was one that struck deep at what was human and what was atevi. He understood Banichi's priorities and took no offense at them. He wasn't in the mood to explain. He wasn't in the mood now to doubt his own security.

Just the dowager's.

Not a cheerful thought.

"Can you ask them what the schedule is?" Jase persisted.

"We were just told what the schedule is."

"For tomorrow, I mean."

He turned and fixed Jase with a glum stare. "I'll tell you a basic truth of atevi, nadi. If there were no real need for you to know that, yes, you could go, or I could go, and ask anyone around us. But because there *is* some question of good will here, and since that's why you need to know, no, it wouldn't be prudent to ask. Never make your hosts lie to you, Jasi-ji. Once that starts, you don't know what to believe."

"They're not lying?" Clearly Jase was not convinced.

"Not yet, I think. Not likely. But I haven't seen Cenedi. I haven't seen the dowager. I haven't seen anything but one servant, and our own security."

"What does that tell you?"

"Nadi, in response to your far too blunt question, it tells me either that people are busy because we've come here on short notice and quite clearly they've had to move even food up this hill to have anything on hand—or—there's something going on and they're too polite to offer us the possibility of a question."

"Meaning *what?*"

"Again too blunt, nadi." He was determined to push, in coldly correct, even kindly atevi fashion, to see whether Jase was capable of holding his temper. "But in response to your question, and in hopes your next question will be more moderate, they may avoid our presence rather than put themselves in the position of lying or us in the position of needing to be polite." He changed languages. "A new word for you: *naigoch'imi.* It means feigned good will."

"*Naigoch'imi.* Is that what we're dealing with?"

"We? Now it's *we?* A moment ago you wanted to kill me."

"I wanted the *truth,* dammit. And I still don't know if this includes you."

"Is that the way they get the truth on the ship? With fists?"

A silence. Several small breaths. "I won't apologize, Bren."

"Fine."

Back into the ship's language. "Friendship wouldn't have hurt, you know. From the beginning, friendship wouldn't have hurt."

Now Jase wanted to talk. He'd had enough from his brother. And he wasn't in the mood for sentiment, dammit, he'd turned it off between him and Jase at the beginning.

"Frankly," he said with coldness that amazed himself, "I don't know that you've ever offered any such thing. Not since we first spoke on the radio before you came down here. You were bright, interested, pleasant. But since you landed, since then—"

"I tried!"

"And I have a job to do, which means hammering words into your head, like it or not—no, I'm not always pleasant. I can't be! *You* were a teacher—I'm not. So I do the best I can, even in the intervals when you had the luxury to be annoyed at me."

"So I've learned. I have learned."

"So you've worked at it. Good for you. You've also gotten mad. But *I* didn't have the luxury to be mad, no matter what you said, no matter what you did. So I've taken it. I've taken anything you wanted to hand out, because I know my way around, I have the fluency, and *I'*m used to being the diplomat in touchy situations. — But friends, no. A *friend* would have met me halfway. A *friend* would have advanced some understanding that I'm crowding teaching you into the spaces where—never mind my leisure time—the spaces where I was getting *sleep,* nadi. Friendship wasn't in the requirements, I haven't asked it and I damn sure haven't gotten it!"

"You don't give me a chance."

"It was your choice, from the first day you landed. You weren't pleased with me or anyone else. You've made no secret of it. You never have trusted me. Why are we talking about it now? What do you want from me?"

"I expected . . ." Jase stopped, a need for words, or just a shaky breath. "Things were not what you promised from the moment we landed!"

(Hanks yelling, Don't trust them! The whole plain afire. Atevi armed to the teeth and clear evidence of an armed conflict.)

"You had some reason to think that, I'll grant."

"And they're not what you said *here!*" Jase flung a gesture about him, at the stones, the situation. "Every time I trust you! Every damned *time* I trust you, Bren, something blows up in my face! You're the one that keeps the peace between your people and the atevi— but your people aren't speaking to you, have you noticed that?"

"You've trusted me once to come down," he said restrainedly, "and once to come here. At no other time have I asked you—"

"Oh, it's *believe* me, *trust* me, *I know what I'm doing,* every time I draw a breath, Bren! I trusted you into that damn party. I trusted you into that interview. Well, where in hell is the ocean?"

"You'll have to trust me again."

"I believed you enough to come down here! Do you know how many parachutes, Bren? Did you notice how many parachutes? The first chute *failed,* Bren!"

Jase outright ran out of breath. And seemed to want something in reply. He saw Jase's eyes fixed on him as they'd not steadied on anything in the chaos of the trip up.

"I know," he said. "I *saw* that. I'm glad you made it. I'm personally glad you made it. If that needs to be said."

"Personally glad."

"I wouldn't have wanted you to die."

"That's kind of you."

"What do I need to do? Name it for me. What would satisfy you?"

"An expression. Have an expression on your face. Tell me the truth for once."

The remark about his lack of expression stung: it was probably true. But it clarified the source of objections, too. "I've tried," he said with labored patience, "to teach you a language and a way of dealing with this world. And you ignore my lessons. Your repeated insistence on questions I've pointedly ignored is rude in atevi eyes, and on such points of misunderstanding with atevi we began a war that killed a great many people. *Do* you understand that?"

"Then cure my misunderstanding. Why in hell are we on this hilltop, in this place?"

"For a good time. Which we will have. Relax."

"What are we down to? *Trust* me? *Trust* me, one more time?"

"Yes!"

"God." Jase ran a hand through his hair and walked to the window. Stark daylight painted him in white as he stood there staring out. And as he stood straight, as if he'd seen the devil. "There are mechieti out there!"

Atevi riding animals. Jase had had that experience on his first hour on the planet.

"Doing what, nadi?" he asked Jase.

"Eating the grass. Inside the wall."

"That's fine," Bren said. "They're the dowager's."

"What does she need them for?"

"Getting down to the sea, maybe."

"I'm not riding!"

"I think you'll do what she says," Bren said calmly. "Whatever it is. She's a lord far higher than I am. And this is, in all important senses, her land."

"Bren—" Jase turned, became a shadow against the white light of outdoors. There was a moment of silence. Then: "All right. All right. Whatever you say."

"We're here to enjoy ourselves. Make an effort at it. And get your wits about you. Complain to me in private if you must. *Don't* offend her. This is not a lesson. This is not an understatement. This is by *no* means a game."

Prolonged silence from the shadow in front of the light.

Then, coldly: "Oh, I don't take it for that, nadi."

It was sunset outside. The hilltop felt the chill of evening. But the fireplace functioned, the long table

had a white cloth and the benches had folded blankets
to keep the splinters from ruining clothes. There was
crystal, there were candles, there was the aiji's banner,
red and black, and the banner of Malguri, red and
green, within the candle and firelight, and there was a
respectable, even a splendid dinner in front of them.
Ilisidi sat in the endmost seat; Banichi and Jago and
Cenedi were seated, privilege of rank; Tano and Algini
were seated but on duty, even here, so Banichi said;
and the paidhiin were seated, one on one side, one on
the other.

No one sat endmost to match Ilisidi. But then, no one
ranked that high in the Association but the aiji himself.

There was pastry, there was a vegetable course—
immense quantities disappeared, which Bren helped,
and Jase discovered a vegetable dish he favored,
clearly, while it remained a wonder where Ilisidi put
the quantities she tucked away; certainly it wasn't evident on her spare and (for an ateva) diminutive frame.

It must go into sheer energy, Bren decided. For a
while there was no discussion, only food, and then the
main course arrived, the seasonal fare, which was fish,
and a delightful tart berry sauce.

"So," Ilisidi said, "did you settle your disagreement,
you two?"

The woman missed nothing.

"Jas-on-paidhi?"

"Nand' dowager, I am told not to talk except the
children's language. I apologize for my inability in
advance."

"Oh, risk it. I'm not easily shocked."

God, Bren thought. "Nand' dowager," he said. "Jase-
paidhi is at a great disadvantage of vocabulary."

"As the nation heard." Ilisidi tapped her glass and a
servant poured. "Water. Pure spring water. Perfectly
safe. —But, do you know, Jase-paidhi, I would have
bet against your learning the language so quickly.
Yolanda-paidhi, on the island, of course, had no such
requirement."

"No, nand' dowager."

"And she's been turning over the precious secrets—at a greater rate of speed?"

Pitfall, Bren thought and opened his mouth and didn't dare say a word.

"Not so, I think, if you please, nand' dowager. Engineering diagrams are the same with both the island and Bren-paidhi."

"One hears also of sad news from that quarter. One regrets your loss, Jas-on-paidhi."

Jase ducked his head. "Thank you for your good will, nand' dowager."

"And how *is* nand' Yolanda? Is she faring well? I get *no* news from my reprehensible grandson."

"I believe she is well, nand' dowager."

"You believe she is well."

Jase looked toward him, disturbed, likely not sure he'd followed her around that corner or used the right word. He had.

"He doesn't understand, nand' dowager," Bren said. And didn't add, thinking of those illicit radio transmissions, Nor do I.

"Oh, well. How do you find the fish, Jas-on-paidhi?"

"The fish is very good, nand' dowager."

"Good. —Such an innocent. What's it like on the ship, Jase-paidhi? Tell me. Satisfy an old woman."

"It's—a lot like being indoors."

"Oh, well, boring, then. Give me the open air, I say. Do you like it there?"

"I hope to go back there. When the ship flies, nand' dowager."

"And when will that be?"

"I'd say sooner rather than later, aiji-ma," Bren said, anxious to divert Ilisidi from her stalking and probing for reaction, one damned jab after another. She was *not* on her best behavior and she was enjoying every second of it.

"Another damned machine roaring and polluting the fields," Ilisidi said, and had a bite of fish. "Now, one could make a ship to go beneath the sea and see the wonders there. Have you ever thought of that, nand' paidhi?"

"It could be done," Bren said, and broke every law on the books.

"You might persuade me to go on a ship like that. I'm less sure about this spaceship. What do you think, nand' Jase?"

"About what, nand' dowager? I'm not sure I follow."

"Do you think I'm too old to fly on your ship?"

"No, nand' dowager. You ride. I'm sure you could fly."

"Wise lad. Flattery is the essence of politics. One wondered whether ship-folk are as wise as Mospheirans. Possibly they are."

"They can learn," Bren said, before Jase could think of words. "Don't you say yourself, aiji-ma, that he's quick?"

"Oh, not so quick as you, nand' paidhi."

"One tries, aiji-ma." It was a fencing match from start to finish. "So what do you have in store for us?"

"A brisk ride, a little outing. —More fish, nand' paidhi? I'll assure you simpler fare tomorrow."

He recalled Ilisidi's brisk rides and hoped Jase didn't break his neck. And had the other helping, taking that for a warning.

Jase, fortunately, said nothing. But seemed not to have as great an appetite.

"Well, well," Ilisidi began.

And of a sudden Banichi, Cenedi, and Jago were simultaneously leaving the benches in a fast maneuver, and Tano and Algini, rising, had guns visible in their hands. So did two of the servants. Something was beeping.

"Perimeter alarm," Cenedi said, with a slight sketch of a bow toward Ilisidi. And started giving orders to persons unseen in the room.

"Piffle," Ilisidi said, and rose slowly from the only chair. "What a pest!"

As a gunshot popped somewhere in the distance.

And Cenedi said, after recourse to his pocket com, "One individual. They have him."

"Him, is it?"

Oh, God, Bren thought with a sinking feeling.

"They haven't killed him, have they?" Bren asked, and held his breath until Banichi had asked and received an answer.

"No. He flung himself to the ground and surrendered. Quite wisely so, nadi."

Bren sat down again and had another sip of his drink.

The island of Dur was, he recalled from the map, off the northern coast of the promontory—down a great steep bluff that one would take for a barrier to sensible people. But it was there.

And after witnessing an ungodly persistence in a culture where a young man knew he was risking his life, he had a sinking feeling of a persistence that, measured against a minor air traffic incident, no longer made sense.

17

They were, Banichi said, over the dessert course, *questioning* the young man, and would have a report soon.

Jase looked entirely unhappy, and concentrated on the cream pastry with mintlike icing.

Pastries disappeared by twos and threes off atevi plates, and Bren poked at his with occasional glances at Jago, who returned not a look in his direction. Ilisidi had said nothing further; Cenedi wouldn't. Banichi wasn't communicating beyond what he'd said.

"The boy is a fool," Ilisidi said, out of no prior question, and added, "Do you know, lord Geigi invited us fishing, and offered to meet us with his boat on the southern reach by the airport. But I think this silliness may divert us to the north."

That brought a glance up from Jase, and Bren suffered a turn of the stomach. Nothing at this moment was chance, not Ilisidi's remark, not the boy's intrusion into a government reserve, not the mention of lord Geigi, and Bren recalled all too well the radio traffic to the north, which was to the north—of the island of Dur.

Which was not beyond reach of Mogari-nai and the earth station. Which was not beyond reach of the town of Saduri. Which was not beyond reach of the fortress where they were having holiday with a mostly invisible security with pipe and board scaffolding and an excess of dust in the shadows yonder.

Deana Hanks and her damned radio talk.

And her connections to Direiso and her ambitions to move against Tabini?

Direiso and her cat's-paw Saigimi, who was now dead, thanks to Tabini?

Direiso, who wished to be aiji in Shejidan, and who was a neighbor to Taiben?

Taiben was not only Tabini's habitual retreat and ancestral holding, but also the wintering-place for Tabini's aged and eastern-born grandmother who herself had twice nearly been aiji, but for the legislatures concluding her ascendancy would mean bloody retributions for past wrongs.

Their Ilisidi, their host tonight, sitting demolishing a third cream pastry.

The situation had so many angles one wanted tongs to handle it.

"So," Jase said, where angels and fools alike feared to tread. "Nand' dowager, but we *are* going fishing?"

Going fishing, Bren thought in disbelief. *Going fishing?* They had a young man under interrogation for invasion of a perimeter only slightly less touchy than that around Tabini himself, Ilisidi talking about lord Geigi joining them, and Deana Hanks talking to two atevi on radio who were probably Direiso's agents, and Jase asked were they going fishing?

His roommate, however, was neither clairvoyant nor briefed on matters, and the last statement he'd heard uttered regarded lord Geigi and a boat.

Ilisidi never batted an eye as she looked in Jase's direction and said, "Perhaps."

Oh, God, Bren thought, feeling that the conversation was going down by the stern. He tried to catch Jago's eye, or Banichi's, and got nothing but a stare from Cenedi as uninformative and sealed as Ilisidi's was. He looked the other direction down the table, at Algini, and Tano, and a cluster of the dowager's young men, as she called them, all Guild, all dangerous, all doubtless better informed than he was.

"I would like the Onondisi bay, nand' dowager," Jase said. "I've heard a great deal about the island. I saw it from the air."

Ilisidi quirked that brow that could, were the Guild under such instructions, doom a man to die, and smiled at Jase.

"We may, I say, go north, nadi."

Bren dropped his knife onto the stone floor, necessitating a scramble by servants to retrieve it.

"Foolish of me," Bren said with a deep bow of his head, and allowed its replacement with a clean one without comment. "Perhaps it's the drink, nand' dowager. May I suggest my associate go to bed now."

"Early start tomorrow," Ilisidi said. "These young folk. Cenedi-ji, were we ever so easily exhausted?"

"I think not, aiji-ma," Cenedi said quietly.

"This modern reliance on machines." Ilisidi made a wave of her hand. "Go, go! No one should leave the table before he's done, but get to bed in good season, else I assure you you'll pay for it tomorrow!"

Jase at least comprehended it was a dismissal and, Tano and Algini clearing the bench for him, he was able to extricate himself. Bren worked his way out, having been similarly freed by two of Ilisidi's security. The two further benches rose in courtesy to the departing paidhiin.

"Go, go," Ilisidi said to the offered bows, and gave another wave. "In the morning, gather at the front steps."

"Nand' dowager," Jase said with a further bow, and not a thing else. Bren escorted him from the hall, up the steps, to their room, and inside, into the candle-lit dark and chill of an unheated room.

Jase turned. Bren shut the door.

Jase said, humanwise: "Trust you, is it?"

"What's the matter with you? Were you *trying* to foul things up or was it your lucky night?"

At least Jase shut up, whether in temper or the mild realization that things might be more complicated than he thought.

"Do me a great favor, if you please, nadi. Go to bed."

"Are you coming back?"

"I assure you. Take whichever side you wish, nadi, and I will gladly take the other."

"Where are *you* going?"

"To try to patch up the dowager's good regard and find out what the boy from Dur is doing here, at the real risk of his life."

He might have been mistaken by candlelight; but there was a little reckoning of that latter statement on Jase's part, and maybe a prudent decision not to ask a question he had in mind.

"Will they tell you that?" Jase asked.

"They'd have told *you* if you hadn't set the evening on its ear. You do *not* question the dowager and you do *not* question her arrangements! Jase, what in hell's the matter with you? This is your associate here, me! This is the person with an equal interest in seeing that ship fly! What are we fighting about?"

He expected an explosion at least of equivalent magnitude. "Nadi," Jase began in Ragi, and then again, "What do I have to do to have you on my side, nadi?"

"I *am* on your side!" He dropped his voice, moved close and seized Jase by the lapels long enough to bring his lips to Jase's ear. "Bug," was all he whispered, and Jase went wooden in his grip and very quiet.

"Just stay here," Bren said aloud and let go.

And left.

Downstairs again, toward their makeshift banquet hall, where nothing had much changed except most of the security was on their feet, the servants were cleaning up, and Ilisidi was still seated, her cane, however, in her hands, and her chair angled at forty-five degrees to the table.

"Well," Ilisidi said, as if he satisfied expectations by appearing.

"Tano-ji," he said in passing, though it was an act of temerity to give orders to Tano, or to give orders to anyone in Ilisidi's hall, "keep an eye on Jase, please."

"Yes," Tano said as Bren came to Ilisidi.

"Dowager-ji," Bren said, "first, forgive my associate his lack of understanding."

There was a nod, with amiable quiet.

"And forgive me mine. But, nand' dowager, is there anything I may ask in confidence?"

"What do you wish to know, nand' paidhi?"

"Why is that boy here, aiji-ma?"

Ilisidi braced the ferrule of her cane against the irregular stones of the floor and leaned forward. "A good question. Cenedi-ji, *why* is this boy here?"

"He is young, he is intemperate, he lacks all finesse, and he believes he alone holds vital information about a threat to global peace."

He guessed, then, what that information might concern: a dweller on the island, near the runaway transmissions.

"Well-intentioned, then," he said.

"One believes so."

"Nandiin," Algini said quietly, Algini, who tended to pick up the small details, "he has repeatedly attempted to reach the paidhi—or the aiji. He seems not at all particular."

"Well, well," Ilisidi said. "Let's have a look at him. Nand' paidhi, do you wish to hear the matter, or not?"

"I shall gladly hear it," he murmured, "aiji-ma." His brain was racing meanwhile and he had Jago but not Banichi or Tano within the field of his vision. He thought that if there were a problem developing between him and Ilisidi he would see Jago's signal to withdraw once Ilisidi said that.

But at a certain point he had to rely on them and *their* man'chi to Tabini. He had never quite so much realized what it might be to stand in the middle of a sort-out of atevi loyalties, blind in his human heart of hearts to what might be going on in atevi; but knowing emotionally, human-fashion, that his heart was with Banichi and Jago, that his duty insisted on Tabini, and that friendship, yes, *friendship,* wanted Tabini and Ilisidi both to listen to him and not tear the world apart.

Stupid, stupid, to have it any other way, and he would not *believe* that Ilisidi was ready to make such moves, or that Tabini had so misread his grandmother in sending them out here.

Cenedi had made a call on his pocket com, and in

not very long black-uniformed security came in from the front door, among them Banichi and several of their own, among Ilisidi's; and with them, a figure in black—the fool, Bren thought—handcuffed and disheveled, and looking for all the world like a scared kid.

"Nand' paidhi!" the boy said.

"Young fool," Ilisidi said, and had his attention—at which point said young fool seemed to realize (surely he'd known the paidhi was here when he invaded the place) that he was in far deeper trouble. The boy grew quiet, and bowed as respectfully as one could in handcuffs and being restrained by two of the largest of Ilisidi's young men.

"The paidhi-aiji has a question for you," Ilisidi said. "Perhaps you will give him the courtesy of an answer?"

"Aiji-ma, yes, if it please your ladyship."

"Nand' paidhi?"

"Nand' Rejiri of Dur-wajran?"

"Yes, nand' paidhi."

"Why did you—?" Attempt to fly into my plane? That was surely not the intent. That was just a pilot inexperienced at that airport. "—come to Shejidan?"

"To tell the aiji there's treason."

"Then why pursue *me?*"

"Because your lordship could tell the aiji I wasn't a fool!"

There was a circular argument.

"I truly never expressed to the aiji that you were one." But the case was clear to him, now: the boy, humiliated, his plane impounded after near collision with the aiji's own plane, couldn't even hope for a hearing that wouldn't involve a plane, the ATC, and his father, a lord of the Association.

And this was a very upset young man, as shaken and as distraught as he'd ever seen an ateva become. "So," he said to the young man, "the aiji-dowager is listening to every word. What will you say, regarding this treason?"

And hope to God the treason wasn't something

Ilisidi was involved in. The boy couldn't know, any more than he could, unless his information accidentally involved Ilisidi's associates or activities, which he truly didn't think.

"Radios," the boy said. "And *humans*, nand' dowager. I'm not making it up."

"Go on about these radios and humans," Ilisidi said, seated like an aiji in court, indeed, with her silver-headed cane in her wrinkled hands and her yellow eyes sharp and absolutely uncommunicative. "What do you say, nadi?"

"That—" Having gotten permission, the young man lost all control over his breathing. "That a plane keeps going out and flying over the ocean, aiji-ma, and you can hear it talking with somebody who speaks Ragi, but who sounds like a human."

"Female, nadi?" Bren asked.

"On the radio—I don't know. I think it might be, nand' paidhi. One—one would hesitate to say—"

Bang! went the cane on the paving-stones. "And you were *where*, when you heard these things?"

"In my father's plane, aiji-ma."

"So you immediately flew to Shejidan and scared hell out of the aiji's pilot."

"Aiji-ma—" The young man was rattled. Badly.

"Could you not have made a phone call?"

"I was afraid—I was afraid it had to go through somewhere—"

"You could have told your father, young man."

There was a flicker of fear, real fear, in the young man's expression. "I stole the plane, aiji-ma."

"Keeping your father out of the notoriety, are you, nadi? The hell you stole it!"

"Aiji-ma, I stole his plane."

The paidhi himself would not like to have been the recipient of that look, in that position; and he had been, both.

"So," Ilisidi said, "what else do you know? *Not* from this plane. From your own sense and the gossip of your elders, what do you know?"

"The man'chi of my house is to the descendants of Barjida, nand' dowager."

That was a neat piece of evasion—to the Barjidi, meaning Tabini's line at the time of the War. Ilisidi was *married* into that line, not born to it, and it was a man'chi predating the present Ragi aiji but including him. He was in a damned machimi play and the kid was doing a piece of footwork either his father regularly did or that he'd seen on television, the classic cousin-to-the-line who turned out to have a knife on his person.

But it wasn't television, and the smile Ilisidi gave him was a dangerous, dangerous thing, while—the human tumbled to the fact slowly, being dead to atevi emotions—*he* was in exactly the same position, appointed and protected by the Barjida's descendant, Tabini-aiji.

Who had sent him here. Who had sent—God! *Banichi and Jago*—here.

The same team the aiji had sent to kill Saigimi— here, inside Ilisidi's defenses. *He'd* seen this game before, the extreme gesture, this insertion of someone deadly dangerous as Banichi and Jago along with the very vulnerable paidhi inside Ilisidi's defenses— challenging the dowager to make an overt move against him.

Or to take his pledge of alliance.

It was hard to keep his calm. But he stood there expressionless, having realized *exactly* what he'd been playing with when he'd taken Jase to Ilisidi.

He'd walked right into an operation of some kind, a thorn-patch where atevi could feel their way and he had to find it by sheer logic.

Did it *feel* right to Banichi and Jago right now? Did it *feel* right to Ilisidi and Cenedi? Or were atevi on one side or the other reaching some pitch of decision that would come crashing down?

Hadn't he said it? The ship would send another one. So would the island.

No. *No.* Tabini couldn't count on *anyone* more on his side than he was if he shot Deana and demanded the backup to *her*. Which might say something about his own sanity—but it *was* an atevi consideration, for a species that *felt* something about man'chi and its direction: a lord didn't attack his own—ask them to die, yes, send them to die, yes, but not without gain to him and his partisans.

Either Tabini was very sure of Ilisidi—now—or ready to take a loss that would not be inconsiderable to his power, a sacrifice of a very major piece for *no* gain commensurate with the loss.

"So," Ilisidi said in a tone of restrained anger. "If your man'chi is to the Barjidi, *if* you have sought the paidhi-aiji, perhaps you will deliver your information to the paidhi."

The boy's glance at him was instant and distraught. "I wish you to deliver what you have to say to the aiji-dowager," Bren said, "as a lord in whom I have confidence."

Clearly the boy looked marginally relieved. But scared. And going through layers upon layers in his mind, surely. He bowed one more time."I heard people plotting against the aiji, nand' dowager. I haven't lied, nand' dowager."

"Young and foolish," Ilisidi said. "What have you observed?"

"This human person. These pilots. Radios that move about the countryside and operate on the trains."

On the *trains*, Bren thought in surprise. Of *course* that would be one way to get a broadcast into some remote village, trains passing through, radios operating on the public bands, on or off by turns.

But Tabini had to be aware of such things going on.

So must Ilisidi.

"Who would do such things?" Ilisidi asked.

"People who say the aiji is turning us over to humans."

"Oh, and one day, one certain day some internal computer chip will make all our machines fail as the ship rains death-rays down on us and the humans pour off the island to ruin us—have you heard that one, nand' paidhi?"

"No, aiji-ma, I have not."

"More rational ones say that the ship itself is meant to fail, to bring down the government by that failure, and that the means will be a technical fault introduced through the designs themselves."

He had heard that argued soberly in the council rooms of the legislature. "There are numerous reasons that's not the case, nand' dowager."

"One has confidence in your confidence, nand' paidhi. But you are *so* persuasive. —What do *you* say, young man?"

"About—"

The cane banged the pavement. "Your wits, boy! What *were* we talking about?"

"About the aiji turning us over to humans, nand' dowager."

Ilisidi leaned forward, her hands clasped on the cane. "Do *you* believe it?"

"No, nand' dowager."

"Does your father the lord of Dur-wajran believe it?"

"No, nand' dowager. We are—"

"—in the man'chi of the Barjidi."

"And to all who support the aiji, nand' dowager."

"Does birthing the ingrate's *father* settle me in the Barjidi man'chi?"

"If you will it to, nand' dowager."

Clearly the boy was losing his composure but not necessarily his wits. But a game of wits with the dowager was not one any boy could win.

"Say that my ingrate grandson and I should have the same interest," Ilisidi said, leaning back, carefully skirting the question of whether she had an overlord, which was private and privileged information, but she admitted, for the first time he had ever heard, to *association* with Tabini. After years living among atevi a human could begin to hope he had the straight of it. "And say that your father, within the man'chi of the Barjidi, has sent his son to Shejidan—"

"My father never sent me—"

Bang! went the cane. "The hell, boy! Your father sent you when the assassination of lord Saigimi shook the inattentive out of bed from here to Malguri! You flew immediately to Shejidan, accidentally arriving *in* the flight path of the aiji's plane, and were involved with the tightened security so you could by no means deliver your message, which you have regularly attempted to inflict upon the paidhi! Am I correct!"

There was a small silence, a chastened demeanor. "Yes, nand' dowager."

"Why now? Why not earlier?"

"Because we didn't know the aiji might not know. Because if it *was* important, the aiji should know, nand' dowager."

"Going quickly and by stealth through the skies."

"Yes, nand' dowager." The boy bowed his head. "I broke the law. I knew I broke it."

"And broke it again coming here!"

"No, nand' dowager. I took the train."

Rarely did anyone get a reaction from the dowager when she was in *this* mood. The brows went up and crashed down, hard. "I mean coming through the barriers, young man! How did you know to come here!"

"It's all over—" The boy took a breath. "All over the province, all over the country, I think, nand' dowager."

"You, young man, will go with my security, you will stay in your room, and in the stead of your father, who is in the man'chi of my ungrateful grandson, you will take orders *from me,* do you hear, or I will shoot you with my own hand."

"*Yes,* nand' dowager."

"Take him elsewhere!" Ilisidi said, and members of her staff collected the young man. "See he gets supper."

The boy put up no argument about it. And Ilisidi, leaning on her cane, rose with a frown on her face.

"By train, indeed. Before we took off this morning, the boy left the capital. And changed trains. —Nand' paidhi."

"Aiji-ma."

"Radios. *Radios,* do you understand?"

"I have heard the rumor."

A wave of Ilisidi's hand. "To bed, to bed. Don't

concern yourself with tomorrow. We'll go riding. Perhaps we'll have a look at the sea and satisfy this intemperate young man you've brought me. He's beginning to be interesting."

He hesitated, then thought better of questioning Ilisidi.

"Aiji-ma," he said, and turned and went for the steps, thinking that he had to get a few minutes alone with his security.

He heard someone behind him. He didn't want to look and find out until he reached the privacy of the floor above.

Then he turned.

"Jago-ji."

"Nand' paidhi."

"Nand' paidhi," he echoed, in not-quite-mock despair. "*Talk* to me, Jago-ji."

"My room," Jago said.

He *wasn't* eager, now, to get himself into interpersonal maneuverings. But *he* had a roommate. So did she, but Banichi was downstairs. Jase was in bed, and not, besides, the person he wanted to overhear a frank talk between himself and the aiji's security about the aiji's grandmother—besides, twice, his room was probably bugged.

He walked in that direction. She did, and opened the door and let him in.

He stood while she lit a match, and a candle. It was a room no different from his, except for the stack of baggage in the corner, a stack of mostly black objects.

He shut the door. And Jago looked at him, her eyes reflecting a disconcerting shimmer of gold.

"Are we safe with the dowager?" he whispered.

"One believes so, nand' paidhi."

Nand' paidhi. He was vaguely disappointed. About what, he didn't know, and told himself he was a fool, but he couldn't but be conscious of her as someone he'd intimately trusted half a year ago; and he felt—he wasn't sure. Set aside. Something like that.

"The aiji is aware of the situation," Jago said, and then, straight-faced. "Should we whisper?"

At first he was moved to laugh and then thought of Jase next door.

"Our hearing isn't that acute," he said in a low voice. "What's going on, Jago-ji? As much as you can tell me. I'll rely on you to care for the rest."

"In brief, nadi, it's common knowledge the paidhiin are vacationing in the province. It was a news item yesterday evening, so the boy's appearance is far from amazing."

"Tabini is using us for hunting-bait."

"One would hesitate to put it so inelegantly."

"But true. Is it not?"

"True."

"Meaning persons of ill intent will flock here. — Mogari-nai and the earth station are right across the hill, nadi! We'll draw harm to it!"

A small pause. "Tabini-aiji has considered that proximity."

Not among things the paidhi should know, then. Gunshots on the lawn.

Or such a lawn as this fallen-down place had.

"Don't be out of countenance, nand' paidhi. There is a purpose."

"What purpose?" He tried not to become emotional, which only set atevi on the defensive with that, and not the issue. "I ask you, nadi, whom I greatly respect, are our interests protected?"

"By us, nadi."

"I always have confidence in that, but, nadi—" He didn't know what to say that Jago would understand. After all they'd been through they were back to that, and it was late, and he was not as sharp as he might have been an hour ago, or he was emotionally rattled and trying to think in too many different directions at once.

"What do you wish to say, nadi?" Jago asked.

He looked up at her, in the dark and the dim light that picked out the sparks of metal on her jacket, the gloss of her black skin, the gold shimmer of her steady gaze. And looked down and aside, because there just was no rational approach and the translator had no words. He wanted to ask what Tabini had in mind and he didn't. He found himself in emotional danger, was what, and he had every reason to be concerned for himself.

"I'd better go," he said, and reached back to the latch and ran into the door edge on his way out of this room.

"Nadi?" he heard behind him, quietly. Jago was confused, in itself a sign of the dangerous way he was dealing with things.

He went to his own room, and inside. The candle had burned down to half. Jase was in bed, a lump in the blankets, and didn't react to his coming in.

He stripped down to his underwear in the biting cold from the slit window, was a little conscious of the exposure to that window, and snipers, even as small as that exposure was, and then told himself that there was some kind of electronic perimeter that had warned them of the boy's approach, and that there was probably one of Ilisidi's men posted to guard all those windows, which were certainly too small for an adult ateva, so the hell with it, he said to himself. He had to trust the security. He had no choice.

He sighted a line between there and the end of the bed, and blew out the candle. He managed the transit most of the way, bashed his leg on the far corner post of the bed, and drew a deep breath from Jase.

"Is that you?"

"So far as I know," he muttered, settled from cold air to a cold bed and pulled the covers up to his chin. Jase was a warmth beside him. He shivered and tried not to.

"Find out anything?"

The brain wasn't primed to work. Other things had been in operation. He tried to recover where he'd left Jase in the information flow. "Kid's not a threat," he said. And remembered Jase didn't know anything about anything except they weren't at the beach and Jase wanted to go fishing.

God save them.

"I imagine we'll go riding tomorrow morning. Just be patient. We might ride down to the beach."

"Can you get there from here?"

"Far as I know. Or we might go up to Mogari-nai. It's near here. There's an old site there."

"Why are we visiting all these old things?"

The question astonished him. But professional judgment cut in and informed him that it might be ship-culture at work.

And where was Jase to learn the value of anything historic, if his world was the ship?

And where was Jase to derive the value of rare species? Or the concept of saving the ecology, if Jase's view was that of a steel ship and lights that kept a computer's schedule?

Where did one start?

"Understand," he said calmly, into the dark above his head, "that the preservation of all life on this planet is of great value, the animals, the plants, all valuable. So is the record of what lies in the past. Accept that this is valuable, not only to the dowager, but to me. Can you imagine that? They're not just old places."

"I—" Jase said. "I found it very strange to handle the descent pod. To walk in the station corridors. It was—a very lonely place. Very old."

"Atevi feel the same about such places as this. Only add a thousand years to the account. On Mospheira, when you walk into the old earth base command center, and you see all the clocks stopped, on the minute the power went—in the War—Mospheirans feel something like that. So don't call it 'old places.' They're more than that. And you know more than that. Clearly you do."

There was a long silence. Just a living presence in the dark.

"We anticipated—a great deal—" Jase said in a quiet voice, in the human language, "getting here. We didn't know what we'd find. We imagined there'd be changes. But when the station didn't answer our hail, we feared everyone had died."

He tried to imagine that. "It must have been a frightening moment."

"Frightening for a long time, while we were moving in. The systems wouldn't respond. Shut down, on conserve, was what we found. But we didn't know. We were really glad when we found there were human beings alive down here."

"And when you knew atevi had advanced so far?" It was amazing that they hadn't had this conversation already, but they hadn't. "How did you feel?"

"Hopeful," Jase said. "Really hopeful. We were *glad* of it, Bren, I swear to you."

"I think I believe that." He did. "Unfortunately it's not a hundred percent that way on Mospheira."

"The resources," Jase said, "are on *this* side of the strait."

"There are powers on both sides," Bren said, "that want something besides atevi in space." He took a chance. "What does the ship want?"

A little silence there, just a little silence. "The ship wants *somebody* up there that can repair what's broken."

"Wasn't that why the colonists and the crew went separate ways at the beginning? Colonists wouldn't *be* a cheap labor force?"

"It's not like that," Jase said. "It won't *be* like that."

"Damn right," Bren said, "it won't *be* like that."

But they meant, he was sure, different things.

There was silence, then. Maybe Jase thought the topic was getting too dangerous. Maybe, and it was his own notion, there was just nothing they could say to each other until that ship flew, and until they had options.

His mother might have had surgery by now, he thought. He didn't know. He thought, hell, he was within driving distance of the biggest communications post in the world, and he couldn't get a damn telephone? The communications his security had was instant and connected to everywhere but Mospheira. He should have asked for a phone.

He had the whole weight of the atevi government if he wanted to try to extract information, but the whole weight of the atevi government had to be used for atevi purposes and affairs of state, not, dammit, news from his family.

He stared at the dark above him and asked himself what kind of an impression he'd made on Jago, bolting from the room the way he'd done.

He'd have been warmer, distracted from his other problems, at least.

But Banichi would have come in for the night.

He didn't know what he'd have done, or said, or what he'd have explained. Likely Jago and Banichi both would have been amused. He wasn't sure he was capable of laughing at the joke. Not tonight, not now, not as things were.

He heard a quiet snoring beside him. Jase at least was tired enough to sleep. He thought of elbowing Jase in the ribs so *he* could rest; but he decided it wasn't that likely he would for a while.

Rest, however, just lying on his back on a surface that didn't move, piled high with blankets in a bed that was getting warm in air that was almost cold enough for frost. . . .

He heard an engine.

Distant, but clearly an engine where none belonged.

No reason to be alarmed. There was a perimeter set.

His security was not going to allow anything to slip up on them. Neither was Ilisidi's.

But what in hell? he wondered.

He heard it come closer, and closer, and finally saw the faintest hint of light touch the wall and vanish.

More engines—than lights.

Vehicles were moving about inside the perimeter.

The snoring had stopped.

"What's that?" Jase asked. In Ragi.

"I don't know." He flung the blankets aside and got up, barefoot, in his underwear, and felt his way around the end of the bed. He went to the window, in the cold draft, as Jase got up on his side of the bed and joined him in looking out.

"Security, maybe?" Jase asked.

"I don't know. Nothing Jago made me aware of."

"You suppose everything's all right?"

It was on a side of the building not exposed to their

view. The back side, he thought. As the vehicles had come up from that side.

There was a time he'd have run to Jago a couple of doors down and asked for explanation. But this time the conspiracy was of his arranging, and he still didn't know the extent of it.

He had a sinking feeling if he asked Jago she wouldn't know, either. And that if anything were wrong he'd hear about it from Jago and from Banichi.

Hell, he *hadn't* survived this long by leaving assumptions lie.

"Stay here," he said to Jase and, numb beyond feeling, snatched a blanket for decency and went out into the hall.

It was dark, excepting the candles.

And one of Ilisidi's young men, who stood in the shadows, whose eyes cast back the light.

"What is it?" he asked the man.

"Supplies and such," the man said. "Sleep peacefully, nand' paidhi."

"Banichi," he called out, worried that the mere opening of his door hadn't brought his security out of the soundest sleep. "Jago?"

"One believes they're helping below, nand' paidhi."

"I'll talk to them," he said. "You have communications."

"Yes, nand' paidhi." The man drew the pocket com out and flicked the switch. "Nandi. The paidhi would wish to speak to his security."

There was a reply he couldn't hear: the man had it against his ear. But he gave it to Bren.

"Banichi-ji?" he asked.

"Bren-ji?" It was Banichi, he had no doubt of that voice. *"Is there a problem?"*

"Is there reason for us to get dressed and come down?"

"No, nadi. Go to sleep. Everything is fine. We'll be early to rise."

"Well enough, then. Good night. Take care, nadi-ji." He handed the com back to its owner, feeling foolish on the one hand, himself with frozen feet and one frozen shoulder, and gave a courteous sketch of a bow, having doubted the man's authority, before going back to the room.

Jase had lit a candle. It was something Jase had seen servants do. From him, it was a piece of ingenuity. Jase stood there holding it, in his underwear, shielding the light from the gust produced by the door and the window.

"What's happening?" Jase whispered.

"It's all right." He didn't whisper. He whisked the blanket off and put it back on the bed. Tucked the foot of it in.

And got in. Jase said, "I hurt my leg getting the matches."

Jase had. He could see the skinned knee. Jase had taken a fall in the dark and he was mad.

"Sorry. Want a bandage? I'm sure the man outside can get one."

"No," Jase said, brought the candle to bed and then went back after something, probably the matches. It wasn't natural to think of both. Not in Jase's world.

Jase blew the light out and, Bren guessed, set the candle and the matches on the floor beside the bed and got in, half frozen, Bren was sure. He felt Jase's silence as a reproach. He'd deceived Jase too often, too long, and now Jase took for granted that was the final answer: it wasn't just Jase's rules-following soul.

"I'm a little worried," he said to Jase.

There was no answer. Jase *was* mad; and shivering beside him, which might be the cold sheets; and might be the situation.

"I don't think they want us to know everything that's happening," Bren said. "Jase, I'm telling you the truth, things may be all right. But there's been a lot going on in the world, and it's just possible things are a bit more complicated than seemed."

"You want me to ask."

He didn't even know what he was trying to say. "I just want you to know—I asked the dowager to show you the old ways. I wanted to help you. I wanted you to have the advantage I've had—in learning about atevi."

"So I won't make a fool of myself?"

It was his turn to be quiet. Jase had a knack, as he supposed he did, for taking the most delicately offered sentiment, and turning it inside out.

"Thanks," Jase said after a while. "Thanks for the thought."

Bren was still mad. And still didn't think Jase remotely understood him. And didn't want to get his adrenaline up any higher when he was trying to sleep.

"I've done the best I know how," he said to Jase finally. "I've tried to teach you."

The silence hung there a moment. From both sides.

Then Jase said, "I've tried to learn."

"I know that. You've done a brilliant job."

"Years left to get better at it," Jase said. "Got to. Ship's got to fly."

"Yeah," he said. It was disappointing, in his view, that he couldn't make Jase like life *here,* where he was. But whatever motivated Jase to study, whatever kept him wanting to go back, that was what he ought to encourage.

And Jase wanted to get back to his mother. He understood that part. Obligations. Divisions. Desperation.

He didn't know how his own was doing, or whether calls might have come in—if anything went wrong, surely Toby would call him.

"So what's going on out there?" Jase asked him.

Deep breath. "I think a number of vans or something came in." More motors than lights. He didn't mention that. One running with lights. The rest without. The electronic perimeter admitting them.

"So what did the guard say?"

"Supplies. Breakfast, maybe." He couldn't but think of the geography of the place—Mogari-nai, which was reachable by air and by a road up from the modern town of Saduri; and the town and the airport down one face of a steep rise on which this ancient fortress was posed, that faced Geigi on one side; and on the other side, the island of Dur.

Whose young heir was locked in for the night, he supposed. They didn't have keys for the bedrooms, but he'd about bet they'd found one for wherever they were keeping the boy.

What might be going on out there might involve calling the lord of Dur-wajran and informing him they now had a young idiot who could be reclaimed for suitable forthcoming information on the other side.

Politics. Tabini. The dowager. And those damned radio transmissions.

18

They walked out the front door and down the steps together, with the dawn coloring the sky, Ilisidi and Cenedi in the lead, and the rest of them, except the servants, all in casual hunting clothing, meaning heavy twill coats with the back button undone for riding, and trousers and boots that would withstand abuse far beyond that of the casual walk down a hallway. Jase, Bren had discovered early on, could wear his clothing and, their outing being on too short a notice for tailor-work, he'd contributed all his outdoor wardrobe to the adventure and packed for two.

Now, borrowed riding crops tucked beneath their arms, he and Jase walked down the steps in the middle of the company. Jago was walking with Banichi, just ahead of them, carrying the computer. Even in this event he didn't leave it.

He wished that he'd had a chance this morning to speak with either of them at length—he wished this morning that he'd not bolted last night, though he was still unsure it wasn't the wisest thing to have done—and now he wasn't certain that Jago hadn't intended to keep him busy and away from hearing and seeing whatever had gone on last night.

They'd not had a formal breakfast, and they'd had not a single hint what that noise had been last night. A lot of transport moving about. But no sign of it this morning. And as for breakfast—here in the open air came servants passing out cups and rolled sandwiches. Bren took one, and when Jase didn't think he wanted a sandwich, Bren nudged him in the arm. "Yes, you do."

"They're fish!"

"Eat it," he said, and Jase took one and took the drink. So they had their breakfast standing there. Tea steamed and sent up clouds into the morning air all about the crowd at the foot of the steps.

Meanwhile he tried to catch Jago's eye, but she didn't look at him. On one level, probably not sensible, he feared he'd offended her last night by ducking out in such a hurry, or looked like a fool, or possibly he'd just amused or disappointed her.

But on another level common sense told him that the little business between himself and Jago last night *had* had no time to resolve the deeper questions between them, and that he'd been very sensible to be out the door before it became something else under what amounted to the dowager's roof. At the very worst that might have happened, he could have gotten himself into an adventure he was neither emotionally nor personally quite sure of—and possibly she'd invited him in for the simple reason they needed to keep him away from information. Ironically that reassured him that his own security was involved in whatever was going on. To them he would commit his life without a question.

Maybe they didn't know that.

Maybe they didn't understand how he *liked* Jago, that dreadful word, and was attracted, he began to admit it; and did wonder certain things which could only be resolved by trying them.

But last night hadn't been that time.

He handed over his cup as the servants passed back through collecting them. He kept near Jase.

Fact: they had a young atevi in detention in their midst, an uncertain situation on their hands with Ilisidi, and somebody had been rummaging about the hilltop last night in motorized transport of which there was no sign nor acknowledgement.

So their lives just might be at some risk, not an uncommon situation in the last year but a situation that didn't need the additional complication of his distraction with Jago.

He had caught Banichi for one fast question in the upstairs hall: "Is there a reason for this rush? What in hell was going on last night?" and Banichi had said, "None that *I* know, nothing I can say, but we're going with the dowager, nadi: what *dare* we say?"

Banichi had been in an extreme hurry at the time. And Jago had been ahead of both of them. Banichi had only caught up to her in the downstairs hall and then they were out the door.

Bren looked around now counting heads. Tano and Algini hadn't shown up yet, in the general flow of Ilisidi's men outside. There were about twenty such men, in all, that he'd counted last night—doubtless a felicitous number, but one rarely saw all of Ilisidi's men on any occasion: the activity of communications and guard that surrounded her was the same as that around Tabini, and the number of them was just not something either Ilisidi or her guards freely unfolded to view.

He did see that the boy from Dur had come out with them, no longer in handcuffs, just a silent presence in that foolish and very dangerous black clothing he'd chosen, and closely escorted by two guards.

Presumably, in this outing, this proposed ride out to look at the countryside and to take the air, it was necessary that young Rejiri come along with them. That was very curious.

But something had Tano and Algini *not* meeting them out here, *not* already outside, and that was also curious.

Possibly Banichi had given them a job to do. A message to run down to the airport or, silly thought, up to Mogari-nai, which not only had the earth station that had monitored the space station for decades; but was the major link in a web of electronic communication.

It had the earth station and also a set of dishes aimed all along the coast toward Mospheira, as Mospheira aimed a similar array toward the mainland.

It was a nerve center, his security had informed him, which was run by the Messengers' Guild, which had not been outstandingly cooperative with him, or with Tabini.

Jase said, in a fit of depression over his father and the party and his own situation, I'd like to go to the ocean. *He'd* said to himself, foolish as he was, why not go to Geigi's estate for a little fishing, and catch that fabled yellowtail? And maybe a little riding. The mechieti hadn't gone back to Malguri for the summer.

So he'd gone to the dowager to see was she willing to back him up, with the notion *she* could teach Jase what he'd learned—and *she'd* said, well, of course it had made sense to come to the government reserve just across the bay rather than to go to Geigi's house asking hospitality—much more politically sound a move, Geigi could visit them here, by boat, an easy trip, the airport and van service lying just right on the water.

The hell! Bren thought to himself. He'd not appreciated the vertical scale, when Ilisidi had said the government site practically overlooked the airport.

He hadn't truly appreciated at all how close it was to Mogari-nai, whose situation atop high bluffs overlooking the sea he *did* know.

He hadn't appreciated the involvement of Dur, either, and *its* proximity to the illicit radio traffic in the north—saying that Dur was near the site was like saying Mospheira was. When you were on the coast there were islands, and nothing was that unreachably far from anywhere else if you wanted to derive trouble from it.

He hadn't expected the boy from Dur to show up last night.

But neither had Ilisidi—at least—if she had, she'd pretended well.

Traffic in the night—that his own security had expected, or not been overly dismayed by, so either it was routine and it *was* kitchen supplies coming up for some surprise banquet tomorrow, or it was something that lay within their man'chi—and *that* came down to very few items.

Knowing Ilisidi's general penchant for intrigue, however, either they were being gotten out for the day so that the cooking aromas wouldn't betray the surprise, or something was damn sure going on. He looked out past the crowd at a vast rolling grassland, gravelly ground with tough clumps of vegetation that grew in what might be quite a fragile ecology, up here on the ocean bluffs.

One of those national hunting reserves, to look at it. Atevi wouldn't eat commercially produced meat. There were immense tracts where no one built, no rail crossed, no one disturbed the land.

Perimeter alarms. Electronic fences. This place.

Had they ever notified the boy's parents, Bren asked himself, shortening his focus to the crowd ahead. Had *anyone* who might worry any idea the boy was with them?

He doubted it, the way he began to be concerned that there was something specifically afoot that had taken away Tano and Algini. From the steps, a head count turned up fourteen of Ilisidi's young men besides *his* small party.

He had brought in his luggage the gun he very illegally owned—under Treaty law that forbade the paidhi to carry a weapon, a gun that *was* Tabini's gift—and Banichi's. He hadn't dared leave it in the apartment with uncle Tatiseigi staying there; finding that in the bureau drawer would have sent the old man through the highly ornate ceiling. But he had tucked it into his baggage for safe-keeping, knowing his luggage never had to go through a security check. He'd never believed he'd need it on this outing and now he wished he dared go back inside to get it from his luggage, not that he knew what he'd want it for, but everybody else but himself and Jase, the boy from Dur, and the dowager herself, was armed.

Wind battered them, sweeping off the sea, across heights broken not even by a fence. Jase was cold, clearly, shoulders hunched, hands in pockets. The wind whipped his hair. He looked up and scowled into the gusts with the cheerfulness with which he might gaze into an enemy's face.

As a snort and a squall broke out from around the corner of the building.

Mechieti.

The huge, black creatures came around the corner, high-shouldered, massive in the forequarters.

Mechieti, the riding beasts that had carried atevi across the continent, that had carried them into war and on their explorations. Mechieti were vegetarian, mostly. But Jase stepped back up on the porch steps, and he thought about his own safety for the space of a heartbeat before pride made him stand his ground. They were a herd into which only their regular riders walked with assurance. Ilisidi's men started sorting the throng out, as the riders, three in number, who had brought the herd around to the steps added to the company of Ilisidi's men.

"You'll have the same mechieta as last time, I think," he said to Jase, who was glum and apprehensive of the whole affair. "Watch the nose. Remember?" Those blunt teeth on the lower jaw, the length of a human hand, could kill a man quite messily, or knock a novice stupidly flat on his back if he was fool enough to press down on the nose of an animal that regularly rooted up its food.

He counted himself still fortunate to have survived his own initial mistake with the beasts unscarred, and he had warned Jase half a year ago: those rooting tusks were blunt-capped to protect potential riders from being disemboweled in their ordinary herd behavior.

And if they fought, and this band had, a different kind of cap, war-brass, went on those tusks to make them sharp as knives.

"Nand' paidhi." One of Ilisidi's young men came to the steps to take charge of Jase, specifically. "Please come with me. Follow closely."

"Remember to keep your foot back," Bren called after him. Some mechieti learned that feet were in reach of a bite. Jase's mount the last time had come close to succeeding; and he never gave odds that his own twice-upon-a-time mount, Nokhada (his own, by generous gift of the dowager) would disdain such a nasty trick.

But he was excited. He had looked forward to a ride during this trip as his own enjoyment, far more than any fishing trip, and he was prepared to enjoy it if he could keep Jase from mortal injury. He was anxious to find Nokhada and renew acquaintances, and, thinking he'd spotted her, he went a little into the herd and whistled.

"Nokhada!" he called out, as riders called to their mounts. "Hada, hada, hada!"

The head turned, an eye observed, and with the surly inevitability of a landslide the neck followed, the body turned, and the whole beast moved—checked for a moment by another moving mountain.

Then, with an ill-tempered squeal that thundered against the eardrums, Nokhada *did* remember him and shoved her way through the others with such energy that one of Ilisidi's men had to pull his mechieta back to avoid a fight.

Prudence might have said to go for the steps. He stood his ground and Nokhada shoved and butted him in the chest, smelled him over and then rubbed her poll against his shoulder, prompting a human who'd been laid out flat and stunned once to step to the side and jerk smartly on the single rein to get that huge, tusked, and devoted head out of the way of his face.

The head came up, which indeed would have knocked him a body-length away if not sent him to the hospital, and then as the whole herd shifted, he was in danger of being squeezed between Nokhada and Cenedi's mount. He instantly lifted his riding crop, putting it end-on between Nokhada's shoulder and the oncoming mass. The steel-centered, braided leather crop stood the impact and shied the two apart again: it was a trick he'd learned his last trip out, it worked; and he jerked on the long, loose rein, which had one end fastened on Nokhada's jaw-piece and the other end slip-tied to a ring on the saddle, to get Nokhada to lower her body for a mount-up in the bawling chaos that was their setting-forth.

They were working out an agreement, he and she, or he was getting better at it. Nokhada extended a foreleg, and the other side of that *getting better at it* was his speed in tugging the rein's slipknot free of the restraining ring, getting hold of the saddle and being ready when Nokhada heaved upward with a powerful snap that pitched her rider up with the same force.

The stopping of said force allowed the rider, at apogee, to subside into the saddle if the rider had aimed himself appropriately at the seat and not to the side.

He had. Jase—was making the mount he'd made when he'd begun, being boosted up and into the saddle of a standing animal. Banichi was up; so was Jago, and the boy, last, who made a mount like Jase's, and made a wild snatch after the rein.

At that point Nokhada made an unsignaled full about turn and used that momentary inattention to get more rein and start her way toward the front of the column.

Ilisidi was on the steps, and came down to her mechieta, Babsidi, who held sole possession of the area around him: mechiet'-aiji, herd-leader. Babsidi came to the steps, and at a genteel tap of Ilisidi's riding crop extended a leg as Ilisidi tucked her cane into a holster made for it and stepped aboard, coordinating her step and Babsidi's rise with a grandeur no machimi actor he had ever seen achieved. This *was* a rider. This *was* the rider of this animal, for all the years of his dominance over the herd and hers over her followers. This was real; and a human found his breath stuck in his throat as Ilisidi brought Babsidi about, every other mechieta following and adjusting position, and tons of muscle moving as one creature.

Bren took tight grip on the single rein and held Nokhada hard from advancing, twisting her head as much as her long neck permitted. He pulled her full about and let her straighten out. He could see Jase, whose mechieta Jarani was one of the lower-rank mechieti, a quieter beast which wouldn't put him to a contest for the lead and which wouldn't lose him, either; the boy from Dur had a similarly quiet beast, so he trusted. But Cenedi's mechieta, who was second in the herd, and Nokhada, who thought she should be, were the two principle difficulties in the whole herd. Cenedi, used to being by Ilisidi, stayed with her. But Nokhada, if ridden, would try to get next to Babs if it killed her rider. He kept a tight rein.

Jase struggled just to keep his balance. He'd been chancy half a year ago and he seemed no abler at balance in the saddle after half a year on the world's surface. He held on with both hands; and Bren reined Nokhada in that direction, able to do so, and, he admitted it, showing off and fiercely proud of it.

Jase was not happy.

"If I die on this ride," Jase said, "I hope you can handle the manuals."

"You won't die. —Foot! Watch it."

Jase tucked it out of convenient reach of Jarani, who, frustrated in his aim, sidled over and bared teeth at Nokhada.

Nokhada ripped upward with the tusks at Jarani's shoulder, who returned the favor half-heartedly, and for a moment there was a sort-out all around them; but Jarani gave ground and ducked and bobbed his head as mechieti would who'd just been outmuscled by one of their kind.

"Damn it!" Jase said, shaken and mistakenly trying to prevent that head movement.

Meanwhile Banichi and Jago had moved to be near both of them, *their* security in a cluster of Ilisidi's young men.

"Where's Tano and Algini?" he asked finally, having something like privacy in the squalling confusion.

"On duty," was all Banichi said, meaning ask no further.

So presumably they were staying behind to guard the gear, or the premises, or were catching sleep in preparation for going on a round the clock alternation with Banichi and Jago.

Which sometimes happened. And from which he might take warning. All hell might break loose here before they got back—and their leaving might be a ploy to get the paidhiin to safety. They *might* have learned something from the boy that Banichi wasn't saying.

Ilisidi started them moving, not at a walk, but at least not at a breakneck run, toward the gap in the low fence by which the vans had come in. At that moderate pace Nokhada had no difficulty reaching the front; but even with Jase and the boy from Dur trailing them there was no chance of losing them. Putting a prisoner or a guest atop an associated mechieta was the best way in the world to guarantee that individual stayed in sight and placed himself wherever the herd-status of that particular mechieta encouraged it to travel. You couldn't leave unridden ones behind, either; they'd follow at the expense of any structure that confined them, breaking down rails or battering through gates, and injuring themselves if they couldn't.

Man'chi. In its most primitive evocation.

At Malguri he'd seen his first primitive model of the behavior and as a human being achieved his first gut-level understanding, with Nokhada under him battling to keep up, risking life and limb—primal need that had roused enough primal fear of falling and enough personal response to that ton of desperate muscle and bone carrying him at a frantic pace that he'd had no trouble *feeling* the emotional pitch. His heart still beat harder when he recalled that first chase. *He'd* been damned glad to have caught up to Ilisidi and not to have broken his neck; all through that long ride he'd been glad to catch up to Ilisidi, and he'd learned to think, gut-level, of the niche Nokhada wanted as the safest place he could be without even realizing the mechanics of what was going on in either the mechieta or in him: the mechieta going to its leader and the primate finding a safe limb, thank you, both at the same destination.

They still had some unridden mechieti with them today; but they were carrying equipment, canvas bundles.

What's that for? he asked himself.

But he had no answer, and didn't figure the paidhi

was going to find out from his own security, not
without bringing him into play, where *his* security
didn't want him to be.

So they maintained his ignorance for his protection
and Jase's, he feared. And they held their sedate gait,
good enough riders to keep Jarani and Nokhada
together, by urging Jarani and getting in Nokhada's
path, while he was getting good enough at least that he
wouldn't let Nokhada have the piece of Jarani's hide
that Nokhada, by her little tensions and shiftings under
his legs, wanted. The single rein always seemed to him
small restraint to the mountain of an animal she was,
but taps of the riding crop for some reason distracted
her from mayhem, possibly because earlier in her life
an ateva arm had wielded it, or just that she paid attention to her rider naturally.

And he was getting better at doing it at the precise
instant it had most effect, too, which he had discovered
to be right before she started to do something overt.
That required a rider reading those little muscle
twitches and the set of her ears and tapping her hard
enough to get her attention.

Jase, however, who had ridden once, from the
landing site to Taiben, was clinging with both hands to
the saddle, not doing much with the rein, which was a
good thing. He bumped about like a sack of laundry,
and was probably annoying hell out of Jarani.

But this was the man who found a window-seat on
an airplane a challenge to his sense of balance.

"Relax the spine," he said to Jase. "You won't fall.
Relax."

Jase tried. It was difficult for him, but he tried.

And at this speed there wasn't a tendency for the
herd to form into hierarchical order: individual
mechieti dipped heads unexpectedly, snatched bits of
green. Which scared Jase when it happened.

"Relax."

Jase's hands were, in fact, white-knuckled, and
Jase's mouth was a thin, straight line as Jarani took a
snap at another mechieta moving up on them from the

rear. That mechieta nipped back, and Jarani bumped Nokhada in sheer surprise.

The boy from Dur drew close, or his mechieta did: he was clearly another non-rider. He appeared to have notions what to do, but he wasn't winning the argument; and his mechieta shied into Banichi's, who gave it a head toss that was audible on impact.

"I'm sorry, nandi, I'm sorry."

"Rein!" Banichi said, and the boy tried, to the inconvenience of all around him as he mis-signaled and sent the well-trained creature off to the side.

He was better than that, Bren thought, with perhaps too much pride; but he patted Nokhada's hard shoulder and quietly gave Jase instruction what to do with the rein and with his feet.

And his spine. "Sit easy—easier than that," he said. "Dammit, Jase—*try* to fall off!"

Jase looked at him as if he'd misunderstood.

"Try," he said syllable by syllable, "to fall off. You can't. You're balanced. Relax, dammit. Rock. Sway. Do it!"

Jase sucked in a breath and let go his death-grip on the saddle. And leaned a little one way, and then the other. And gave another deep breath.

Banichi, damn him, crooked an easy leg across the saddle front, watched the performance, and grinned.

"Better," Banichi said. There was nothing in the entire universe that Banichi, who stood solid and square as a wall, could not do, and do gracefully. And Banichi laughed, waved his riding crop at the boy from Dur. "You listen to the paidhi, nadi. Sit like a living creature, not like a load of baggage."

Then—then for some reason unannounced—the pace increased.

And increased, until mechieti were moving together, almost in unison, stride for stride. Bren looked back as the old fortress fell behind them.

He saw, from the angle they'd achieved in their riding away, the back of the building and vans parked there, maybe six, seven of them.

Damn, he thought. He shortened his focus to Jago

riding close behind him, and knew she knew and no one was talking. They were headed upslope, now, up the general pitch of the rolling, fragile sod, on which a little brush grew, but not much, and never a tree. They were out here in an area reminiscent of riding the ridge at Malguri, climbing, and climbing.

He thought of the bluffs that overlooked the sea, and the installation of Mogari-nai that sat atop them.

He thought of the boundary out there beyond the horizon, that invisible demarcation of sea and air that marked where Mospheira began. They were moving toward it. He didn't think by the direction they were going they'd come in view of it. But they would come close.

And the speed and smoothness with which the mechieti traveled even walking in this grassy, open land was something he'd never felt in the rough land around Malguri. It was wonderful, a traveling pace that let even Jase find his sense of the rhythm in the movement. The boy from Dur gave up holding on and rode easily in the saddle.

And slowly, inexorably, predictibly, Nokhada lengthened stride and came closer and closer to Ilisidi and Cenedi. Banichi and Jago moved with him, up through the herd.

There was never a word said. Ilisidi, a competition rider, rode with that easy grace that put them all to shame, and Babsidi's long strides challenged all of them that followed her, reminding them that Babsidi *was* quality, from his finely shaped head to his powerful rump. No one got ahead of Babsidi. And Nokhada's joy was dampened only by the presence of Cenedi's mechieta, her chief rival, who *always* had a rider, an entitlement of some kind Bren had never figured out. Unridden, Nokhada hung back and caused no trouble; with him aboard, she aspired, that was all, she aspired to the front line—and made her rider feel guilty that he was so seldom there.

But he had no idea, absolutely no idea what drove her, or whether she'd been glad to see him when she recognized him after an absence or whether her fierce mechieta heart just saw justification for raising hell. He patted her shoulder. It got a flick of the ears; but no understanding of her. He said to himself he had to arrange to ride more often, somehow.

Among other dreams.

The mind could grow quiet, watching that motion, hearing the noise of mechieti at that comfortable pace all about them. Watching that horizon. Watching the shadows that had been in front of them slowly, slowly overtake them until the sun beat down on their heads.

Then Ilisidi took the group to a slower pace, and to a stop. Jase caught up to him for the first time in over an hour, and Jase had done it—had stayed on, had even, with encouragement from the riding crop and his feet and the rein, gotten Jarani to move through the crowd.

"Good for you," Bren said as they sat on the hard-breathing mechieti. "How are you doing?"

"Alive," Jase said, and seemed to be in pain.

Jago and Banichi moved up close. Meanwhile two of the men had slid down and were getting one of the mechieti to kneel, to let them reach the pack it carried.

"Do we go back now?" Jase asked.

"Not yet," Banichi said; and the men hastily getting into the pack had come out with a bag of sandwiches, which they passed about, beginning with the dowager.

They ate the sandwiches, and the mechieti under them grazed the sparse vegetation, and wandered as they grazed, taking them in whatever direction or association the mechieti chose. They never got down. Canteens were an ordinary part of their equipment, and they drank. After that, the men afoot adjusted the canvas on the one pack they'd gotten into, remounted, and Ilisidi started moving again.

Not back toward the fortress, but dead ahead as they'd been bearing.

They'd started at dawn, they were going on past noon—they weren't going to be back by dark, that became clear as they kept going.

But now that Jase failed to besiege him with questions he began to have questions of his own, no longer *where* they were going: that was, he suspected almost beyond question, eventually, Mogari-nai.

Why should they be going there? Considering the contingent of vans that had moved in behind them, coupled with Tano's and Algini's absence, he had a notion, too, of that answer: that Tabini-aiji was not pleased with the establishment at Mogari-nai, or the Messengers' Guild.

Dared the aiji take on a Guild, and what would happen if he did? The Astronomers had fallen from highest of all the Guilds when they'd misinterpreted the Foreign Star, when the ship had appeared in the heavens the first time and slowly built the station. In the time when the Astronomers had predicted the future, they had entirely failed to know the nature of their universe, and they had fallen.

Possibly the Messengers had failed to know the nature of *their* universe, and the aiji had resolved to see that his messages flowed accurately. But to take on the Messengers when the political situation was so difficult and so fraught with trouble, with Direiso urging his overthrow and Hanks and her radio broadcasting to atevi small aircraft.

Yet there it was, if he thought about it. The radio. Another *communications* problem: another problem that could be laid right in the Messengers' laps. Radio traffic was a problem of which the Messengers were in charge, which Mogari-nai could have heard, especially situated where they were, near the coast.

If there were difficulty with one Guild, what other Guilds would stand by the aiji most firmly? What Guilds *had* stood most firmly by the aiji? The Mathematicians—and the Assassins.

Direiso had benefit in that illicit radio. *She* would stand by the Messengers, if they were turning a blind eye to the problem.

The government had potential difficulties up here. And Banichi and Jago weren't saying a thing.

Maybe it was Ilisidi's orders. He had the sudden sinking feeling Ilisidi had found their vacation a fine

excuse to be out here, and the paidhiin might be superfluous to her intentions to visit Mogari-nai.

Certainly Jase was.

But dammit, there were things he needed to know
too. And he was going to find out, if they could just
shake loose some answers.

19

It was a long, long ride at a fair clip after that. Nokhada disliked eating dust and fought to get forward, which Bren fought to prevent, not wishing to leave Jase alone, even if the spacing necessary to the mechieti for their sheer body size made conversation difficult.

That meant that the strangers to Ilisidi's company all rode in a knot that strung out at times, but never broke entirely apart so long as Bren kept a tight rein on Nokhada, who eventually seemed to resign herself to the notion that due to some failure of ambition or temporary insanity on her rider's part they were not going to dash forward and attempt to occupy the same space as Cenedi's mechieta—for maybe this little while.

Ilisidi, meanwhile, ignored them to hold consultation with the armed young men who took her orders, and one or the other would fall back to the rear guard. Bren kept glancing at the horizons, asking himself what was going on. There was no recourse to the pocket coms, nothing to indicate any problem. But something had changed.

There was a wicked, angry streak in this woman, not just in a human opinion but in *two* species' ways of looking at it. Ilisidi had been genial at the dinner last night; that was the velvet over the steel. Ilisidi was the gracious lady, the lame old woman—and the aristocrat, lord of her scaffold-supported hall. She'd arranged that crystal-laden table simply because it was difficult, and because her staff, too, did the impossible at her whim.

This morning she'd ceased to make things difficult for her staff and, astride Babsidi, whose four strong legs carried her with more speed, agility and strength than any man alive, she began to make things difficult for *them*. It was her way of saying to the world, he began to think, Those who follow *me* have to follow at disadvantage and difficulty. It was the condition of her life. She was *not* aiji. But those who served her treated her wishes as if she were.

And to the powers around Tabini she said, When you who rejected *me* as aiji suddenly want my help, damn you all, you'll bleed for it.

So the aiji's security (along with the paidhiin, who were excused from the normal considerations of man'chi and courtesies due, but not from the suffering part of it) didn't get full information from her, either: they were simply supposed to follow in blind obedience whenever fortune and chance, those devils of Tabini's designs, put his agents temporarily under her instructions.

That was one way Bren summed it up, having seen it in operation at Malguri and again in the Padi Valley.

Or possibly it was nothing of retribution on Tabini at all.

Perhaps it was just the native style of the old-fashioned, unabashed atevi autocrat she was—as old-fashioned in some ways as the fortress of Malguri off in the east—to make them follow her only under her terms.

As if, ateva to the core, she *proved* the direction not only of the man'chi of the mechieti she lent them, but that of the men she led.

Bren reasoned his way to that precarious point, while slowly stretching muscles he only used when he skied and when he rode, and bruising points of contact he *only* contacted when he rode. He'd asked for it. He'd asked for it for good reasons, but he'd forgotten how badly one could ache after a ride with Ilisidi.

There was, however, the suffering of the boy from Dur, who now rode with inexpert desperation and, being taller, leaned more, with a more committed center of gravity.

The boy from Dur fell off, and fortunately held to the harness on his way down.

The dowager kept going, as Bren reined in, as the boy's mechieta tried to keep going, as Banichi and one of Ilisidi's men reined in and Jago went on with Jase, who had no success stopping Janari at all: if the herd was going, Jase was going.

"Bren!" Jase called back in alarm, as if he were being kidnapped.

The boy from Dur meanwhile proved that one of atevi weight and from a standing start (or from upside down with one foot still in the bend of the mechieta's neck and the other on the hither side of the beast, while hanging onto the saddle straps) could not leap or even crawl back into the saddle. To a likely devotee of television machimi, it was surely an embarrassment.

"I'd get off," Banichi said dryly, as he, Bren, and Ilisidi's man Haduni all watched from mechieta-back. "I'd make him kneel and get up from the ground."

One suspected if anyone could *do* the television trick, Banichi might, but the boy from Dur gave up his foothold on the mechieta's neck and hopped to the ground, whereupon the mechieta decided he was through for the day and decided to wander off.

The boy was clearly mortified, took a swat with the riding crop while holding to the rein and the mechieta bolted, jerking the rein from the boy's hand and flinging him flat.

Haduni rode after the mechieta, which was on its way to join the herd.

The boy nursed a sore palm and bowed and bowed again.

"I'm sorry, nandi. I'm very sorry."

"Shouldn't have hit him," Banichi said. "That's for running."

"Yes, nadi." The boy, a lord's son, bowed, clearly in pain.

Meanwhile Haduni had caught the mechieta and brought it toward them.

Banichi tapped a strap on his mechieta's saddle. "Hold and tuck up," Banichi said, and that was something Bren had seen in the machimi, too. For the short distance they had to go, the boy held to the saddle strap while Banichi swung to the other side and counterbalanced, and they met Ilisidi's man and the recovered mechieta.

Then the two men gave the boy a very quick lesson on how to get the mechieta's attention with a tug on the rein, where to touch the crop to get it to kneel, how fast to get his foot into the stirrup, and how to use the animal's momentum to settle on, with what tension of the rein. It was familiar stuff. And it was a good lesson, which the boy from Dur seemed to take very gratefully.

"Very much better, nandi," Ilisidi's man said.

"You have a chance," was Banichi's judgment, and they set off at a brisk clip toward the rest, who were now over the horizon of a land that didn't look all that rolling. But it was. And the dowager, Jago, Jase, and the rest were as invisible as if they'd sunk into the sparse, gravel-set vegetation.

It wasn't the only time they had to stop for the boy from Dur, whose mortification was complete when, at one such crisis, the mechieta led him a chase, body-length by body-length, as it grazed on the fine spring growth and the boy would almost lay hands on it only to have it move on.

There was laughter.

"Someone should help him, nadi," Jase said, as if suggesting he should do it; but Bren shook his head. "They laugh. If they meant ill, they wouldn't. If the boy laughed it would be graceless and impudent."

"Why?"

"Because, nadi, it would signal his mastery of the matter." The mechieta eluded the boy another body-length, and the boy this time made a sprint for it. The mechieta, almost caught by surprise, bolted, and the boy went sprawling, clutching his leg. There was laughter at that, too, but fainter, and one of the men got down to see to the boy and another chased down the errant mechieta.

"Good try, boy," the dowager said. "Bad timing."

The boy, clearly in pain, bowed. "Thank you, nand' dowager." And limped over to the mechieta the man brought back for him. He properly had it kneel, had it hold the posture, the lesson of his last fall, and got on with dignity.

"Good," Ilisidi said shortly, and Bren guessed there was—if not devotion forming in a young atevi heart, for atevi reasons: man'chi would determine that—at least a knowledge that respect could be won from her.

As good as a ribbon, that was. A badge of honor.

"Nandi," the boy said, and bowed with a modern conservatism, not going so far as the arm-waving extravagance of the riders of such beasts on the television. He managed not to look foolish.

From Jase there was silence. If they were lucky, Bren said to himself, there was deep thought going on.

Midafternoon. There was one break for, as the atevi put it, necessity, at which they all dismounted (it was Banichi's comment that in less civilized days they didn't dismount at all) and went aside with two spades from the packs, men to one side of a small rise, women to the other.

"Nadi," Jase said in a faint, unhappy voice, "I can't do this."

"You'll be terribly sorry in a few hours if you don't," Bren said with no remorse at all, and Jase reconsidered his options and went and did what he had to do.

He came back happier. Embarrassed, but happier. They rejoined the dowager and Jago, the mechieti having waited quite happily without a boy chasing them. Babsidi came to the dowager's whistle, and riders sorted the rest out.

The boy from Dur and Jase were the last up, but they managed on their own.

Definitely better, Bren said to himself, safe and lord of all he saw, from Nokhada's lofty back; and Babsidi started moving, which meant Nokhada had to try to catch him.

He let Nokhada win for a while. Jase was doing well enough back there, and was not slowing them down.

At no time yet had they hit an all-out run: they had mechieti carrying the packs, and that, he began to realize, was the primary reason. But the pace they did strike ate up the ground.

They were going west. And they reached a point that the sun burned into their eyes, and still the mechieti kept that steady gait.

He had shut his eyes to save them pain from the light when a hitch in Nokhada's rhythm warned him of change ahead, and his eyes flashed open as they topped a low roll of the land.

The horizon had shortened. The land fell away here into golden haze.

The sea stretched out in front of them hardly closer than they'd seen from the plane. Rocky hills across a wide bay were only haze. An island in blued grays rose from the golden sheet of water.

The mechieti stopped as Babsidi stopped, on the rim of the land.

"That's Dur!" the boy said, and added meekly, in courtesy, "nand' dowager."

"That it is," Ilisidi said, and signaled Babsidi to go down. She was quicker to dismount than Cenedi, snatching her cane from the loop in which she had kept it, and with a hand on Babsidi instead of the cane, waved the stick at the immediate area. "Make camp."

"What direction are we facing?" Jase asked quietly.

"West. That's the sun. Remember?"

Jase pointed more directly at the sun, which was slightly to their left, and near a knoll of rock and gravel that shadowed dark against the sun and broke the force of the wind. "That's west."

"North." Bren signaled the direction. "We're facing west northwest."

"West north," Jase said.

"West northwest."

It wasn't a concept Jase got easily. But Jase repeated

it. "West northwest. Dur to the north and west.
Mospheira west. Shejidan is tepid."

"South. Actually southeast."

"South," Jase amended his pronunciation. "East. Can
the mechieti go down to the sea?"

"On a road or a trail they can. Trail. Small road." He
didn't see one at the rim, which looked sheer to his
eyes. "But we've done enough traveling for the day.
Supper. I hope." In fact the order was going out now to
make camp, and he heaved a sigh, feeling a definite
soreness that was going to be hell tomorrow.

"She said sit down?" Jase had heard it too.

"Settle for the night, nadi. Camp is the word."
Talking with atevi was a constant battle to have the
numbers felicitous. Talking to Jase was a continual
questioning of one's memory on what words Jase knew
would carry a thought.

"We go down to the sea in the morning."

"Nadi, remember manners. Don't bring up the matter
at supper. The dowager gives. She won't have things
demanded of her or she'll say no. Face."

Jase was disturbed. But he mended his manners, made his face void of thoughts, and bowed
slightly. "Nadi. I shall remember. North. Northwest.
South. Southeast. Is there a northeast, nadi?"

"There." He pointed. "Taiben is in the northeast.
Southwest is Onondisi Bay. This water is Nain Bay."

"I know. It was on the map."

Nain Bay was on the map. The sun wasn't. And Shejidan was tepid.

One hoped, Bren said to himself, that this whole
adventure would express itself only in Jase's striking
vocabulary. He hoped the night to come would be
quiet, that the vans had been the caterers', that Tano
and Algini had stayed to manage the details of a
welcome-home banquet—all possible—and that none
of the things added up the way they might.

"Also," he said, trying to think of everything with a
man for the first time loose among the hazards of the
outdoors, "nadi, be very careful of the cliff edge.
Weather weakens the edge, do you understand? The

earth could crumble and you could fall a long way if the edge is weak."

"Then how do we get down?" Jase asked.

"Carefully," Bren said. "And on a road if one exists. That's what one does with roads."

The packs began to come off the mechieti. Canvas bundles came down.

And sprang up rapidly as tents—spring-framed, modern tents, arising with blinding quickness.

For a woman who favored the ancient, Ilisidi certainly didn't disdain the latest in camping gear. He *knew* those atevi-scale tents. Northstar, the same brand of Mospheiran-made tenting that had served Mospheiran campers for generations, was a big export item to the mainland in atevi scale, a very, very popular export that helped Mospheira secure aluminum. The paidhi's mind was full of such helpful eclectic data.

But a tent like this modern thing of aluminum and nylon certainly wasn't what he expected the dowager to be using. And in hunting camouflage, not the house colors. They sprang up, arched, immediate, ground-sheeted, and pegged down with toothed lightweight pegs that went into soft ground like this like daggers into crusted bread.

"What are we going to do?" Jase asked, he thought somewhat obtusely, and he answered with a little impatience: "I suppose we're going to have supper, nadi-ji."

The packs gave up not only tents, but well-packed modern thermal storage, so there was no need of fire, and the mechieti, grazing, wandered off to join the mechiet'-aiji and to have Ilisidi's men take off their harnesses.

Jason sat himself down on a hummock of grass and was examining a stem of bristle-weed as if it were of significance—and of course it was a curiosity, to him. The boy from Dur, Rejiri, had appeared to settle on Jase as a person of great interest and minimal threat and, having nothing else to do, had settled down opposite Jase, the boy talking to him rapidfire in a way that looked to have Jase engaged but confused. There was no knowing what Jase said, but Jase looked embarrassed, and the boy laughed.

But, Bren said to himself, Jase could handle himself. The boy who'd nearly bashed a plane into him wasn't one to talk about taking offense at the paidhiin.

He could draw breath, at least, and allot concern about Jase to someone else as the sunset, beyond the picturesque spire of rock, drowned in a bank of leaden cloud.

He walked about at peace and off duty, stretching out muscle—doing nothing for bruises near the bone, but it did seem to prevent the worst stiffness. Banichi and Jago were talking with Cenedi; Ilisidi was talking to three of her young men who were about to set out the thermal containers. As a rough camp, it was a lot more grand than the night they'd spent dodging bombs in Maidingi's hills.

And there was still nothing ominous on the horizon behind them. One could hope, maybe.

They were up here, notably, with the establishment at Mogari-nai, which had not made Tabini happy. And if they were up here to rattle the foundations of Mogari-nai and the Messengers' Guild, that Guild was not a warlike crew. Their hostilities mostly expressed themselves in the paidhiin's fouled-up mail.

There was also the matter of the tower up by Wiigin, and the pilots and the communications regulations. That as well as the communications fallouts he was sure was on the agenda, if they were paying an official call on Mogari-nai, and he certainly didn't rule it out.

And if he got all that straightened out, he might possibly get another chance to make a phone call, this one with the weight of the aiji and the aiji-dowager behind him, to crack the phone system.

He wondered what had happened with his family now. No calls, he was reasonably sure, at least nothing that had gotten past Mogari-nai, through which the incoming calls from Mospheira were all routed. By the luck that dogged him in that department, there was a good chance any incoming call that Toby sent was hung up in politics. Ilisidi, if she was planning a housecleaning at Mogari-nai, couldn't head the agenda of the aiji of Shejidan with a query from the paidhi-aiji. It just wouldn't look right. But he might get that call through after other business was finished.

So he walked and he stretched his legs. He walked closer to the sea than he would have liked Jase to come, and he shouldn't have done it. Jase followed him, with the boy from Dur trotting along with him, pointing out the sights, telling them there was, approximately, Wiigin, in that haze across the bay, and there was Dur, one could just see the lights in the gathering gloom, and that was the fishing port, but his father's house at Dur-wajran, *that* was on the height of the island, which had been a fortress in the days of the first sailing ships, but the inhabitants of Saduri on the body of the mainland, with their deeply inland harbor, had attempted to take the trade, even if they'd had to dredge the bay, because of the deeper draft of modern ships.

It was all done with scarcely a breath. And Jase looked a little desperate.

"Supper," Jago came to say, "nadiin-ji."

They had set the tents in a semicircle, the back of each to the wind that escaped the knoll. The company settled down to a lightless supper as the dusk settled about them, and there was good hot food from the insulated containers.

There was also a wind getting up that, in Bren's estimation, was going to make two humans glad of their jackets and the insulated tents before morning. The synthetic canvas fluttered and rippled in the wind, and the clouds flew in rags above their heads, gray in an apricot sky.

The mechieti grazed in apparent contentment. Jago had stowed the computer, little good that it was besides mental comfort, and had put it in his tent. They passed out sandwiches and had tea from instant heat containers in insulated cups.

When the dowager *wanted* modernity, it attended her. Clearly so.

"So, Ja-son-paidhi," Ilisidi said. "How do you fare?"

"Well, nand' dowager, thank you." Jase was on his very best behavior, and bowed with courtly grace.

"And you, son of Dur-wajran?"

"I am well, nand' dowager. Very well."

"And *you*, nand' paidhi?"

"Curious, nand' dowager, about your purpose here."

"Ah." Dark was coming down on them. "Curious. I thought you might be. What do you *think* we're doing out here besides pasturing the mechieti and enjoying the sea air?"

"Annoying Mogari-nai."

He took a chance. He was relatively certain of that much.

And he amused the dowager, whose shoulders rose and fell as she leaned upon her silver-headed cane. "The earth station, they call it. This unsightly great bowl. An offense, I say."

"A shame they put it on such a lovely view. But how else could it also watch Mospheira?"

They sat crosslegged. On ground still cold and damp with spring. And ate fish sandwiches.

"Do you think so?" Ilisidi asked, and he had the feeling that it was no casual, habitual challenge, but a question very much to the point of the hour. "Let me tell you, nadiin, before the aijiin sat in Shejidan, before humans were a suspicion in the skies, before foolish atevi had made stupid smoking machines to run on rails across the country and frighten the creatures that lived there, and before that eyesore of an earth station existed or a petal sail had dropped down to annoy us, there was war in this place. Where we sit, there was death and bloodshed." Ilisidi held out her hand for a refill of her cup, and a young man ducked close and low to refill it. "Bones probably underlie this very hilltop. And do you know why, heir of Dur?"

"The island of Dur," the young voice said, "was held by the heresy of the Gan, and they used to send ships up and down the coast to collect gold and grain, and they killed anybody that opposed them. They held the whole coast and they raided on Mospheira. But aijiin

from several townships began to follow the aiji of
Wiigin, and they raided the island and set up—set up
our line."

"Wiigin it was," the dowager mused. And pointed a
dark forefinger. "Source of this traitorous tower, this
hotbed of conspiracy."

"But now," the young man said, "nand' dowager, we
follow the Barjidi."

"Since the War of the Landing. That *now*. Two hundred years of *now*. "

"Since the War, nand' dowager." The boy had
become very quiet, very wary, sensing that he was
being stalked, Bren was sure, and asked himself to
what end Ilisidi was proceeding.

"The petal sails came down on Mospheira," Ilisidi
recalled, "the wandering machines tore up the land and
the stones of the Gan, and for a time that was convenient for Barjida-aiji, that the last stronghold of the
Gan should fall to such an unforeseen threat. The
grandmother stones were downed not by fleshly hands,
but by these reeking machines. Machines struck down
the heresy."

"Yes," the boy said. "And all the atevi on Mospheira
left and settled on this coast."

"Foolish politics," Ilisidi said. "The Gan lords
attempted to deal with what they thought were men
descended from the moon. And it killed them. Did it
not, nand' paidhi?"

He did not want part of any quarrel, ancestral or otherwise. The atevi of the coast held just reasons for dislike
of humans: many of them had moved off Mospheira to
escape human contact, human ways; more had moved
off when the War of the Landing had ravaged the island;
the last had left when the Treaty of Mospheira had given
the land to humans, the whole of a vast and once pros-
perous island.

"We did each other great harm, nand' dowager." A
gust battered them.

"A good night to be under canvas," Ilisidi said. "And
a strong wind rising. But what would you tell our guest
from Dur, regarding humans? Should he fear them?"

Loaded question. Very.

"Yes, nand' dowager. At least one should remain prudent."

"Are all humans on the island reasonable people?"

"Some are, nand' dowager. Some are very well disposed to the peace. And I have discovered some are not."

It was an infelicity of two, unbalanced, positive and negative. It could not be allowed to stand. It was, in its way, a question. But by inviting the posing of two, the dowager had encouraged it. *This* was the difference between competency and fluency: *this* was the line he'd begun to cross in his off-the-cuff negotiations, the line across which humans who'd dared it had frequently blundered. *He* felt a kind of elation, aware of what he was doing as Wilson-paidhi never had figured it, aware the dowager was getting responses with which *she* could know she was understood.

And with a twist of her mouth, as at some sour taste, the dowager added,

"The Kadigidi are *fools*."

"I agree."

"It lastingly troubles me that I did not shoot that woman."

Direiso was a possibility. But he knew *that woman* had one meaning to Ilisidi. "Hanks-paidhi, aiji-ma?"

"Hanks." Definitely a sour taste. "Melon-headed, my ally, did I tell you?"

Jase had to wonder about his vocabulary.

"Lord Geigi?" Bren asked.

"One had an excellent chance to shoot Hanks-paidhi," Cenedi interposed. "And Geigi protected her."

"Melon-head," Ilisidi said.

"So what *did* happen, aiji-ma?" It was a point of his extreme curiosity. "One hears that there was breakage of small objects."

"Nothing of taste," Ilisidi said. "Oh, it was easy for Geigi to gain admittance to Direiso's estate. Direiso had offered Geigi money to pay off a certain"—a waggle of Ilisidi's fingers—"oil investment gone bad. Saigimi had the extreme impatience to call it due immediately. Saigimi's wife is, you may have heard, Geigi's cousin. And *she* held the financial note on the house at Dalaigi. She had no idea that Geigi dared come to me with the matter." By now a smile was tugging at Ilisidi's lips. "Silly mistake. And of course Direiso had involved herself with that detestable human woman who had embarrassed them all. Saigimi had taken her from the capital, so my sources say, and brought her to Direiso's estate somewhat against his will."

One *had* to be aware of the lord of Dur's son, who was sitting still as a stone. And themselves, Tabini's for certain, when Tabini himself had not been able to discover the things Ilisidi was saying.

Ilisidi held out her cup, and more tea arrived in it.

"Well, well, and having taken her from the capital before she spoke any more such foolishness and proposed death rays coming from the station," Ilisidi said, "he was of a notion to take her to his house in the Marid, from which she would only speak at his permission. Covering his embarrassment over the faster-than-light notion, as happened. When you were able to explain the paradox, it was clear that houses would topple, and *not* Geigi's. Meanwhile Direiso had gained Hanks as her guest. She called Geigi's cousin, Saigimi's wife, up to her house in the Padi Hills, and things were moving very rapidly. Murini, Direiso's heir, had gone to the Atageini—*his* nerve was weakening when it came to such an outrageous provocation of the aiji; but Tatiseigi locked him in a storeroom and refused to deal with him. Tatiseigi phoned *me* saying he had apprehended vermin in his cellar, meaning that he had some prisoner, of course, and was notifying me, and *that* was when that fool Saigimi shot up the lilies."

He felt his heart beating faster and faster.

"To be rid of me?" he asked in the silence the dowager left for a sip of tea.

"The action would at one stroke have embarrassed the Atageini, whom Saigimi saw as dangerous, and if it had eliminated you, who were seen as in my grandson's man'chi, it would have elevated the value of the human woman. They were planning an attack on nand' Jase at the landing site, and would thus have all the paidhiin, a situation which looked quite impressive.

"At this point I approached them to contest with Direiso—as Direiso privately thought—to try to take leadership of her movement, and sent Geigi as my emissary, having myself paid his debts not an hour before.

"But the transfer of funds had not reached Saigimi, who was, of course, out of his district, being involved with the lily matter. So he didn't know, need I say, that Geigi was free, and in *my* debt, and gave no warning when Geigi showed up to see whether the way was clear for me. Silly man, he thought Geigi had come to see his cousin, who was there for, well, *safe-keeping* in Direiso's care.

"It was quite a little conference. And, not wholly relying on Geigi's inexperienced judgment, why, I showed up at the door and asked admittance before Geigi had even made his report to me. The foolish woman was distracted from the back entry. I always *said* Direiso had no qualifications for high office. And *she* said she was electable as I am not. Well, well, she probably was electable, being *of* the Padi Valley and a westerner. If she didn't look a fool."

Now he knew why Ilisidi had spoken freely in front of the boy from Dur, who was probably terrified of hearing so much detail of conspiracy against the aiji.

Twice the national legislature had voted against Ilisidi becoming aiji in Shejidan, the story was, because she was believed apt to take bloody revenge on enemies *in* the legislature; twice that he *knew* of, now, Ilisidi had been involved in conspiracy that might have led to Tabini's overthrow, and this time had made a thorough fool of Direiso. If she had ever admitted what she had said in others' hearing, his security hadn't reported it and Tabini had professed to him not to know.

As Tabini might *not* know. Ilisidi would delight in putting Tabini in a place where he had to rely on her simply because maneuvering the aiji of Shejidan into such a position exercised muscles and gave the dowager pleasure, damned if not. The plague of my life, Tabini called her; and never, that he knew, *never* made a move against his grandmother.

"Dowager-ji," he said softly, "you *are* amazing."

"Ah, but I should have shot that woman."

"As seems now," Cenedi said, "but then—who knew what would come from the sky?"

Hedging her bets against the ship keeping its word. Cenedi hadn't revealed that, either, without the dowager's implied permission, but far fewer in this company would understand it in all its meaning.

"One needs ultimately," Ilisidi said, "to draw all these elements together. But this distasteful human woman, one takes it, *with* the help of the *Presidenta* of Mospheira, is continuing her meddling. She knew contacts. She knew where to send such messages to have them fall on willing ears. She evidently gathered such information quite freely while she was dealing with Saigimi—whose demise was timely. I dare say, timely."

What does *that* mean? he wondered in some distress, but consciously didn't frown.

The rags of cloud had flown over them. There was thunder, definitely, in the distance. The sky flickered over their heads, reminding one of metal tent frames and their situation at the crest of the promontory—save the knoll behind the tents.

"It was well done," Ilisidi said, and chuckled softly. "So was Badissuni's indigestion."

"Nand' dowager," Jago said as if she had received a compliment.

He at least had suspected. He *was* at least keeping up with situations. Badissuni might have joined Direiso in her adventurism in the north. Badissuni was in the hospital—but alive—and Ajresi still had Badissuni to worry about, so *he* was out of the game.

"Time for bed," Ilisidi said, and the woman who used a cane to get about and who had complained for years that she was dying used it now to lever herself up with smoother grace than a much younger human whose muscles had stiffened from sitting on the ground. "Early to rise," the dowager proclaimed, looked up, and smiled at the lightning. "Lovely weather. A new year. *Spring* on the coast."

20

"What was she saying?" Jase asked in a whisper as they went toward the tent. Jase caught his arm. "What was going on?"

"A little information," Bren said. Thunder rumbled above them, and he could feel Jase flinch. He saw Banichi and Jago in converse a little distance away, and guessed that they had heard detail they had never heard, the same as he had. "Banichi and Jago killed lord Saigimi," he said to Jase, "at Tabini's order. But the dowager said she took Deana Hanks away from Direiso when Direiso kidnapped her last year. That dispute was what you parachuted into."

"Factions." Jase knew that word.

"Factions. She's saying that Saigimi's wife was trying to get lord Geigi's land and title, and she prevented it. So Geigi helped *her* get Deana away from lady Direiso. Tabini let Deana go. Now Deana's behind some radio broadcasts to Direiso's followers, talking against Tabini. And I wouldn't be surprised if, sometime during our trip, we don't go up to Mogari-nai and express the aiji's *and* the dowager's discontent with them losing our mail and not acting aggressively to prevent those broadcasts. That's a huge electronics installation. If it's letting some little handheld radio communicate with the mainland—" Thunder cracked and Jase jumped, his face stark and scared in the lightning flash. "—it's not doing its job very well."

"Will they shoot?"

"Mogari-nai? No. That's not their job. The Messengers' Guild holds Mogari-nai. The Assassins' Guild is with Tabini. Open conflict isn't going to benefit the Messengers' Guild, I can tell you that. Better get inside." He'd seen Banichi leave the brief conversation and go out into the dark, possibly for nothing more than call of nature; but he wasn't sure. "I'll be there in a minute. Don't worry about the thunder. Lightning's the threat. But it hits the tallest thing around. Keep lower than the tent roof and you're fine."

It wasn't true. But the mechieti were in more danger.

"Where are you going?"

"To talk to our security, nadi. Go inside. Don't worry about it." Wind was battering them, ruffling and snapping the canvas. A fat, cold drop splashed down on him as he went to that endmost tent.

Jago had seen him coming. She waited for him in the pelting early drops of rain.

"Is everything all right?" he asked, fearful, despite the assurances he'd given Jase, that there might be more going on than he knew about.

"Yes," Jago said, and caught his arm, pulling him toward the inside of the tent. "Come in out of the rain, Bren-ji."

It was their tent. Hers and Banichi's, compact for atevi, affording her no room to stand. It was warmer, instantly. Softer than the ground, insulated by an inflated bottom fabric. Black as night. He couldn't see a thing. Possibly she could.

"You did very well," Jago said in a hushed tone. "You did *very* well, Bren-ji."

"One hoped," he said.

"She wished to say such things in the boy's hearing, and you afforded her the audience she needed. You asked about Deana's kidnapping. Did it occur to you to ask about your own?"

The thought had crossed the depths of his mind, while Ilisidi was confessing to things Tabini's security had worked hard to learn. "I feared it might divert us. I take it that it *is* a second matter."

Lightning showed her shadow against the dim fabric of the tent. Something hard and dangerous and metal met his hand. His hand closed on a pistol grip. "This is yours, Bren-ji. I took it from your luggage. Keep it inside your coat."

His heart was beating fast enough to get his attention now. "Are we in such danger?"

"Do you remember the getting of this gun?"

"Tabini gave it to me."

"No. *Banichi* gave it to you."

It was true. He couldn't tell one from the other. On holiday at Taiben, he and Tabini had shot at melons and broken Treaty law––before he'd ever met Ilisidi.

Tabini had given him a gun he shouldn't have, by Treaty law; and he'd been anxious when he returned to Shejidan. He'd not known what to do with it in his little garden apartment, with two servants who were *not*—he understood such things far better now—reliably within his man'chi. He'd tucked it beneath his mattress.

He'd fired it at an intruder that had appeared at his curtained door, in lightning flashes, on such a night as this.

Banichi and Jago had replaced his security that night. Banichi had replaced the gun—in case, Banichi had said, an investigation should link it to Tabini.

Banichi and Jago had taken over his apartment, wired his door, replaced his servants, and brought in Tano and Algini, whom at that time he hadn't trusted.

From that hour forward he'd been in Jago's and Banichi's care.

And immediately Tabini had sent him, with Banichi and Jago, to Malguri, to Ilisidi's venue.

He'd been in danger of his life. He believed that then. He believed it now, sitting in this tent with Banichi's gun tucked into his jacket.

And he went back to the simplest, most ground-level question he had used to ask them: he, the paidhi, the expert. "What should I know, Jago-ji?"

"That in the matter of Deana Hanks, Ilisidi did very well, and has only credit. But the night the intruder came to your bedroom, one of her faction had exceeded orders and attempted to remove you. We did find out not the name but the man'chi. And that you, yourself, bloodied this reckless person; that was a profound embarrassment to the dowager. She had refused Tabini's offer to negotiate until that happened and until, against her expectations, Tabini declined to expose the author of the attack and asked again for her to accept you in trust. But before he sent you to Malguri, he filed Intent against persons unnamed, which was a gesture toward the Guild, which caused the Guild to take official notice and regularize the paidhi's rank within Guild regulations. And *that* made illegal any second move against the paidhiin. It was coincidentally a situation which complicated his dealing with Deana Hanks when she arrived in the capital while you were absent at Malguri.

"Meanwhile Ilisidi was trying to determine whether she would believe Tabini's urgings that neither he nor humans had betrayed the association—or whether she could agree to lead an attempt to remove Tabini from office. Some eastern conspirators believed her assessment that you were honest—and some were convinced by questioning you."

"Was *that* what that was?"

"The matter in the cellars? Yes. We could *not* prevent it. The rebellion was going forward. A certain lord moved without the dowager, attempting to overthrow *her*, and she brought down Tabini's forces on their heads. *Here*, in the west, however, the situation was exactly as you apprehend: there was a fear *of* humans, and once that was allayed—Tabini was more popular than before with the commons, as was the prospect of even closer cooperation between humans and Shejidan, a deluge of technology from the heavens, and more centralized power to Shejidan. Direiso and others who want to sit in Tabini's place, and the peninsular lords who don't want a centralized government, all saw that if they didn't move soon, they'd never dare. So they approached Ilisidi in the theory she might have been coerced into returning you. And Ilisidi acted to rescue the paidhiin and keep them out of Direiso's hands. That much was clear. Ilisidi does not want Direiso as aiji.

But where does Ilisidi herself stand? The answer, nadi-ji, was out there tonight. I suspect Saigimi, from the peninsula, attempted to get Ilisidi to overthrow Direiso—who *is* from the Padi Valley, as Ilisidi is from the remote east."

"Can we rely on her? It pains me even to ask, Jago-ji, but dare we rely on her? Or is there some *third* choice?"

There was silence out of the dark. Lighting showed him Jago, elbow on knee, fist on chin. And a break of that pose in that flicker of an instant.

"The aiji tested *her* by sending you to her at Malguri. Now she tests *him* by demanding both paidhiin in her hands. *That* is where we sit tonight, Bren-ji. And we don't *know* the answer."

"I asked her to bring us here."

"Not as Cenedi told me the story."

It was not, he recalled now, accurate. "I asked her to go with us to Geigi's house."

"And she then suggested Saduri."

"She did."

"And Geigi had invited you to his house."

"He did. He had."

"Geigi is within her man'chi, Bren-ji. Tabini's maneuvering helped him pay his debt to Ilisidi. But she had already rescued him financially. However— you— whom the dowager favors—and who have man'chi to Tabini, as you have stated, saved his reputation. Geigi is in an interesting three-way position."

One of the things that humans had done most amiss in the days before the War was to make what they thought were friendships across lines of association that could not otherwise be associated: they'd ripped atevi society to shreds and killed people and ruined lives, never realizing what they'd done.

"Damn," he said, with a very sick feeling; but with a little inaccuracy in the dark, Jago touched his hand.

"This is not necessarily bad, Bren-ji."

"It was damned foolish on my part."

"Ah, but not necessarily bad. Once *you* wished her to come to Dalaigi, which Tabini's actions against

Saigimi had made unwise—she was free to suggest Taiben. Which Tabini expected. But she wished you to go to Saduri, and now we know why: Deana Hanks is coming to the mainland and the aiji-dowager already knew it."

"To the *mainland!*"

"We don't know how. Boat or small plane. It could be anywhere on the coast."

"*Why,* nadi-ji?"

"One would ask the paidhi *that* question. But this information is since last night, Bren-ji. Tabini didn't know, and Ilisidi may yet know more than we do."

"To ally with Direiso. A second establishment—to challenge Tabini's government. That's what Deana's up to. God! But where's Ilisidi in this?"

"With the aiji. We hope."

He had recently realized there were new players in the game. Dangerous ones. He recalled the controversy with the pilots forming a Guild. The opposition of the Messengers. "And the Messengers' Guild? The Guilds in general?"

"The Guilds in general stand with the aiji. We expressed that fact in the Marid, when we carried out our commission. Meanwhile Hanks is coming to the mainland for reasons we don't know; but we do know that Direiso has not yet explained to her that she has much less support than previously. *Now* Hanks is an asset which Direiso *must* have to demonstrate to her wavering followers that she has the resources to deal with Mospheira; and we think that is exactly what she intends. Mospheira seems weak, lacking in resources—its ship will not fly in advance of ours. And could Direiso secure her own position by dealing with Mospheira, she would do so. That she dislikes humans would only make it sweeter to her."

"That Hanks' faction dislikes atevi wouldn't stop them, either. She's coming here to make a deal for resources Mospheira can't get without those rail lines and the northern shipping ports. Where Direiso is strong right now."

"It would accord well with our suspicions."

"*Dur* wouldn't support this—would it?"

"The boy? Completely innocent. And aware of far more than young ears should hear. His father wished to keep the island out of difficulty, I suspect. Or told the boy that wiser heads would settle it. Dur is not reckless. It's an island that used to live by smuggling and now wants tourism. They're far too small to matter in most accounts. But the boy—is a boy. He stole the plane, and with a map six years out of date, he flew out of Dur at night and followed the railroads to Shejidan, which brought him over the rail terminal. And right across your approach route."

Rain suddenly hit, rattling hard on the canvas.

On the edge of that downpour a shadow appeared in the doorway. Bren's heart jumped.

"Nadiin." Banichi squeezed into the dark, dripping wet. "Have you explained everything, Jago-ji? Made clear the universe?"

"Almost," Jago said. "And given him the gun. Which you will use, Bren-ji, at your discretion."

"I hope not to need it."

"Traceable only to me," Banichi said. "But such details matter very little in the scope of this situation."

"How did she get me to ask her to come here?" He still struggled with that thought. "Am I so transparent?"

"Immaterial that you asked *her*. One believes the aiji would have packed you up and sent you, all the same," Jago said. "She didn't *need* you to ask her. She came back to Shejidan to get you. The party was the excuse. She was feeling out Tabini, feeling out your position— and observing Jase."

He had a sinking feeling. "Tatiseigi. Where is *he* in this?"

"Ah," Banichi said. "Uncle Tatiseigi. Bets are being laid. Very high ones."

Thinking what he'd been meddling with, in that crazed business with the blown lightbulb, he felt cold all the way to the pit of his stomach.

"You still don't know where he is in this."

"Bren-ji," Jago said quietly, "Saigimi didn't know

where *he* was. Even we make mistakes of man'chi. It is not always logical."

"And he can't find the television set," Banichi said somberly. "One hopes."

He laughed. He had to laugh.

"*I* shall sleep with Jase," Banichi said. "Just—be prudent, nadiin. Keep the noise low."

"Banichi," he began to say. But it was too late. Banichi was out the door into the rain, headed for his tent, *his* roommate, and leaving him nowhere else to be for the night.

He was in the dark. In utter silence. And there might be more briefing for Jago to do. "So what else is there to ask?" he inquired of her.

"I've said all I can, Bren-ji."

A silence ensued.

"We should rest," Jago said.

"Jago," he began, and had to clear his throat.

"One is not obliged, nadi-ji. Banichi has a vile sense of humor."

"Jago—" He reached for her hand in the dark, found what he thought was her knee, instead, and knew how he'd possibly rejected her and embarrassed her, last night, after what seemed a set-up. He didn't *know,* that was the eternal difficulty, even what signals he sent now, and he thought about her, he thought about her in his unguarded moments in ways that made this touch in the dark the most desirable and the most reprehensible thing he could do.

Her hand found his with far more accuracy, and rested atop his, warm and strong and its gentle movement occupying all the circuits he was trying to use to frame an objection of common sense.

"Jago," he began again, and Jago's hand slid across to *his* knee. "I'm really not sure this is a good idea."

And stopped.

To his vast distress. And disappointment. But he was able then to find her hand and hold it. "Jago," he said for the third time. "Jago-ji. I am concerned—" Her fingers curled about his thumb, completely throwing his logic off course. "Propriety," he managed to say. "Banichi. The dowager. I want you, but—"

"She is outside your man'chi. Not far. But outside. And it's safer, tonight, if you're here and Banichi is with Jase, if anything untoward should happen."

"What might happen?"

"Anything. Anything might happen. Whatever pleases you. I would be inclined to please both of us."

He could feel the warmth from her. The lightning showed him her shadow, close to him. "Then should we—" he began, in the glimmer of a self-protective thought.

"We should be careful of the guns," she said with what he was sure was humor, and her fingers searched the front of his jacket.

He felt a rush of warmth, shifted position and took hold of her to defend himself from her exploration in search of the firearm. "Is this a good idea?" he asked, reason sinking fast. "Jago-ji, if you do that, we may both scandalize the company."

"Not this company," she said, and somehow they were past each other's defenses and he was no longer thinking with complete clarity of purpose, just exploring a territory he'd not seen and didn't see, alone and not alone for the first time in his life. She was doing the same with him, finding sensitive spots, and presenting others he might have missed. Clothes went, on the somewhat bouncy and thin mattress— "We have to look presentable," was Jago's prudent warning, and with clothing laid carefully to the side, caution went. He moved his hand along smooth expanses in the darkness, to curves that began to make sense to his hands, as her hands were traveling lightly over him, searching for reactions, finding them.

God! Finding them. He brought his hands up in the shock of common sense that said danger, harm, pain— and at that moment Jago's mouth found his and began a kiss both explorative and incredibly sensual.

He had never known atevi did that. She *tasted* foreign; that was odd; but matters now reached a point of no-thought and no-sense. They were in the dark, neither knowing in the least what hurt and what didn't, but efforts to consummate what was underway began to be a rapid and frustrating comedy of errors that at first frustrated and embarrassed him and finally started her laughing.

Her good humor made him less desperate. "We have to practice this in daylight," he muttered. "This is exhausting."

It won a finger poke in the ribs, which she'd discovered got a protective reaction. He curled up—and at a thunder boom, jumped against her and held on. They were, he thought, both out of their minds, in a tent, halfway to the lightning-laced heavens, under a metal frame, and in earshot of Ilisidi's men. Then—then, maybe it was the plain admission he was being a fool, or maybe it was Jago's changing position—a sudden and by no means coordinated reaction sent him toward release. She shivered oddly and didn't complain; and his eyes shut and the dark went darker and red and black.

For a moment or two then he just drifted in space, half aware of the warm body wrapped around his, tasting the strange taste that was Jago, and feeling, well, that he'd managed enough. She seemed to have found something enjoyable out of it, and he was appalled at the thought she'd tell Banichi and make a funny story of their night.

Which it was, dammit. She was right to laugh. Thank God she could laugh. It made it all less serious, what he'd gotten into, and he tried to set it in perspective as they lay together with the lightning turning the walls transparent. She was curious; he'd answered her question. She'd surprised the hell out of him about the kiss—he felt warm even thinking about it—and he wondered whether she'd done a little research of her own or whether atevi just did that.

And she hadn't given up on the night. Bad trouble, he said to himself, as Jago's fingers wound curls in his hair, as she fitted her body against his just for comfort and seemed satisfied. In that moment his human feelings slid right over the edge of a cliff more dangerous

than the one outside. She brought him no recrimina-
tions, found no fault—maybe had an agenda—but this
was the woman he'd trust for anything, and whose
good will he wouldn't risk for anything.

Evidently, by those fingers making curls out of his
hair, he still had her good regard. He'd risked everything and hadn't lost, and there might be other nights,
when he'd thought he'd reached a safe numbness to his
personal affairs. Oh, *God,* it was dangerous.

"Was it pleasant?" she asked him.

He drew a breath. "I enjoyed it."

"It was not very responsible of us. But Banichi knew
we would do it."

"*Did* he?" he asked, but he was sure of that, too.

"Of course. But we should get dressed, in case.
There was no danger early on. But toward morning we
should be a little on our guard, in case we must move."

"Direiso?"

"Possibly."

"What's going on? *Where* are we going and what are
we up to?"

"Cenedi and the dowager know that for certain. But
Mogari-nai, most likely. Which Direiso-daja will not
like." She unwound herself upward and tugged on
his hand.

Will not like? he asked himself. Getting to his feet,
he agreed with. But she ducked out of the tent stark
naked into driving rain and pulled him out with her. It
was cold rain. They were standing in water. Lightning
was still going on, the wind was still fierce and Jago,
her black skin glistening in the lightning, sluiced over
by the rain, and her braid streaming water, acted as if
she were in the safe, warm showers at home.

He followed her example, unwilling to think himself
more delicate than she was. He scrubbed and rubbed
and was oh so glad she ducked back inside in a hurry.
She flung his insulated sleeping bag at him for a towel,
and they both cleaned up and dressed and snuggled
down with one of the open bags beneath them and one
zipped out flat above them, both shivering and holding
on to each other.

"Better than a roof in the peninsula," she said, and hugged him close. "Get some sleep."

He tried. He didn't think he could, after the shock of cold water; but the shivering stopped, her warmth was comfortable, her embrace was trustable as anything on earth, and he found himself drifting.

Not love, he said to himself. And then thought, with one of those flashes of insight his professional mind sometimes had, maybe they'd had such rotten luck with the love and man'chi aspect of relations because that word in Mosphei' blurred so many things together it just wasn't safe to deal with.

They were lovers. But Ragi said they were sexual partners.

They were lovers. But Ragi said they were associated.

They were lovers. But Ragi said they were within the same lord's man'chi.

They'd made love. But Ragi said there were one-candle nights and two-candle nights and there were relationships that didn't count the candles at all.

They'd made love. But a Ragi proverb said one candle didn't promise breakfast.

He and Jago would be lucky to have a breakfast undisturbed by the trouble that might come tomorrow, but he'd know his back was protected, come what might, by her *and* Banichi. So if their languages didn't say quite the same thing and their bodies didn't quite match and the niches they made that said *this person satisfies enough requirements to make me happy* were just a little different-shaped in their psyches, the center of that design might match, leaving just the edges hanging off.

But didn't his relationship with Barb have unmatched edges? Didn't every close relationship?

He was quite out of his depth in trying to reckon that. But with Jago he certainly wouldn't count the candles. Whatever they could arrange, as long as it could last from both sides, that was what he'd take.

He was happy, right now, where he was. He didn't swear it would bear the light of the sun. He didn't let himself hope—the way things in his personal life that had looked as if they were going to work had tended not to—that it would stand the sun.

But he trusted that Jago would protect herself.

That thought let him relax, finally, listening to her breathing. In dim-brained curiosity he began timing his breaths to hers and seeing if they could be brought to match. He could force it—but it wasn't quite natural. She seemed asleep, so that might not be a fair test.

He went on trying to make a match, but it eluded him.

21

"Good night?" Banichi asked them, in the cold, rainy dawn, when Ilisidi's men were off to saddle the mechieti.

"Quite good," Jago declared with a tilt of her head. "For the curious, *yes,* Banichi-ji, and you'll go begging for the salacious details."

Bren tried to keep an expressionless face as Banichi glanced at him for information. And didn't think he succeeded.

"Shut out," Banichi said. "Abandoned."

"Fled," Jago said. "Having set the scene."

"*She* was the one who said we needed to set separate guard last night," Banichi said. "But I heard no appeals for rescue."

"Be decent!" Jago said, finally rising to the defense. "My partner has no shame, paidhi-ji."

Banichi strolled off quite happily, while the servants hastily struck tents. Ilisidi and Cenedi had gone out to get the mechieti; until Babsidi came to his rider, no other would. The boy from Dur had found Jase and was tagging him on a course toward them.

Jase was limping: it needed no guess to say why, in a beginning rider. Jase looked worried. Likely he was going to ask why they'd been separated last night.

And he didn't know how he was going to explain it. The truth was going to have repercussions. There was no way it wouldn't.

"I have duties," Jago said, and deserted him.

"Bren?" Jase said.

"Good morning, Jasi-ji. Sorry about the change of arrangements last night."

"The rain. I know." Jase rushed past that item. "Where are we going? Nand' Rejiri says west. West, am I right, nadi? Mogari-nai? Not fishing. Not down to the sea?"

The boy from Dur looked as if a glimmering had reached him that he had just possibly said something out of line. And Bren tried to recall what he'd told Jase on the other side of a mountain of new information.

"You promised me the ocean," Jase reminded him, "nadi. We were going to go fishing. You said political problems at Mogari-nai. Nand' Rejiri says his father should bring guns there and I should ask you to ask the dowager if he can go to his father and bring guns."

"Ask the dowager," Bren said to the boy, "nadi."

"One has asked, nand' paidhi. But she won't rely on me."

"Possibly she has other reasons, nadi, such as intentions she holds in secret, and I would suggest that you remember she is old because some of her enemies are dead."

Rejiri's face grew quite sober. "Nandi," he said.

While an aggrieved roommate with a good deal more than that on his mind waited to have *his* question answered.

"Jase," Bren said, "we are going to Mogari-nai, and I am increasingly certain we have a difficulty."

"We are not on vacation."

"I do not think we are on vacation, no, Jase."

"Where were you last night?"

The boy was there, all ears.

"Talking," Bren said.

"But not to me," Jase said, and walked off.

"Jase!" he said, but Jase kept walking down what had been a line of tents and now was a set of bundles of baggage.

He couldn't run after after Jase in front of the whole camp. He couldn't start a quarrel. Jase was *not* a diplomat. He didn't know how far it would go, or where it would end if Jase blew up, and blew up at the wrong people.

Meanwhile Ilisidi was up on Babsidi and she and Cenedi were bringing the herd in to the place where the gear waited.

"I suppose I talked too much, nand' paidhi," Rejiri said shamefacedly.

He'd never dealt individually with atevi youngsters. Certainly not with a boy verging on independence.

And he had no wish to humiliate the boy, who had probably heard his faults enumerated by Banichi. "Did nand' Banichi give you advice?" he asked.

"Yes, nand' paidhi."

"Was it good advice?"

There was a moment of silence. "Yes, nand' paidhi."

"He's a wise man," Bren said. "I take advice from him, frequently. Even the aiji does. I'd watch *him* and do what he does."

He wasn't thinking about the boy. He was thinking about Jase, and how to patch his own mistakes, and maybe it was a little revenge for Banichi's jokes to aim the innocent in his direction. But the boy said, enthusiastically,

"*Thank* you, nand' paidhi," and set off in Banichi's direction.

He wondered what he'd just done; and then it struck him that Ilisidi and all her men were eastern, and he and Jase were the only officials here whose man'chi was really clearly Tabini's. He'd just confirmed to the confused lad that, indeed, he could rely on Banichi, and recommended he do so.

At least it was the truth, and he hadn't misled the boy or done any harm to the situation.

If he could only be so lucky with his own species.

Jase didn't look at him as he walked up. The camp was a snarling confusion as the dowager's men saddled the mechieti.

"Well, well, well," Ilisidi said cheerfully, as Babsidi moved up to tower against the gray-ribboned sky, "good *morning*, nand' paidhi."

Was she upset? Bren asked himself. Did she know?

Ilisidi knew every sneeze in her vicinity. And that courtship game they'd played, he and Ilisidi. Did it mask real possessiveness? An old woman's real inclinations?

Disaster?

"You inspire so *many* questions," Ilisidi said from her height of vantage, and signaled Babsidi to go past him. Nokhada was saddled. So was Jase's mechieta, and there was no place to talk, no *time* to talk with the mechieti waiting for riders and the men who were doing the saddling wanting to get riders up and out of their way.

He made Nokhada bend down for him, got himself up with that unique pain of the second day in the saddle. Jase was no better, he was well certain. He was sure the only ones immune were Ilisidi and her men.

He kept Nokhada under tight rein and knew he wasn't going to have a chance to talk to Jase in anything like the length and complexity of topic that could calm Jase down.

Jase knew he'd been lied to. Not by intent, maybe, but he deserved Jase's anger at being left literally in the dark last night. Banichi would be good-humored and a quiet bedfellow, *very* quiet, meaning Jase would not have gotten any information out of him. He'd indicated he'd come back. Lie number one.

He'd not told Jase where he'd been. Lie number two, at least by omission, and he hadn't remotely *thought* about Jase's state of mind in terms of anything but the storm and the lightning he knew Jase feared. Banichi *wasn't* always good at reassuring a man, Banichi and his jokes. Banichi had probably given him the statistics on people hit by lightning on camping trips.

He had to get his wits together. He couldn't treat Jase that way. He was solidly in the wrong this time, because he'd been distracted by personal affairs, and it was just too damn serious a matter to say *I forgot.*

The last of the company mounted up. The sea was a misty gray beyond the cliffs. The island of Dur showed indistinct in a morning haze.

Ilisidi kept it on her right as she led off at a fast clip.
They were headed west.

And they clearly weren't going fishing.

The clouds kept blowing overhead from some inexhaustible source beyond the horizon, wave after wave
driven by stiff winds aloft; but the sun began to win the
battle toward midmorning, and light and shadow
played on the velvet-textured rolls of the land.

Beautiful. A distracted mind couldn't but notice.

Bren said as much to Jase as they rode, trying to set
up a friendlier mood for the rest stop he knew was
coming, when he hoped to have a chance to talk.

"Yes," Jase said; but nothing more, and when they
did get their stop, and did get down, Jase listened to his
"I'm sorry," and said, "Where is the truth, nadi? How
do I tell the truth?"

"I was with Jago," he said in the lowest voice that
would carry. "I'm sorry! I wasn't thinking! I was
stupid! Will you *listen* to me?"

"Go ahead." They weren't that far from Banichi. But
that meant they weren't far from the boy from Dur,
who'd attached himself exactly as he'd said. And
Jase's tone didn't invite confidences.

"There's a rumor Deana Hanks is coming to the
mainland. I suspect Mospheira is going to try an independent deal with Direiso of the Kadigidi to peel the
northern provinces *out* of the Western Association, but
I'm not sure I can make atevi see entirely what Hanks
thinks she's doing: it's too foreign to their instincts.
The whole east is shaky, held mostly by Ilisidi's influence. Do you follow me?"

"Is that what you discussed in bed?"

"*Yes,* dammit, among other things. Listen to me.
We've got a problem a hell of a lot larger than my mistake. I *admit* it was a mistake, all right, I was a damn
fool, but I was trying to find out the situation last
night—"

"Among other things."

"Yes, *among other things.*" He was getting madder.
He was so mad already his muscles were shaking, and

his breath was short, and it didn't help communication. He shifted to Mosphei'. "Can you for God's sake quit keeping score on who's wrong and who's right and hear what I'm saying?"

"I do hear what you're saying. If you're not lying one *more* time, what are we doing out here in the middle of it? Why did they bring us here, if this was going on? Can you answer *that?*"

"I'm trying to!"

"What does it take? More *research?*"

"Use your head, dammit! This is serious."

"I don't take it for anything else. Where are Tano and Algini? Why are we suddenly with *these* two? Bren, give me an answer!"

The dowager was getting back in the saddle. They had to follow or it was certain the mechieti would go and leave them stranded.

"I assure you they're all right," Bren said. "They're working back at the fortress, securing the area."

"Easy answer."

"These are partners of theirs!" The man assigned to help Jase up was waiting. They were almost the last. "Consider man'chi. Consider everything I've told you. Banichi and Jago aren't going to see anything happen to them."

"Meaning you don't *know* why they didn't come."

Question begot question begot question. "I can't argue with you. We *have* to go." He went to Nokhada, so charged with temper he hardly felt the effort it took for bruised muscles to catapult him into the saddle. He reined about to be sure Jase made it as the man boosted Jase up, then assisted the boy from Dur into the saddle.

Jase didn't understand him. Given professional experience, he ought to be able to achieve an understanding with Jase with far less trouble than he had with atevi; and it didn't work that way. It hadn't worked that way all year.

Why are we with these *two?* Stupid question, ignoring everything he'd said.

But Tano and Algini had been there while Jase was in the apartment, and Banichi and Jago hadn't been there for a long while. Tano and Algini were the reliable figures in the household that Jase knew of, the ones *he* would go to; so from Jase's viewpoint there was attachment quite as valid as his—admitted—attachment to Banichi and Jago.

In that reassessment of Jase's obstinacy he rode Nokhada near him, hoping that he would choose to talk; but Jase said nothing to him nor seemed to care he was there. Jase sometimes rode with his eyes shut, maybe ignoring the pitch and heave of the land, maybe motion sick: he had complained of it a great deal when he'd first come down.

"Pretty clouds," Bren said.

No answer.

"This whole land tilts," Bren said. "There aren't that many roads. The fortress watches the slope up off the plains. If it weren't there, someone could drive up undetected. They're back there to warn us. That's what they're doing." It dawned on him then in cooler temper that a man who had trouble with a flat surface wouldn't intuitively grasp warfare and its tactics. "Like the foyer at home. Stand in that door and nobody can come in. Just like them staying in the foyer office. As long as they're there, nobody can come up on this land. And Tano and Algini might do that if we *were* out here on vacation. The aijiin never assume no one's after them. Ever."

Jase didn't answer. But Jase did at least look at him.

"Four, five hundred years ago," Bren said, "before humans on this planet, atevi rode mechieti to war." He pointed to the rolling land ahead of them. "Five hundred riders could be just up there, close as the gardens to the apartment. You couldn't see them. That's why men keep riding ahead of the dowager. Ordinarily the mechieti don't like to do that—get ahead of the leader. But they do it for short rides out and back, looking to see the way is clear."

Jase *was* listening. He caught the quick and worried glance at the horizons, and saw Jase's whole body come to a different state of tension. In that distracted moment Jase suddenly synched with the mechieta's moving and seemed to feel it.

"That's how you *ought* to ride," Bren said, "Jase."

Jase looked at him, lost his centering and found it again; and lost it.

The fact Jase *had* somehow coped with being out here didn't mean Jase knew a thing, Bren thought, not about the mechieti, not about the concept of land, or tactics, or how to stay on or how to protect himself if someone did come up on them and mechieti reacted as mechieti would do. Politics and language and living in an apartment was what he'd taught Jase. It was *all* he'd taught Jase.

"If the mechieti have to run," he said, "—in case they do." He changed languages and went rapid-fire. "The atevi riders stay on by balance. *You* just hunch down tight and low and hold to the saddle. It won't come off. Get as low as you can. If they *can* jump something they will; otherwise they can turn very fast, and if you're not low you'll fall off. Join his center of mass. All right? If he jumps, his head will come back, and if your face is too far forward he can knock you cold. If they jump, center your weight, lean forward, head down while he's rising, lean back while he's landing and duck down again. We're small. Nothing we do affects them as much as an ateva's weight. Don't pull on the rein and don't try to guide him. It can turn his head and blind him to the ground and kill you both. If you do nothing with the rein, he'll follow Ilisidi's mechieta come hell or high water."

"Are we going to run?" Jase said. "From what?"

"It's just an 'in case.'"

Jase gave him one of those looks.

"It's a possibility, nadi," Bren said, and then wished he hadn't said. He wished he'd said, To hell with you, and not shaved the meaning one more time. "You're not going to find absolutes in this situation. There aren't any. I'm sorry. I knew I was asking for a hard time up here when I turned matters over to other people. I knew last night things were getting complicated. I figured—maybe we'd get a chance to go down to the water. Somehow. And things might not even involve us."

"Once we left the fortress," Jase said in Mosphei', "*I* knew we weren't going fishing."

"Because you knew I'd lie? You don't know that."

There was lengthy silence.

Then Jase said, "We were still going fishing? All around us, people with weapons. People on radios. Hanks. We were going fishing."

"Well, we will." It sounded lame even to him, in what he began to see as a long string of broken promises, broken dates, incomplete plans—not professional ones, but personal. He couldn't explain all that was going on. Jase didn't understand the motivations. And God knew what conclusions he'd draw.

The silence persisted some distance more. He wasn't there for the moment. He was across a table from Barb. Barb was saying, When? When, *really*, Bren?

"You really *tell* yourself we're going fishing," Jase said, "don't you?"

"Jase, if I don't plan to do it, we'll damn sure never get there. At least," he added, beginning to be depressed, "if you plan a dozen trips, one happens."

"Are all Mospheirans like you?"

He'd like to think not. He liked to think, on the contrary, that he was better than the flaws that frustrated him in his countrymen. But it was an island full of people living their safe routines, their weekend trips to the mountains, their outings to the market, like clockwork, every week, sitting on a powder keg, electing *presidenti* who lived the same kind of lives and left decisions to their chief contributors rather than those with any knowledge or insight.

Delusion played a large part in Mospheiran attitudes.

Delusion that they had a spacecraft, or could build one, with no facility in which to do it.

Delusion that they could fix their deficits when there was suddenly a great need and all their bets came due.

Self-delusion to which, apparently, he was not immune.

"Lifestyle," he said, with self-knowledge a bitter

lump in his chest. "But I still do plan to go fishing, Jase."

"Just not this trip."

"Even this trip, dammit! Security alerts go on all the time. I *live* with it! In between times, I relax, if I can get a few hours. Nine tenths of the time nothing happens or it happens elsewhere and life goes on. If you've planned a fishing trip, it might be possible. We can rent the gear. And hire a boat."

"It's a nervous way to live."

"It is when you park a bloody huge ship over our heads and offer the sun, the moon, and the stars to whoever gets there first! It makes the whole world a little anxious, Jase!"

"Was life more peaceful before we came?"

"Life was absolutely ordinary before you came. You've set the whole world on its ear. Don't you reckon that? Absolutely ordinary people's lives have been totally disrupted. Absolutely ordinary people have done things they'd never have done."

"Good or bad?"

"Maybe both."

They rode a while more in silence. He watched Jago ahead of him, by no means ordinary, neither she nor Banichi.

He *loved* Jago. He loved both of them.

"A *lot* of both," he said.

And a long while later he asked, "*Why* did the ship come back?"

"Weren't we supposed to?"

He thought about that a moment, thought about it and wondered about it and said to himself of course that was what the ship did and was supposed to do: go places between stars. And this was where other humans were, and why wouldn't it come here?

But he always argued the other point of view— everyone's point of view: Barb's, his mother's, Jase's. He'd elaborated in his own mind Jase's half-given answers in the days when Jase hadn't been able to say much in Ragi and after that when the pressure mounted to get the engineering translation settled. They'd talked fluently about seals and heat shields. But when he'd asked, in Mosphei', as late as a handful of days before his tour, Where were you? Jase had drawn him diagrams that didn't make any sense to him.

And he'd said to himself, when he hadn't understood Jase's answer or gotten any satisfaction out of it, well, he wasn't an astronomer and he didn't understand the ship's navigation; or maybe space wasn't as romantic as he'd thought it was—or maybe—or maybe—or maybe.

Well, but. But. But.

Did delusion play a part in it? Or a human urge to fill out Jase's participation and make excuses for behavior that otherwise wasn't satisfying his expectations.

The ship was doing as it promised. The spacecraft was becoming a reality.

But in his failure to find the friendly, cheerful young man he'd talked to by radio link before the drop, he'd insisted on making that side of Jase exist in the apartment.

He'd done all Jase's side of the conversations in his head, was what he'd done. He'd made up all sorts of answerless answers Jase *might* give, if Jase had the vocabulary, if he had time to sit and talk at depth. Naturally Jase was under stress: language learning did that to a mind. Or maybe—or maybe Jase had been doing the same, filling in between the lines to suit *his* initial impression; and when those expectations didn't match reality, he felt betrayed.

"Jase," he said.

"What?"

"Where *was* the ship?"

"I told you. A star. A number on a chart."

"You know the feeling you had we weren't going fishing?"

"Yes?"

"It's what *I* feel when you tell me that."

Silence followed. It wasn't a happy silence. He wished at leisure he hadn't come at Jase with that.

He wished a miracle would happen and Jase would come out of his sulk and be the person he'd thought he was getting, the person who'd help him, not pose him problems; the person who'd stand by him with reason when the going got tough.

But Barb had done that until she'd had enough. She'd run to marry Paul Saarinson. Maybe Jase didn't want a career of keeping the paidhi mentally together, considering they had to share an apartment.

Maybe in meeting him, the astonishing thought came to him, Jase hadn't found the man *he'*d thought he was dealing with, either. The breakdown of trust might be rooted more deeply than any dispute over truthfulness, in failings of his own. He managed so *well* with atevi. His personal life—

Ask Barb how he got along. Ask Barb how easy it was to deal with him.

He remembered Wilson-paidhi. He remembered saying to himself he wouldn't ever get to that state. The bet had been among University students in the program that Wilson couldn't smile. That Wilson *couldn't* react. Grim man. Unresponsive as hell.

But at the same time those of them going for the single Field Service slot learned to contain what they felt. You learned not to show it. You *studied* being unreadable.

Barb had complained of it. Barb used to say—he could remember her face across that candlelit table— You're not on the mainland, Bren. It's *me,* Bren.

It gave him a queasy feeling to realize, well, maybe—*maybe* it had something to do with the falling away and the anger of humans he dealt with. But he'd told Jase. He'd tried to teach Jase to do it. Jase should realize why he didn't show expression.

Shouldn't he realize it?

Move that into the category of fishing trips.

Fact was, he'd told Jase *not* to show emotion with atevi, and when Banichi and Jago walked in, he'd been laughing and lively and all those things he'd taught Jase not to be.

Maybe they should have thought a little less about language early on, and more about communication. Maybe they should have learned first what they expected of each other instead of each resigning himself to what he'd gotten.

"You and I," he said in Mosphei', "you and I need to talk, Jase. We need it very badly."

"We were going to do that out here."

"I'm *sorry*. I didn't remotely know what I was getting you into. I knew it was a chancy time. It's *always* a chancy time, especially when the pressure mounts up and you want to get away. I knew present company was the chanciest thing on the planet but the people who can *do* anything always are. It's the way it works, Jase."

"I trust you," Jase said in a curiously fragile tone—had to say it loudly, with all the thump and creak of the mechieti. "I do *trust* you, Bren. I'm trying like hell to."

"I'll get you back in one piece," he said. "I swear I will."

"That isn't what I'm worried about."

"What is?" he asked, thinking he'd finally gotten one thread that might pull up a clue to Jase's thinking.

But Jase didn't answer that.

And in the next moment he saw Cenedi rein back while Babs kept going. Something was going on. He thought Cenedi had done that to talk to Banichi.

But he was the target. Cenedi fell all the way back to him and Jase.

"Bren-paidhi," Cenedi said, as Bren restrained Nokhada from a nip at her rival. "The dowager asks why you avoid her. She told me to say exactly that, and to say that Nokhada still knows her way, nadi, if you've forgotten."

22

Nokhada indeed knew the way, and with a little lax-
ness on his part thought she was being sly about
moving forward. Had he touched her with the crop,
he'd have been there at the expense of every mechieta
in front of her.

As it was, Nokhada announced to the mechieti in her
path she was coming through with small butts of her
head, a little push with the rooting-tusks against an
obstinate flank. Mechieti hide was fortunately thick,
and tails lashed and heads tossed, but no blood
resulted, just ruffling of well-groomed hair.

Cenedi had lagged back. Nokhada achieved the position she wanted, next to Babsidi, and became quite
tractable.

"Ah, well," Ilisidi said, sitting with that easy,
graceful seat. She deigned a sidelong glance. "One can
only imagine."

One didn't dare say a thing.

"Oh, come, come, nand' paidhi. *Are* we like
humans? Or are humans like us? Is it—how am I to put
it delicately—technically feasible?"

"One is certain we are not the first pair to have made
the—" That led, in Ragi, to a difficult grammatical
pass. He was sure he blushed. "To try."

"Was it pleasant?" she asked, delighting, damn her,
to ask.

"Yes, nand' dowager." He wouldn't retreat, and met
her sidelong glance with a pleasant smile.

Her grin could blind the sun. And vanished, in

pursed lips. "Now that the world knows the paidhi has such interests, there'll be *such* gossip. My neighbor who loves to spy on my balcony will be absolutely *convinced* of scandal in our little breakfasts, now. We must do it again."

"I would be delighted, aiji-ma." He had no need to feign relief to have her take it well. "I treasure those hours you give to me."

"Oh, not that I have any scarcity of hours! I languish in disuse. My hours are such a little gift."

"Your hours and your good sense are my rescue, aiji-ma, and so I trespass egregiously on them, but never, never wish to impose."

"Languishing, I say. And now, now you drop young men from the heavens and expect *me* to civilize them. —Did I detect strife, nand' paidhi? Do I find discord?"

"He doesn't expect fish at this altitude."

Ilisidi laughed and laughed.

"Ah, paidhi-ji, a fish is what we hope for. A great gape-mouthed fish of a Kadigidi, which thinks to wreck us. I wanted you with *me,* Bren-ji. I *like* the numbers we've worked with this far; and I *never* tempt an Atageini beyond his virtue."

He was shocked. Outright shocked. Banichi and Jago had ridden up on his right and he wondered if *they* had accounted how great a temptation the paidhiin posed inside an Atageini perimeter, with the dice in motion, the demons of chance and fortune given their moment to overthrow the order of the world.

Baji-naji. The latticework of the universe, that allowed movement in the design.

Tabini was sleeping with the Atageini: Tatiseigi had made his move to get into the apartment to get at *them,* for good or ill or just to make up his mind, and Ilisidi had moved in. Ilisidi had possessed herself of the greatest temptation that might tip the Atageini toward a power-grab of their own, just flicked temptation out of Tatiseigi's reach at the very moment it might prove critical to his choice of direction in these few dangerous days.

Believe that Tabini didn't see it? Possible. Remotely possible.

But *if* Tabini should miscalculate, if he should wake up stabbed by an Atageini bride, the Atageini and the Kadigidi alike had to reckon that getting rid of Tabini didn't kill Ilisidi.

And *twice* the Padi Valley nobles had politicked to keep Ilisidi from being aiji.

Dare Tatiseigi move on Tabini now, or move on Ilisidi, who had the paidhiin in the middle of an action that could put them all, if it failed, in Kadigidi hands?

Tabini's rule was a two-headed beast. He saw that now with crystal clarity.

Bane of my life, Tabini called Ilisidi.

And Tabini had resorted to her in what seemed reckless action when he knew he had to contemplate war with Mospheira.

She hadn't gone home since.

"Any news?" she asked Cenedi now.

"Quiet still, aiji-ma."

"Well, well, so long as it lasts."

The dowager called rest, and Bren actively *rode* Nokhada back through the company as it drew to a halt, a choice he was sure, in the way he'd come to understand how Nokhada did think, that Nokhada perfectly well understood. She expressed her dislike with flattened ears and a bone-jarring gait which he had come to understand he had to answer with a swat or she'd think her rider wasn't listening.

But not with the heel, or he'd be through the company like a shot: he used the crop at the same time he kept a pressure on the rein. The gust of breath and the shift into a smooth gait was immediate as she moved through mechieti establishing rights over their small patches of green grass, a touchy business of snarls and status in the herd; and Nokhada breezed past lower-status mechieti with scarcely a missed beat, back to where Jase and the boy were already dismounted.

He stopped Nokhada at the edge of the herd and slid down, keeping the rein in hand and the crop visible, against what otherwise might be a tendency slyly to wander closer to Babsidi during the stop.

The head went down; she snatched mouthfuls of grass.

Jase didn't ask him, What did the dowager want? The boy didn't, either. But the boy wasn't his partner.

Maybe, the amazing thought dawned on him, Jase was waiting for *his* ally to say something.

And, dammit, the boy was underfoot and all ears, he was sure. He couldn't send the boy to Banichi. They were talking to Cenedi on matters the boy didn't need to hear, either. He looked in that direction and met the boy's absolutely earnest gaze.

And saw the escort. "Nadi," he said to the man, "Haduni, please brief the young gentleman: we may have to take a faster pace."

"Nand' paidhi." Haduni gave a nod as if he perfectly understood and had been waiting for such an order, then smoothly collected the all-elbows young lord and steered him to the side.

Bren heaved a sigh and with a sharp jerk of two fingers against the rein in his left hand, checked Nokhada's intent to gain a few meters on her agenda. "He's very anxious," he said to Jase. "He sees the reputation of his house at stake."

"What did they want up there?" Jase obligingly asked the question. Jase did the obvious next step.

"To be sure I knew things were all right," he said and told himself to relax, let his face relax, *use* expression.

And what in hell was he supposed to do? Grin like a fool? He looked at the grass under his feet and looked up and managed a little smile, one he trusted didn't look foolish. When he knew damned well he hadn't been shut down with Ilisidi. He just let Jase touch off his defenses, *that* was what he was doing, and it was a flywheel effect of distrust and guardedness.

"Jase, she said Tatiseigi might—*might*—have moved against us. I'd hope he wouldn't, but she said his virtue was a lot safer if we weren't in his reach. I didn't think that. But I did think things in Shejidan were going to go a lot more smoothly without us in the way. So it was the same move, two reasons."

Jase was listening, at least, without the anger he'd shown.

"We *are* going to Mogari-nai, nadi?" Jase switched back to Ragi.

"I have no doubt of it. The Messengers' Guild has been pulling at the rein—" Source of his metaphor, Nokhada tried a different vector and got another jerk of the rein he held, hands behind his back. "And Ilisidi intends to make it clear the authority is in Shejidan, not in the regional capitals. That's an old issue, the amount of power Shejidan holds, the amount of power the regions have. They've fought over it before. Your ship dumping technology into Tabini's hands has raised the issue again. That's *why* the tension between some of the lords and the capital."

There followed one of those small, tense silences, Jase looking straight at him as if thoughts alone could bridge the gap.

"Thank you," Jase said then, carefully controlled. "*Thank* you, nadi."

"Why?" was the invited question. He asked it, angry in advance.

"It's the first time," Jase said, "that I've ever felt I've heard the truth."

"I have *not* —" —lied, he almost said. But of course he had. And would. "I haven't known what I *could* say." He changed back to Mosphei' to be absolutely certain that Jase understood him. "Jase, if I told your ship enough to let them think they could guess the rest and go hellbent ahead, I *knew* they could tear the peace apart. You can *see* now what the stresses in the atevi system are, and I don't know the quality of people in office on your ship. But the people in my government who've cut the Mospheiran Foreign Office off from communication with the Mospheiran public have completely written off the majority of people on this planet as of no value to them. They're not pleased with my continuing to operate as *the* Foreign Office, such as it is, but here I am, and here I stay. That, I *have* told you.

For what you can see with your own eyes, look around you. See how it works. *See* the land. See the people. See everything you came here to see. It's all I've got to offer you."

And even while he said it he was hedging his bets, telling himself—just get that spacecraft built, get it flying, get atevi up there before politics shuts atevi out of the meaningful decisions.

If he could get help—he'd take it.

But jeopardize that objective? No.

Jase didn't answer him. He decided that was a relief. He couldn't debate trust with Jase. It didn't exist. It might, eventually, but it didn't, not here, not now. He daren't debate it with Ilisidi, either, but he did trust her, as far as he could reason what she was doing.

Banichi and Jago—there was his one known quantity, though Tabini never was: believe that those two, who were right now deep in conversation with Cenedi, would bend Tabini's orders a little to save his neck. He was sure they had done that very significantly at least once. Believe that Tabini valued him *and* his objectives? So far he was irreplaceable.

One of Ilisidi's men came close to him, Haduni, bringing the boy back. He looked in that direction and saw them offloading the baggage from the mechieti.

Are we camping here? he wondered. That didn't accord with his knowledge of the situation.

No, he thought, seeing men adjusting mechieti harness, we're going to move.

Harness adjustment was something he didn't venture to do. There were straps he knew what to do with: mechieti shed a little of their girth after a morning start, especially when they were traveling this hard; and a saddle that slipped more than Nokhada's had been doing just before the dismount was a problem he didn't want. Expert handlers moved through the company seeing to any mechieta the rider for one reason or another wasn't able to see to; and just as the young man was attending to Nokhada's harness, the discussion the senior security officers had been holding among themselves was breaking up. Banichi had left the group and was leading his mechieta along the edge of the company at a very purposeful stride while Jago and Cenedi went to speak to Ilisidi.

"Banichi-ji?"

"Everything is fine," Banichi said cheerfully. "Our enemies are being fools."

"Doing what?"

"Oh, nothing up here. Down the coast. The authorities have *caught* one of Direiso's folk on the Wiigin-Aisinandi line."

On the train, Banichi meant.

"Illicit radio? Saying what?"

Banichi shot him a guarded, assessing kind of look. "That Tabini-aiji is fortifying Saduri plain and preparing to bomb Mospheiran cities. That he's seizing Mogari-nai to have absolute control of the radar installations during the aforesaid operation, because he knows a retaliation is coming immediately after he bombs the island and the northern provinces are going to take the brunt of it."

"That's absolutely insane!"

"We're quite sure it is, but it *is* indicative of Direiso's objective. She wishes to seize Mogari-nai and the airstrip and say there's nothing there because she's thwarted the plot."

"The plant at Dalaigi." He had a sudden great fear of harm to Patinandi. "What if it's a diversion, Banichi-ji? Are we protected there?"

"Oh, we are protecting all such places," Banichi said. One of the men was adjusting harness, and Bren gave a distracted yank on Nokhada's rein as she swung her hindquarters and refused cooperation. "We have very heavy security on those plants, especially in facilities where you've very diligently pointed out security problems, Bren-ji, and your eye is becoming quite keen in that regard."

"One is grateful to know so, nadi-ji."

"Once the report said bombs would fall, we became very much more concerned that the reserve here is a major target—because maintaining that falsehood means controlling this area within a certain number of hours or attacking government facilities within the same time, so they can say we moved the equipment. And Direiso has adherents among Messengers' Guild officers, but *not* necessarily among the membership. That we silenced that radio and were ready with statements laying out Direiso's plans will at least throw water on the fire. Our press release *is* being routed through Mogari-nai and the local stations *are* carrying the official broadcast. It may be significant, however, that Mogari-nai was the last major communication center to pass the aiji's press release to the broadcast stations."

It was ominous. Very much so. He made a motion of his eyes toward the heavens. "If *they* have bombs—"

"No, Bren-ji. I assure you, *no* aircraft will reach us. There are aircraft sitting ready to take action against any craft Direiso can send against us. We learned at Malguri, and we have taken precautions. Not mentioning Tano's position, which is quiet, but very capable of defending itself. The fortress *is* ancient. But for you alone to know—though possibly Direiso does—even the dust of Saduri is modern. They blow it on. For the casual hiker. This is more than a game reserve. If we've kept that secret from Mospheira, numerous people will be surprised."

He was mildly shocked; and no, his government didn't tell him everything: particularly the Defense Department with its touchy secrets. His mind raced through memories of dilapidated halls, a row of doors facing their bedrooms that didn't open and didn't have windows.

In this vast, open government reserve there were fences, he guessed, that were far more than low stone walls. And he had no idea what other electronic barriers might exist out here, or what those vans he'd seen parked behind the old fortress might contain, but Tano and Algini were surveillance specialists, he had guessed before this, while Banichi and Jago were surely what the Guild so delicately called, with entirely different meaning, *technicians*.

"We aren't using the pocket coms to transmit any

longer," Banichi said. "Though I assure you reception is no problem. We listen to a mobile unit up near Wiigin talk to one east of the fortress and know all we need. *This* time, Bren-ji, we are not using a defense heavily infiltrated with the opposition, as we were at Malguri. As for what we need *worry* about, there's one other road that goes up the cliffs from Saduri Township. It supplies Mogari-nai, and tourists use it to tour the cannon fort. The aiji's forces will keep that road open. Meanwhile—" Banichi's voice, from rapidfire cataloging of assets, took on an airy quality. "Meanwhile, the dowager will assert her prerogative, as a member of the aiji's household, to tour the facility. But we have to be careful. To dispossess the Messengers' Guild of Mogari-nai would tread on Guild prerogatives. Even to save lives, *our* Guild will not countenance that kind of operation. Politics, you understand. And in the balance of powers, it *is* wise to preserve those prerogatives."

"One understands that much." A Guild disintegrating would be very dangerous to the peace. As the fall of the Astronomers from credibility after the Landing had been catastrophic for atevi stability: for lords there were successors, but for the Guilds there were not. "Banichi-ji, the aiji does know, I hope, that we can receive data without the earth station. Surely he does know."

"Yes. But Guild prerogatives demand it go through the Messengers' Guild no matter where we receive it. The Messengers will bend, nand' paidhi. Their rebellion will go on precisely as long as that Guild sees other entities defying the aiji with impunity, or until the fist comes down on them. The aiji can no longer ignore Hanks' challenge to his authority."

"So we are going to fight, there? The dowager is truly on our side?"

"Fight, nand' paidhi? *Ilisidi* is on holiday at Saduri. The television says so quite openly. The television says, during her holiday, she will tour Mogari-nai." The call was going out to mount up. "Saigimi's death was a serious blow to Direiso. Tatiseigi's appearance

on television was a second. Badissuni's attack of heart-
burn was a third, leaving Ajresi unopposed in the
Tasigin Marid, and Badissuni very cooperative with
the aiji, if he's wise. The Messengers' Guild admitting
Ilisidi for a tour is a fourth. Direiso may strike in *any*
direction, but it's the business of aijiin to settle their
affairs and then the Guilds have no difficulty arranging
their policies. Believe me that the Messengers are no
different from *our* Guild."

Banichi made his mechieta extend a leg and got up,
in that haste the maneuver needed. Others were getting
up. Bren had Nokhada kneel and as he rose, turned
and landed in the saddle, he saw Jase attempt to do
the same.

Attempt. Jase failed, was left clinging to the saddle
ring with one foot hung and the other off the ground as
the mechieta rose and tried to turn full circle in
response to Jase's unwitting grip on the rein. It was a
dangerous halfway, from which a man could fall with
his foot still trapped; but Haduni was there instantly to
put a hand under Jase and boost him up, disheveled and
with his braid loosening, but safe. Jase still pulled, and
the mechieta resisted, lifted his head and turned
another circle until Jase apparently realized it was his
own fault and slacked the grip on the rein.

"It took me a while," Bren said.

Jase still looked scared. Well a man could be. And
dizzy. For a man who had trouble with the unclouded
sky and kept taking motion sickness pills, the mechieta
turning while he was off balance was not, Bren was
sure, a pleasant thing.

"You're doing fine," Bren said.

And with no warning but a ripple of motion through
the herd Nokhada spun and joined the others in a rush
after Ilisidi, who had taken off. Bren looked back,
scared for Jase, but he had stayed on. Jago fell back to
join him as the herd sorted itself out, Nokhada fought
the rein to get forward, and Banichi rode ahead of him.

But the rush settled into a run for a good long while.
Ilisidi, damn her, was having the run she'd wanted, a
perverse streak she had, a desire to challenge a man's

sense of self-preservation, never mind Jase was fighting to stay on and scared out of good sense.

He dropped further back, a fight with Nokhada's ambitions, and came past the boy from Dur, who was riding with a death grip on the saddle straps and excitement in his eyes. He came alongside Jase, then, who was almost hindmost in the company. Jase was low and clinging to the saddle, his whole world doubtless shaking to the powerful give and take of the creature that carried him.

"What are we *doing?*" Jase yelled at him. "Why are we running, nadi?"

"It's all right!" he yelled back. And yelled, in Ragi, what he'd said on the language lessons when Jase had reached the point of anger: "Call it practice!"

Jase, white-faced and with terror frozen on his features, began suddenly to laugh, and laugh, and laugh, until he wondered if Jase had gone over the edge. But it *was* funny. It was so funny he began to laugh, too; and Jase didn't fall.

In a while more, as Babsidi ran out his enthusiasm for running, they slowed to that rocking pace the mechieti could hold for hours, and then Jase, having been through the worst, grew brave enough to straighten up and try to improve his seat.

"Good!" Bren said, and Banichi said, riding past him, "Well done, Jase-paidhi!"

Jase glanced after Banichi with a strange look on his face, and then seemed to decide that it *was* a word of praise he'd just heard. His shoulders straightened.

The mechieti never noticed. The boy from Dur dropped back to ride with them and with Haduni and Jago. But then Nokhada decided she was going to go forward, giving little tosses of her head and moving as if she could jump sideways as easily as forward, meaning if she found an excuse to jump and bolt, she would.

Bren let her have her way unexpectedly and touched his heel to her ribs, which called up a willing burst of speed around the outside of the herd and up to the very first rank. She nipped into place with Ilisidi and Cenedi, where she was sure she belonged.

"Ah," Ilisidi said. "Nand' paidhi. Did he survive?"

"Very handily," he said, and knew then the dowager had kept *one* promise she'd made in coming here, to give the new paidhi the experience he'd had.

And Jase had laughed. Jase had sat atop a mechieta's power and stayed on, Jase had been told by a man he hadn't trusted that he had done quite well, and Jase was still back there, riding upright and holding his own under a wide open and cloudless sky.

And by that not inconsiderable accomplishment Jase was better prepared if they had to move: it *was* practice; and practice like that had been life and death for him—in a lot of ways.

The sun declined into the west until it shone into their eyes and made the land black, and nothing untoward had happened. The sun declined past the edge of the steep horizon toward which they were climbing, and the light grew golden and spread across the land, casting the edges of the sparse, short grasses in gold.

Suddenly, with the topping of a rise, a white machine-made edge showed above the dark horizon, far distant.

Mogari-nai: the white dish of the earth station, aimed at the heavens. Beyond the dish in that strange approach to dusk, the blue spark of warning lights. Microwave towers aimed out toward the west, a separate establishment.

They rode closer, and now the sky above the darkening land was all gold, the sun sunk out of sight. One could hear in their company the sounds that had been their environment all day: the moving of the mechieti, in their relentless, ground-covering strides; the creak of harness; the rare comment of the riders. Somewhere below their sight the sun still shone, and they discovered its rim again as, between the shadow of cliffs falling away before them, the ocean shone faintly, duskily gold—no longer Nain Bay, but the Strait of Mospheira.

The last burning blaze of the sun then vanished still *above* the horizon. The mountains of Mospheira's heart, invisible in the distance, were hiding the sun in haze.

"A pretty sight," Ilisidi said.

If they had not struck their traveling pace when they had, they would have arrived well after dark. Ilisidi, Bren thought, had wanted the daylight for this approach to the earth station and its recalcitrant Guild.

A peaceful approach. Banichi had said that was her intent, at least.

23

A prop plane, a four-seater, sat beyond the dish of the earth station, marking the location of the airstrip, and beyond it, a low-lying, modern building, was the single-story sprawl of the operations center.

The vast dish passed behind them, the dusk deepened to near dark, and the company stayed close around the dowager as they rode. Bren eyed the roof ahead of them and had his own apprehensions of that long flat expanse, and the chance of an ambushing shot from that convenient height. He was anxious about their safety and hoped Banichi and Jago in particular wouldn't draw the job of checking out the place. It looked like very chancy business to him, and chancier than his security usually let him meet.

They stopped. A good thing, he thought.

But the mechieti had scarcely gotten their heads down for a few stolen mouthfuls of grass when the door to the place opened, bringing every mechieta head up and bringing a low rumble and a snort from the mechiet'-aiji, Babsidi, who was smelling the wind and was poised like a statue, one that inclined toward forward motion.

"Babs," Ilisidi cautioned him. One atevi figure had left the doorway and walked toward them at an easy pace, nothing of hostility about the sight, except the black clothing, and the fact that the man—it *was* a man—was armed with a rifle which he carried in hand.

But about the point that Bren was ready to take

alarm, the man lifted a hand in a signal and one of Ili-sidi's men rode forward to meet him.

Not even of Tabini's man'chi, Bren thought, though Banichi had said Tabini was moving; it seemed to be all Ilisidi's operation. But it was reassuring, at least, that they had had someone on site; perhaps, as Banichi had also said, preparing security for Ilisidi's tour, much as Tabini's security had prepared the way for him on tour.

There was some few moments of discussion between the two, then a hand signal, and a few more of Ilisidi's security went up to the door.

A shiver began in Nokhada's right foreleg and ran up the shoulder under Bren's knee. Otherwise the mechieti were stock still. Creatures that had been inter-ested only in grazing at other breaks were staring steadily toward the building, nostrils wide, ears swiveling. They had not put on the war-brass, the sharp tusk-caps that armed the mechieti with worse than nature gave them; but the attitude was that of creatures that might take any signal on the instant and move very suddenly.

But Cenedi and Ilisidi together began to move quite slowly and the rest of the mechieti came with them, across the narrow runway, onto the natural grass of the building frontage.

Men slid down. Ilisidi signaled Babsidi to drop a shoulder, and stepped down from the saddle, retrieving her cane on the way as Cenedi swung down.

Bren tapped Nokhada's shoulder, nudged her with his foot and as she lowered her forequarters, swung off, keeping his grip on the rein until he was sure that was what he should have done. But everyone was getting down and while Banichi moved off to talk to Cenedi, Jago showed up, and called Jase and the boy in close.

"One expects no difficulty," Jago said. "But fol-low me."

They let the mechieti go, merely tying reins to the saddle ring, and Bren was acutely conscious of the gun he carried in the inside pocket of his jacket as more than a nuisance and a weight that thumped when

Nokhada hit her traveling gaits. He was armed and able at least to shoot back. Jase and the boy were not. He gave no odds on Ilisidi, who passed into the building surrounded by rifles and sidearms.

So did they, into a double-doored foyer and into a broadcast operations center, one side wall with two tiers of active television screens and six rows of consoles, some occupied and active despite the presence of armed guards.

An official had joined them, bowed, and offered courtesies, offering drinks and a supper, which the official swore were under the guard of Guild security.

"I'll see this place first," Ilisidi said and, walking with the aid of her cane, toured the long rows of counters and consoles with Cenedi beside her, with a handful of her young men around her, as others took up posts on all sides. The technicians couldn't quite remain oblivious to what was going on, or to the fact that guns were visible: nervous glances attended her movements and those of the men on guard.

There was, the dowager was informed, in a stillness so great there was no need of close eavesdropping, this central command center; and there were, down that hall, the offices, the rest areas, and through the door, the adjacent staff barracks. Her men had been there, one said, and they had posted a guard there and at the outlying service buildings.

"I assure you, aiji-ma," the director said, "everything is in order."

"And the paidhi's messages?"

"Nand' dowager?" The director seemed dismayed; and *whack!* went the dowager's cane on a console end. A score of workers jumped. One bent over in an aborted dive under the counter, which she turned into a search after an escaped pen, and quickly surfaced, placing the pen shamefacedly before her.

Scared people, the Messengers, with officers of their Guild trafficking with the other side, and the Assassins' Guild guarding the aiji-dowager, a gray eminence in the chanciest atevi politics. Ostensibly she was on a holiday tour including the old fortress, which this

communications nerve center had to have known was
coming, and the nature of that old fortress some here
had to know.

They had to believe she was *probably* on the aiji's
side at a moment when other things were going chancy,
rapidly, in electronic messages sailing all over the
continent.

"Where," Ilisidi asked, in that shocked silence, in
which only Ilisidi moved, "*where* is the paidhi's mail
and *why* has the communication run through *this center*
gone repeatedly amiss? Is this the fault of individuals?
Or is this a breakdown in equipment? Does fault lie in
this place? Can anyone explain to me why messages lie
in this place and do not move out of it in a timely
manner? Is it a spontaneous fault of the equipment?"

"No, aiji-ma," the director said in a voice both faint
and steady. "There is no fault of the equipment. I have
taken charge of this facility in the absence of the senior
director."

"You are?"

"Brosimi of Masiri Province, aiji-ma. Assistant
director of Mogari-nai by appointment of my Guild."

One did not miss the *aiji-ma,* that was the address of
someone at least nominally loyal; and Ilisidi, diminutive among her guards, was the towering presence in
the room.

Ilisidi walked further, looked at one console and the
next, and all the while Cenedi and Banichi were near
her; but so was a man named Panida, whose talents and
function in Ilisidi's household had always seemed to be
very like Tano's. Panida was generally, in Ilisidi's
apartment in the Bu-javid, near the surveillance station
that was part of every lord's security. And now he
paused here and there at certain idle and vacant consoles. Once he flipped a switch. Whether it had been on
or off, Bren did not see.

"Nand' director," Ilisidi said. "This is a very thin
staff I see. Are there ordinarily more on this shift?"

"Yes, aiji-ma. But they went down to Saduri
Township."

"Well, well, and will that improve the efficiency of this staff?"

"I assure the dowager such will be the case." The director made surreptitious signals to his staff, who uncertainly rose from their seats and, almost as a body, bowed in respect.

"Nadiin." Ilisidi nodded, and said, by way of introduction: "Bren-paidhi. Jase-paidhi. And their devoted escort, the heir of the lord of Dur."

"Nand' director," Bren said as faces turned toward them. "Nadiin."

A second round of bows and nods of heads. And the hasty but respectful movement of a young woman who gathered up a heavy stack of paper and proclaimed it, "Nand' dowager, here are all the messages routed through this station in the last ten days. With great respect, aiji-ma."

"And the messages for the paidhiin?"

A middle-aged man moved to a desk and carefully, with an anxious eye on the behavior of security, gathered up a smaller handful of printout. "This is the phonetic log and transcript, aiji-ma, during the same period, but the translators have all left."

"One assures you, nadi, the paidhiin do not need translators." Ilisidi with a casual backhand waved the man in their direction, and the man brought the log and bowed.

The dowager wanted the record read, Bren said to himself. "Thank you, nadi," he said to the anxious technician, took the thin volume, and set it down. It was the end of the record he wanted, and he was accustomed to the phonetic transcription. He sat down and flipped the pages over to the latest messages.

There were Deana's transmissions, as late as this morning, included in the limited transcript although they were in Ragi. A cursory glance proved them more grammatical and careful than her conversation in the language—but then, on Mospheira, Deana had her dictionaries at her elbow.

Deana, however, could wait for a moment. For a moment he was on a search for things *not* necessarily on government matters, things personal to him, which, if he could find while doing his job—

He was aware of Jase leaning on the counter, reading over his shoulder.

He was aware of his hand trembling as he turned the pages back and on a deep intake of breath he discovered the fear he'd not *let* surface since he'd failed to get through on the phones was still very much alive.

More of Deana's junk. It made up the bulk of the stack and it made him mad. He wanted his own messages. He wanted answers from Toby, what had happened, how his family fared.

He found it.

It said, *Bren, mother's out of surgery. They said it was worse than they thought. But she's going to be all right. I tried to call. The lines went down. I hope . . .*

The line blurred and he blinked it clear.

. . . hope you get this. I hope you're all right. I was sorry we were cut off. I shouldn't have said the things I did, and I knew it, and all that other crap came out. I wanted to say I love you, brother. And I said that nonsense.

His hand shook uncontrollably. He couldn't see. He couldn't think for a moment, except that it wasn't allowable for him to show disturbance in front of a roomful of atevi, in the service of the dowager. Too much was at issue. He had too much to do. He shoved his way out of the seat, told himself a restroom might give him a moment to get himself together without anyone being the wiser if he just moved slowly and showed no distress. *Lives* rode on his composure. He couldn't become the subject of gossip or disgrace to the dowager.

"Jago-ji," he said. His eyes were brimming and he tried not to blink. "It's a little warm. Where's a restroom, please?"

"Nandi." Jago moved past Jase and, thank God, between him and the rest of the room. "This way."

"Bren?" Jase asked him.

"Stay there!" he said to Jase, and found he could talk, and if he could get privacy enough to clear his eyes without making a fool of himself, he'd be fine and back before anyone questioned his reactions.

Jago, meanwhile, brought him to the side hall, and to a restroom door, and inside, all the while one could have heard a pin drop outside.

"Bren-ji?"

"It's all right." There was a wall basin, and he ran cold water and splashed it into his face. Jago handed him a towel. Atevi restrooms had no mirrors. He trusted he hadn't soaked his hair. He'd gotten his eyes clear but his gut was still in a knot. "Jago-ji, I'm sorry. I'm fine. How do I look?"

"Ill," Jago said. "What did you read, Bren-ji?"

He tried to frame an answer. *Good news* seemed a little extravagant. He truly wasn't doing well.

The door cracked. Jago held it with her hand, protective of him. Jase said, "Bren?"

"In a moment, Jase." Adrenaline surged up, annoyance, anger, he didn't know what. But Jase persisted.

"I have to talk to him, nand' Jago. *Please.*"

"Let him in, nadi-ji," Bren said, thinking by the tone of Jase's voice he might have found something urgent in the record. Jago let the door open and Jase slipped in, while he knew the room outside would be concluding something was direly wrong.

"I need to talk to you," Jase said. "I read the message. I need to talk to you. Alone."

He didn't understand. He damned sure didn't want to discuss his personal life. He had a great deal else weighing on him.

But part of that great deal else was Jase's cooperation.

"Jago," he said.

"I will not leave you, Bren-ji."

Nor should. Jago took herself to the side, however, and back a pace to the wall.

That left Jase as alone as he could manage in a tiny space; and Jase ducked his head and took a breath in the manner of a man with an unpleasant task in front of him. "Bren," Jase said in a low voice, and went on in his own language, "Yolanda's trying to get away. She's coming here. She's going to try."

That took several heartbeats to listen to. And a few more to try to figure. Yolanda Mercheson, Jase's partner from the ship, was going to *leave* Mospheira?

"Why?" was the only thing he could say, not When? Not How? which were backed up and waiting, but at that point, Cenedi opened the door.

"Nandiin. Is there a problem?"

"We're all right," Bren said. His nerves were still wound tight, and he realized that the dowager was being kept waiting. "A moment, Cenedi-ji. Please excuse me to the dowager for just a moment." One didn't *do* such a thing; but he did. "Jase. Why? What's going on?"

"I don't know the details. I just know she's coming here. It's her judgment she can't work with the island."

Giving up on Mospheira? The ship was writing off the human population.

"I don't understand," he said. "And we're going to have to explain this to the dowager. When is she doing this?" Jase's sudden passion for the seashore began to nag at the back of a mind grown suspicious, over the years, of every anomaly. "Where did you make contact? When?"

"On the phone," Jase said in a faint voice; and Jase was white-faced and sweating. "We had it arranged before we came down, that if one of us found the place we were in impossible, if demands were being put on us that we couldn't accept, we'd cross the water somehow. And she—called me on the phone and that was how I knew. I knew I had to come at least to the coast. And then if she made it I was bound to find out about it if I was with you, so I could get her—get her to the capital. But I didn't know it was so big out here. I didn't know it—"

"Jase, that story's got so many holes in it—"

"I'm not lying."

"You were just going to flit over to the coast and pick her up—on *what?* A boat? A plane? Or is she going to hike over?" He was too shaken right now to be reasonable. Temper was very close to the surface. "How did you know? And don't tell me you made a phone call I don't know about. Anything that came into the apartment I *do* know about, unless it walked in on two legs."

"No. It didn't. We had it arranged, Bren, we *didn't* know what we were putting ourselves into, and we knew there was a potential for problems with the atevi side; we knew there was a potential for problems on the island, too, but we really thought if things broke down they'd break down here, not there. So we said— if we had to signal trouble—one of us would say— would say there was a family emergency. We figured it was the one thing even atevi might understand and let one of us reach the other. And whoever—whoever had to run for it, it was going to be the other one who had somebody get sick. Or die, if it was a life and death situation. She said my father *died,* Bren. She's in real trouble."

He *might* have let expression to his face. He wasn't entirely sure. He was angry. He was embarrassed, and angry, and had a clear idea Jago followed most of it. He'd been through the entire government with Jase's lie. He'd intervened in an already touchy situation with a Guild half of whose local members had fled the site they were standing in.

"I didn't know the atevi," Jase said. "I didn't understand the way things are set up here. I didn't know you had *real* problems yourself, and then I did know and I didn't know how I was going to make it work and get her to the mainland when you had far worse troubles than I could claim to and you weren't getting your family out. I knew it wasn't going to work the way we'd planned, and I felt like hell about your situation, and I didn't know what to do except get over here somehow and get to the shore and know if she made it I'd be here—"

"You know," Bren said, with far better control of his voice than he thought he'd have, "you know I could take about any of it, piece at a time. I could understand your lying to me. I could accept you had to. But you took after *me* about lying, Jase. You went all high and holy about *my* lying, and you wanted *me* to apologize

to you, when you damned well knew it was the other
way around, Jase, that's what I can't understand."

"I didn't know I could believe you!"

"And now you can."

"Now I *do*," Jase said.

"Wasn't the plan that we'd *send* for her? Or was this
something else, Jase? Are we hearing one more story?"

"I didn't want to call for her to come over here into
something worse than she was in. And I didn't dare
give her a come-ahead. I was with strange security. I
couldn't get you for *four days*, Bren. I couldn't ask the
staff. You said be careful with them. By then it was too
late. My call to my mother—the ship hadn't heard from
Yolanda. Not in four days. And I didn't know what
to do."

"So you want to come out here. And it's not what
you expected. And *now* you trust me."

"Everything you've told me," Jase began, but now
his voice was shaking. "Everything so far makes sense.
I believe Yolanda's leaving the island is tied to what
Deana Hanks is doing, it's tied to everything you've
told me. I've been trying all the way out here to find a
way to tell you what was going on, but every time I
tried I ran into something *else* that wasn't what you'd
led me to think. I didn't know but what Yolanda was
leaving the island *with* Hanks. But I don't think so,
now. By everything I've heard, I don't think so. These
people outside don't make me think so. The business in
the apartment didn't make me think so. The dowager
doesn't. But I just haven't known what to do, Bren. I
tried to find out the truth—and at the first you were
lying to me, and you work for the Mospheiran government, *and* for the aiji, and I didn't know where you
stood, and everything was coming apart."

That made sense. The fishing trip. The damned
fishing trip. Every lie they'd told each other, every difference of perceptions two hundred years of separation
made in two sets of humans.

And if Yolanda Mercheson was pulling out of
Mospheira, there were going to be some angry and desperate people on the island, who were only going to

make matters more tense and more desperate for all of them remotely involved.

Forces on various sides of atevi concerns were moving on the mainland. Everything that had been going forward was still in motion and now human troubles were linked into it.

"You and I had better level with the dowager, is what we'd better do," Bren said. "There are operations going on all over the coast. It may be a hostile reaction Hanks *means* to stir up, if your partner's given away her intentions. If she and Hanks have had a falling-out, it could be *why* Hanks is doing what she's doing in the first place, trying to start a war here so the ship won't deal with us. Or it may be as simple and stupid as I think it is: she doesn't know what in hell she's messing with. Years in the program and a week being *with* atevi and she still doesn't figure it. —Jago-ji, nadi." He changed languages, and went for the door, concerned at the time slipping away from them. "How would Yolanda come, Jasi-ji? By boat? By plane?"

"She can't fly. That's certain. She *could* steal a boat. But the storm—"

"Handling a boat's no given, either. Stay with me." He walked into the communications center, walked past concerned technicians and the boy and the dowager's security to speak to Ilisidi herself. "Nand' dowager," he said, "my partner says that the other ship-paidhi has quit her post."

"Quit."

"And is leaving the island and coming to the mainland for refuge. Likeliest by boat. We don't know when. We don't know where."

"And *that* is in these messages you read?"

"No, nand' dowager," Jase said for himself. "I knew by a phone call days ago. Nand' Bren had *no* knowledge of it. I wished finally—" Jase's voice was trembling, and steadied. "I wished to tell it before now. I apologize, nand' dowager."

"It was a code by conversation," Bren interjected, "aiji-ma. Security couldn't possibly detect it. *I* didn't."

"Well," Ilisidi said, and while a foul temper was

possible, when it was entirely justified, in fact, it didn't happen, though nerves all around were drawn tight. "Well." Ilisidi stood leaning on her cane. "And in this night of human secrets, in this night with serious consequences on every hand and fools attempting to overthrow all established order, what will happen on the island, nand' paidhi? What *has* happened? Disasters? Or better news."

Bren found his hands trembling again. He didn't want to go into the business with his family and he was sure someone on Ilisidi's staff had read the message by now, since it had sent Jase rushing after him, and had stalled everyone until he could sort matters out in the restroom.

"I'm sure that they'll try to stop her, nand' dowager." He had one resource left, one thing Shawn had given him, and as best he could figure it was time to try it.

It was a connection into the international phone system he'd done everything to avoid making: the National Security people had had their hands on his computer during his last visit, and *something* had happened when he'd stopped on his way to the airport to update his files: a huge amount of information had flooded into his computer storage, data and programs he'd downloaded onto removable storage once he'd realized it. And the Foreign Secretary having gone so far as to slip the codes he had under his cast to get them onto the mainland with him, he figured that Shawn intended them for a dire emergency and not just a phone-home-soon, Bren.

He also figured that by the time he'd found the note, far later than Shawn had intended, things were vastly changed and the people in the State Department and in the Defense Department who were in charge of such things had probably put something lethal on that access, something that would render his computer worse than useless.

He'd no facilities or knowledge to figure out such destructive actions. He'd not dare connect it in again to any computer system for fear of what he might bring with it. He just hoped the contact he was trying wouldn't destroy the computer's unconnected usefulness to him, in his translations and the other things he used it for, right down to his personal notes.

But, foreseeing the day, he'd backed up what he could. And he couldn't avoid the direct contact. It was a reciprocating set of operations that would flow back and forth—if he got in.

He used the keyboard. He entered what he had. He sat, with a human by him who *was* a computer tech from a system vastly more advanced than his, who didn't, Jase said, know as much about what Jase called *these early machines* as he knew about atevi. Jago was there. Banichi was. Cenedi was. And at the critical keystroke, the computer telltales lit up, flickered, and kept flickering. He sat and listened for the vocal output, which he didn't believe would come.

But relays were clicking. It sounded as if relays were clicking. On the State Department lines, if that was how he'd gotten in, there was a robot, not a human operator. If the numbers were good, the call went to another robot.

But if what he feared was true, the second robot would be deactivated, the one that once had been able to get him through to the Foreign Office.

Next relay. He expected a voice. He could hardly believe it.

Then another click dashed his hopes. Click. Pause. Click. Click. Click.

"They must be routing the call to the far side of the island," he said to Jase, and even as he said it, he suspected the call was doing exactly that: those were repeated long-distance connections, his codes still burrowing through walls and routing itself, please God, to the State Department and the Foreign Office, where if he was very, very lucky, at this late, after-dark hour, he might find the system routed itself *without* an operator, as could happen if your codes were very, very clean, to Shawn, wherever he was.

It rang.

"You have reached—" It was the damn recording. He punched a manual code. And it rang another number.

"Foreign Office."

It was a young voice. Female. Very young. His heart sank.

"Shawn Tyers," he said. "Code check. This is an emergency."

"Sir?"

"The Foreign Secretary." God, God, they were hiring fools. "Put me through to the Foreign Secretary. You punch code 78. You have to do it from your console."

"Is this Mr. Cameron?" There was alarm in the voice. Excitement. And he didn't want to admit it, but he saw no choice.

"Yes. It is. On diplomatic business. Life and death. Put me through."

"He's gone home. I mean—he's gone home up to the coast, Mr. Cameron. They shut the office."

"They shut the office."

"Well—" The voice lowered. Sounded shaky. *"Mr. Cameron, the State Department shut it down. They've fired everybody in the whole Foreign Office, except I worked for both offices. I'm the night operator."*

"Polly?" He remembered a dark-complexioned young woman with a part down the middle of her head.

"Yes, sir, Mr. Cameron. And they're going to fire me, too. They record all the calls. I can't call out. Is there something you can tell me that I can tell somebody?"

"Good night, Polly."

"Yes, sir." The voice was very faint. Hushed as it was, she sounded like a child. *"Have a good evening, sir."*

Damn, he wanted to say. And wanted to slam the receiver down. But he didn't. He drew a deep breath and calmed his nerves.

"Nand' dowager, the State Department has discharged everyone in the Foreign Office. Even the Secretary has gone home. That's what I'm told, and I believe the young woman who told me. Yolanda-paidhi

may well have gone somewhere. But I'm very fearful
she hasn't."

Jase, leaning on the counter, hung his head and
looked utterly downcast.

"So," the dowager said.

"I know where she'd come," a young voice said.

And with one accord everyone looked at the boy
from Dur.

24

There were maps. Ilisidi's security had very detailed maps, which they had brought into the small, glass-walled conference room just off the main communications center. Out there beyond the glass, technicians of the Messengers' Guild kept routine broadcasts going and, being mostly Saduri locals stranded away from their homes by the crisis, gratefully had their suppers off the official buffet. In this room, standing around the conference table with the chairs pushed back to the glass, all of them that had to make the plans were the crowded but willing audience as Rejiri of Durwajran ran his hand over a profusion of numbers and topographical lines on the shoreline of Mospheira— including this area, which was not detailed on most atevi maps.

"Most illegal boats come from the Narrows, here," Rejiri said with his fingers on the narrowest part of the strait, that nearest Aidin. "And there's a very bad current in the Narrows, so it looks like a real good place to go across but it isn't. Freighters know, but they come down from Jackson and catch the current and drive hard. They have the big engines, too. But the little boats, they can't carry that much in their tanks, nand' dowager, and if they go too hard they'll run their tanks dry and especially if they don't have a lot of extra tanks aboard they'll be in a lot of trouble. If they leave out of Jackson and go with the current and the wind's not in their faces off Aidin headland they can cut across and the current will just carry the little boats to

Dur. But the sneaky thing is if you don't know anything but boating in safe water and you don't know you're in the current and you think you're going across, and you aren't, you're going way, way south. You want to have a lot of cans of fuel, a whole lot of cans. But if you run out or sometimes if you go out of Bretano—if you do that, and some do, they all come in right here." The boy pointed to a spot on the outer shore, at the place where it turned in to Saduri Harbor—and drew a second breath. "That beach. If you drop a bottle in at Jackson or Bretano it's got to come here. You can find all sorts of stuff after a storm. Just junk, most times. But if there's a boat tried to smuggle stuff in, or if they don't make Dur, they'll break up on the rocks at the point or they'll make landfall somewhere right along here. And weather's been bad. Which could help them along but the seas are going to be awful, too."

"What does he say?" Jase wanted to know. The boy had a rapid patter, an accent, and he was using words Jase didn't know. Bren gave him the condensed version in Mosphei'.

"He's saying the current through the strait is very strong. Boats starting from Mospheira if they don't reach Dur, it carries them onto a beach near Saduri."

"Water current."

"Yes." *He* didn't know what caused a current. It wasn't the time to find out. He had a council of war around him and Jase. The dowager was looking grimly at the map over which he was sure her knowledge of plans that might be affected was superimposing other considerations, and the boy went on.

"Nand' dowager," the boy said. "I could take the plane out there. I could get to Dur and tell my father you need help."

Ilisidi scowled at the boy. "You don't have a key."

"One doesn't need a key, nandi."

"One forgot. Stealing airplanes is your trade. How *does* one start it?"

"One pushes a button, nand' dowager."

"A security disaster. Stay here. I plan to charge your father your hourly keep."

"But I could help!"

"Gods felicitous, boy, this is the communications headquarters for half the continent! Do you think we can't *phone* your father?"

"But they might tap the phones. Mightn't they, nand' dowager?"

There was quiet for a moment, and Cenedi said, "It might be a useful diversion. And the boy's presence on the radio could get four men in unannounced."

"A damned fool of a boy whose welfare is in *my* hands."

"Nand' dowager, I could go right off the cliff and *be* on approach. *I* could fly men into Dur! And we'll get my father to shut the ferry down, so nobody can go from Wiigin to here! If you send men, he'll believe me!"

"Wari-ji."

The man so named leaned a hand on the table. "One does see it as possible, aiji-ma. And the boy has a point."

"Instruct him. If he can start the thing, *if* it has fuel— let him go. And go now. We haven't touched Dur, so as not to involve them, but Dur has touched us. So let them act, if they will."

"Yes," the man said. Nawari was his entire name. "Boy."

The boy darted to the man and toward the door, remembered to bow, and went where the man beckoned him to go. There was a silence in the glassed-in room until the door was shut. On the end of a console counter outside in the communications center, the carefully prepared buffet laid in the path, and the boy pocketed a sandwich as he passed that table, against, Bren supposed, famine on the way to Dur.

It was safe food: their own people had brought it, as Bren understood, when they came in to secure Mogari-nai. Even if everyone but the paidhiin had had the foresight to tuck emergency rations into their pockets once they left the baggage behind.

"There's fuel in the plane," Ilisidi said. "As happens. Our staff flew it here." There were men still on guard on the roof and about the area of the transmission towers, men who had certainly gotten up to Mogari-nai somehow, but there were too many for one small plane. "One would leave the young fool here, but one can lay odds he'd be in the midst of matters." The dowager's fingers rested on the map, on the aforenamed beach and the island of Dur. "Dur-wajran and its position has been a concern. I do rely on the boy's assessment of his father's man'chi, and I am relieved on that score. We *have* a number of men on Dur. They came in two days ago on the ferry from Saduri, but they're there as tourists unless they receive orders or see trouble. Nawari will provide them orders for quiet and specific actions and, with the active cooperation of the lord of Dur, we can close off Wiigin from Saduri by water. The boy *can* be useful in that regard. As is his advice useful. Trust every local youth to know that beach. And if that *is* the case, so do the Kadigidi know it. They *may* have advised a boatload of otherwise inept human sailors to put out from Jackson Harbor with enough fuel just to keep the bow to the waves. Smugglers have used Dur, generally, since the stretch of beach in question is government reserve. So Cenedi informs me."

"Trust every local youth to have been *on* that beach," Cenedi said. "Nandiin, we had not relied on holding Dur, because its beaches are too broad and it's a wooded, populated island rife with smugglers' caches the locals don't want found. We believe a landfall on the Aidin headland would be far safer for the rebels. We do not have sufficient resources in Aidin to prevent a landing at village airstrips or movement at train stations or other routes that might bring Hanks-paidhi into friendly hands. If she comes by air she could possibly come in at the city airport at Wiigin and leave by train without our people being able to prevent her. But if she comes by boat—and we hope our heavy air activity up over Wiigin has discouraged an air route and forced her to that—we know now it will be a small boat, and *that* can't reach Wiigin. There's been a diplomatic snag in clearance for freighters, ours or theirs, to leave Mospheiran ports: the aiji has withdrawn permits as of yesterday. They've been warned, and they're a cautious breed. The last freighter in transit turned back to Mospheira this morning. If another leaves port, we can spot it. A small boat, however, has a good chance of getting through the net unseen, and they know that."

That freighter ban was very serious, Bren thought. Extremely serious, following the pattern of the attack on Mospheira the rebel radio had foretold. Atevi would be using surveillance planes out over the strait, probably overflying the harbors and provoking more alarm. The aiji did have customs boats, a number with guns of a range and power sufficient to sink another ship.

Mospheira also had such boats. There was a danger of confrontation if this state of crisis went on too long. "What does the *presidenta* say?"

"There is a protest from the Trade Office regarding the aiji's action," Banichi said. "If they're officially aware of Hanks-paidhi's provocations, they're being very quiet about the matter. There's no signal they're willing to correct the problem."

"One suspects they *are* aware," Bren said, and was conscious he now contemplated treason; his stomach knotted up—but so did his nerves, from years of coping with the administration. "But they're not very brave, dowager-ji. They'll please their contributors until the first consequences show up where the voters can find out. Then their attention will be on keeping the voters from finding out and keeping their contributors from being exposed. They'll pull back. The main thing is keeping the customs boats away from each other. That's where people at lower levels could worsen the crisis."

"If they link up with Direiso," Ilisidi said, "she'll lead them on much more precipitate courses."

Or she'll be driven mad with frustration trying to deal with the Mospheiran government, Bren thought. Unless Direiso planned to invade Mospheira if she became aiji.

Which was not a joke. Direiso might indeed have such a notion. The island was ill-prepared to resist, precisely as it had been ill-prepared and ineptly led in the War of the Landing. It was, potentially, the same situation: a mushrooming crisis and most of the human population in slumberous disregard of the danger of a rebel ateva seizing power and running with it.

The same way one decree from Tabini's pen had swept away all debate, all studies, all partisan delays in relocating Patinandi Aerospace and reconfiguring the space program, so events around them now could replace Tabini, who tolerated humans, with Direiso, who would wipe them off the face of the earth.

Bad news multiplied and Mospheira blamed the Foreign Office which told it things that didn't match its expectations; Mospheira then refused to listen to the paidhi in the field and, rather than face down human agitators who now thought they were winning political points, Mospheira had withdrawn police protection from his mother's apartment, or worse, politics infiltrating the police departments had made it impossible for the Mospheiran government to do anything about political thugs and lunatics if they wanted to.

He'd seen it coming. He'd watched it barrel down on them like a train headed down the tracks.

This time there was a strongly centralized power in Shejidan. *This* time the Edi and Maschi atevi of the peninsula weren't raiding the Padi Valley. *This* time they had a ship over their heads that was definitely a player, but which couldn't reach them or get its people out. This time atevi were *very* well advised on human habits and internal divisions, and *this* time there were paidhiin.

All of which might—or might not—tip the scales.

Outside, he heard the sound of the plane starting up.

The boy was on his way. With the means to take the island of Dur for their forces. That was one stretch of beach, if the lord of Dur was on their side, they were relatively sure they could win.

And one of the men outside the glass walls came

in and handed Cenedi a note. Cenedi's expression changed as he read it.

"Nand' dowager," Cenedi said, "the warehouse down in the town is moving its trucks out. Down the harborside road to the west. Do we stop them, or allow them to clear the harborside?"

Ilisidi frowned and looked down at the maps.

"Maintain the peace," Ilisidi said. "For the next hour or so."

So now atevi forces were moving. Bren didn't know where, or how many, but the consoles out there were manned by loyal Guild and watched over by loyal Guild, and he tried to sit in one of the soft chairs in the lounge, lean his head back on the back of the seat and rest, when he wanted to be up pacing the floor.

Jase came into the little nook with a cup of tea. He had a worn, grim look, and found even the padded chair uncomfortable—at least he'd winced when he sat down, and Bren would have done so when he'd sat down, if he'd had the strength left. He eyed the arrival, muttered to indicate he didn't mind Jase being there, and shut his eyes, thinking that in Shejidan it would be about bedtime.

Their company was getting the little rest they could. Not all of them: Banichi and Jago were in close conference with Cenedi, and the dowager had taken possession of the director's office to rest, having taken a map with her.

He'd rather, personally, have stayed in the briefing; but it was Guild business in there, not the Messengers, but the Assassins, and when Banichi said in that very polite tone, "Nand' paidhi, you need to rest," he supposed even aijiin took that cue and went to nurse their headaches.

And watch over their other responsibilities.

Mospheira didn't care so much, Bren told himself, if it let both its Ragi-speaking paidhiin, him *and* Deana, travel out of its grasp; there were other students in the University. Someone's son or daughter could replace either of them. Of course.

Jase shifted. Bren heard the creak of the other chair. Jase was worried about Yolanda. Justifiably so.

As Mospheira's allowing Deana Hanks to cross the water meant risking her life. If Mospheira lost her, that meant they had no translator who'd actually been in the field advising them, and their maze of security precautions was going to operate very slowly in giving anyone outside the State Department access to documents: the aiji's blockade order, which *he* hadn't translated, must either have come in Ragi and sent them scurrying for advanced translation, or in atevi-written Mosphei', which wasn't supposed to exist. He did wonder which.

But the readily obvious fact was, the government didn't give a damn whether it talked to atevi so long as it thought the ship up there would deal with them.

It would, however, panic at the thought of Yolanda Mercheson leaving its shores or the ship aloft cutting them off cold from the flow of technology that was coming to the atevi. There was a level of self-preservation in the President's office that hated adventurous doings, and that wouldn't *let* Deana Hanks take Yolanda with her. He reasoned his way to that conclusion.

There *were* also people in charge of Deana: Deana who did not have the intelligence or the authority she dreamed she had. She was not a random and stupid threat until she was in the field dealing with atevi. *They,* the *they* who controlled her, didn't know how bad her handling of the translation interface was, which was their major flaw. If there *were* atevi experts able to know how bad she was, there wouldn't *be* an intercultural problem. They liked her because what she told them would work was shaped exactly to fall into their plans, and that was their blind spot and her reason for getting the post.

But they had to be restraining her from her wilder notions, or God knew what would happen.

And *somebody* could keep Hanks on the island. George Barrulin could, if he could get through to him.

But the paidhi-aiji was out of phone numbers that

would mean anything, and he *couldn't* get through to George. *They fired everybody in the whole Foreign Office*. God!

"Bren," Jase said.

He opened his eyes a slit. And saw Jase sitting opposite him, elbows on knees, cup in both hands, with a downcast look.

"Bren," Jase said in human language. "I want you to understand something."

He had to listen. Jase's voice had that tone. He sat up, tucked a foot across his knee, and tried to look as if his brain were working.

"The business about my father," Jase said. "I don't have one. Fact is—fact is, he *is* dead."

"I'm sorry to hear that." Politeness was automatic. Understanding what Jase was getting at wasn't.

"No," Jase said. "He *died* hundreds of years ago."

A glimmering of understanding *did* come, then. "Taylor's Children. Is *that* what you mean?"

The ship had had its heroes—those *everyone* owed their lives to: the original crew and the construction pilots, the ones who'd mined and fueled the ship in the radiation hell they'd first had to survive, had left their personal legacy in cold storage, all they knew they'd send into their ship's uncertain future.

And such individuals, drawn from that cold-storage legacy, had *not* been the lowest members of the Pilots' Guild, when the modern crew let them be born.

When—rarely—they'd let them be born.

He was sitting in an ordinary chair in an ordinary lounge in a tolerably exotic facility, but the man he'd been dealing with was *not* ordinary, as he understood history.

The man he'd almost called a friend—brought a bit of the cold of space with him into this little nook.

What the ship had sent them in Jase wasn't the lowest, most expendable crew member. It was one of the elite, one who wouldn't be seduced by any planetary—or personal—loyalties.

The people of the Landing, Mospheirans, hadn't been outstandingly fond of the breed. The privileges of that elite was one of the issues that had led to the Landing. And now the ship sent one down to the planet?

"I must say," Bren said mildly, "I'm surprised. I take it you do have a mother."

"One I'm very fond of. One I want to get back to."

"One can understand how much you want to get back. One can understand very well."

Jase looked at him a little curiously, and didn't ask. But maybe, he said to himself, Jase didn't know there'd been a rift between the ship's crew and the colonists. Maybe that was one of the informational dropouts over time—things like weather, and currents, and sunrise.

"What I want to tell you," Jase said, "is that I *am* telling you the truth. I'm not keeping secrets from you. And I'll tell you all of it. But I want your help."

"For what?"

A slight move of Jase's eyes, a gesture to the side, to the communications center, he supposed. "To talk to the ship. To warn them what's going on and to tell them to send someone else down here, if something happens."

"*Is* that what you'd tell them? I'd think it would be 'Get the hell out of here. They're crazy down here.' "

Jase shook his head. "That's not my conclusion. I don't know what's on the other side of the water. Yolanda said at first she was all right. She was having a lot less problems than I was. But things starting going bad. I've heard other codewords, that just meant worry. When she gave me this one—I was scared. You weren't there. And then things started blowing up. I don't think it's coincidence she called me about the time your government started making trouble over here."

Your government. Mospheira. It was a hell of a thing, that statement, he'd had to parse that to know *which* government Jase meant.

"Telling you the family crisis story was supposed to get you to get Yolanda over for a sympathy visit. And it went wrong. It just went wrong. The ship knows there's something wrong on her side of the water. But if I don't call soon they'll think there's something wrong on this side, too."

"What would they do about it?"

"They'd attempt to deal with it, most probably attempt to deal with atevi in the notion some of them do understand Mosphei' and maybe I'd made a mistake."

He was considering that possibility. "Let's try some critical truth. Is the ship armed?"

"It has weapons. It doesn't have atmospheric craft."

"Coercion occupies absolutely no place in their planning? A little piracy, perhaps?"

"No. If they get involved in this situation, it's possible they can withhold information from one side or the other and get cooperation. It's my recommendation that they cooperate with the atevi and withhold all help from Mospheira."

"You know," Bren said, on a breath that made his voice sail higher and more casual than he wished. "You know," he said more soberly, "I think that's a reasonable position, but I haven't had a lot of luck persuading human governments about it, and we've *lived* on this planet a couple of centuries."

"You want the truth?"

"I think it would be a really good idea, Jase."

"If Yolanda goes—" Emotion clouded Jase's face and ruffled the calm in his voice. "If she doesn't make it, it's important to me. But not to the ultimate outcome of this business. Neither of us is that important to the outcome unless we can do our work. They give us a lot, that's what they say. But they ask a lot of us."

"You're not a computer tech who's studied languages and taught kids."

"I know computers. We had two engineering texts in the library, one French, one German. They didn't teach me a lot about planets. But I learned how languages work. That's the truth, Bren."

"You in love with Yolanda?"

"I suppose so. Yes. I am."

"But disregarding all this, *if* we lost you, what would your ship do?"

"Right now, they'd go on pretending everything was fine, and see if you built the spacecraft."

"And then?"

"If atevi got up there, my captains would negotiate. They'd have done what they want. They'd negotiate with atevi. They'd probably keep on giving them tech. As much as they wanted."

He had a very, very bad feeling that he wasn't understanding everything, and that Jase wanted his full attention for the next item.

"Why?" he asked.

"They want the atevi in space."

"Why?"

"Because—" Jase's voice was faint. "Because we're not alone. We're not the only ones in space. And they're not friendly. And we're not sure, but they could come here."

He sat, having heard that. Having heard it, he didn't want to believe it.

"You said," he recalled, "there was another station out there, at the other end of—wherever you've been."

"There was one. It's gone. We don't know who the aliens are. We don't know what they want. We tried to contact them. We had a few passes, months apart. Just a streak on one tape. And some transmissions. We tried scanning the area where we thought they were coming from. We'd moved *Phoenix* out. And when we got back, the station was—was wrecked. Everyone was dead. It hadn't infallen. But it was going to. We took a vote. We decided—we decided we'd better get out of there."

"And come *here*."

"It was the only place."

"Oh, you could have lost yourself in space. You could have gone the hell *away* from us!"

"It's not that far, Bren. It's about eighteen, twenty years light. You're in their neighborhood. We did *nothing* to these people. People—whatever they are. We did *nothing* to provoke them."

"We did nothing to provoke the atevi into attacking the colony, either, but we made it damned well *inevitable!*"

"You know that. You dealt with this situation. Maybe you have a skill—maybe you have a skill we don't. We need you."

"God, look around you! My government's not doing outstandingly well at the moment!"

"If they'd listen to *you,* they'd be better off."

"But failing that miracle, you want the atevi in space. You want us, or you want the atevi."

"This is the atevi star. This is their world. There's something out there that kills people it doesn't know anything about, that never did anything to them. And the atevi need to know that. We could have gone off in space somewhere and hoped they never found us. We could have tried again—"

"No, you couldn't. *You* thought there'd be a thriving colony here. You thought you'd get fuel for the ship here. *You* thought you'd rally the colony to the defense and you'd have everything the way you used to have it, with us doing the mining *and* the dying for you to run the ship."

There was a small silence. But Jase didn't flinch. "We thought we'd have your help, yes. But we thought we owed each other a mutual debt—a warning, and a chance for us to get out of here if you want to take your chances."

"That's a lousy patch on exactly what I said."

"That's fine. That's the situation. *Now* what do you do?"

He let out a long sigh and fell back into the chair cushions to look at the room beyond, communications that could indeed talk to the ship.

Then at Jase.

"Damn lot of choice you've given us."

"I'm giving you a choice, Bren. The people at the other station didn't have any."

"What in hell provoked it?"

"We don't know. We just don't know. Maybe they're just that way. That's always a possibility, isn't it?"

"Not one I accept!"

"That's what I count on."

What Jase had already said began to sink in. Unwelcomely. "Don't you lay *that* on me! Good *God,* no."

"Let me call the ship. We have armed atevi and probably armed humans and airplanes and boats and mechieti and no one knows what else. None of us may get out of this. Yolanda's already told them don't rely on Mospheira for anything. If you don't want to leave the matter of the atevi to blind luck, baji-naji, Bren, let me talk to them. I'll give them codewords to tell them I'm not compelled and I'll tell them first to trust you, to trust the aiji and the aiji-dowager and whoever they recommend. And if it comes down to Direiso and the rest of them, maybe they'll give the outsiders indigestion if they come here, I don't know. But if we die here, everything is left to chance. They could end up trusting this Direiso person."

"You're not inept, yourself, Jase."

"I've tried to learn from you. Will you let me do it?"

25

"**B**anichi," Bren said at the door of the little room in which the Assassins held private consultation and, having drawn Banichi a little out of earshot of the guard the Guild had placed on the meeting room, he tried to tell a man who last year hadn't known his sun was a star that aliens were hunting in the neighborhood.

"There are other suns," was the way he put it to Banichi, "and one of them is a very bad neighbor. Jase is an officer in the Pilots' Guild and he's made up his mind we're preferable to Hanks."

"A man of good taste," Banichi said calmly. "What about these bad neighbors?"

"They fly in space," he said, and Banichi said, "I think Cenedi should hear this."

Banichi called Cenedi and Jago out of the room. After three more sentences, Cenedi said, " 'Sidi-ji needs to hear this."

Jago went to wake the dowager, and in a very short time indeed Ilisidi herself had come out of the office she had chosen as her retreat, immaculate, stiff-backed, and frowning.

"More foreigners," Ilisidi said, then. "With bad manners, is it? And Jase-paidhi wants us to ally with his people, who provoked them?"

"I think we can avoid alliance," Bren said, with a hollow feeling in his stomach. "Or manage it to our advantage. But I do think the call to his ship would open options otherwise at risk should he—or I—be unlucky tonight."

"The risk seems on his side," Cenedi said, "aiji-ma, since we could then remove him from consideration were we so inclined."

"He is very well aware of the hazard," Bren said, "and has expressed the wish that the aiji-dowager take Mercheson paidhi under *her* personal protection as he himself is under the aiji's."

Banichi gave him a look. So did Jago, at this yielding up of rights Tabini might have contested. But contest was the operative word. There was no option without extensive negotiation if Ilisidi was the leader in the field, as she was, and there was a certain advantage in having Ilisidi step in. Having her as protector of one paidhi created a new position of authority if somehow they should fail and if Ilisidi had to contest with Direiso.

And for all persons concerned in the transaction including Yolanda Mercheson it brought *paghida sara,* mutual leverage. It meant negotiable positions.

Meant a place, a man'chi, a salvation—if they could stop the slide toward unreason.

A message had come in. A white paper went from an operator to one of Ilisidi's junior security to Cenedi, to Ilisidi.

And to Banichi.

Banichi picked up a sandwich from the table. And pocketed it. And another.

That, Bren thought, that was the action of a man who didn't expect a regular breakfast.

"We've just had an indication from Dur," Banichi said, "that the boy did get down safely. One thought you would wish to know. Whether he'll be safe when his parents lay hands on him is another matter, but we do at least have a confirmation that they're being met by his father's staff. Tano and Algini report movement, however."

That was worrisome.

"The fortress hears at some distance," Jago said.

"Not far enough to give it another hour," Cenedi said. " 'Sidi-ji."

Ilisidi gave a wave of her hand. "Whatever one does to make the earth link work," she said, "do. How long does this talking to the ship take?"

It took very little time, the director said. And gave the orders.

Then it was a matter of settling Jase at the console in the communications center. Jase was visibly anxious.

It was disturbing for the workers, too, Bren was sure, a human not only occupying that post, but giving his own protocols and codewords to the ship in a language they had, for one reason and another, no translators here to interpret.

The ship answered. The foreign voice went out over the speakers so all the room could hear.

Then with full knowledge that the conversation was going to be monitored by a very similar center on Mospheira, Jase had to inform his captain that things were both better and worse than the ship might have feared.

"Sorry to call at this hour," Jase said, and his voice steadied. "But I've thought it over and I really need Yolanda over here."

"Yes," the answer came back. *"How are you?"*

"Doing very much better, sir. I've received sympathy from the atevi and I've made recommendations to the atevi government which they've accepted. I need Yolanda, though. Everybody means well, but it's hard. I want her here. I'll try to negotiate that myself, but I wonder if you can't explain to the island that I really need her for a while. Urgent persuasion. That kind of thing. Tell Sandra not to worry about me."

The whole speech was laced with codewords. If he'd had any concern that Mospheiran cooperation was still a possibility, he'd have expected a following and angry phone call. But they knew. He knew. Jase wasn't even taking pains to bury them too obscurely in ordinary conversation. He was just delivering the words and all of them could hope they were the right ones.

"Do you want to talk to your mother?" the captain asked, after hearing all of that with no comment.

"Absolutely no need to, sir."

"I'm here anyway," another, female voice cut in. *"I miss you."*

"Good to hear your voice, mom." This time there was a little shakiness. "I'm fine. I really am. How are you?"

"Worried about you. When am I not? How are you doing?"

"A lot better. I can't talk too long. I'll call when I get back to the city. I'm on what they call a vacation. You'd be amazed. I was rained on by a weather system and I'm sore from riding. And it's beautiful down here. But I've got to sign off now. I love you. You take care, mom. And you can take a call from me *or* from Bren."

"You take care. —Jase? Jase?"

"Yes? I'm here."

"Jase, are you keeping your hours regular?"

Jase ducked his face and wiped a hand over his mouth as if that last was some unexpected and embarrassing item. "Fine, mom. I'm doing fine. You just take care. All right? I'll call you maybe in three or four days. Tell the captain solid fix and green lights on the report and *please* look out for Yolanda. Whatever you hear from this side, rely on the people I've been dealing with to tell you the truth. Good night."

"Good night, Jase," was the signoff, and Bren stood there, the most fluent listener to the exchange, on whom all the others most relied.

And *he* couldn't tell. There wasn't a way to crack a verbal code, no way but fluency and a specific knowledge of the situation.

"So?" Ilisidi asked.

"I take no alarm, aiji-ma. Codewords were certainly all through it, which I expected. There'd have to be to make assurances valid. He seemed to want his captain to pressure Mospheira to get his partner out. He also asked his captain to listen to his associates down here as reliable people."

"A very good thing," Ilisidi said, leaning on her cane. "A very wise thing."

And they waited, while technicians revised settings and threw switches and consulted checklists.

Jase took out a folded sheet of paper that had already seen a great deal of crumpling, and spread it out on the console in front of him—Jase's own writing, but two paidhiin had collaborated on it to eliminate infelicitous remarks; and Banichi and Cenedi had read it, with one good suggestion, but Ilisidi by her own choice had not.

The director cued Jase, and Jase, smoothing his piece of paper flat on the counter, perhaps because his momentary attempt to hold it in his hands did not produce a steady view of it, began:

"Nadiin of the aishi'ditat, this is Jase-paidhi with news of the current situation—" Risky word. Jase pronounced it with only a slight stammer. "I have spoken with the ship and have learned that Mercheson-paidhi on Mospheira has concluded that the unsteadiness of the Mospheiran government and haphazard management make it impossible to continue there. She has appealed to the ship to leave Mospheira and to come to the mainland. The Mospheiran government is attempting to prevent her from doing so and has attempted to stir up political rivalries among atevi of the aishi'ditat to cover their own failures. The ship however, on the advice of Mercheson-paidhi and of myself, has concurred: the ship is withdrawing Mercheson-paidhi from Mospheira and calls on the Mospheiran government to allow her to join me on the mainland. The ship is continuing its association with Tabini-aiji and will deal solely with Shejidan. It sends good will to the aishi'ditat, and to the aiji, and to the aiji-dowager, who has stated she will take Mercheson-paidhi under *her* protection, to preserve the felicity and the wisdom of the arrangement that has established *three* paidhiin, myself, Bren-paidhi, and Mercheson-paidhi, as representatives. Thank you for your kind attention. I shall now repeat this message in Mosphei' for the information of Mospheiran listeners on the other side of the strait."

Technicians scrambled in the silence of a broadcast area. Coughs were smothered. Switches were thrown off, others were thrown on, and a tower aimed at Mospheira punched out the next message at a power level reserved to announce impending war.

Jase got his next cue.

"Citizens of Mospheira, this is Jase-paidhi with news of the current situation—"

Atevi stood very still throughout the whole length of the message. Technicians jumped at one point, and made adjustments. Jase was speaking rapidly and it inevitably took Mospheiran technicians a moment to respond to an electronic provocation.

This version, however, was going up to the ship as well. And *if* they received the ship's support and that message came back down from the sky, there would be receivers tuned to it, and if they jammed every broadcast on the island, *someone* in an island full of various-minded and argumentative humans was going to get that message recorded and passed out hand to hand on faxes and copy machines.

This time there was a consequence and a crisis George Barrulin couldn't head off from the President's door.

The President's morning golf game might not take place tomorrow.

Jase finished. A technician cut off the microphone and shut down his console and spoke to him. Then everyone dared talk—and take a breath. Small coughs broke out, held until now.

"He did it exactly," Bren said to Ilisidi. "And the University will *know* he damned Hanks' numbers in what he said."

"Hanks' numbers *and* Direiso's." Ilisidi was very pleased.

Jase meanwhile had gotten up and left the console. He looked very solemn and pale as he came down the aisle between the long rows of consoles.

He looked very lonely.

Atevi might not understand two humans embracing

in a crowded room. They did understand an offered hand.

Jase took it like a drowning man. Squeezed it hard.

"Just a little shaky," Jase said. "Sorry. Did I do it?"

"You did it."

Jase's voice sank to near-nothing. "Codeword, for the ship: ask to speak to Constance." And sadly, desperately, "Is there *any* word, Bren?"

As if information might be forthcoming from them now that Jase had done what he could on their side— and made Mercheson-paidhi suddenly a very valuable piece in a very deadly game. Bren reluctantly shook his head. "I wish I could tell you yes."

"We may not get her out," Jase said quietly.

"If she comes ashore anywhere from Dur southward, the aiji's people will bring her in, no question."

Or, the unspoken possibility, Direiso's people might try to lay hands on her if they had any *inkling* she might be attempting a crossing. If Hanks' people were holding her, a possibility he didn't discount, he was sure they'd hear from them, maybe *claiming* to hold her, after they'd held their meetings and managed a decision about it.

"How long does it take to cross?" Jase asked.

"Varies. Depends on the weather. Freighters, about two days."

"If she was out there during the storm—"

"You just point the bow at the waves and keep the engine running enough to let you steer. She didn't come down here knowing, but she could find that out among the first things she'd learn. The wind would be constantly at the back of someone trying to cross. That would save fuel. A lot of it. The storm was out of the west—it would *help* her, not run her out of fuel."

"The captain's gotten the word from me to apply pressure to get her over here. I didn't get anything from him on what she might have told him about her situation and, most of all, the captain didn't cue me at any time that he knew where she was or that she's safe. — What's going on? What's happening?"

There was movement, suddenly, in the room: security headed for the stairs that led, they had all learned, to the roof.

Cenedi was looking not entirely displeased.

Jago came to him, and Banichi close behind. "Lord Tatiseigi," Jago announced, "has moved forces to Saduri headland, nandiin. That was the movement Tano reported. Tano and Algini have agreed to let them pass. However, the dowager says we would be prudent to retire our force to Saduri Township down the road, and get the staff down to the town as well."

Banichi said, "Either he's approved the marriage or he's tracked down the television set."

The plain of Saduri was a smallish peninsula, shaped like a triangle, and the sea made a deep indentation in one of the legs with the old cannon fort and Mogari-nai on one side of the indentation and a flatter, more rolling land on the other, where rail ran. Onondisi Bay, with its resorts, was one face of the pyramid. Much larger Nain Bay, barriered by the isle of Dur, was to the north.

And the town of Saduri was below them, down at the bottom of a winding one lane road, out of sight from this position and in the dark, but Bren standing at the front entry to the station, with the mechieti moaning and spitting about the night-time summons to the herd, was very sure he had a good description of it.

"I'm glad it's night," Jase said. Jase had taken two of his motion sickness pills before he came out, and he fastened his jacket now with multiple tries at the buttons.

"They give you bonuses for this, I'm sure," Bren said; and Jase, who didn't get paid any more than he did nowadays, gave a nervous laugh, even a grin.

Jase wasn't in any wise as anxious as the Messengers' Guild, whose local assistant director, nand' Brosimi, and two junior staffers, came to the dowager and wished to stay on to protect the equipment. But Brosimi, who did not at all relish the notion of resistance to an armed lord's political intentions or simple misuse of the equipment, obeyed Ilisidi's instruction to send the junior personnel down to safety and to obey all orders lord Tatiseigi gave.

"So long as they aren't damaging to the equipment," Ilisidi added, while her men were out calling in the mechieti and the staff that were going to walk down the road were shutting down their consoles.

All nonessential communications ceased when those switches flipped. Phone service was going to be limited in the region. The local province was going on the Emergency Network for such things as fire and ambulance, which one hoped didn't prove necessary.

But other things were happening. Among the last messages to come in over the news service, there was a train stopped on the tracks near Aisinandi, effectively blocking the northern rail from reaching the area. By amazing coincidence, a switching error derailed another car in Aidin. *Something* had started moving, and that event wasn't on Cenedi's list or Banichi's.

There was beach on the northern face of the peninsula, running all the way around, broad and flat and such that motorized transport could operate, but it couldn't get to the beach the boy named, on the Saduri headland, because the stretch where the point of the jut of headland met the waves of the strait was sheer jagged rock. If a ship grounded there, it was very bad news.

It was good news for them, however, because if the small force they now knew was safely on Dur could keep either of the two ferries from operating and also keep boats from landing on Dur's sandy north shore, they'd assure that Deana went south right into the aiji's hands.

Motorized transport had moved *in* Saduri, earlier, and Ilisidi hadn't stopped it, fearing, Bren judged, that a fight would break out inside town limits with innocent citizens at risk.

That much made tactical sense. But he didn't figure even yet that he knew all of what was proceeding. Humans in the War had had the advantage of their high tech neutralized by the assumptions they made about *what* atevi might do and when they would do it.

Studying atevi campaigns, as he'd done, didn't tell him why, for instance, they left some of this station active instead of shutting it all down, no matter Tatiseigi's annoyance. It might be technical, the need to keep personnel at hand to keep certain functions going and to be sure a lord didn't go ordering things turned on and off that one of the least technologically minded lords in the Association didn't understand.

The reason might also lie in the insult it might accord that powerful and influential lord if one didn't accept his gesture of help in the spirit in which, if they were lucky, it was truly offered.

One wondered where Direiso's heir was at the moment, whether he was again under Tatiseigi's roof, or whether Saigimi's daughter, claimant to Saigimi's lordship, was with the force almost certainly coming at them.

One wondered exactly where Ajresi, Saigimi's brother and that daughter's bitterest rival, happened to be at the moment, and whether Badissuni's indigestion had swayed his opinions.

If Ajresi wanted to stay neutral, he probably could, with Tabini's tolerance. If he saw Tabini fall, however, and Direiso rise, the first debts Direiso would have to pay off would be awarding the Tasigin Marid to Saigimi's wife and daughter, and that meant dispossessing Ajresi, who was too young for peaceful retirement and whose quarrel with Saigimi's Sarini-province wife was too bitter for him to survive her daughter's lordship in the Marid.

Add to that tangle of relationships lord Geigi, who had a grudge against the wife for her attempt to dispossess him from his seaside estate at Dalaigi.

There was one thing a great deal different than the last time, at the start of the War of the Landing, when the northern provinces had gone against Mospheira. In that long-ago day the south, the Peninsular lords, had joined the north and the dispossessed Mospheirans in their assault against the island.

This time most of the former atevi inhabitants of Mospheira were running resorts at Onondisi, fishing on the Dur coast, or scattered up and down the Aidin headland, a Gan minority that had not fared as well under the lord of Wiigin as those had fared who had settled near the old fortress at Nain, on the Barjidi grant of that vacated lordship that had made the Treaty possible. Tabini's ancestor had deserved well of the Gan.

And Tabini's sudden removal of Saigimi, he began to understand, had made the south less, not more likely, to join Direiso.

The coastal ethnic minority around old Nain wasn't fond of the northern provinces and *they* wouldn't side with Direiso, who couldn't shake her long-time association with Wiigin.

And Dur? Dur, famous mostly for a ferry connection and for smuggling? Dur through its teenaged heir swore itself consistently loyal to Tabini's house.

Ilisidi, in the light from the foyer door, got up on Babs, and men searched out their various mounts. Haduni had lost one of his charges, who had flown down to Dur, but he was there to take charge of Jase; and Bren whistled for Nokhada who was *not* delighted to see her rider at this hour when she was full of grass and roused from sleep. He hoped the handlers had gotten the girth tight.

He got up in Nokhada's surly sketch of a bow. There were complaints of mechieti all around them, and Banichi and Jago glided close to him, shadows in the single-source light from the door, as the Messengers' Guild staff that was going down the road with them afoot moved nervously into a knot by the door.

He had the gun in his coat pocket. The paidhiin were supposed to be unarmed and innocuous. Neither of them fit the latter description.

But defend the third of them? He didn't know how they were going to find a woman from space who'd possibly launched out from Jackson with no skill and no chart and no knowledge of a sea that overmatched even the occasional smuggler.

He knew the dangers *and* the numbers of people who drowned in that crossing. Whenever some enterprising

fool of a human or atevi thought he'd circumvent the
import restrictions, and failed in the crossing, the fact
if not the grim details reached the paidhi's desk as a
complaint from one authority or the other. Fishermen
and, very rarely, pleasure boaters got caught by a
squall and if they were very, very lucky, the paidhi got
to straighten out the international paperwork and get
them escorted to the middle of the strait, aimed at the
appropriate harbor.

There were the sad inquiries to which the paidhi had
had to say, no, no one had been picked up, no boat had
reached shore.

He didn't want to think about Yolanda trying it alone
in some harbor runabout she'd found the key left in.

Deana Hanks, on the other hand, could easily get
expert help, either some 20 meter yacht with a crew
hired from her rich father's friends or, more useful and
far more likely to reach the port she aimed at, some
Mospheiran smuggler who supplied mainland antiques
and jewelry, two items no one could identify as smuggled, to the parlors of that crowd who otherwise disdained atevi culture.

God, he wanted his hands on Hanks!

Preferably before Hanks ended up in Direiso's camp.

Without warning Ilisidi started out, and they were
moving. One of Ilisidi's men told the communications
staffers who were walking down to stay to the inside of
the road so a mechieta didn't shoulder them off a cliff.

Better to hit the rocks on the inside of the curve than
the ones at the bottom of the cliff, was the way the man
put it, to a collection of people, mostly young, already
scared by their situation; but they fell in, keeping in a
group as they walked and trying to stay clear of the
mechieti.

"The staff will have to tag after us as best they can,"
Banichi said. "I have a feeling we'll out-pace them
considerably; and that may be best for their sakes."

"What's waiting for us down there?" Bren asked as
they moved into the dark and the starlight of the road.

"Tabini's men, nadi, and some of Ilisidi's who came
in by train from Shejidan, if, baji-naji, we have fortune

on our side for a few more hours and they've met up without shooting each other."

They passed the split in the road, that which led around the rim to the cannon fort, the route the tourists used. Another mechieta shouldered in, with Jase aboard and Haduni leading it by the rein. "Nadiin," Haduni said, "the dowager has lent Jase-paidhi Nawari's mechieta for the trip down."

Nawari had left in the plane. Nawari was one of those who ordinarily rode close to Ilisidi.

"Jasi-ji," Jago said out of the dark by Bren's left, "he means when we run, you take the rein from him, stay low and hang on. He's holding the rein now because if he lets go you'll be up there with the dowager very fast."

"Yes." Jase acknowledged an order with atevi brevity. And to Bren. "I'll certainly hang on, nadi."

The head of the party had reached the fork of the road that slanted sharply down in the starlight, down and down into dark. As yet they kept a moderate pace, but the first hairpin turn came a good deal sooner than Bren expected, the mechieti still moving briskly, but not so the staff walking down couldn't stay with them.

The next hairpin and the next tier of the road brought the town lights into view, not as many lights as one saw looking down, say, from a plane on a *Mospheiran* city by night.

But those lights might be fewer than ordinary tonight, since one could well suppose the townsfolk were not unaware of the crisis, and were probably listening to radio and television in hopes of news or public safety announcements.

It was a steep road at the next turn. Very steep for the tourist buses that were the summer traffic up this road; but one paved lane was very broad for mechieti; and the front rank at the fourth hairpin turn struck a faster downhill pace that would leave the group afoot behind very quickly. Nokhada was in a far better mood, pricking her ears forward and hitting a stride that advanced her just marginally through the pack.

Her rider didn't stop her. That made her happier still; and Jase's mechieta stayed with her.

Next switchback. "Nadiin," Jago said, riding near Bren, as Banichi came on Jase's far side. "If we come under fire, stay on. Our security is holding the road into town, and it will not be Guild opposing us, but all the same, present as low a profile as possible. There is a chance of Kadigidi partisans."

It was never hard to pick out the leaders in an old-fashioned atevi cavalry charge. It never had been. It was part of the ethic—and maybe, Bren thought, among other fearful thoughts, that risk kept wars to a minimum, in a species where the leaders went first, not hindmost. The gun knocked hard against his ribs as the dowager let Babsidi gather speed. Nokhada was right on the front rank with Babsidi. Cenedi's mechieta was; and Jase's; and Banichi's and Jago's. As they reached the lowest part of the road they were running nearly all-out, security maneuvering only to put their bodies between their charges and the likelihood of snipers as the road let out onto a town highway.

A human might not be wired to know what passions it could touch off in the hearts of atevi instinct-driven to follow such a leader as Ilisidi was. He'd seen the maneuver in the machimi plays, he recalled that, the mad dash of riders across a landscape, a move *he'd* understood for a dramatic convention, but which often preceded a sort-out, a realization of atevi loyalties.

But as they came into the streets of the township of Saduri, he felt real emotion gathering in him. Hadn't the waving of a flag, the call of a trumpet meant something to humans once? They couldn't but follow. No matter whether Ilisidi or the atevi she led rationally *knew* what she was invoking—*this* human felt it.

A shot from somewhere blasted white chips of plaster from a building onto what was now black, starlit pavement ahead of them; and fire racketed back at that source from riders all around him. From another answering source more fire broke out somewhere ahead on the road. He was aware every smallish rider in their group was a target. He knew he was supposed to keep his head down and he knew that using the gun he carried and putting his head up to do it was a stupid risk—but in his heart-pounding excitement Jago's warning at the start was all that held him from such foolishness.

Do what Jago said. Listen to his security. Get through this alive and take down the ones who'd threatened him and his the way *he* could deal with them, not with a gun, but by getting to what they wanted before they did, and interdicting them from everything they intended tonight.

A flare went off behind them, a brilliant burst of light that threw them all into silhouette. Then he hoped the Guild workers, caught on the road above this fire-fight, had the sense to take cover. They'd stirred no random fools but an ambush. Tabini's men were *not* in possession of this area. They passed side streets that would lead to the harbor, each one of which could become a shooting gallery.

Then a single small light blinked ahead of them and a second red one, twice, to the right.

That might surely be signals of their own allies. Abruptly, Ilisidi took Babsidi around a corner, down a ghostly deserted street, and rode hellbent through the heart of a not-quite-sleeping town toward the harbor.

"Aiji-ma!" someone cried from a window above the street and others yelled it. But the street was dark.

"Go!" shadows yelled at them from an intersection, in utter darkness. " 'Sidi-ji! Go! Go! *Go!*"

The darkness of the streets gave way to open night sky and hills and the sheen of water, and they went toward that gap. A light flashed in a window above the street, near the end of the block, and when they reached that open harborside, other atevi shadows appeared with that same flashing of lights, some white, some red, in a pattern that must silently tell Ilisidi and the Guild with them what was critical for them to know.

Ilisidi stopped on harborside against a weather-shelter. A sign by the water and another on the railing said *Ferry,* and gave a departure schedule, but there was no ferry there for them.

A boat was coming, however. Not a ferry, if one could judge who'd only seen them on television, but a fair-sized boat, just the same.

"Is that someone we want?" Jase asked faintly, having seen it too, as mechieti all around them breathed and blew and harness creaked. One could just make out the spreading disturbance of the boat's wake, as, against a shadow of low hills well across the water, it made its way on a diagonal toward them.

"*Late,*" Ilisidi breathed. "After all these years, every damned appointment, Geigi is still *late,* damn him!" She signaled Babsidi to extend a leg, and got down—a glistening dark trail was on her hand, and Cenedi wanted immediately to see to it, but: "It's a damned plaster-chip," she said. "The man's revised his arrival time three times—half an hour more, he says, and he's *still* late!"

Bren slid down and Haduni got down, but in the meanwhile Ilisidi was back among the mechieti, looking for more injuries.

One mechieta had taken a fairly extensive injury on the flank. Two riders had been hit, one a trivial matter, one man with a serious amount of bleeding and a broken arm, which by no means improved her mood.

"I want this woman," Ilisidi said. "*Damn* this fool! Damn, damn, *damn!* —Can someone get this man to hospital?"

"Help is coming," Jago said. They had risked the pocket coms, she and Banichi, so it seemed.

And indeed dark figures were moving on the street, figures that shouted to each other and brought timid ventures from the buildings along the way. More supporters joined them, townsfolk or maybe Guild. But by this time the victim was swearing that he could very well walk to the hospital, which was just down the street. They could see the lighted sign from here. People who called themselves local residents were offering respects to the aiji-dowager in an outpouring of support, loudly wishing to carry the wounded man and to take the injured mechieta to the doctors, too.

Haduni provided them answers and directions.

Cenedi and Banichi were giving orders to the ferry personnel, who had shown up uncertain whether their services could be of use, and very willing to support the woman they recklessly called 'Sidi-ji.

In the meanwhile Jase was safely down and on two feet, and Ilisidi was muttering about the modern age and modern leaders sitting safely in estates and offices looking at computer screens, as lord Geigi's boat cruised up to the ferry landing with a powerful slow thump of engines and a boil and wash of water.

For a fishing boat, Bren thought, it was pretty damned impressive.

Security came ashore first. Lord Geigi followed with an amazingly agile leap, as the ramp manned by the ferry personnel attempted to adjust to the height of his moving gangway.

"Late!" Ilisidi cried.

"The wind *is* up, nandi-ji! A hard west wind beyond the breakwater, which does make a difference! Was I to forecast intent to join you? The *aiji* was late, so I was late, the whole *countryside* is late, so the Kadigidi will be late, too!"

"You were to take the train and borrow the boats here!"

"Well, and the village of Kinsara has a carload of spring vegetables derailed on the grade on this side, so we had to take the boats all the way, and I've come to order boats out from Saduri, if I can get some of the good fisherfolk to give us a hand. —And good *evening,* paidhi-ji. Good evening to your associate. Come aboard! We've a cold supper if you've been in a hurry. It's a good half hour back to the breakwater against the wind. 'Siri's going to call in debts up and down the harborside. We'll get boats out there tonight, as many as you like."

Bren recognized Gesirimu among the handful who had come ashore, as shouts went out to get boats away and get the coastal road blocked.

"We have three boats out there holding off shore, but it's a dark, wide sea," Geigi said, "and I'll not say we can keep the Kadigidi from getting a boat past us. If we can intercept the rascals on the water we'll take fewer casualties."

"Some Kadigidi *are* here," Banichi said, "in the township. If we're unlucky we'll just have chased them to positions up the shore to warn their allies."

"Nothing for it," Cenedi said. "Sitting here gains us nothing. With a west wind blowing, lord Geigi, where would a Mospheiran craft come in, between here and Aidin?"

"Is it only Hanks-paidhi, all this mysterious goings-on?"

"*Only* Hanks indeed," Ilisidi said in disgust and, with Geigi, led the way to the heaving plank. The wind blew cold off the harbor, and the buffers squealed and groaned as the boat heaved against the shore.

"We're going looking for Hanks," Jase said faintly, at Bren's side. It was a question. It was despair. "What about any other boat? Can you ask him—"

"Take your pills," Bren said. "I'd take a double dose."

"You don't think she'd have survived the storm," Jase said. "Do you?"

"I don't know." He had resolved not to lie to Jase, but Jase had a way of going head-on to questions with bad answers. "She might not have gone out with the weather threatening. There've been planes out, and boats, all up and down the middle of the strait. Somebody could have picked her up if she did try. I don't give her up."

"Neither do I," Jase said resolutely. And added, with a desperate grip on the gangway rail. "But, Bren, the pills are gone."

"You can't have taken all of them!"

"I didn't. The bottle fell out of my pocket."

26

Geigi had been communicating delays since the derailment of vegetables, which had happened, Geigi said, while he was at the train station at the Elijiri ferry dock waiting to take the train over the hills to Saduri to keep his appointment. At that point, realizing the train connection would not work, he'd made a call to his private boat, which was on its way back to Dalaigi, and advised them to come back to get him. The three neighbors who were stranded with him had called for *their* boats to fill the tanks for a long haul, and to come across to pick them up at Elijiri. Having crossed the Bay, their small fleet (consisting of two retired gentlemen, the lord of Dalaigi, and a middle-aged lady who had made her fortune in the jewelry business) had fueled again at the resort marina at Onondisi, so they were going to be capable of staying out.

Now, seated on soft cushioned chairs and couches, the dusty and sweaty company watched the lights of Saduri Township retreat from the stern windows. A strange way to go into a fight, Bren thought, as Geigi himself poured Ilisidi a small glass of cordial: the arm was, Ilisidi confessed, uncomfortable.

"I also have," Geigi said, "the name of the resort manager of Mist Island Tours, who says if there is a need that serves the man'chi of Sarini Province, he will publish a need for boats. The seas are rough and I would hesitate to encourage small craft tonight, but there are the harbor tour boats and their crews would willingly bring them out. They lack onboard radar, but they do have radio. I have only to give the orders."

"Do so," Ilisidi said. "I don't think we are operating in overmuch secrecy now. What the wind brings us, the wind will bring."

"May one—" Bren said quietly, "may one also request we call Dur at this point? There *is* more than Hanks. There's some chance that Mercheson-paidhi has fled the island, and if she's done so, it would be a very light craft. With the storm, as I remember the map—she'd be blown straight west."

"Southeast, nadi."

"I've heard how strong the current is," Bren said. "But the wind—"

"Out of the northwest. The storm *and* the current, nand' paidhi, one assures you."

"The storm was out of the west. It was in our faces when we were camped. Was it not, nadiin-ji?"

"Northwest, Bren-ji," Jago said. "The Mogari-nai headland doesn't lie parallel to that of the south. It faces northwest."

His whole land-sense had been wrong. He'd looked at the map and *believed* west.

"The cliff is weathered, nand' paidhi," lord Geigi said, "by uncounted storms that wear away the headland. By waves that dash against those rocks. It's a dangerous place in a heavy sea. But since centuries ago, when atevi made the breakwater to protect the harbor from silting, the sand has come in all along that stretch and stopped against the stones. What flotsam comes in there is washed out by the next storm, but with that blow night before this, I'd look at Saduri Beach above all else. And I'd say every other sailor on this coast would make the same conclusion."

"It's a government reserve," Ilisidi said. "Does *no* one on this shore respect the signs?"

"Certainly the wrecks don't," lord Geigi said. "Baji-naji, they come there, 'Sidi-ji. And so will anyone who needs to find them."

"Direiso's lot had a freighter in here two days ago," Cenedi said. "A shipment of four heavy trucks. They moved out tonight and headed up the road to the break-water. So they are thinking in the same direction."

Lights were showing in the windows. Boats were standing away from the shore. Gesirimu had rallied the fishermen. Lord Geigi had ties to Saduri as well as to his neighbors in Onondisi Bay.

The Peninsula's north shore had joined Shejidan, this time, in *opposing* the dissolution of the northern provinces.

"Well, well," Geigi said, looking back over the cushion, "we shall have help." He turned and picked up his glass. "In the meanwhile, if anyone would care to wash away the dust of travel, there is a lavatory just forward and to the left."

Jase got up and went forward. Quickly.

"Excuse me," Bren said, and Banichi came with him, across a deck he didn't think too unsteady; but he feared Jase's stomach did. The door was shut.

Bren gave a weary sigh. And leaned against the wall as they waited.

"At least," Banichi said, "he's not as sick as you were with the tea."

He'd forgotten that.

Mercifully.

"Have we," he asked Banichi, because it was the first chance he'd had since they'd made contact with Geigi, "any difficulty at Patinandi?"

"No, no, no," Banichi said softly, "Geigi could hardly put on tight security, as if he had any reason to fear his good neighbors. But certainly if the dowager has requested lord Geigi's assistance here, with smugglers, Tabini *has* to provide support and security." Banichi flashed a grin. "How *did* you and Jago get along?"

Banichi caught him utterly by surprise, and speechless.

The door opened. Jase was there, water soaking his face and the front of his hair, which strung mostly loose.

"Can one go out on deck?" Jase asked. "I want to look at the water."

"One can, but you might fall in. It's quite deep. And it's dark out there."

"I want to go outside," Jase said.

Bren looked at Banichi, who slid a glance toward the door not far removed from where they stood. It let out on the deck and a narrow walk to the fishing deck at the stern or the foredeck in front of the bridge.

They were in the middle of the harbor and it was cold out there in the wind, he fully anticipated that; but he nodded, and went back to the group in the salon to catch Jago's eye.

"We're going outside a moment," he said. "Jase needs air."

"One does understand," Jago said, and joined him in his going back to the door and out onto the deck.

Banichi and Jase had gone to the foredeck. Jase stood at the very point of the bow, in the wind and the spray. He'd be soaked, Bren thought. Banichi was out of his mind, standing by him like that.

He and Jago walked up to the rail.

"How deep is it?" Jase asked, over the rush of water and the noise of the engines.

"Oh—" He had no real idea. He guessed, since security didn't come up with the answer. "About thirty meters."

"We're high up, then."

It was an odd way of looking at the ocean. "I suppose we are."

"If you fall in, do you go to the bottom?"

Now he knew the direction of Jase's thoughts. And didn't like it.

"The waves bring you to the shore," he said, and didn't know how to explain that fact of oceans to a man from space. "Jase? Don't give up on her."

"I'm not giving up," Jase said. "I won't. I couldn't be sick, Bren. I thought I was. But it's better at night. You can see the stars."

One could. The land was black on either side of them. The water shone. There was a black line reaching far out across the harbor mouth; a light stood at the end of it and a line of light shone across the waves. That was the breakwater, extending south from the cliffs. That was where the beach was,

"There are boats out there in the distance," Jago said, she of the sharp eyesight. He couldn't see them.

"Beyond the breakwater," Banichi said, and lifted an arm. "We'll go out and around, paidhiin-ji. The road is running beside us at the moment, at the foot of the cliffs over there. If we'd dared rely on Saduri or the Atageini lord, we should have left you both in the township."

"No," Bren said. "I'm glad we're here. Just—how are we going to get in to shore in this boat, nadiin? We can't beach it."

"A good question," Banichi said, but didn't answer. Bren tried again.

"Can we get ashore, nadiin-ji?"

"*We* will go ashore, Bren-ji," Jago said. "If we have to go in, which is by no means certain yet."

"With us, you will!"

"Listen to your security, Bren-ji. Always listen to your security."

"Damn it, I was with you at Malguri, I was with you at Taiben."

"My partner," Jase said. "Nadiin, *my* partner and Hanks-paidhi. Out there."

"Bad numbers," Banichi said. "No."

"You're not a 'counter," Bren said, "nadi. I know you're not. Four is a perfectly fine number."

Banichi laughed and looked at the open sea ahead of them.

"You need translators, if it's humans involved."

"Jago-ji," Banichi said, "you stay with them. Felicitous three."

"No," Jago said.

"Your duty, Jago-ji. Someone has to keep them aboard."

"I am going," Bren said.

"No," Banichi said, "you are not, nand' paidhi. But you can watch."

He fell silent then, dejected, telling himself it was

not fair of them, but neither was he of any use if he took Jago away from her partner simply to watch them.

"Then trust, Jago-ji, that I can remain safe with the guard aboard, and I will not risk Banichi's life by holding you here. You saved him at Malguri and again in the Marid—"

"An exaggeration," Banichi said.

"I want both of you back," Bren said. "Nadiin." The wind was like ice this far out in the harbor. The breakwater was very close. The boats were running dark. There was only the one light showing, that at the end of the breakwater rocks.

"Best get inside," Banichi said. "All of us. We'll be passing close to a sniper vantage, if they've positioned anyone to hold the harbor."

Banichi herded them back, back to the door. Against the glow from Saduri Township, even human eyes could see the fishing boats running behind them, six, seven, maybe more behind.

The light inside the salon was out. They were dark as all the other boats now. Bren felt his way the short distance to the salon, with Jase and Banichi and Jago behind him.

"Best everyone get down, nandiin," Banichi said. "We're coming up on the breakwater."

"A very good idea," Cenedi said. " 'Sidi-ji?"

"Damned nuisance," Ilisidi said. "*You* stay inside, 'Nedi-ji. There's nothing to be gained out there. Down!"

The dowager sat down on the floor. That settled the matter. They all sat down, low, beneath the woodwork, while the engines thumped placidly away.

And all of a sudden surged, as the fishing yacht proved what it had in reserve. They had to be passing the breakwater light, the one vantage for ambush.

Jase was tucked down. Bren held his breath as the deck tilted sharply to port under the power of the engines; and all of a sudden the boat shook and rocked and something exploded against the hull and the super-structure at once.

"Damn!" Geigi cried, as the diesels roared and the

deck pitched hard on the beam on the other tack. Starboard, this time, canted way over. The boat's course was an arc. And they were surely beyond the breakwater. "We've not lost an engine," Geigi said, which was the first thing to think in a veering motion. By the sound, that was correct, but the pilot up on the bridge must have jammed the wheel all the way over to starboard and if they were past the breakwater they had to be turning back to—

The boat's keel hit something, the engines kept driving, one roaring dry as the starboard side hull hit and bounced along rock. Cushions and bodies and glassware and the remnants of the stern window all traveled toward the bulkhead as Jase and Bren slid down the hall toward the door that swung wildly on its hinges.

"Get out!" Banichi shouted as motion slowed. "We're full of fuel!"

"Do it!" Bren cried, shoving at Jase. They were closest to the door, and the door had come open, the whole boat listing over hard as it swayed and bobbed and scraped along the shore, pushed by the sea and its last working engine. "Get out!"

Jase moved, half-fell through the open door and slid against the rail, Bren right with him and someone else close behind him. Gunfire hammered at the hull as they went over the rail and dropped into waist-deep water.

Someone and a second someone landed beside them with two distinct splashes. "Keep down," Banichi's voice said. "Keep below the tide line! Stay *near* the water unless the tank blows!"

He took the advice, his hand in the middle of Jase's back as they moved aside to give others room to exit the still-moving boat, which was grinding and scraping its way along rocks, its engines both dead now, the waves pushing at it. They were on the breakwater. Others of their group splashed down and they made their way further toward the bow. Fire was still coming at them.

"Where's Lasari?" Geigi's voice cried. "Lasari! Casurni, he's not answering."

"Get clear, nandi!" someone said. "I'll get him out!"

Gunfire boomed out, a large gun, from somewhere astern and in the dark.

It hit the cliffs.

"I've got him," someone said. "Geigi-ji, I have him, I'm coming down!"

A hand found Bren's arm. "Move, nadiin! That rock!"

He couldn't see what she wanted. But he moved ahead, keeping low, and Jase was with them. Someone, two or three, splashed past the three of them, and flattened down on the rocks and got up and ran again, as gunfire aimed at the boat thumped and echoed off the cliffs.

'They're trying to blow the boat up," Jago said.

"Where is the dowager?" he asked. "Where's Banichi?"

"Just go, paidhiin-ji!"

He could see cover ahead now, Jago's rock, a huge boulder embedded in sand; and sand kicked up where bullets hit it.

He dived behind the rock and Jase went down with him, Jago atop them, for a second. Then Jago was seeking targets in the rocks at the foot of the cliffs, the height above them that of Mogari-nai. He remembered—for the first time remembered—he had a gun. It was jabbing him in the ribs; and he dragged it out and slipped the safety off.

"Can you see anything?" he asked.

"We are—"

Jago shoved herself around the rock, slammed them into the rock and the sand, and a shot went off to their right flank, and a second, answering shot banged out right beside him from Jago's gun, so close to his face he was in danger of powder burns.

He couldn't see. "Stay down!" Jago said, and used her pocket com, telling Banichi something in vocal code.

An answer came back. He couldn't hear. His ears were still ringing from the gunshot. Jase was breathing hard, Jago's elbow and a lump of rock were both in painful places, but he didn't move, nor did Jase.

Another paired set of shots resounded near at hand as Jago's body jumped, and a succession of shots went off, two of them hers. He saw a gun flash: he fired back; and heard a scatter of gunfire elsewhere.

Then in a thump of sound and glare that cast the rock breakwater and the sand in stark light and shadow—the boat's fuel tanks blew. He saw a figure, the man he must have shot, lying flat on the beach near them.

Then other atevi figures started running across the rocks from the boat and toward the action.

"That's Cenedi," Jago said, with no breath. And he hoped to God she meant the running ones.

"Are you hit?" he asked Jago. "Jago-ji, are you all right?" He shook at her, and then for whatever reason she caught a breath. "Are you hit?"

"Bruised—bruised, nadi." Gunfire was still thumping and popping from further away, as in the continuing, fainter light of the burning boat, he probed past her fingers where the leather of her coat was shredded. His hands met the bulletproof lining beneath that, and that fabric had a stiffened dent where kinetic reflex fibers had absorbed the force and taken that shape permanently.

One of the new plastics. For the space program.

"Stay in shadow," she said, and held her side and braced herself to reload. "One is grateful, nadi," she said between her teeth. "But if Banichi finds us sitting here, I will hear about it often. We need better cover."

The water was lit like a carnival. Gunfire was coming at them from along the bottom of the cliffs, where the sandy beach offered dunes and cover. And there, at the limit of the light from Geigi's boat, another sail-driven yacht lay in a wreckage the mirror-image of their own, heeled over on the sand. Inflatable runabouts were beached near it, three of them.

"God." He nudged Jago. *Jago* hadn't seen the wreck, either, until then. She made a call on the pocket com, and this time, crouched very close to Jago and in a lull in the gunfire, he heard Banichi's voice:

"I see it," Banichi said. *"I see no sign of movement."*

A concentrated fire swept the beach and knocked chips off the boulder.

"One would suggest you stay down," Banichi said.

"One would suggest you do the same," Jago retorted, and did not seem happy—evidently not believing Banichi would take his own advice. She turned on one knee, crouching low, and took a fast look.

Very fast. Fire blasted back and kicked up sand that Bren spat and wiped from his face.

"We are in a predicament," Jago said. *"I* have position. I'm going to move quickly, Bren-ji, and I must ask you stay here. You have your gun. I want you to fire ten shots, above my head, please, while I run for the rocks a little closer. Then I will lay down fire to cover Banichi and Casurni, who will move. Ten will empty your clip." She pressed a clip into his hand. "Reload as rapidly as you can and please aim above me."

"Jago—"

"I must trust you to do this, nadi," Jago said. "Can you see the gunflashes?"

Fire was going on. He did see, risking a look. "Yes."

"Begin firing, Bren-ji. Now!"

She didn't give him a chance to protest. She ran. He fired, putting shots as accurately as he could toward that mark, and someone else was firing, he thought maybe Banichi and maybe someone else.

But fire came back. Jago staggered and went down, and got up, and he fired, pacing his shots. Jago was hurt, trying to run; and then someone from their side broke from cover and reached her and swept her along just as *he* ran out of bullets.

"Damn!" he gasped, and tried to reload calmly, rammed the clip in and fired as rock shattered and something stung his chin. He saw the two figures reach cover and then open fire—two discharges of weapons.

"She made it! They made it!" Jase said beside him. "Incandescent."

He held his fire maybe two seconds, having maybe seven, eight shots left. Then fire started up again, Jago's and, he guessed, Banichi's, which was covering

Geigi's man, Casurni. It was too rapid for just one. He opened fire to support them.

Then—

"Bren!" Jase said, and distracted him to the side, where firelit movement out on the water caught his eye.

Something huge was coming in from the sea, past the wreck of the yacht, like some floating white monster with a mouth gaping dark and wide, an incredible sight, lit by the fire of the burning boat.

It rammed itself onto the sand between them and the wrecked yacht down the beach. A broad ramp came thumping down and a tide of atevi poured out onto the beach, guns in hand. The sign on the superstructure said *Dur-Saduri*.

"God," he said, as fire spattered across the beach.

"What *is* it?" Jase asked.

He said, faintly, not quite believing his own conclusion, "I *think* it's the Dur island ferry."

27

There were black-uniformed Guild among the new arrivals. Bren could see them walking across the beach, saw the use of pocket coms, and held his breath and hoped. For a moment firing was very intense and he shouted aloud, "Finesse, nadiin! We have people out there!"

Someone came directly toward their shelter, not rapidly, a little bent and limping, and he ducked in fear of having mistaken the situation. He was about to advise Jase to run for one of the inflatables, when a shadow came to the rock, leaned there, black leather sparking firelight off metal studs, and—he was sure it was Nawari, of Ilisidi's service—said, "Are you all right, nandiin?"

"Perfectly fine," Bren said, and stood up as Jase rose to his feet beside him—if Nawari was standing up, he dared. "Jago and Banichi and I think Cenedi went that way!" Fire was still going on. He was shaky in the knees. "Can you spare a clip, nadi?"

Nawari gave him one, and took off running.

"Come on," he said to Jase, and ran after the man, toward the bank of rocks that, he saw in the firelight, supported a paved road right at cliffside, until pavement lost itself on the beach.

That was where the intense fighting had been going on. That was where he found others of their group, lord Geigi among them, and Ilisidi; and Jago, who had a bloody bandage just above the top of her boot and who was getting off shots down into the dark. As he and

Jase slid in beside her, he could just make out the tops of a group of trucks in that direction, between them and Saduri Township. She spared only a dart of her eyes toward them.

"What target?" he asked her.

"Those trucks," she said. "Aim high! My partner's a fool!"

He was alarmed. "Where's Banichi?" he asked. He saw gun flashes out in the dark where he thought was water, and realized then it was the fishing boats. Geigi's other Guild protection, Gesirimu, had been with them, and *they* were running close to shore, firing from the water toward the trucks on that road.

"He said he'd get the trucks!" Jago said, stopping to shove in another clip.

"Are we sure who's out there in the trucks, Jago-ji? Jase's partner is missing!"

"We're sure. Hanks has a pocket com. She's appealed to all of us to disintegrate and abase our weapons."

It was surreal. The paidhiin were shooting at each other. His *friend* Banichi was out there in the dark with bullets flying from the water and from their position, and he opened fire high, with the thought of knocking rock down off the cliffs above those trucks. He was scared of hitting Banichi.

Jago's fire joined his, lower and more dangerous to the enemy, he was sure. And another someone joined them.

"Nandiin!" a young voice said. "My father *believed* the dowager's men! I have a gun! Where do I shoot!"

"Above the trucks!" Bren said. "Aim at the cliff. Produce ricochets!"

"Yes!" Rejiri said, lifted his high-caliber rifle, and fired.

Fire blossomed in the trucks, and in a flash that imprinted trucks and figures on the retina, light stained the cliffs, the sand, the sea, lit the boats and the rocks they were using for cover. The shock went through the ground and into their bones and before the light died a piece of the cliff was peeling away and headed down toward the trucks. There was the sound of one truck engine, speeding away.

"Ten, ten," Jago said anxiously into the com.

"Got them," Banichi's voice came back. "All but one, damn it."

That truck was headed back to Saduri, by the sound of the motor fading. Jago rattled off a string of verbal code that Bren guessed was their identities. It ended with, "The Dur island ferry," and drew an astonished and rude remark from the com.

A hand closed on Bren's shoulder, Jase's, in the silence of the guns. He reached his own out and closed on Jase's arm, shaky, feeling the chill of the wind now that the area was quiet. Jago went on, apparently trying to talk to someone else.

Then a voice came back and Jago said, "Ten, ten, four, sixteen. Headed your way."

"Mistake on their part," a voice came back. And something exploded in the distance, another shock echoing and echoing off the cliffs.

There was silence after, except the ringing in the ears.

"Lord Tatiseigi's compliments," the com said distinctly.

Deana Hanks was dead. Banichi said he could verify that and it was probably better not to go down to the trucks, but Bren did. The place stank of smoke, of oil, and ocean—of burning, mostly, and while he was there, a small rock gave way high up the cliffs and fell with a pelting of gravel.

Six humans. At least—he was relatively sure it was six. More atevi. Twisted metal, the paint burned off. Banichi had gotten them with a grenade he'd gotten from up at Mogari-nai.

And Tatiseigi's forces, while the elderly lord had ridden down in the van, had occupied the township proper and thrown up a roadblock with the help of residents. So they heard on the radio.

Fishing boats had come in as close as they could to shore within Saduri Harbor. They were anchored there.

One could just see the lines that ran down to the water. Bren began to be aware of the dawn, as he and Banichi walked back toward the beach.

Jase and Jago waited for him where the paved road gave way to sand and a view of two wrecked boats, the beached island ferry, and a sea full of pleasure yachts and working boats, all in the shadow of the Saduri headland.

Jago had his computer. The case was mostly melted. It was a wonder the strap held.

"Bren-ji, I did my best," Jago said.

"Jago, you did wonderfully well." He took it, such as it was. What it could do, it had done. Data recovery might turn up something, but he doubted it. "How are *you* doing?"

"Nothing serious, nadi. The dowager is well, lord Geigi is well. Cenedi has a cut from glass. *We* have taken no serious injuries. Lord Geigi's pilot has cuts and both arms broken, but he did excellently well to steer us about into the shore when the bridge was hit."

"One is *very* glad, Jago." Bren leaned against the rock and caught his breath. Or tried to. He pointed to the ferry. "Did you know about that?"

"One had *no* idea, nadi," Jago said. "Our people there were under orders not to use radio, and they didn't. The boy—and his father—called in certain of the island folk. And saw the fires and came in."

"Definitely it was Hanks," Bren said. "It's a mess down there. We won't know what happened—but she *must* have hit the rocks at the point." He was looking out to sea as he said it. And saw, among the atevi yachts in the haze of smoke and morning, a motor-sailer, a tall-masted boat that didn't belong in this company, gliding along under sail.

It didn't belong in this company.

It didn't belong in these waters. It belonged up on the north shore of Mospheira.

"My God," he said, and then in Ragi: "That's my brother's boat!"

* * *

"Bren!" a male voice yelled, and he knew the man who'd come running toward him from the grounded runabout—a man in a pale fishing jacket and a hat, a ridiculous hat stuck about with fishing floats. Yolanda Mercheson stepped over the side of the orange fabric boat, with him, and third was Shawn Tyers. Yolanda was trying to run, not quite steady on land-legs; and about then Toby was all his field of vision, Toby unshaven, looking as if he'd had no sleep for days, and grinning from ear to ear.

"God, it's good to see you!"

"Good to see you," Bren said, and Toby hugged him; he hugged Toby. Atevi had to wonder at them, and he didn't care.

"What are you *doing* here?" Bren managed to ask.

"What are *you* doing?" Toby asked. "Are we at war or something? We were doing fine but a gunboat escorted us down here. "

"They're ours. How's mama?"

"She's doing fine. We couldn't bring her. But Jill's with her. And the kids. We brought Shawn's family, though."

Shawn was there, in a puffy insulated jacket, bright blue, the most informal thing he'd ever seen Shawn wear. He let go of Toby and recovered wit enough to hold out his hand.

"Welcome ashore, sir. I take it you had something to do with this."

"It was getting uncomfortable," Shawn said, and nodded over his shoulder where Jase and the other ship-paidhi were giving atevi another exhibition, oblivious to all else. "I figured it was easier to talk to the aiji than to George, truth be told. We just assembled down at Bretano and Toby flew up to the coast and got the boat. Got my wife, my kids, a Ms. Johnson who said you sent her—"

"God, Sandra made it."

"Showed up at my door with two plants in a grocery sack as I was leaving for Bretano. I said come along, we'd explain it. She said she didn't want to go this far, but it sounded safer here." Shawn cast a look around the beach. "She's probably changed her mind."

Bren looked behind him, where a row of atevi stood, Banichi, and Jago, and Cenedi, expressionless, uniformed, and armed.

He suddenly realized how they must look to Toby and Shawn. And blinked again and saw his dearest friends.

28

The wind came in from the sea, in a summer warm and pleasant. The leaves sighed in a lazy, sleepy sussuration on the face of the wall, where the djossi vine had spread itself wide.

Lord Geigi was bringing the boat. His new, two meters *longer* boat, gratefully donated by Murini, lord of the Kadigidi. It was a short walk down to the water.

"Quiet day," Jago said, leaning elbows on the rail. She made hand-signals. The paidhi could just about bet that Banichi was below, watching over the boat dock.

Jago made a furious sign then, and a sign of dismissal, but not in anger, in laughter. Banichi's unseen comment was, he was sure, salacious.

"The boat's coming in," Jago said.

"One thought so," Bren said, and stood up and looked over the the rail himself.

Toby was joining them—that was the second boat, tied up just down the row. Geigi especially favored Toby: a fine sailor, Geigi called him, a true fishermen. Toby had an invitation in his own right; and he'd brought their mother for a three-day visit coinciding with the paidhiin's two weeks at Geigi's estate. Jill, who was pregnant, had flung herself valiantly into the breach, and was, with Shawn's wife, not only entertaining their mother, but escorting a children's birthday party (Shawn's oldest) to the beach, which had Tano and Algini occupied.

"Nadi." Jase joined him, with Yolanda, coming out

of the house. "Are we promised fishing gear? One wants to be sure."

"There is, nadiin," Bren said. "I assure you it's on the boat."

"I'll be sure before I board," Jase said, and the two of them took the steps quite rapidly for spacefarers.

The ship—it was up there. The government of Mospheira was dealing quite politely nowadays, having apologized for the misunderstanding—one knew they would. The aiji had threatened an embargo of more than aluminum if they didn't come up with a passport for anyone the paidhiin requested—an offer the validity of which Sandra Johnson had tested, returning once for a visit, and a night of live machimi theater in Shejidan, the experience of her office-bound life. Now the State Department wanted Yolanda to come back and lecture to the Foreign Studies program at the University. One was absolutely sure she would not accept the offer, although Shawn said with Eugene Weinberg in as Secretary of State it was a certainty they'd honor her passport.

The telling matter was that the government of Mospheira, no longer able to pretend it had a space program, was dealing for Patinandi to build an expansion plant on the mainland to build a second spacecraft, part of a fleet of five such craft, that being the only way humans were going to get up to the station; and the ship did want them.

Shawn, however, was not going back to Mospheira. Emissaries came to Shawn, who said he'd wait for the next elections to see whether the voters had really acquired some sense. The Progressive Unionists wanted Shawn to run for President of Mospheira in the fall, but he said he'd think about it. Meanwhile Sonja Podesty was a very good candidate for Foreign Secretary if they'd use their heads. He wrote letters to Weinberg suggesting Weinberg run for President for the Unionists and appoint Podesty to the cabinet post.

Mospheira had to revise its notions of the universe, quite as much as Geigi had—and with far more disturbance to their expectations.

A radio show on the far side of the island, on which George Barrulin was a frequent guest, still maintained that atevi were going to pour across the straits and murder them all; but tell that, this summer, to the traders who saw their markets opening up, tell that to the companies which were making across-the-straits deals. The Foreign Office and the State Department were beginning to issue trade permits and companies would cut throats to be in early on the market—even if the aiji would not issue patent protection beyond three years for any product. The aiji *was* protecting certain Mospheiran patents, where it served the interests of atevi or where the paidhiin recommended exceptions. Everything among atevi was both patronage *and* merit. It always had been. And Gaylord Hanks wasn't on the aiji's list.

Tides ebbed and flowed in that blue water, and the one that had carried Deana Hanks to the heights of influence was ebbing. Her father still had money; and the old money still gathered at the Society meetings and talked about the unfairness of it all, but money meant less when the ideas it bought and backed were on the ebb of their fortunes, gotten down to the tide-pools and creatures that skipped away for deeper, safer water.

The aiji was in Shejidan, the heir of Dur was attending University, grandmother was riding mechieti at Malguri on the lake, and uncle Tatiseigi was in Shejidan politicking with the fragments of the association which had revolved around Direiso and now wanted very much to be seen with Uncle *and* with lord Geigi, who was the guest of the season in social circles.

As for the bad neighbors out in space, those who needed to know were warned. They were working on it. Nobody mentioned it. Yet.

Bren picked up the lunch basket that had rested on the terrace and joined Jago on the way down the steps.

They had gotten fairly good at certain things. Practice, Jago called it.

The aiji-dowager had invited the paidhiin and their staff for a season at summer's end—the aiji-dowager had promised *them* boating, too, and a bedchamber guaranteed to be as haunted as the lake.

The ghost bell has been heard this summer, Ilisidi had written them, in that careful, delicate hand Jago said was the old school of penmanship. *I propose to spend the night in the old watchman's tower on the island in the lake. If we find no ghosts the view of the stars will still be extraordinary, and if it rains, the fireplace is intact.*

I assure you of the safety of the old tower and the caution of our cuisine as well as the security of our boundaries. The shell holes are patched. The banners fly. There's a nest of wi'itikiin on the roof this summer.

The damned creatures have taken advantage of the repairs and are getting entirely too impertinent.

CJ Cherryh
The Foreigner Novels

"Serious space opera at its very best by one of the leading SF writers in the field today." —*Publishers Weekly*

"Her world building, aliens, and suspense rank among the strongest in the whole SF field. May those strengths be sustained indefinitely, or at least until the end of Foreigner." —*Booklist*

To Order Call: 1-800-788-6262

www.dawbooks.com

DAW 8

CJ Cherryh

Classic Novels in Omnibus Editions

THE DREAMING TREE
Contains the complete duology *The Dreamstone* and
The Tree of Swords and Jewels.   0-88677-782-8

THE FADED SUN TRILOGY
Contains the complete novels *Kesrith*, *Shon'jir*, and
Kutath.   0-88677-836-0

THE MORGAINE SAGA
Contains the complete novels *Gate of Ivrel*, *Well of
Shiuan*, and *Fires of Azeroth.*   0-88677-877-8

THE CHANUR SAGA
Contains the complete novels *The Pride of Chanur*,
Chanur's Venture and *The Kif Strike Back.*
      0-88677-930-8

ALTERNATE REALITIES
Contains the complete novels *Port Eterntiy*, *Voyager
in Night*, and *Wave Without a Shore*   0-88677-946-4

AT THE EDGE OF SPACE
Contains the complete novels *Brothers of Earth* and
Hunter of Worlds.   0-7564-0160-7

To Order Call: 1-800-788-6262
www.dawbooks.com

C.S. Friedman

The Best in Science Fiction

THIS ALIEN SHORE   0-88677-799-2
A *New York Times* Notable Book of the Year
"Breathlessly plotted, emotionally savvy. A potent
metaphor for the toleration of diversity"
—*The New York Times*

THE MADNESS SEASON   0-88677-444-6
"Exceptionally imaginative and compelling"
—*Publishers Weekly*

IN CONQUEST BORN   0-7564-0043-0
"Space opera in the best sense: high stakes adventure
with a strong focus on ideas, and characters an intelligent reader can care about."—*Newsday*

THE WILDING   0-7564-0164-X
The long-awaited follow-up to *In Conquest Born*.

To Order Call: 1-800-788-6262
www.dawbooks.com

Tanya Huff

The Confederation Novels

"As a heroine, Kerr shines. She is cut from the same mold as Ellen Ripley of the *Aliens* films. Like her heroine, Huff delivers the goods." —*SF Weekly*

in an omnibus edition:

A CONFEDERATION OF VALOR
(*Valor's Choice, The Better Part of Valor*)
0-7564-0399-5
978-0-7564-0399-7

and now in hardcover:

THE HEART OF VALOR
978-0-7564-0435-2

To Order Call: 1-800-788-6262
www.dawbooks.com